Blueprints of Desire

Redesigning Elizabeth

Julie Freebush

SFD Publications

Contents

CHAPTER ONE

"Staring at Ceilings"

5:14 AM. Liz Donovan opened her eyes to the familiar landscape of her bedroom ceiling, its smooth expanse unmarred except for the hairline crack that had appeared last winter. The alarm wouldn't sound for another sixteen minutes, but her body had long ago internalized the schedule, rendering the actual device unnecessary. Beside her, Mark's heavy breathing had devolved into a rumbling snore that seemed to vibrate through the mattress.

She turned her head to study her husband's profile. In sleep, with his features relaxed, she could still glimpse traces of the handsome college athlete she'd fallen for fifteen years ago. The sharp jawline had softened, the flat stomach had rounded, but the sandy hair—though thinner now—still fell across his forehead in the same boyish way.

Liz eased herself from bed, careful not to disturb him though experience had taught her that little short of an actual marching band could penetrate Mark's weekend-caliber snoring. She padded across the plush carpet, navigating the geography of their divided bedroom by memory.

Mark's side exploded with memorabilia. Framed jerseys. Team pennants. The basketball from that legendary game senior year—the one where his buzzer-beater shot had clinched the conference championship. The one he still mentioned at every dinner party. The trophy shelf that had somehow expanded beyond its designated corner to claim nearly an entire wall.

Her side, by contrast, was a study in minimalism. A single framed photo of her parents. A sleek lamp. Three novels stacked neatly on the nightstand, their spines uncracked despite weeks of residence there. No evidence of the Preston Academy valedictorian runner-up. No hint that she'd graduated summa cum laude from Northwestern with a double major. Her academic achievements had been tidily packed away in storage boxes, while Mark's athletic glory dominated their shared space like an invasive species.

In the bathroom, Liz went through her morning routine with practiced efficiency. Splash water on face. Brush teeth. Apply toner, serum, moisturizer with SPF. She studied her reflection—the hazel eyes that looked more amber than green this morning, the chestnut hair cut in a sleek bob that framed her face in a way that required minimal styling. She looked put-together. Professional. And utterly unremarkable.

She slipped into her running clothes and headed downstairs. The house was silent except for the distant hum of the refrigerator and Mark's muffled snoring from above. Liz started the coffee maker—programmed to begin brewing at 6:15, but she was early again. As the machine gurgled to life, she leaned against the counter, suddenly caught in the undertow of memory.

Their first apartment. Barely six hundred square feet with a kitchenette that could barely fit one person, let alone two. Mark making coffee on Sunday mornings while she read the paper aloud to him. The way he'd kiss her mid-sentence sometimes, just because he couldn't help himself. Planning adventures for the weekend. Making love on the cramped couch because they'd been too lazy to walk the ten feet to the bedroom.

When had that stopped? When had they transformed from passionate partners into polite roommates who shared a bed?

The coffee maker beeped. Liz poured herself a cup, added no cream, no sugar, and carried it to the back porch. The early summer air held a promise of heat later, but for now, it wrapped around her with gentle coolness. She sipped her coffee and watched the sun illuminate their meticulously landscaped yard—another item on the checklist of suburban success they'd been so eager to achieve.

Her morning run through Lakeside Park was brisk and mindless. Five miles at a steady pace, her thoughts churning faster than her feet. By the time she returned, showered, and dressed in tailored slacks and a silk blouse, it was nearly 7:30. Mark would be up soon—if his internal weekend clock held true.

She was buttering toast when he stumbled into the kitchen, hair sticking up at odd angles, eyes still puffy with sleep. He made a beeline for the coffee pot without a word of greeting.

"Morning," she offered, sliding a mug toward him.

Mark grunted something that might have been "morning" if one were feeling generous in their interpretation. He poured coffee, added three sugars, and took a long gulp before his eyes fully focused on her.

"You're dressed up for Saturday," he observed, his first complete sentence of the day.

"I told you last night, I need to go into the office for a few hours. We're finalizing the quarterly marketing strategy on Monday."

"Right." He nodded vaguely, making it clear he hadn't registered this information when she'd shared it. "What about dinner? Kevin and Lisa invited us over. Game night or something."

Liz felt a flicker of irritation. "I mentioned that too. I'll be back by four, plenty of time."

Mark shrugged and opened the refrigerator, staring into it as if expecting its contents to have magically changed overnight. "We need groceries."

"I put a list on the counter. Thought you might grab them while I'm working."

He closed the refrigerator door and leaned against it. "Got plans with the guys. Golf, maybe hit the sports bar after to watch a game." He took another sip of coffee. "Can we do it tomorrow?"

The familiar knot of dissatisfaction tightened in her stomach. She'd predicted this response with such accuracy she could have written the script. "Fine. I'll go tomorrow."

Mark nodded, mission accomplished, and shuffled toward the living room where the massive television awaited. "What time did you say for the Barnes' thing?"

"Six-thirty. We're bringing wine."

"Cool." He was already reaching for the remote, his attention shifting away from her like water flowing downhill, following the path of least resistance.

Liz gathered her purse and keys, hesitating in the doorway between kitchen and living room. Mark had settled into his designated spot on the couch, the cushion permanently molded to his form. ESPN was already blaring.

"I'm heading out," she said.

He raised his coffee mug in acknowledgment without turning. "Later."

The front door closed behind her with a quiet click that felt somehow more final than a slam would have. In the driveway, Liz sat in her car, hands gripping the steering wheel though she hadn't yet started the engine. The knot in her stomach had expanded, climbing up into her throat.

When had they become strangers? When had their conversations devolved into logistics and grocery lists? When had she stopped expecting more?

She thought about the office awaiting her—the empty weekend halls, the marketing strategy she'd already revised three times, the mounting pressure from Catherine to deliver something "revolutionary" for the next campaign. Was this truly all there was? Shuttling between a house that felt increasingly like a museum to someone else's past and an office where her creativity was channeled into selling products she didn't care about?

A text notification chimed. Probably Mark asking her to add something to the grocery list he wouldn't be tackling. She didn't check it.

Instead, she closed her eyes and took three deep breaths, the way her yoga instructor always recommended for "centering yourself in moments of emotional turbulence." The air filled her lungs, held, released. Again. Again.

When she opened her eyes, nothing had changed. The same driveway. The same house. The same life constructed of careful compromises and lowered expectations. But something had shifted inside her—a hairline crack in her own foundation, not unlike the one on their bedroom ceiling. Small. Almost imperceptible. But once noticed, impossible to unsee.

Liz started the car. Whatever awaited her at Meridian Enterprises today, it had to be more fulfilling than the empty house behind her. At the very least, it was a place where her intelligence was acknowledged, where her contributions mattered. For now, that would have to be enough.

She backed out of the driveway, leaving behind the colonial house with its perfect landscaping and hollow rooms, carrying the weight of her dissatisfaction like a familiar companion.

CHAPTER TWO

"Mechanical Motions"

L iz's key turned in the lock at precisely 4:42 PM. Her shoulders ached from hunching over marketing projections all afternoon, and a dull throb had taken up residence behind her left eye. The quarterly strategy wasn't coming together. Catherine had rejected her first two drafts as "predictable" and "safe," words that felt increasingly like indictments of more than just her work.

The house greeted her with the blue-white glow of the television and the distant roar of a crowd. Mark hadn't moved from his spot on the couch since that morning, though he'd apparently showered and changed into fresh athletic wear—his weekend uniform of team logo t-shirt and basketball shorts.

"Hey," she called, dropping her keys in the ceramic bowl by the door. The sound echoed through the foyer.

Mark's eyes remained fixed on the screen where men in colorful jerseys scrambled across a court. His hand absently reached for a beer on the coffee table—his third, judging by the empties lined up like sentinels. "You're late."

"The marketing strategy needed more work than I thought." She shrugged off her blazer and hung it in the coat closet. "We still have time before Kevin and Lisa's."

He grunted in response, eyes never leaving the television as a replay showed in slow motion. "Got caught in a scoring drought in the third quarter, but they're rallying now."

Liz stood for a moment, waiting for him to ask about her day, about the project that had kept her at the office on a Saturday. The question never came. She moved toward the kitchen, surveying the day's damage—dishes in the sink, crumbs on the counter, an empty pizza box abandoned on the island.

"Did you eat the leftover pasta?" she asked, opening the refrigerator.

"Wasn't enough for lunch. Ordered pizza."

Liz grabbed a yogurt and leaned against the counter, watching her husband through the doorway. There was a time when Mark would have waited to eat with her, when they would have prepared meals together, laughing and bumping hips in their tiny first apartment kitchen.

"I need to shower before we go," she said, more to herself than to him.

The hot water sluiced over her tired muscles, washing away the day's frustrations. She closed her eyes, trying to summon enthusiasm for an evening of forced socialization with the Barnes. Kevin would talk about his promotion. Lisa would show off her latest home renovation project. Mark would relive his college basketball glory days with Kevin, who'd never tire of hearing about that championship game.

And Liz would smile and nod and ask all the right questions, while a voice inside screamed that there had to be more to life than this.

She emerged from the bathroom wrapped in a towel to find Mark standing in the bedroom, remote in hand, eyes still fixed on the portable TV they'd installed on his insistence.

"Almost ready?" he asked without looking at her.

"Give me ten minutes."

Fifteen minutes later, they were in the car, Mark behind the wheel, Liz clutching the bottle of Cabernet

they'd received as a Christmas gift and had been saving
for "a special occasion" that never seemed to arrive.

"So my fantasy league is looking solid this season," Mark began as they pulled out of the driveway.
"Got Embiid as my center, Mitchell at shooting guard.
Kevin's team is stacked too, but he's weak at point
guard."

Liz nodded, gazing out the window at the identical
houses lining their street. "Catherine rejected my marketing strategy again today."

"That sucks," Mark replied without inflection.
"Anyway, I'm projected to score higher than anyone
this week if Mitchell keeps his hot streak going."

And so it continued for the entire fifteen-minute
drive—Mark's monologue about player statistics, draft
picks, and league standings flowing uninterrupted
while Liz's thoughts drifted elsewhere. By the time
they arrived at the Barnes' colonial-style home—nearly
identical to their own but with gray siding instead of
blue—she had given up on steering the conversation
toward anything meaningful.

Dinner was exactly as she'd predicted. Lisa's pot
roast. Kevin's promotion story. Mark's animated
retelling of his buzzer-beater shot, complete with
standing demonstration of his form.

"It was all instinct, you know?" Mark's eyes lit up
as he pantomimed the shot. "Clock winding down,

defense all over me, but I just felt it. Knew it was good the moment it left my hands."

Kevin nodded appreciatively, having heard this story at least twenty times before. "Man, that must have been something."

"Best moment of my life," Mark declared, sinking back into his chair with a satisfied smile.

Liz felt a twist in her chest. Their wedding day hadn't even made the list.

"How's work going for you, Liz?" Lisa asked, refilling wine glasses. "Still at Meridian?"

"Yes, Senior Marketing Director now. We're actually working on a new quarterly strategy that's been challenging. The CMO wants something revolutionary, but within very specific parameters."

"Sounds complicated," Lisa offered with polite interest.

"It's like trying to be innovative while wearing handcuffs," Liz continued, suddenly desperate to engage in actual conversation. "The corporate philosophy is all about 'progressive tradition'—embracing innovation while respecting established practices. But in reality, they want something new that looks exactly like what's always worked before."

She realized she'd been speaking too long, too intensely. Mark was staring at her with a mixture of boredom and annoyance.

"It's just marketing," he said dismissively. "Not like you're curing cancer."

The table fell silent. Liz took a long sip of wine, feeling heat rise in her cheeks.

Kevin cleared his throat. "So, who's watching the playoffs tomorrow?"

The conversation returned to sports, leaving Liz to push food around her plate and smile at appropriate intervals. By the time they made their excuses and headed home, her face ached from the effort.

The drive home was silent except for the sports radio station Mark had tuned to for score updates. Liz leaned her head against the window, watching suburban houses blur together into a monotonous landscape.

At home, Mark immediately reconnected with the television while Liz changed into her nightclothes—silk pajamas that had once been chosen with care for their appeal but now served merely as comfortable sleepwear.

She was brushing her teeth when Mark appeared in the bathroom doorway. The sports program had ended, and his expression had shifted from distant to focused in a way she recognized all too well.

"Coming to bed?" His voice had dropped half an octave, his intent clear.

Liz rinsed her mouth. "In a minute."

In the bedroom, Mark had already stripped down to his boxers and was waiting beneath the sheets. Liz slipped in beside him, and his hand immediately found her waist, pulling her closer.

"You look good in those," he murmured, fingers already working at the buttons of her pajama top.

She allowed herself to be undressed, responding to his touch with practiced motions. His kisses landed on her neck, her collarbone, moving downward with predictable progression. The foreplay was perfunctory—a checklist of actions performed without genuine attention to her responses.

His hands skimmed over her breasts, stomach, between her legs, touching all the right places but with the efficiency of someone following an instruction manual. There was no discovery, no genuine curiosity about what might please her tonight, as opposed to any other night in the past fifteen years.

"You're so beautiful," he whispered, the words as routine as his touch.

Liz closed her eyes, trying to summon desire from memory. She made the appropriate sounds, moved in the expected ways, while her mind drifted to tomorrow's marketing presentation. Perhaps if she restructured the third section, emphasized the sustainability angle Catherine had mentioned...

Mark's weight shifted above her, his breathing quickened. His movements were rhythmic, focused entirely on his own building pleasure. Liz wrapped her legs around him, angled her hips in the way she knew would hasten his climax.

"God, Liz," he groaned, pace increasing.

She gasped and moaned on cue, performing her role in this familiar dance while mentally reviewing bullet points for Monday's meeting. When she felt him tensing, she clutched his shoulders and cried out, providing the affirmation he expected.

Mark collapsed beside her, satisfaction evident in his heavy exhale. "That was amazing," he murmured, already rolling away, eyes heavy with approaching sleep.

"Mmm," she responded, pulling the sheet up to cover herself.

Within minutes, Mark's breathing had deepened into the familiar cadence of sleep. Liz lay awake, staring at the ceiling, at the hairline crack that seemed to have grown imperceptibly wider since morning.

How had they arrived here? She remembered the early days—passionate encounters in their cramped apartment, on the couch, against the wall, in the shower. Mark's hands learning her body with reverent attention, his eyes locked on hers as they moved together. The whispered confessions, the laughter, the genuine connection of two people discovering each other.

Now they performed like actors in a long-running play, reciting lines without emotion, going through motions without meaning. She had become a prop in Mark's performance, a means to his satisfaction, her own pleasure an afterthought if considered at all.

When had she started faking her responses? When had she stopped expecting more? When had she begun to drift away during their most intimate moments, her body present while her mind escaped to anywhere else?

The worst part wasn't Mark's selfishness or her own dishonesty. It was the hollowness afterward—the empty space where connection should be, the silence filled only with his snores and her regrets.

Liz slipped from bed and padded to the bathroom. She turned on the shower, letting steam fill the room before stepping under the hot spray. She scrubbed herself methodically, washing away the physical evidence of their encounter while the emotional residue clung stubbornly to her skin.

She avoided the mirror as she dried off, unwilling to confront her own reflection. Who was this woman who moved through life like a ghost, who performed intimacy without feeling it, who had gradually surrendered her desires until they became distant memories?

When had she become a stranger to herself?

Liz pulled on fresh pajamas and returned to the bedroom. Mark had rolled onto his stomach, claiming two-thirds of the mattress, one arm flung across what should have been her space. She carefully maneuvered around his sprawled form and slipped under the covers on the edge of the bed.

Above her, the ceiling crack seemed to mock her with its imperfection in an otherwise flawless surface. Like her life—structurally sound, aesthetically pleasing, and fundamentally flawed in a way that couldn't be patched or painted over.

She turned away from Mark, curling into herself at the edge of the mattress, and waited for sleep that would be long in coming.

CHAPTER THREE

"The Announcement"

Liz checked her reflection in the elevator's polished doors. Monday mornings at Meridian Enterprises demanded a certain armor—today she'd chosen a charcoal pencil skirt, cream silk blouse, and the burgundy blazer that Catherine once mentioned brought out the green in her hazel eyes. The slight bags beneath those eyes were expertly concealed, evidence of another restless night staring at ceiling cracks.

The elevator chimed at the executive floor. Liz stepped out, nodding at the receptionist while mentally reviewing her quarterly marketing presentation. She'd revised it three times over the weekend, each version attempting to thread the needle between Catherine's demand for "revolutionary" and Meridian's institutional aversion to genuine risk.

"There she is!" Derek appeared beside her, coffee in hand. "Thought you might need reinforcements before the firing squad."

Liz accepted the cup gratefully. "Is it that obvious I was here until nine last night?"

"Only to someone who's known you for five years." Derek fell into step beside her, his boyish face belying his thirty-six years. "Besides, I saw the light under your door when I left. The cleaning crew was taking bets on whether you'd actually gone home Friday."

"Your concern is touching."

"Not concern—admiration for your dedication to selling software integration solutions to middle management." Derek's eyes crinkled. "Though Paul mentioned Mark called looking for you around seven."

Liz took a long sip of coffee, avoiding Derek's gaze. "Budget meeting ran long."

"Of course." Derek's tone made it clear he understood the subtext—another evening avoiding the hollow space her marriage had become.

They reached the Conference Room where executives were already gathering. Catherine Wilkes stood near the head of the table, her sleek silver bob catching the morning light as she reviewed documents with laser focus. At forty-two, Catherine embodied everything Liz had once aspired to—sharp, efficient, respected. Lately, Liz wondered if that aspiration had been misplaced.

"Elizabeth," Catherine looked up, "we're adjusting the agenda. Howard has an announcement before your presentation."

Something in Catherine's tone made Liz straighten. "Everything alright?"

"More than alright. Just be prepared to pivot." Catherine's eyes flickered with rare excitement before returning to her tablet.

Derek whispered, "Cryptic much?"

Before Liz could respond, Howard Meridian strode in. At sixty-two, the company founder still commanded attention without effort, his salt-and-pepper hair and tailored suit projecting success without ostentation.

"Good morning, everyone," Howard called out as executives settled into their seats. "I know we have Elizabeth's quarterly marketing strategy to review, but I'd like to begin with something that will shape Meridian's future for the next decade."

The room quieted immediately. Howard wasn't known for hyperbole.

"As you know, our current headquarters has served us well for twenty-three years. But as our company has evolved, our physical space hasn't kept pace." Howard activated the room's display screen, revealing an aerial view of an industrial property on the city's revitalized riverfront. "I've acquired the old Westfield manufacturing site. We're going to build a new Meridian headquarters that embodies our corporate philosophy of progressive tradition."

Murmurs rippled through the room. Liz leaned forward, a spark of genuine interest igniting for the first time in months.

Howard continued, "This isn't just a building project. This is about defining who Meridian is for the next generation. The architecture, the sustainability features, the workspace design—everything will tell our story." His eyes swept the room with unusual passion. "I've allocated significant resources to ensure this becomes a landmark project, not just for our company but for the city's architectural landscape."

Liz found herself studying the property outline with growing excitement. A blank canvas. A story waiting to be told. Something substantial after years of incremental marketing campaigns for software upgrades.

"We're establishing a project committee with representatives from each department," Howard explained. "Catherine will oversee marketing integration, and she's recommended Elizabeth as the department's primary representative."

Liz's head snapped up, meeting Catherine's know-ing gaze across the table. For once, surprise rendered her speechless.

"Elizabeth's background in both marketing and lit-erature makes her uniquely qualified to help translate our corporate narrative into physical space," Catherine added smoothly. "The committee will work directly with the architectural team we select."

Howard nodded. "The timeline is aggressive. We want groundbreaking within three months, comple-tion in eighteen. Catherine has the detailed brief for committee members." He looked directly at Liz. "This project will define Meridian's identity for decades. We need our best people fully committed."

The meeting continued, but Liz barely registered the subsequent discussions. Her mind raced with pos-sibilities—brand integration within architectural el-ements, narrative-driven spatial design, experiential marketing that lived in physical form rather than dis-posable campaigns. For the first time in years, a profes-sional challenge stirred something beyond mere com-petence.

When Howard finally adjourned, executives filtered out discussing implications. Catherine approached Liz with a slim folder.

"Project brief. Committee meets Wednesday morn-ing." She studied Liz with shrewd eyes. "Howard specifically requested you after seeing your work on the client experience initiative."

"I'm surprised," Liz admitted. "And grateful for the opportunity."

"Don't be grateful yet. This will double your workload while maintaining existing responsibilities." Catherine's voice lowered. "But it's the kind of project that makes careers, Elizabeth. Don't waste it."

After Catherine departed, Derek sidled up, eyebrows raised. "Well, look who's suddenly the golden child."

"Hardly." Liz clutched the folder like a lifeline. "Just the designated sacrifice to the architecture gods."

"Please." Derek rolled his eyes as they walked toward her office. "I saw your face when Howard made the announcement. You lit up like Times Square on New Year's. When's the last time anything about quarterly software marketing made you look that alive?"

Liz couldn't argue. The familiar hallways of Meridian seemed different somehow—as if the promise of creation had already begun transforming the space.

In her office, Derek closed the door and dropped into the visitor chair. "So, what does Mark think about his wife becoming an architectural muse?"

"I haven't told him yet." Liz set the folder on her desk, avoiding Derek's gaze. "It just happened."

"Right." Derek's tone softened. "How are things on the home front anyway?"

Liz busied herself organizing papers. "Fine. The usual."

"The usual meaning you work late to avoid going home, and he watches sports to avoid noticing?"

She shot him a warning look. "That's not fair."

"Isn't it?" Derek's usual playfulness vanished. "Liz, I've been with Jacob for twelve years. I know what partnership looks like, and I know what two people sharing space looks like. You and Mark stopped being partners a long time ago."

"We're just in a phase." The words sounded hollow even to her ears.

"A five-year phase?" Derek shook his head. "Look, I'm not trying to pry. I just hate seeing my friend disappear into her work because her home isn't a place she wants to be."

Liz sank into her chair. "It's complicated."

"It always is." Derek stood, squeezing her shoulder. "But hey, at least you finally have something interesting to do around here. Maybe building a new headquarters will help you rebuild other things too."

After he left, Liz opened the project folder, scanning requirements and timelines. The scope was ambitious—sustainability targets, workspace innovation, brand integration throughout. Howard wasn't just building an office; he was creating a legacy.

She found herself thinking not of Mark or their stagnant marriage, but of who she'd been before—the girl who devoured literature and analyzed texts with passionate precision, who thrived on intellectual challenge, who once believed her mind was her greatest asset. Somewhere along the way, that girl had been packed away like her academic achievements, stored in boxes while Mark's trophies claimed the walls.

By late afternoon, Liz had rearranged her schedule to accommodate committee meetings and dived into research on architectural firms rumored to be bidding for the project. She created a spreadsheet comparing their portfolios, sustainability credentials, and design philosophies.

The Thomas Building caught her attention—an award-winning sustainable office complex that had generated both acclaim and controversy for its radical approach. She clicked through to the architect's defense of the design, finding herself nodding at the elegant argument balancing innovation and practicality.

The next link made her freeze.

The Calloway Design Group, founded and led by James Calloway.

The name hit her like a physical force. Her cursor hovered over the firm's profile as memories cascaded through her mind—intense debates in AP Literature, competing research papers, the hushed tension when class rankings were posted. James Calloway with his infuriating confidence and brilliant mind, always one step ahead, always the counterpoint to her arguments.

James Calloway, who had edged her out for valedictorian by decimal points.

James Calloway, who had won the prestigious Beckman Scholarship to Rice University, the scholarship she'd also applied for, coming in second place.

James Calloway, whose victory had tasted so bitter she'd abandoned her plans for literary studies and chosen Northwestern instead.

The last time she'd seen him was graduation day. He'd approached her after the ceremony, extended his hand, and said, "It was an honor having you as competition, Mitchell." She'd shaken his hand with cold formality, turned away, and spent the next twenty years trying not to measure her achievements against his shadow.

And now, his firm was bidding to design Meridian's new headquarters—the project that might redefine her career and possibly her life.

Liz closed the browser window and leaned back in her chair. The knot in her stomach wasn't entirely unpleasant. It felt strangely like anticipation, like standing at the edge of something monumental.

For the first time in years, Elizabeth Donovan felt fully awake.

CHAPTER FOUR

"Ghost from the Past"

L iz arrived at the Chicago Conference Room thirty minutes early, arranging presentation packets
with methodical precision. She'd spent two days researching each architectural firm, preparing questions
that would reveal their true capabilities beneath polished pitches. Her notes were color-coded, cross-refer-
enced, and highlighted with the thoroughness that had
once earned her the nickname "Mitchell the Meticulous" at Preston Academy.

"Someone's prepared." Catherine entered, eyebrows
raised at Liz's elaborate setup.

"Just doing my homework." Liz straightened a slightly misaligned folder. "Howard's staking Meridian's future on this building. We can't afford to be dazzled by flashy renderings."

Catherine studied her with that penetrating gaze that made junior executives quake. "I've never seen you this invested in a project before."

"It's important."

"Yes, but there's something else." Catherine set down her tablet. "This is personal for you."

Liz busied herself with the projector settings. "It's professional. I want to do a good job."

"Elizabeth, I've watched you 'do a good job' for five years. This is different." Catherine's voice softened slightly. "It's good. You've been on autopilot too long."

Before Liz could respond, Howard arrived with the facilities director and CFO. Soon the room filled with stakeholders, each clutching coffee and opinions about what the new headquarters should represent.

"Three firms presenting today," Howard announced once everyone settled. "Each has thirty minutes for presentation, fifteen for questions. We'll deliberate next week." He glanced at Liz. "Our project committee has prepared evaluation criteria focusing on innovation, sustainability, and alignment with Meridian's philosophy."

The first presenter was Martin Wells, a corporate design specialist whose portfolio screamed safe efficiency. His renderings featured glass and steel with token green spaces—competent but forgettable. Liz noted how he directed his answers primarily to the men in the room.

The second firm, led by a husband-wife team, presented a more thoughtful concept emphasizing employee wellness. Their questions about Meridian's culture showed genuine interest in alignment, earning them approving nods from Howard.

During the break before the final presentation, Liz reviewed her notes, satisfied with the thoroughness of her analysis. Neither firm had truly impressed, but both had viable approaches. She was comparing sustainability metrics when Howard called everyone back to their seats.

"Our final presenter is Calloway Design Group," he announced. "They're known for innovative sustainable architecture with their 'functional beauty with purpose' approach. The Thomas Building downtown is their work."

Liz's pen stilled. Despite two days knowing this moment would come, her pulse quickened. She kept her eyes fixed on her notepad as footsteps entered the room.

"Thank you for the opportunity to present today. I'm James Calloway, founder of Calloway Design Group."

The voice struck her like a physical force—deeper than she remembered but with the same precise diction that had once delivered devastating debate rebuttals. Liz raised her eyes slowly, professional mask firmly in place.

James stood at the front of the room, commanding attention without apparent effort. At thirty-eight, he'd grown into his features—the lanky teenager now a tall, broad-shouldered man in an impeccably tailored black suit. His dark hair showed distinguished touches of silver at the temples, and reading glasses hung from his shirt pocket. A small scar through his right eyebrow was the only imperfection in his appearance.

Then he saw her.

For a microsecond, James Calloway's practiced composure faltered. His eyes, still that intense blue she remembered, widened slightly, his presentation momentarily forgotten. The recognition flickered across his face before disappearing behind professional polish so quickly Liz wondered if anyone else had noticed.

"Before I show you what we envision for Meridian," he continued smoothly, "I want to understand what you're truly building. Not just a headquarters, but a physical manifestation of your company's identity and future."

As he spoke, Liz was suddenly sixteen again, sitting in AP Literature while James dismantled her analysis of Gatsby's symbolism with surgical precision. The classroom disappeared when Mrs. Abernathy announced the quarter's class rankings—James 98.73%, Elizabeth 98.67%. The sickening lurch in her stomach when the Beckman Scholarship committee announced their decision.

James had moved to the presentation screen, revealing concept sketches that blended bold innovation with practical functionality. His design incorporated sustainable elements as integral features rather than afterthoughts, living walls that served as natural air filtration, kinetic exterior panels that harvested energy while providing dynamic shading, a central atrium that eliminated traditional departmental silos.

"Architecture isn't just about creating space," James explained, his passion evident beneath his controlled delivery. "It's about shaping how people interact, how ideas flow, how a company's values become lived experience."

Despite herself, Liz was impressed. The concepts weren't just beautiful, they were thoughtful, researched, rooted in understanding of workplace dynamics. As he discussed how the design would evolve with Meridian's growth, she found herself leaning forward, drawn into his vision despite the complicated emotions churning beneath her professional facade.

A particularly innovative solution for integrating client spaces with work areas made her inadvertently nod in appreciation. James caught the movement, his eyes meeting hers for a fraction of a second. Something passed between them, recognition, challenge, the ghost of their former rivalry.

"Now for the technical specifications," James continued, transitioning to sustainability metrics that exceeded their requirements by significant margins.

Howard looked genuinely excited, asking questions that revealed his growing investment in James's vision. Other stakeholders followed with enthusiastic inquiries about timeline, materials, and adaptability.

When the formal Q&A began, Liz waited until others had spoken before raising her hand. James nodded to her with perfect professionalism, though something in his eyes suggested he'd been waiting for her question.

"Your design emphasizes transparency and connection," Liz began, her voice steady despite her racing heart. "But Meridian handles sensitive client data requiring security and confidentiality. How does your open concept address the practical need for information protection without creating the very silos you're trying to eliminate?"

A small smile touched James's lips, the same expression he'd worn before dismantling her arguments in debate club. "An excellent question, Ms. Donovan."

The use of her married name confirmed he'd done his homework. Of course he had.

"The apparent contradiction between openness and security is precisely what makes this design innovative," he continued. "Rather than relying on physical barriers, we've incorporated graduated security zones using advanced materials with variable opacity, sound-dampening technology that creates auditory privacy bubbles, and directional lighting that naturally guides movement patterns without obvious restrictions."

He approached her side of the table, pulling up detailed schematics. "The psychology of space security is about creating intuitive boundaries people respect without feeling constrained. It's the architectural equivalent of guiding a conversation rather than censoring it."

The literary reference wasn't lost on her, it was from her own senior thesis on narrative control in modernist literature, which had beaten his for the department award. Her only clear victory over him.

"Theoretical applications don't always translate to practical implementation," Liz countered, ignoring Catherine's surprised glance at her challenging tone.

"Your Thomas Building had similar security concepts that required significant modification after implementation. How have you addressed those lessons learned?"

James's eyes narrowed slightly, the only indication her barb had landed. "The Thomas modifications resulted from the client changing requirements mid-construction. We've since developed a more robust stakeholder alignment process specifically to prevent such issues." He held her gaze. "I believe in learning from mistakes, Ms. Donovan. It's how we improve."

The double meaning hung between them, visible only to them.

"Our team would work closely with your security specialists to ensure both the letter and spirit of your requirements are met," he added, addressing the broader room while maintaining eye contact with her. "Perfect design isn't created in isolation—it emerges from productive tension between vision and practical constraints."

The phrase "productive tension" lingered in the air as he returned to the front of the room. For the remaining minutes, Liz felt hyperaware of his every movement, caught in the strange vertigo of past and present colliding.

When Howard finally concluded the meeting, stakeholders gathered around James with follow-up questions. Liz busied herself collecting her notes, determined to escape before any direct interaction became necessary.

"Elizabeth." Catherine appeared beside her. "What was that?"

"What was what?" Liz kept her voice neutral.

"That exchange with Calloway. I've never seen you so..." Catherine searched for the word. "Combative."

"I was being thorough. The security question is legitimate."

"Of course it is. But there was something else happening." Catherine's shrewd eyes studied her. "You know him."

It wasn't a question. Liz considered deflection before recognizing the futility. "We went to high school together. Academic rivals."

Catherine's eyebrows rose. "Well, that explains the interesting dynamic. Whatever history you have, set it aside if he gets the contract. Howard was practically salivating over that design."

"I'm a professional," Liz replied stiffly.

"Good. Because that man is likely designing our future headquarters, and you'll be working closely with him." Catherine glanced toward James, who was showing Howard something on his tablet. "Though I must say, watching you two spar was the most entertaining part of these presentations."

After Catherine left, Liz gathered her materials with mechanical precision, keeping her back to the room. She'd nearly escaped when a familiar voice spoke behind her.

"Elizabeth Mitchell. Though I suppose it's Donovan now."

She turned slowly, professional smile fixed in place. "James. It's been a long time."

Standing closer, she noticed details invisible from across the room—the faint lines at the corners of his eyes, the perfect knot in his tie, the subtle scent of his cologne.

"Twenty years, two months." His smile didn't quite reach his eyes. "I didn't expect to find you in corporate marketing."

The observation carried an edge. He'd known her as the girl determined to become a literary scholar, who'd mocked "corporate drones" in their senior English journal.

"Life takes unexpected turns." She met his gaze steadily. "I didn't expect to find you defending the Thomas Building's security flaws."

Something flashed in his eyes—annoyance, respect, she couldn't tell. "Still direct as ever. The Thomas was a learning experience."

"I'm sure it was."

An awkward silence stretched between them, filled with unspoken history.

"Your question was valid," he finally said. "If we get the contract, I'd welcome your input on the security zones. You always had a knack for finding the weak points in my arguments."

Before she could respond, Howard called James over to introduce him to the CFO.

"We should catch up properly sometime," James said, already backing away. "For old times' sake."

"Of course," Liz replied automatically, knowing neither of them meant it.

She watched him walk away, struck by the strange sense of time compressing—the brilliant, arrogant boy now a successful man, still occupying the space just ahead of her, still the measuring stick against which she couldn't help comparing herself.

In the bathroom, Liz splashed cold water on her face, avoiding her reflection. Her hands trembled slightly as she reached for a paper towel. The woman who had entered that conference room—composed, prepared, professional—had momentarily vanished, replaced by a seventeen-year-old girl still smarting from coming in second.

Worse was the unexpected reaction she couldn't quite name—the involuntary admiration for his work, the sharp thrill of intellectual sparring after years of

conversations that never challenged her, and something else entirely when he'd held her gaze across the
conference table.

"Get it together," she whispered to herself, finally meeting her own eyes in the mirror. Water had
smudged her mascara slightly, a crack in her perfect
presentation. "It's just a project. He's just an architect."

But as she repaired her makeup with practiced
movements, Liz knew she was lying to herself. James
Calloway had never been "just" anything to her. And
now he was back, about to become entangled in the
project that might define her professional future.

The woman in the mirror looked both terrified and
more alive than she had in years.

CHAPTER FIVE

"Selection Committee"

T he conference room buzzed with opinions as Liz arranged her evaluation materials with methodical precision. After a week of architectural presentations, the selection committee was finally convening to make their recommendation. Howard had assembled a diverse group: Liz representing marketing, the CFO for financial oversight, the head of operations, HR director, and Gerald Matheson, a board member whose silver hair and Brooks Brothers suits telegraphed his fifty years in corporate America.

"Let's begin with the evaluation criteria," Howard said, taking his seat at the head of the table. "Elizabeth has prepared a comprehensive matrix comparing all firms across our key requirements."

Liz distributed her analysis—twenty pages of detailed comparisons on sustainability metrics, space utilization efficiency, timeline feasibility, and brand alignment. She'd worked through the weekend on it, telling Mark she had a deadline. He hadn't questioned her, absorbed in a basketball tournament.

"Each firm was scored objectively against our stated requirements," Liz explained, pointing to the executive summary. "I've highlighted areas where performance significantly exceeded or fell below expectations."

Gerald Matheson flipped through the document with barely concealed impatience. "Very thorough, Ms. Donovan, but these technical details don't capture the intangibles of selecting a partner for such a significant investment."

"The 'intangibles' are on page twelve," Liz replied evenly. "Cultural alignment, communication style, adaptability to feedback—all scored based on their presentations and follow-up materials."

"Still," Gerald continued, "there's something to be said for proven reliability. Martin Wells has designed headquarters for three Fortune 500 companies without controversy or complications."

"Without innovation either," Liz countered before she could stop herself. "His designs are functionally adequate but offer nothing distinctive."

Howard leaned forward. "That's precisely what we need to discuss. Are we building an adequate headquarters or a distinctive one? The difference matters to our identity as a company."

For the next hour, the committee debated the merits of each firm. The CFO raised concerns about Calloway Design Group's premium pricing, while Operations praised their functional efficiency. HR favored the wellness features from the husband-wife team.

"Calloway's approach is untested at this scale," Gerald insisted, tapping his pen against the table. "The Thomas Building controversy should give us pause. Do we want to be an architectural experiment?"

Liz took a measured breath. "The Thomas Building won three sustainability awards and increased tenant productivity by twenty-two percent. The 'controversy' was about pushing boundaries, not failure."

"You seem particularly defensive of Calloway's work, Ms. Donovan," Gerald observed with raised eyebrows.

Catherine intervened smoothly. "Elizabeth is defending data, Gerald. The metrics speak for themselves."

"Metrics don't capture risk," Gerald countered. "Wells offers certainty. Calloway offers potential—with all its attendant risks."

"Meridian wasn't built on certainty," Howard said quietly. "We've always balanced innovation with pragmatism."

The debate continued through lunch, catered sandwiches growing stale as positions hardened. By mid-afternoon, the committee had effectively split: Gerald, the CFO, and Operations favoring Wells; Howard, Catherine, and HR leaning toward Calloway; with Liz maintaining a facade of neutrality despite her internal certainty.

"Perhaps we should adjourn and reconvene tomorrow," Howard suggested as the discussion circled back on itself.

"Before we do," Gerald said, "I'd like to hear Ms. Donovan's personal recommendation. She's analyzed the data most thoroughly, yet has been curiously reserved about stating a preference."

All eyes turned to Liz. She felt a familiar tightness in her chest—the pressure of judgment, of being evaluated not just on her analysis but on her allegiance.

"My recommendation is based solely on which firm best meets our stated objectives," she began carefully. "While Wells offers proven reliability, Calloway Design Group demonstrates superior innovation, sustainability integration, and alignment with our 'progressive tradition' philosophy. Their design doesn't just house our company—it expresses it."

Gerald studied her with narrowed eyes. "And your recommendation has nothing to do with your personal history with James Calloway?"

The room fell silent. Liz felt blood rush to her face.

"What personal history?" Howard asked.

"They attended the same high school," Catherine explained before Liz could respond. "Academic rivals, I understand."

Gerald's smile didn't reach his eyes. "My grandson attended Preston Academy a few years behind them. The Mitchell-Calloway rivalry was apparently legendary. Something about a scholarship competition?"

The Beckman. The memory hit Liz with physical force—standing on stage at the awards ceremony, certain she'd won the prestigious full scholarship to Rice University. She'd applied on a whim, her essay on literary narrative as architectural space earning her finalist status alongside James. When the foundation's president announced James's name instead of hers, the shock had been visceral. Later, she'd learned the margin between their scores had been decimal points.

"That was twenty years ago," Liz said, her voice remarkably steady. "And completely irrelevant to this discussion."

"Is it?" Gerald pressed. "Professional objectivity is difficult when personal history is involved."

"If anything," Liz countered, "my history with James Calloway makes me more critical of his work, not less. I've scrutinized his proposal more thoroughly than anyone's."

Howard raised a hand to silence further discussion. "Elizabeth's analysis speaks for itself. Let's take a day to review the materials again and reconvene tomorrow morning."

As the committee dispersed, Liz gathered her materials with deliberate calm, avoiding eye contact. She'd nearly escaped when Catherine caught up with her in the hallway.

"You should have told me about the scholarship," Catherine said quietly.

"It wasn't relevant."

"Gerald Matheson just made it relevant." Catherine steered them toward her office. "What else should I know before tomorrow's vote?"

Inside Catherine's office, Liz sank into a chair. "We were competitive in high school. Top students in our class. The Beckman Scholarship was the culmination of that rivalry."

"And you lost."

"By three-tenths of a point." The bitterness in her voice surprised her. "But that has nothing to do with my professional assessment of his firm's proposal."

Catherine studied her with those penetrating eyes. "Doesn't it? We're shaped by our histories, Elizabeth. Pretending otherwise doesn't make for good decisions."

"What are you suggesting? That I'm sabotaging James because of a twenty-year-old grudge? Or favoring him to prove I'm over it?"

"I'm suggesting you acknowledge the complication instead of denying it exists." Catherine leaned forward. "Your analysis is excellent. Your recommendation is sound. But Gerald has created doubt about your objectivity, and that could sway the vote against Calloway."

Liz rubbed her temples. "So what do I do?"

"Address it directly. Acknowledge your history, then demonstrate how your analysis compensates for potential bias." Catherine's expression softened slightly. "And maybe examine whether you're truly as objective as you believe."

That night, Liz worked late in her office, refining her presentation for the next day. The building had emptied hours ago, leaving her alone with fluorescent lights and the weight of tomorrow's decision.

On her computer screen, images from Calloway Design Group's proposal rotated in a slideshow. James's vision was undeniably brilliant—integrating Meridian's values into physical space with an elegance that made Wells's design look pedestrian by comparison.

Was she supporting his proposal because it was superior? Or because some part of her still needed to prove herself his equal?

A memory surfaced—the Preston Academy debate finals, senior year. The topic: "Tradition versus innovation in institutional design." James had drawn the tradition position, Liz innovation. The irony wasn't lost on her now.

She'd prepared meticulously, crafting arguments about the necessity of breaking from outdated forms. Her opening statement had been flawless, earning approving nods from the judges.

Then James had risen, adjusted his tie, and systematically dismantled her position—not by defending blind tradition, but by reframing the debate entirely.

"The question isn't whether to choose tradition or innovation," he'd argued, "but how to honor the purpose behind traditions while evolving their forms. True innovation doesn't reject history—it builds upon it with respect and understanding."

He'd won. Not because his argument was inherently superior, but because he'd seen beyond the false dichotomy the prompt presented. It was the moment Liz realized James didn't just think differently than she did—he thought beyond conventional frameworks entirely.

Now, staring at his architectural vision for Meridian, she recognized that same quality. He hadn't designed just a building but a philosophy expressed in physical form.

Her phone buzzed with a text from Mark: "Dinner in microwave. Don't work too late."

The perfunctory message emphasized the distance between them. Once, Mark would have asked about her day, offered encouragement about her project. Now they exchanged logistical information like room- mates managing a shared space.

Liz closed the presentation and gathered her things. Tomorrow would determine not just Meridian's archi- tectural future but her professional trajectory as well. The thought should have terrified her. Instead, she felt strangely energized by the challenge.

The selection committee reconvened at nine the next morning. Liz arrived early, setting up her revised presentation with coffee-fueled precision. She'd barely slept, rehearsing her approach until dawn.

"Good morning, everyone," Howard began once all members were seated. "Before we continue yesterday's discussion, Elizabeth has asked to address the committee."

Liz stood, meeting Gerald's skeptical gaze directly. "Yesterday, Mr. Matheson raised a valid concern about my objectivity regarding Calloway Design Group. I want to address that transparently."

She clicked to her first slide—a photograph of the Preston Academy debate team, James and Liz standing at opposite ends, trophies in hand.

"James Calloway and I were academic rivals throughout high school. We competed for everything from class rankings to the Beckman Scholarship, which he won by a narrow margin. Our history is real, and it would be dishonest to pretend it doesn't exist."

She advanced to the next slide—her evaluation matrix with a new column.

"That's precisely why I developed this bias-controlled methodology. Each firm was evaluated using blind scoring on technical requirements, with secondary review by Derek Townsend from my department. Where subjective judgment was necessary, I applied consistent criteria across all proposals."

For the next fifteen minutes, Liz methodically demonstrated how her process controlled for potential bias, concluding with a clear comparison of the three finalists that left little doubt about the superior option.

"In conclusion," she finished, "when evaluated objectively across all our stated requirements, Calloway Design Group's proposal offers the optimal balance of innovation, functionality, and alignment with Meridian's values—regardless of any personal history."

The room fell silent when she finished. Even Gerald looked thoughtful rather than combative.

"Thank you, Elizabeth," Howard said. "That was exceptionally thorough."

The subsequent discussion was markedly different from the previous day's. Gerald still advocated for Wells's reliability, but with less certainty. The CFO raised valid concerns about budget contingencies for Calloway's innovative features. Operations questioned timeline feasibility.

Liz addressed each concern with data rather than defensiveness, acknowledging legitimate risks while demonstrating how they could be mitigated.

By noon, the energy in the room had shifted. When Howard called for a final recommendation vote, the result was clear: five to two in favor of Calloway Design Group, with only Gerald and the CFO dissenting.

"It's decided then," Howard announced, looking pleased. "I'll inform the firms of our decision this afternoon. The project committee will transition to implementation phase immediately." He turned to Liz. "Elizabeth, as our marketing representative with the most comprehensive understanding of the proposal, you'll serve as primary liaison with Calloway's team."

Liz maintained her professional composure while her stomach executed a complex gymnastic routine. Primary liaison. Direct collaboration with James. Daily interaction with the man who had once been both her greatest rival and secret measuring stick.

"Of course," she replied smoothly. "I'll prepare a transition briefing."

As the committee dispersed, Catherine lingered behind. "Excellent presentation. You addressed the bias concern perfectly."

"Thank you for the advice."

Catherine studied her with those unnervingly perceptive eyes. "This project will be challenging enough without personal complications, Elizabeth. Whatever history exists between you and James Calloway needs to remain in the past."

"It will," Liz assured her. "This is about Meridian's future, not our past."

"See that it stays that way." Catherine's tone softened slightly. "For what it's worth, I think Howard made the right choice—both in the firm and in you as liaison."

After Catherine left, Liz returned to her office, closing the door before allowing herself a moment of genuine reaction. Primary liaison. The professional opportunity was significant—high visibility with executive leadership, creative input on a landmark project, potential career advancement.

The personal implications were more complex. Working directly with James meant confronting not just their shared history but the divergent paths that had followed. He had pursued his architectural passion without compromise, building a reputation for innovative excellence. She had detoured into corporate marketing, her literary ambitions and creative instincts channeled into selling software solutions and crafting brand narratives.

Howard's email arrived mid-afternoon, copying all committee members: "Calloway Design Group has accepted our offer. Contract negotiations begin tomorrow. Project kickoff meeting scheduled for Monday, 9 AM."

Liz stared at the screen, the reality settling over her. In five days, she would sit across from James Calloway in a professional capacity, expected to collaborate as though they were merely new acquaintances rather than people with a complicated history.

Her phone rang—Catherine's extension.

"Elizabeth, Howard wants you to send the initial communication to Calloway. Professional courtesy before the formal contracts. Just a brief welcome and coordination details for Monday's kickoff."

"Of course. I'll draft something immediately."

After hanging up, Liz opened a new email. The cursor blinked expectantly on the blank screen. How did one address a former rival now turned professional collaborator? How formal should the tone be? How much acknowledgment of their past was appropriate?

She typed and deleted three different openings before settling on professional simplicity:

To: James.Calloway@CallowayDesign.com

From: Elizabeth.Donovan@MeridianEnterprises.com

Subject: Meridian Headquarters Project - Kickoff Coordination

Mr. Calloway, On behalf of Meridian Enterprises, I'm pleased to formally welcome Calloway Design Group to our headquarters redevelopment project. As the marketing department representative on the project committee, I'll be serving as your primary liaison throughout the design and implementation phases. I'd like to schedule a preliminary meeting before Monday's official kickoff to discuss communication protocols, stakeholder management expectations, and initial timeline coordination. Would tomorrow at 2:00 PM at your offices be convenient?

Please let me know if you require any specific materials or information in advance of our meeting.

Regards,

Elizabeth Donovan

Senior Marketing Director

Meridian Enterprises

Her finger hovered over the send button. The email was perfectly professional, appropriately formal, and completely devoid of any acknowledgment of their history. It was also utterly false in its pretense that they were strangers.

After a moment's hesitation, she added a final line:

P.S. Congratulations on the selection. Your proposal demonstrated the same innovative thinking that made our AP Literature debates so challenging. I look forward to working together.

Before she could reconsider, Liz clicked send. The message disappeared into the digital ether, the first thread in what would become a complex tapestry of professional collaboration and personal reckoning.

For better or worse, Elizabeth Donovan and James Calloway were once again in competition—not against each other this time, but against the shadows of who they had once been and the question of who they might become.

CHAPTER SIX

"Professional Boundaries"

The industrial district had transformed since Liz last visited. Once-abandoned warehouses now housed artisanal coffee roasters, tech startups, and creative agencies. The Calloway Design Group occupied a corner building—a former textile factory whose brick exterior gave little hint of what waited inside.

Liz checked her reflection in her car's visor mirror, smoothing an imaginary wrinkle from her navy blazer. She'd chosen her outfit with maddening precision that morning—professional without trying too hard, confident without being showy. The emerald silk blouse beneath her blazer was her only concession to vanity, a color Mark once said made her eyes look like "fancy whiskey."

James's reply to her email had been prompt and formal, accepting her proposed meeting time with a brief "Looking forward to productive collaboration." No acknowledgment of her postscript, no hint of personal connection. Just business.

The building's entrance featured a simple steel door with the firm's logo, a minimalist "C" that somehow managed to suggest both stability and movement. Liz pushed it open, stepping from bright sunlight into a space that momentarily stole her breath.

The interior bore no resemblance to the factory it had once been. Soaring ceilings revealed exposed beams and ductwork, but bathed in natural light from strategically placed skylights. The industrial bones remained, but transformed—like a cathedral to creativity. The reception area featured a floating desk of reclaimed wood, behind which a young woman with purple-tipped hair looked up.

"Ms. Donovan? Mr. Calloway is expecting you."

Before the receptionist could rise, a side door opened and James appeared. Today he wore charcoal trousers and a black button-down with sleeves rolled to the elbows, revealing forearms corded with lean muscle. The casual attire somehow emphasized his authority rather than diminishing it.

"Elizabeth." He extended his hand. "Welcome to Calloway Design."

His grip was firm, professional, the contact brief enough to be proper yet long enough to register the warmth of his palm against hers. Up close, the small scar through his right eyebrow was more noticeable—a jagged white line interrupting the perfect symmetry of his features.

"Thank you for accommodating my schedule," Liz replied, withdrawing her hand and gesturing to the leather portfolio tucked under her arm. "I've prepared some preliminary materials on communication protocols and stakeholder management."

"Always prepared." Something flickered in his eyes—amusement? Respect? "My office is this way."

He led her through the main workspace—an open floor plan with architecture tables and computer stations arranged in collaborative clusters. Designers and architects looked up briefly as they passed, curiosity evident. The space hummed with focused energy, the walls adorned with sketches, models, and photographs of completed projects. The Thomas Building featured prominently—that controversial masterpiece that had established James's reputation for pushing boundaries.

His office occupied a corner with glass walls that maintained connection to the team while offering acoustic privacy. Inside, a drafting table stood perpendicular to a modern desk, both positioned to capture natural light. Behind the desk hung framed architectural awards—impressive without being ostentatious.

"Please, sit." James indicated a chair across from his desk. "Can I offer you coffee? Water?"

"Water would be fine."

As he poured from a carafe, Liz took the opportunity to compose herself. The studio was exactly what she'd expected—and nothing like she'd imagined. It reflected success without arrogance, creativity without chaos. It was, she had to admit, impressive.

"Before we begin," James said, returning with her water, "I'd like to address the elephant in the room."

Liz stiffened slightly. "Which elephant would that be?"

A ghost of a smile touched his lips. "Our history. Preston Academy. The Beckman."

"Ancient history."

"Is it?" He studied her over the rim of his own water glass. "It has been a long time, but not long enough to forget being rivals."

"We're not rivals now, James. We're collaborators on a project that matters to both our organizations."

"Precisely my point." He set down his glass. "I want to be clear that I intend to approach this project as a true partnership. Whatever competitive dynamic ex-

isted between us at seventeen has no place in professional collaboration at thirty-eight."

The directness caught her off guard. She'd expected him to either ignore their past entirely or use it as
subtle leverage. This straightforward acknowledgment
disarmed her prepared defenses.

"I appreciate that," she said finally. "And I share your
commitment to a productive partnership."

"Good." He leaned back slightly. "Now, you mentioned communication protocols?"

For the next thirty minutes, they established project
parameters with brisk efficiency. Liz outlined Meridian's approval processes and key stakeholders, while
James explained his team structure and design development approach. The conversation flowed with professional ease, interrupted only when James's phone
buzzed.

"Excuse me." He glanced at the screen. "My associate
has arrived. I asked him to join us for the tour and
branding discussion."

The door opened to reveal a young Asian man with
intense eyes and a portfolio under his arm. He couldn't
have been more than thirty, but carried himself with
quiet confidence.

"Elizabeth, this is Thomas Chen, my lead designer
on the Meridian project. Thomas, Elizabeth Donovan,

Senior Marketing Director and our primary client liaison."

Thomas's handshake was firm, his assessment of her swift and thorough. "Ms. Donovan. James speaks highly of your analytical abilities."

"Does he?" Liz glanced at James, who maintained a neutral expression.

"Thomas graduated top of his class at MIT," James explained. "He's been with the firm four years and has a particular talent for translating brand values into spatial experience."

"The Meridian philosophy of 'progressive tradition' presents interesting architectural challenges," Thomas said, opening his portfolio on James's desk. "We've been exploring how to physically manifest that tension between innovation and established practice."

His sketches revealed preliminary concepts for the headquarters atrium—a soaring space where traditional materials like wood and stone were employed in thoroughly modern ways. The designs were thoughtful, sophisticated, showing both technical skill and conceptual depth.

"These are preliminary, of course," Thomas continued. "We'll refine based on stakeholder input and site requirements."

"They're impressive," Liz acknowledged. "Though I'm curious about how you'll integrate Meridian's brand touchpoints without making the space feel corporate-generic."

Thomas glanced at James, something unspoken passing between them.

"Perhaps that would be easier to discuss while touring the studio," James suggested. "Seeing our approach might clarify our thinking."

The tour began in the main workspace, where James introduced key team members. Each station featured models or renderings of past and current projects, revealing the firm's evolution. James moved through the space with easy authority, his hand occasionally touching Liz's elbow to guide her—brief, professional contacts that nonetheless left warmth in their wake.

"Our process emphasizes collaborative iteration," he explained as they examined a scale model of a university building. "Initial concepts emerge from deep research into the client's needs, values, and aspirations. We believe architecture should solve problems while creating experiences that elevate daily life."

The tour continued to a materials library where samples of sustainable building components lined the walls. James demonstrated a kinetic facade system similar to what he'd proposed for Meridian—panels that adjusted to sunlight, temperature, and occupancy patterns.

"The building essentially breathes," he explained, his passion evident as he manipulated the model. "Responding to environmental conditions while maintaining optimal interior comfort."

"With significant energy savings," Thomas added. "Thirty percent reduction compared to conventional systems."

They proceeded to a rooftop garden where prototype plantings demonstrated various sustainable landscaping approaches. The space offered spectacular city views while creating a natural oasis above the urban congestion.

"We use this for client meetings and team gatherings," James explained. "It's also our laboratory for testing green roof systems like what we've proposed for Meridian."

Standing beside him at the rooftop's edge, Liz was struck by the contrast between this space and her sterile office at Meridian. Here, ideas seemed to flow as naturally as the breeze that ruffled her hair. James had created not just a workplace but an ecosystem for creativity.

"This would be the view from Howard's office in our design," James said, pointing toward the river. "Morning light, city connection, but with natural elements as a buffer."

"He'll appreciate that," Liz admitted. "Howard talks about being connected to the city without being consumed by it."

"Exactly the balance we're trying to achieve."

As they descended to the main floor, Thomas excused himself to take a call, leaving Liz and James alone as they entered a conference room where renderings of the Meridian project covered the walls.

"These are more developed than what you presented to the committee," Liz observed, studying a detailed section of the proposed lobby.

"We've been refining since the initial proposal." James stood beside her, close enough that she caught the faint scent of his cologne—something subtle with notes of cedar. "The presentation gave us confidence to advance the concept."

"Without client input?" Liz raised an eyebrow. "That's presumptuous."

"Prepared, not presumptuous. We develop multiple options so clients can react to concrete possibilities rather than abstractions." He turned to face her directly. "But you're right—we should have waited for your input on the brand integration."

The admission surprised her. "That's... refreshingly self-aware."

"I've learned a few things over the years, Elizabeth." His use of her full name carried an undercurrent she couldn't quite identify. "Including when to acknowledge a valid critique."

Their eyes held for a moment longer than professionally necessary. Liz broke contact first, moving to examine another rendering.

"These entry sequences emphasize transparency," she noted. "That aligns well with Howard's vision for client experience."

"But you have concerns."

"Not concerns exactly." She chose her words carefully. "Meridian's clients include financial institutions and healthcare providers. Their security requirements might conflict with this open approach."

"Security and openness aren't mutually exclusive." James joined her at the rendering. "We can create layered security without obvious barriers. The experience of welcome remains while controlling access."

"That's the theory. In practice, security always compromises experience."

"Only with unimaginative design." James's voice took on an edge. "Still approaching everything like it's a debate competition to be won, Elizabeth?"

The question landed like a physical touch. "I'm approaching it like a marketing director responsible for brand experience. Still confusing innovation with complication for its own sake, James?"

A beat of silence, then something unexpected—James laughed, a genuine sound that transformed his features. "There she is. I was wondering when Preston Academy Elizabeth would make an appearance."

Despite herself, Liz felt her lips curve upward. "She's never far below the surface."

"Good. She asks better questions." He gestured to the renderings. "Show me where the brand integration fails."

For the next hour, they engaged in detailed discussion of how architecture could embody Meridian's values. The conversation flowed with increasing energy as they challenged each other's assumptions, building on ideas rather than tearing them down. Thomas rejoined them, contributing technical insights while observing their dynamic with quiet interest.

"The central atrium needs to communicate Meridian's evolution," Liz argued, sketching rapidly on tracing paper laid over a rendering. "Not just where the company is now, but its journey."

"A chronological display would be corporate-generic," James countered. "What if instead we embed the narrative in the materials themselves? Older, established materials at the foundation, transitioning to innovative composites as you move upward."

"Physical metaphor as brand story." Liz considered the concept. "It could work if subtle enough."

"We can develop material studies," Thomas suggested. "Showing the transition at different scales."

As afternoon stretched into early evening, their discussion expanded to encompass workspace psychology, client journey mapping, and the politics of corner offices. They'd moved from the conference room back to James's office, where diagrams and sketches now covered his desk.

"Howard will never agree to eliminate private offices entirely," Liz said, circling a section of floorplan. "Executive privacy is non-negotiable."

"We're not eliminating privacy," James clarified. "We're redefining it. Glass walls with programmable opacity, sound isolation through advanced acoustics. Privacy when needed, connection by default."

"It's a significant cultural shift."

"Isn't that partly the point? Architecture that enables cultural evolution?"

The question hung between them—not just about office design but about the nature of change itself. Before Liz could respond, her phone chimed with a calendar alert. Six o'clock—she'd been at the studio for four hours, double her intended stay.

"I should go," she said, gathering her notes. "Mark will be wondering where I am."

Something flickered across James's face at the mention of her husband—so brief she might have imagined it.

"Of course." He stood, professional mask firmly in place. "Thomas, would you prepare the material samples we discussed for Monday's kickoff?"

Thomas nodded, gathering the sketches they'd annotated. "I'll have concept revisions by tomorrow afternoon. Nice meeting you, Ms. Donovan."

After Thomas departed, James walked Liz toward the reception area. The studio had emptied while they worked, the space now quiet except for their footsteps on the polished concrete floor.

"I'll have my team incorporate today's insights into the presentation materials," James said. "Your perspective on brand integration is valuable."

"Your team is impressive," Liz acknowledged. "Especially Thomas. He's extraordinarily talented."

"He reminds me of someone I used to know." James's voice carried a hint of something unidentifiable. "Brilliant, driven, sees connections others miss."

They reached the entrance, pausing in the liminal space between his world and the outside. The late afternoon sun slanted through the door, creating a golden rectangle on the floor between them.

"Thank you for today," Liz said, extending her hand with deliberate formality. "It was productive."

James took her hand, but instead of the brief professional handshake she expected, he held it a moment longer. "It was." His eyes held hers. "I've missed this, you know."

"Missed what?"

"Having my thinking challenged by someone who keeps up." A slight smile. "Not many people do."

The compliment warmed her more than it should have. "Well, we have eighteen months of challenging each other ahead of us. I'm sure the novelty will wear off."

"I doubt that." He released her hand. "See you Monday, Elizabeth."

Outside, the summer evening embraced her with humid warmth as she walked to her car. Through the studio's front windows, she could see James still standing in the reception area, watching her departure with an expression she couldn't decipher from this distance. For a moment, she was tempted to turn back, to continue their conversation that had somehow shifted from professional to something more complex.

Instead, she unlocked her car and slipped inside, sitting motionless for several minutes before starting the engine. The day had left her oddly energized yet unsettled, her mind racing with ideas for the project—and with the disconcerting realization that four hours of intellectual sparring with James Calloway had engaged her more deeply than any conversation she'd had in years.

, As she pulled away from the curb, she glanced in her rearview mirror. James had moved to the doorway, his tall figure silhouetted against the golden light of his studio. For a brief, irrational moment, she imagined what it would be like to return to that light instead of driving home to Mark and their carefully maintained suburban existence.

The thought lasted only seconds before she banished it, turning her attention to traffic and the long drive home. Whatever had sparked between them today was professional chemistry, nothing more—the natural result of two competitive minds engaging with a complex problem.

At least, that's what she told herself as the Calloway Design Group faded from her rearview mirror, replaced by the familiar route back to a house that somehow felt less like home with each passing day.

CHAPTER SEVEN

"Domestic Dissonance"

L iz pulled into the driveway at 7:43 PM. The house windows glowed with the blue flicker of the television—Mark was home, likely settled into his recliner with dinner balanced on his lap. She sat in the car a moment longer, trying to recapture the intellectual energy she'd felt at Calloway Design. The transition from professional stimulation to domestic routine always jarred, but tonight the dissonance felt particularly acute.

She gathered her portfolio and purse, mentally rehearsing how to describe her day. Mark wasn't interested in marketing details, but surely the architectural project would intrigue him. Something tangible, un-like her usual campaigns.

The front door opened to the familiar soundtrack of a basketball game. Mark's Northwestern Wildcats sweatshirt stretched across his broadening midsection as he lounged in his leather recliner, a half-eaten plate of microwaved lasagna on the side table.

"Hey," he called without looking away from the screen. "There's food in the microwave."

"Thanks." Liz set her things on the entryway table. "Sorry I'm late. The meeting at the architectural firm ran longer than expected."

Mark grunted as a player missed a shot. "No prob-lem."

Liz kicked off her heels and padded to the kitchen, where a foil-covered plate waited beside a sticky note with microwave instructions in Mark's blocky hand-writing. Once, she'd found his practicality endearing. Now it felt like evidence of their parallel lives—him handling dinner, her handling work, neither truly en-gaging with the other's world.

She returned to the living room with her reheated food, settling on the couch. Mark's eyes remained fixed on the game.

"The architectural studio was amazing," she offered between bites. "Converted warehouse with this incred-ible open concept. The team seems brilliant."

"That's nice." Mark reached for his beer. "Who's designing the building again?"

"Calloway Design Group. They did the Thomas Building downtown—the one with the kinetic facade system."

"The what system?"

"Kinetic facade. The exterior panels move in response to sunlight and temperature." Liz leaned forward, warming to the subject. "It's brilliant engineering that reduces energy consumption while creating this dynamic visual effect. The building literally changes throughout the day."

Mark glanced at her, then back at the game. "Sounds expensive."

"It's actually cost-effective over time. The energy savings."

"Three-pointer!" Mark interrupted as the crowd on TV erupted. "Did you see that shot? Unbelievable."

Liz fell silent, pushing lasagna around her plate. After a moment, she tried again. "The lead architect went to high school with me, actually. James Calloway. We were academic rivals."

This caught Mark's attention momentarily. "The guy who beat you for valedictorian?"

"Yes." She was surprised he remembered. "He's become quite successful. His firm is doing innovative work with sustainable design."

"Huh." Mark turned back to the game. "Must be weird working with him now."

"It's... interesting. Challenging." She searched for words that might bridge their worlds. "Like playing against a familiar opponent who knows your moves."

"Speaking of which," Mark gestured to the TV, "Robertson's playing like he knows exactly what their defense is planning. Coach should give him more minutes."

And just like that, the conversation slipped away. Liz finished her dinner in silence, watching her husband watch basketball. His body occupied the same room as hers, but his mind might as well have been in another country.

"I'm going to review some project materials," she said, standing with her empty plate.

Mark nodded without looking up. "Game's almost over. I'll be up later."

In her home office, Liz opened her laptop and spread out the notes from her meeting with James. The contrast between the intellectual engagement she'd felt hours earlier and the emptiness of her exchange with Mark created a hollow ache in her chest. When had they stopped having real conversations? When had his eyes last lit up at something she said?

She worked until midnight, losing herself in the Meridian project specifications. When she finally crawled into bed, Mark was already asleep, his broad back turned toward her side. She stared at the ceiling, listening to his steady breathing, feeling the vast distance between them despite the inches separating their bodies.

"Kevin and Lisa are coming at seven," Mark announced Saturday morning, scrolling through his phone at the breakfast counter. "Kevin's bringing steaks for the grill."

Liz looked up from the project documents she'd been reviewing. "Tonight? I thought that was next weekend."

"Nope, tonight. I told you on Tuesday."

Had he? Liz couldn't remember any such conversation, but that wasn't unusual lately. They spoke at each other more than to each other, words passing without landing.

"I'll need to go to the store," she said, mentally rearranging her day. "What should I make for sides?"

"Whatever's easy. Lisa's bringing that pasta salad thing you like."

Liz nodded, closing her laptop. The Barnes were their closest friends in the neighborhood—Kevin, a sales manager at a pharmaceutical company, and Lisa, a part-time real estate agent. Their friendship consisted mainly of shared meals, neighborhood gossip, and discussions of home improvement projects. Pleasant but rarely profound.

"I thought I might work on the Meridian project this afternoon," Liz said. "I need to prepare for Monday's kickoff meeting."

Mark shrugged. "Just be done by six so you can help set up."

The rest of the day unfolded with domestic efficiency. Liz cleaned the house while Mark mowed the lawn. She prepared a salad and dessert while he cleaned the grill. They moved around each other with the practiced choreography of fifteen years of marriage, rarely making eye contact, their conversations limited to household logistics.

At 6:55, Liz changed into a casual sundress and applied fresh lipstick. She studied her reflection, noting the slight shadows under her eyes from late nights working. For a moment, she wondered what James would think of her suburban home with its matching furniture sets and framed vacation photos. The thought was inappropriate and irrelevant, yet it lingered as she descended the stairs to greet their guests.

"There she is!" Kevin's booming voice filled the foyer as he handed Mark a six-pack of craft beer. At 41, Kevin maintained the hearty enthusiasm of a former fraternity president, his receding hairline compensated by an expensive watch and perpetual tan.

Lisa followed, pasta salad in hand, her blonde highlights freshly done. "Liz, you look amazing. Is that dress new?"

"Old, actually." Liz accepted Lisa's air kiss. "Just hasn't seen much use lately."

"Well, it should. The color is perfect on you."

The couples moved to the patio, where Mark immediately engaged Kevin in a discussion about lawn fertilizer strategies. Lisa rolled her eyes at Liz with good-natured exasperation.

"Men and their lawns," she said, pouring herself wine from the bottle Liz had opened. "Kevin spent three hundred dollars on some special seed last month. Three hundred! For grass!"

"Mark's been researching irrigation systems," Liz replied, settling into the familiar rhythm of wives commiserating. "Apparently our current sprinkler placement is 'inefficient.'"

"At least yours has practical hobbies. Kevin's latest thing is collecting vintage beer cans. We have shelves of them in the garage."

The conversation flowed along well-worn channels—neighborhood gossip, children's accomplishments (the Barnes' teenage sons), vacation plans. Liz found herself observing rather than participating, noticing the patterns in their social quartet. Kevin dominated conversations while Mark played affable sidekick. Lisa asked questions but rarely offered personal revelations. And Liz herself performed the role of engaged hostess while keeping her thoughts carefully contained.

As Mark grilled steaks with Kevin's unsolicited advice, Liz watched the two men—the easy male camaraderie, the comfortable sharing of space. When had she and Mark last shared anything beyond household management? When had he last asked about her work with genuine interest?

"Earth to Liz," Lisa waved her hand. "Where'd you go?"

"Sorry." Liz refocused. "Just thinking about a work project."

"The new building thing? Mark mentioned you're working with some fancy architect."

"Yes, Meridian's new headquarters. It's a significant project—eighteen months from concept to completion."

"Sounds exhausting," Lisa said, sipping her wine. "But you always did love throwing yourself into work."

The comment carried a subtle judgment Liz recognized from previous conversations. Lisa had left her corporate job when her first son was born, transitioning to part-time real estate that accommodated school schedules and family vacations. She occasionally made comments suggesting Liz's career focus was a compensatory mechanism for not having children.

"It's actually fascinating," Liz replied, choosing to ignore the subtext. "The architecture firm is doing innovative work with sustainable design. The building will generate part of its own energy through kinetic facades and geothermal systems."

Lisa's eyes glazed slightly. "Well, that sounds... technical. Is the architect cute, at least? That would make eighteen months more interesting."

The question caught Liz off-guard. James's face flashed in her mind—the intensity of his blue eyes, the slight scar through his eyebrow, the way his expression transformed when he was explaining a design concept.

"He's... professional," she managed. "Actually, we went to high school together."

"No way! Old flame?" Lisa leaned forward with sudden interest.

"God, no. Academic rival. We competed for everything—debate tournaments, writing awards, class ranking."

"Like that movie with the two lawyers who hate each other and then fall in love?"

Liz forced a laugh. "Nothing like that. We barely spoke outside of academic competitions."

"Steaks are ready!" Mark called, saving Liz from further questioning.

Dinner proceeded with the usual distribution of conversational labor—Kevin discussing his recent sales triumph, Mark recounting a client golf outing, Lisa updating them on her sons' sports achievements. Liz contributed appropriately, asking follow-up questions and offering congratulations at the right moments.

"How about you, Liz?" Kevin asked eventually. "Mark says you're working on some big building project?"

"Yes, Meridian's new headquarters. I'm the marketing liaison for the design process."

"So what does that mean—you pick the paint colors?" Kevin laughed at his own joke.

"Not exactly." Liz kept her tone light despite the condescension. "I ensure the architectural design embodies our brand values and creates the right experience for clients and employees."

"She's playing with building blocks," Mark interjected with a chuckle. "Big, expensive ones."

The dismissive comment stung more than it should have. "It's actually a complex integration of spatial design, brand storytelling, and functional requirements," Liz said, unable to keep the edge from her voice. "The architecture becomes a physical embodiment of the company's identity and values."

An awkward silence followed. Kevin raised his eyebrows at Mark in a male solidarity gesture that clearly communicated: *Touched a nerve there, buddy.*

"Well, it sounds very important," Lisa said with forced brightness. "Speaking of high school, did I tell you Tommy got selected for the honors program? Following in his mom's footsteps—I was in all the advanced classes back in the day."

"Liz was a total brainiac in high school," Mark said, clearly relieved by the subject change. "All those academic trophies and perfect grades. She was so serious about school, it was kind of adorable."

"Not that serious," Liz corrected. "I had normal teenage interests too."

"Oh yeah? Like what?" Mark challenged with a teasing smile. "I remember that story about your senior prom—tell them, Liz."

She knew immediately which story he meant. "It's not that interesting."

"Come on, it's hilarious." Mark turned to Kevin and Lisa. "So Liz was supposed to go to prom with this guy from her debate team, but the night before, she realized prom was the same day as some big academic competition—"

"The state literature symposium," Liz interjected. "I was presenting a paper that had been accepted for publication."

"Right, some paper thing. So she calls this poor guy and cancels prom to go present her paper. Who does that?"

Kevin laughed appreciatively while Lisa made a sympathetic noise. Liz felt a familiar hollowness expand in her chest. Mark had told this story many times over the years, always with the same framing—Liz the over-serious student, prioritizing academics over normal teenage experiences. What he never included was that the paper had won a prestigious award, opening doors to college opportunities. Or that the "debate team guy" had asked her to prom only after his first choice turned him down.

"The paper was on narrative structure in modernist literature," Liz said quietly. "It was published in an undergraduate journal afterward."

"See what I mean?" Mark gestured with his beer. "Total brainiac. Thank god she loosened up in college, or I'd never have had a chance with her."

The conversation moved on, but Liz remained caught in the dissonance between Mark's characterization and her own memory. He portrayed her academic achievements as quirky personality flaws rather than accomplishments that had shaped her identity. When had that started? Had he always seen her intelligence as something to be teased about rather than respected?

After dinner, the men moved to the living room to watch highlights from a golf tournament while Liz and Lisa cleared the table. In the kitchen, Lisa lowered her voice.

"Everything okay with you? You seem a little... distant tonight."

Liz arranged dishes in the dishwasher with careful precision. "I'm fine. Just tired from work."

"It's more than that." Lisa leaned against the counter. "I've known you for eight years, Liz. Something's off."

The genuine concern in Lisa's voice cracked something in Liz's careful composure. "Do you ever feel like Kevin doesn't really see you? The real you?"

Lisa's expression shifted from surprise to understanding. "All the time. Last month I mentioned wanting to take a photography class, and he bought me a fancy camera without asking what kind I needed. Sweet gesture, completely missed the point."

"Mark told that prom story like it's a joke," Liz said, keeping her voice low. "That paper was important to me. It helped secure my scholarship to Northwestern. But in his version, I'm just the weird girl who chose books over boys."

"Men simplify things." Lisa sighed. "Kevin still introduces me as 'the homecoming queen I married' at his work functions. Never mentions I graduated cum laude or ran the marketing department at Simmons before the kids."

"How do you handle it?"

"Honestly? I correct him sometimes. Other times I let it go." Lisa's eyes took on a faraway look. "Marriage is long, Liz. You can't fight every battle."

"But if you let too many go..."

"You wake up one day wondering who you've become." Lisa finished the thought, then shook herself. "Listen to us—we sound like a bad Lifetime movie. Our husbands are good men. They just don't always get us."

From the living room came the sound of Mark and Kevin laughing at something on TV. The familiar, comfortable sound of their friendship highlighted the unexpected intimacy of the kitchen conversation.

"Does Kevin know about your photography interest now?" Liz asked.

Lisa smiled ruefully. "I don't think he'd notice if I turned the guest room into a darkroom. But that's marriage after fifteen years. The small disconnects accumulate until you're living parallel lives in the same house." She squeezed Liz's arm. "Just don't let work become your entire identity. That's the trap I see you falling into."

Before Liz could respond, Kevin appeared in the doorway. "Ladies, Mark's breaking out the scotch. You joining us?"

The moment of connection broken, Lisa transformed back into the cheerful suburban wife. "Coming! Just finishing up here."

Later, after their guests had departed and Mark had gone upstairs, Liz sat alone in the darkened living room. Lisa's words echoed in her mind: *parallel lives in the same house*. The description fit with uncomfortable precision. She and Mark occupied the same physical space but increasingly different mental landscapes. When had they stopped sharing their inner worlds? Had they ever truly shared them at all?

The house creaked and settled around her, fifteen years of memories embedded in its walls. Photos from their early days lined the hallway—Mark's arm around her at graduation, their honeymoon in Maui, the purchase of this house. She'd been happy then, hadn't she? Or had she just been young, mistaking passion for partnership, potential for reality?

Upstairs, she heard Mark's snores begin, the familiar rhythm that had become the soundtrack to her nights. She should join him, try to sleep, prepare for another week of balancing work demands and domestic expectations.

Instead, Liz returned to her office and opened her laptop. Sleep was impossible with her mind racing between Lisa's observations, Mark's dismissive comments, and the lingering energy from her meeting with James. She needed distraction.

Without conscious intention, she found herself typing "James Calloway Thomas Building" into the search bar. Articles appeared immediately—architectural reviews, sustainability awards, interviews with James about his design philosophy. She clicked on a video interview from an architecture journal.

James appeared on screen, standing before his controversial masterpiece. He looked slightly younger than now, his hair without the silver at the temples, but his presence was unmistakable—confident without arrogance, passionate about his work.

"The Thomas Building challenges conventional thinking about workplace design," he explained to the interviewer. "We're not just creating space for work; we're creating architecture that works, for people, for the environment, for the future."

As he described the building's innovative features, Liz found herself leaning closer to the screen. This was the James she remembered from high school, brilliant, articulate, seeing connections others missed. But maturity had tempered his youthful intensity with something deeper, more considered.

"Critics say the design prioritizes concept over functionality," the interviewer challenged.

James smiled slightly, the scar through his eyebrow catching the light. "That criticism assumes a false dichotomy between beauty and function. The most beautiful architectural solutions are those that solve real problems in unexpected ways. The facade isn't just aesthetically dynamic—it reduces energy consumption by forty percent. The atrium isn't just visually striking—it creates natural ventilation that improves air quality and worker wellbeing."

The clock on Liz's desk showed 2:47 AM. She should close the laptop, go to bed, lie beside her sleeping husband and try to quiet her mind. Instead, she clicked another interview, then another, absorbing James's design philosophy, the evolution of his thinking, the principles that guided his work.

At 3:18 AM, she found an article about the controversy surrounding the Thomas Building's security features—the very issue she'd challenged him about in the Meridian presentation. James had written a detailed defense of his approach, acknowledging the implementation challenges while standing by the conceptual integrity.

"Architecture exists at the intersection of aspiration and reality," he'd written. "When implementation falls short of vision, the solution isn't to abandon innovation but to refine it through iteration. The greatest architectural achievements throughout history emerged from productive failure and persistent revision."

Liz sat back, struck by the humility beneath his confidence. The James Calloway she'd known at seventeen would never have acknowledged failure so openly. The man he'd become had learned from experience without surrendering his vision.

She closed the laptop at 3:43 AM, her mind still churning. In her darkened office, surrounded by the carefully curated artifacts of her life with Mark, Liz confronted an uncomfortable truth: she couldn't remember the last time she'd felt intellectually alive the way she had during those hours in James's studio. The challenge of matching minds with someone who kept pace with her thinking—who pushed her to sharpen her arguments, refine her perspectives, defend her positions—had awakened something long dormant.

Upstairs, Mark's snores continued undisturbed. Liz slipped into bed beside him, careful not to wake him. He rolled slightly, one heavy arm draping across her waist in unconscious familiarity. The gesture should have comforted her. Instead, it felt like an anchor holding her in place while her mind drifted elsewhere.

She stared at the ceiling, counting the hours until Monday morning when she would return to Meridian, to the headquarters project, to the intellectual challenge that had reawakened her curiosity. To James Calloway and the unexpected revival of a rivalry that had once defined her.

Sleep, when it finally came, brought dreams of buildings that transformed themselves, facades shifting like expressions on a face she couldn't quite recognize but somehow knew intimately. And through it all, a voice discussing the intersection of aspiration and reality, of vision and implementation, of who she had been and who she might become.

CHAPTER EIGHT

"Drawing Lines"

The temporary project office had been hastily assembled at the edge of the construction site—a double-wide trailer with the Meridian logo hastily affixed to the door. Inside, folding tables formed a makeshift conference area, architectural plans covered the walls, and the smell of fresh coffee battled with construction dust.

Liz arrived fifteen minutes early for the first official project meeting, her leather portfolio tucked under her arm. Through the windows, she could see earth-moving equipment preparing the site where Meridian's future would rise. The vast emptiness held promise—a blank canvas waiting for creation.

She was arranging her materials when the door swung open. James entered with Thomas Chen a step behind, both carrying rolled blueprints and laptops. James wore a charcoal suit that somehow remained immaculate despite the dusty site, his white shirt open at the collar without a tie.

"Elizabeth." He nodded professionally. "You've found our humble war room."

"It has a certain rustic charm," she replied, gesturing to the folding chairs. "Very start-up aesthetic."

A ghost of a smile touched his lips. "We'll upgrade as the project evolves. Thomas is already designing custom furniture for when we move operations into the foundation level."

Thomas unrolled several drawings on the conference table. "The temporary space actually offers strategic advantages. Being on-site creates immediate feedback loops between design adjustments and implementation realities."

The door opened again, admitting a woman Liz hadn't met—petite with a riot of dark curls and striking amber eyes. She carried an oversized portfolio case decorated with colorful stickers from global destinations.

"Sorry I'm late," she announced without seeming remotely apologetic. "Traffic was biblical. Please tell me there's coffee."

"Just made," James replied. "Elizabeth Donovan, this is Sophia Rodriguez, our interior design lead. Sophia, Elizabeth is Meridian's marketing director and our primary client liaison."

"The famous Elizabeth." Sophia's handshake was firm, her assessment swift and thorough. "James mentioned you were formidable."

"Did he?" Liz glanced at James, who suddenly became very interested in organizing his papers.

"He said you'd challenge our assumptions," Sophia clarified with a knowing smile. "That's rare and valuable. Most clients just nod and pretend to understand spatial dynamics."

Howard arrived with Catherine and several Meridian executives, and the meeting officially began. James presented the project timeline while Thomas explained site preparation phases. Liz observed the easy rapport between the Calloway team—the shorthand communication, the seamless handoffs, the shared vision evident in how they built upon each other's points.

"Now for the critical path decisions," James said, advancing to a slide showing key milestones. "We need marketing narrative alignment before finalizing the entrance sequence design. Elizabeth, I understand you've prepared initial concepts?"

Liz distributed the document she'd prepared over the weekend—twelve pages of brand positioning, narrative structure, and experiential touchpoints. "Meridian's headquarters should tell our story through a carefully orchestrated journey," she explained. "From approach to entrance to interior progression, each spatial moment reinforces our brand promise of 'progressive tradition.'"

James studied the document with an unreadable expression. "You've certainly been thorough."

"That's one word for it," Thomas muttered, flipping through the densely annotated pages.

"The entrance sequence you've proposed," James continued, "emphasizes transparency and technological innovation. But the narrative structure here"—he tapped a section of her document—"leads with Meridian's historical stability and evolution."

"The contrast creates productive tension," Liz countered. "Visitors experience the physical embodiment of 'progressive tradition' through that deliberate juxtaposition."

"Or they experience cognitive dissonance." James leaned forward. "The architectural experience should align with the narrative, not contradict it."

"It's not contradiction, it's counterpoint." Liz felt the familiar spark of intellectual challenge. "Like dissonance resolving to harmony in music."

Sophia looked between them with growing interest. "I see both perspectives. The question is whether clients will appreciate the sophisticated tension or just feel confused."

"Exactly," James said. "Marketing narratives work differently in physical space than in communications. The experiential reality has to be intuitive, not intellectual."

"You're assuming visitors can't handle complexity," Liz replied, her tone sharpening. "Meridian's clients are sophisticated financial and healthcare executives. They navigate complexity daily."

"It's not about their intelligence," James countered. "It's about creating an immediate, visceral understanding that doesn't require conscious analysis."

Howard interrupted. "This is precisely the dialogue we need between marketing and architecture. Elizabeth understands our brand, James understands spatial experience. Find the synthesis."

The meeting continued with discussion of materials and sustainability features, but the tension between Liz and James remained palpable. When Howard and the executives departed for another meeting, Sophia immediately filled her coffee cup and settled back with evident anticipation.

"Now that the clients are gone," she said, "let's get to the real debate. James clearly thinks the marketing narrative is too complicated, and Elizabeth thinks the architectural approach is too simplistic. Yes?"

"I wouldn't say simplistic," Liz measured her words. "But there's a tendency in the current design to prior- itize aesthetic impact over narrative coherence."

James's eyebrows rose. "And there's a tendency in your marketing approach to over intellectualize what should be an intuitive experience."

"The Thomas Building had the same problem," Liz said before she could stop herself. "Brilliant concept, but the visitor experience was disjointed because the narrative wasn't properly integrated."

The temperature in the room seemed to drop several degrees. Thomas straightened, glancing between them with wide eyes.

"The Thomas Building's challenges stemmed from client-driven changes mid-construction," James replied, his voice deceptively calm. "The original con- cept maintained perfect narrative integrity."

"Perfect on paper," Liz countered. "The execution failed to translate that concept for actual users. The security controversy alone demonstrated the gap be- tween theoretical design and practical experience."

"Perhaps we should focus on Meridian specifically," Sophia suggested, though she made no move to actu- ally redirect the conversation.

James ignored her. "You've always had an impres- sive capacity for critique without offering constructive alternatives, Elizabeth. The Thomas Building pushed boundaries precisely because it rejected conventional thinking about workplace design."

"Pushing boundaries only matters if people can navigate the new territory," Liz shot back. "Innovation without accessibility is just self-indulgence."

"And accessibility without innovation is just mediocrity." James's eyes had taken on the intensity she remembered from debate tournaments. "You always did mistake loudest voice for strongest argument."

"And you always confused complexity with depth." The words escaped before she could filter them, the old rivalry flaring with unexpected heat.

Thomas cleared his throat loudly. "Perhaps we should take a short break?"

Sophia was watching them with undisguised fascination. "I don't think that's necessary. They're just getting to the interesting part."

James took a deliberate breath, visibly recalibrating. "Let's approach this constructively. Elizabeth, what specific elements of the entrance sequence do you believe fail to support Meridian's narrative?"

The professional redirect cooled the temperature slightly. Liz opened her portfolio to the relevant section. "The current approach emphasizes technological innovation through the dynamic facade and transparent materials. But Howard specifically wants visitors to feel Meridian's stability and established history first, with innovation revealed as they move deeper into the space."

"The facade isn't just about technology," James countered, moving to the architectural renderings. "The materials themselves tell the history story—traditional limestone base transitioning to advanced composites as the building rises. It's literally 'progressive tradition' in physical form."

"But that's not legible to visitors," Liz insisted. "They won't decode your material symbolism without explicit guidance."

"Then perhaps that's where marketing integration belongs—not in changing the architectural experience but in making its meaning accessible."

The suggestion caught Liz off-guard. It was actually... reasonable.

"That could work," she acknowledged. "Environmental graphics and digital touchpoints could reveal the meaning without compromising the spatial experience."

"Exactly." James seemed equally surprised by her agreement. "The architecture creates the experience; marketing makes it legible."

For the next hour, they worked through the entrance sequence in detail, finding unexpected common ground. Thomas contributed technical considerations while Sophia sketched potential integrated moments where brand storytelling could enhance the architectural experience.

"For the atrium," Sophia suggested, "we could use lighting to highlight the material transitions James mentioned—subtle projections that activate at key moments during the visitor journey."

"And incorporate Meridian's historical timeline into the limestone elements," Liz added, warming to the approach. "Making the company's evolution tangible within the materials themselves."

James nodded, making notes. "That maintains the spatial integrity while enhancing narrative comprehension. Good."

By meeting's end, they had outlined two approaches for next week's presentation—one emphasizing environmental graphics integrated with architecture, the other using digital touchpoints to create an augmented reality layer over the physical space.

"We'll develop both options," James concluded. "Each has merit, and Howard should see the range of possibilities."

As they gathered their materials, Sophia sidled up to Liz. "That was the most entertaining project meeting I've had in months. You two should take that show on the road."

"I don't know what you mean," Liz replied stiffly.

"Of course not." Sophia's smile was knowing. "But whatever that was—keep it coming. It's making the design better."

Thomas and Sophia departed first, leaving Liz and James alone in the trailer. The silence stretched uncomfortably as they organized their respective documents.

"I apologize for the Thomas Building comment," Liz finally said. "It was unnecessarily personal."

James looked up, surprise flickering across his features. "And I apologize for the debate competition reference. That was... unprofessional."

"We seem to bring out old patterns in each other."

"Not entirely old." His voice had softened. "We never used to find compromise this effectively."

"We were more interested in winning than in finding the best solution."

"Weren't we?" A ghost of a smile touched his lips. "I remember a particularly vicious debate about Hemingway's symbolism where you compared my analysis to 'a freshman's discovery that rain represents sadness.'"

Despite herself, Liz laughed. "And you said my interpretation had 'all the subtlety of a sledgehammer with literary pretensions.'"

"We were merciless."

"We were children."

Their eyes met across the table, the shared memory creating an unexpected moment of connection. James looked away first.

"Your marketing insights are valuable, Elizabeth. Even when I disagree with your approach, your perspective improves the work."

The compliment felt weightier than it should have. "Your design vision is... extraordinary. Even when I find it frustrating."

Another silence, this one charged with something Liz couldn't—or wouldn't—name.

"Same time next week?" James asked, returning to professional territory.

"I'll be here." Liz gathered her portfolio. "And I'll have the narrative touchpoints developed for both approaches."

"I look forward to it."

At the door, Liz paused. "For what it's worth, I've always admired the Thomas Building. My criticism comes from wishing it fully achieved what it almost did."

Before he could respond, she stepped outside into the bright afternoon. The construction site bustled with activity—foundation marking underway, earth movers preparing the ground where Meridian's future would rise. Fifteen minutes of heated debate had somehow shifted both her thinking and, apparently,

James's. The synthesis they'd found felt like neither victory nor compromise, but something more valuable—genuine collaboration.

Her phone buzzed with a text from Catherine: *How was the first meeting with Calloway?*

Liz considered how to respond. Challenging? Stimulating? Unexpectedly productive? She finally typed: *Constructive tension leading to better solutions.*

Catherine's reply came quickly: *Good. Keep it professional.*

The warning was unnecessary but not unwarranted. Something had sparked between her and James that transcended professional collaboration—an intellectual chemistry she hadn't experienced in years. It was dangerous precisely because it wasn't sexual or romantic, but something possibly more intimate—the recognition of a mind that both challenged and complemented her own.

As Liz walked to her car, she glanced back at the trailer. Through the window, she could see James still at the table, his head bent over a sketchpad, drawing with focused intensity. Even from this distance, she could see the energy in his movements—the pencil moving rapidly across the paper, pausing occasionally as he considered, then continuing with renewed purpose.

He was sketching something new, she realized. Something that hadn't existed before their argument. Their clash of perspectives was literally reshaping his design in real time.

The realization sent an unexpected thrill through her. In her marriage, her opinions shaped nothing. In her department, her ideas were respected but rarely transformative. But here, in this unlikely collaboration with her former rival, her thoughts had tangible impact—changing not just marketing strategy but the physical reality of what would be built.

Liz turned away and continued to her car, trying to ignore the uncomfortable truth that her argument with James had made her feel more alive than anything in recent memory. That the intellectual spark between them had illuminated not just the project but the dullness that had crept into her life without her noticing.

Inside the trailer, James continued sketching, his pencil moving with aggressive energy across the page. The entrance sequence was evolving before his eyes—not abandoning his original vision but enhancing it with elements that addressed Elizabeth's concerns while maintaining architectural integrity.

The design was better for their argument. He was reluctant to admit it, but her challenge had pushed him beyond his initial concept to something more nuanced, more complete. Her critique of the Thomas Building had stung precisely because it contained a kernel of truth—one he'd privately acknowledged but never publicly conceded.

He paused, studying what he'd drawn. The new approach integrated narrative elements without compromising spatial experience—exactly the synthesis they'd been debating. Elizabeth would approve of some elements, challenge others. The thought brought an unexpected smile to his face.

Thomas would develop the technical drawings tomorrow. Sophia would refine the experiential touchpoints. But tonight, James would continue sketching, driven by the intellectual energy of their clash—and the rare pleasure of engaging with a mind that kept pace with his own.

CHAPTER NINE

"Midnight Oil"

The digital clock on Liz's desk flipped to 9:47 PM. The Meridian offices had emptied hours ago, leaving behind the low hum of air conditioning and the occasional distant ping of the elevator. She rolled her shoulders, feeling the tension of six straight hours hunched over her laptop. The presentation was nearly perfect—forty-three slides analyzing the two narrative approaches they'd developed in last week's meeting, complete with implementation timelines and ROI projections.

She deleted an unnecessary transition animation, then restored it, then deleted it again. The perfectionism that had served her so well academically now manifested as an inability to declare anything truly finished.

There was always one more tweak, one more refinement that might make the difference between good and exceptional.

A soft knock at her open door startled her. Derek leaned against the doorframe, jacket slung over his shoulder.

"I knew I'd find you here," he said, stepping into her office. "Didn't we have a conversation about work-life balance last month?"

"That was before the Meridian project," Liz replied, gesturing to the explosion of architectural renderings, material samples, and sticky notes covering her desk. "Howard's presenting to the board on Thursday. Everything needs to be perfect."

Derek perched on the edge of her desk, eyeing the chaos with amusement. "Perfect is the enemy of done, my friend. Also the enemy of having a life."

"I'll sleep when the building's finished."

"In eighteen months? Your eye bags will reach your knees by then." Derek picked up a material sample—a piece of the limestone James had selected for the building's base. "So how's it going with Mr. Architectural Genius? Still driving each other crazy?"

Liz kept her eyes on her screen. "We have a productive working relationship."

"Mmm-hmm." Derek's tone suggested he wasn't buying it. "That's why Catherine mentioned your 'spirited debates' in yesterday's staff meeting."

"Creative tension produces better outcomes."

"Is that what they're calling it these days?" Derek grinned, then softened his expression. "Seriously though, how are you handling working with him? It can't be easy collaborating with someone who has history with you."

Liz saved her presentation, buying time to formulate a response that wouldn't reveal too much. "It's... challenging. James approaches problems differently than I do. He sees patterns and connections I miss, but he can be frustratingly abstract. I focus on practical implementation, which he sometimes dismisses as unimaginative."

"So basically you're still competing."

"We're not competing," Liz protested, though the words rang hollow even to her ears. "We're pushing each other toward better solutions."

Derek studied her with unexpected seriousness. "Can I ask you something personal?"

"When has asking permission ever stopped you?"

"Fair point." He set down the limestone sample. "What really happened between you two in high school? This feels like more than academic rivalry."

The question caught her off guard. "What do you mean?"

"I mean whenever you mention him, you get this look—like you're simultaneously annoyed and energized. And from what Catherine said about your meetings, there's something electric happening."

"Electric is definitely not the word I'd use." Liz closed her laptop with more force than necessary. "We were competitive teenagers who brought out each other's worst instincts. Now we're adults with a job to do."

"But he got under your skin then, and he still does now."

Liz was saved from responding by another knock. She looked up to find James standing in her doorway, a portfolio under his arm and surprise evident on his face.

"I'm sorry," he said, taking in the scene. "I didn't realize you had company."

Derek stood, extending his hand. "Derek Townsend, marketing deputy and Liz's self-appointed work-life balance enforcer. You must be James Calloway."

"Guilty as charged." James shook Derek's hand, his expression professional but slightly guarded.

"I was just leaving," Derek said, shooting Liz a meaningful glance. "Some of us remember we have homes to return to."

"I'm heading out soon," Liz replied, not meeting his eyes.

"Of course you are." Derek grabbed his jacket. "Nice meeting you, James. I've heard... well, I've heard quite a lot, actually."

After Derek departed, an awkward silence filled the office. James remained in the doorway, as if uncertain whether to enter or retreat.

"I didn't expect to find you here this late," he said finally. "I was going to leave these revised renderings on your desk for tomorrow."

"Deadline prep," Liz explained, gesturing to her workspace. "Howard's board presentation."

"Ah." James hesitated, then stepped fully into her office. "I've been working on the same thing. The entrance sequence modifications we discussed."

"You've been working late too?"

"Thomas would say I'm always working late." A small smile softened his features. "Occupational hazard of caring too much about getting things right."

The unexpected moment of self-awareness created a bridge between them. Liz found herself gesturing to the chair across from her desk.

"Since you're here, you might as well show me what you've done."

James sat, opening his portfolio to reveal hand-drawn renderings more detailed and evocative than the digital versions they'd been sharing. His sketches captured not just the architectural elements but the quality of light, the sense of movement through space, the emotional experience of entering the building.

"These are..." Liz searched for a word that wouldn't reveal too much. "Impressive."

"They incorporate the narrative integration we discussed," James explained, spreading the drawings across her desk. "Environmental graphics embedded in the limestone elements here, interactive displays positioned at key decision points in the journey."

Liz leaned forward, absorbed in the drawings. "You've maintained the spatial flow while adding these storytelling moments. It's exactly what we talked about."

"Your critique last week was valid," James admitted, surprising her again. "The original approach prioritized architectural experience without considering how visitors would interpret it. These revisions maintain the integrity of the space while making its meaning more accessible."

For the next thirty minutes, they discussed the revised designs with growing animation. The professional tension that usually characterized their interactions gave way to something closer to collaborative excitement as they discovered unexpected alignment in their visions.

"The material transition from traditional to innovative elements works perfectly with Howard's philosophy," Liz said, pointing to a detail in the atrium design. "Visitors will literally experience 'progressive tradition' as they move through the space."

"Exactly." James's eyes lit with rare enthusiasm. "And your idea about using lighting to highlight the transition at different times of day adds another layer of narrative without compromising the architecture."

"It's actually good," Liz admitted, surprising herself with the genuine praise. "Better than either of our original concepts."

"That's what happens when we stop trying to win and start trying to solve the problem." James's voice carried no accusation, just thoughtful observation.

The comment hung between them, acknowledging the competitive dynamic they'd never directly addressed. Liz looked up from the drawings to find James watching her with an expression she couldn't quite read.

"Old habits," she said quietly.

"Very old." He leaned back slightly. "Though I've noticed we're better at finding common ground than we used to be."

"We've grown up. Mostly."

The ghost of a smile touched his lips. "Speak for yourself. I still get unreasonably irritated when someone challenges my ideas."

"No," Liz feigned shock. "You?"

The shared moment of self-deprecation shifted something in the atmosphere. For the first time since reconnecting, they weren't performing professional roles or rehashing old rivalries. They were simply two people acknowledging their flaws with unexpected honesty.

"I've been following the Hadley Museum renovation," Liz said, changing the subject to safer ground. "The cantilevered gallery extension is remarkable."

Surprise flickered across James's face. "You follow architectural projects?"

"I've developed an interest recently." She didn't mention the hours spent researching his firm's work, reading architectural journals, and educating herself on contemporary design trends. "The integration of historic preservation with modern intervention is fascinating."

"It is," James agreed, studying her with new curiosity. "The tension between honoring what exists and creating something new is the central challenge of thoughtful architecture."

"Like marketing," Liz observed. "Respecting brand heritage while evolving for contemporary relevance."

"I hadn't considered that parallel." James tilted his head slightly. "Though I suppose both disciplines navigate the space between tradition and innovation."

The conversation flowed with unexpected ease as they discussed current architectural trends. Liz found herself sharing opinions she'd formed during her late-night research binges, while James offered insider perspectives on projects she'd read about. For twenty minutes, they spoke not as rivals or even colleagues, but as two people sharing genuine intellectual interest.

"You have remarkable insight for someone outside the field," James said eventually. "Your analysis of the Thompson Center controversy was more nuanced than most architectural commentary I've read."

The compliment created a warm glow that Liz tried to ignore. "I did my homework. This project matters to Howard, which means it matters to me."

"It's more than homework," James countered. "You have natural intuition for spatial dynamics and experiential design. It's rare in marketing professionals, who typically think in two dimensions rather than four."

"Four?"

"Three spatial dimensions plus time—how people experience space as they move through it." James leaned forward slightly. "Your presentation last week demonstrated sophisticated understanding of that temporal dimension. It's why your critique of my approach was so effective."

Liz felt oddly exposed by his assessment—seen in a way that was both flattering and uncomfortable. "I've always been interested in how environments shape experience. It's why literature resonated with me—the creation of mental spaces through narrative."

As soon as the words left her mouth, she regretted the personal revelation. James's expression shifted subtly, his eyes sharpening with interest.

"That's right," he said. "You were planning to pursue literary theory. What happened with that?"

The question touched a nerve Liz had thought long cauterized. "Life happened. I chose a different path."

"Marketing instead of academia."

"A practical career instead of an impractical passion." She kept her tone light, though the old wound throbbed unexpectedly. "Not everyone has the luxury of pursuing artistic callings."

Something flickered in James's eyes—not pity, which she would have resented, but a flash of recognition. "Architecture wasn't a luxury for me, Elizabeth. It was a necessity. I would have failed at anything else because nothing else would have commanded my full attention."

The simple honesty of his statement caught her off guard. For a moment, she glimpsed the person beneath the professional facade—someone driven by genuine passion rather than ambition or competition.

"I didn't mean to imply—" she began.

"I know." He waved away her explanation. "And I didn't mean to pry. We all make choices that shape our paths."

The conversation had veered into territory too personal for comfort. Liz straightened in her chair, retreating to professional safety.

"Speaking of choices, we need to decide which narrative approach to recommend to Howard." She gestured to the drawings still spread across her desk. "Based on these revisions, I think the integrated environmental graphics are stronger than the digital overlay option."

James accepted the redirect without comment. "I agree. The physical integration creates a more cohesive experience while still allowing for technological elements where appropriate."

They spent the next hour refining the presentation for Thursday's board meeting, their earlier moment of personal connection carefully set aside. Liz adjusted her slides to incorporate James's revised renderings while he annotated the architectural drawings with narrative touchpoints they'd identified.

By eleven-thirty, they had assembled a comprehensive presentation that seamlessly integrated their previ-

ously competing approaches. Liz felt the familiar satisfaction of completing a complex task to exacting standards—a feeling she rarely experienced in her regular
marketing work anymore.

"I think we're done," she said, saving the final version. "This should give Howard everything he needs to
secure board approval."

"Agreed." James gathered his drawings, carefully returning them to his portfolio. "Thank you for staying
late to work through this. The result is stronger than
what either of us would have produced alone."

"Professional collaboration at its finest," Liz replied,
maintaining the careful distance they'd reestablished.

Neither made a move to leave. In the quiet office,
with the city lights twinkling beyond the windows,
they seemed suspended between professional obligation and something more complicated. Liz found herself noticing details she normally suppressed—the way
James's hands moved with precise grace as he organized
his materials, the slight furrow that appeared between
his brows when he concentrated, the subtle scent of his
cologne mingling with drafting paper and coffee.

"I should go," James said finally, standing. "It's late,
and we both have early meetings tomorrow."

"Right." Liz remained seated, reluctant to end the
evening for reasons she didn't want to examine. "I just

need to send these files to Howard, then I'll head out too."

James paused at her door. "Elizabeth?"

"Yes?"

"You would have been extraordinary in academia." His voice carried quiet certainty. "Your analytical mind and capacity for nuanced interpretation—they're rare gifts. Meridian is fortunate to have them directed toward their benefit."

Before she could respond to the unexpected compliment, he was gone, leaving her alone with the ghost of a life she hadn't chosen and the uncomfortable awareness of how easily he had seen through her professional facade to the ambitions she'd abandoned.

Liz sat motionless for several minutes, the empty doorway framing the empty hallway beyond. She should pack up and go home. Mark would be asleep by now, but at least she could get a few hours' rest before tomorrow's meetings.

Instead, she opened her laptop again, reviewing the presentation they'd created. The seamless integration of their approaches was remarkable—neither fully hers nor fully his, but something new born from their collaboration. It was objectively better than what either would have produced independently.

The sound of movement in the hallway drew her attention. James had returned, his own laptop now tucked under his arm.

"I thought you were leaving," she said, surprised.

"I am. But I realized I should send Thomas the updated renderings tonight so he can prepare the technical drawings first thing." He hesitated. "Do you mind if I use your office for a few minutes? The Wi-Fi in the lobby is unreliable."

"Of course." Liz gestured to the small conference table in the corner of her office. "Make yourself at home."

James settled at the table, opening his laptop. For the next twenty minutes, they worked in silence—Liz finalizing her notes for Howard, James preparing files for his team. The quiet wasn't uncomfortable but charged with awareness, each hyperconscious of the other's presence.

Occasionally, Liz would glance up to find James focused intently on his screen, the blue light highlighting the angles of his face. Once, their eyes met briefly before both returned to their work, the momentary connection sending an unexpected current through the room.

The situation was objectively innocent—two professionals working late on a shared project. Yet Liz couldn't shake the feeling that some boundary had shifted, some line had blurred between their carefully maintained professional relationship and something more complex.

Outside her windows, the city continued its nighttime rhythm—office lights blinking out one by one, taxis flowing through streets, the distant wail of a siren. Inside, the quiet hum of two laptops and the soft sound of breathing created an intimate bubble that felt increasingly dangerous.

"Sent," James announced finally, breaking the silence. "Thomas will have everything he needs for tomorrow."

"Good." Liz closed her own laptop. "I've finished my notes for Howard."

Neither moved to leave. The late hour and empty building created a strange space where normal professional rules seemed suspended, where the walls they'd built between past and present, between rivalry and respect, felt suddenly permeable.

"We should go," Liz said, though she made no move to stand.

"We should," James agreed, equally stationary.

Another moment of silence stretched between them, filled with unspoken awareness.

"Elizabeth—" James began.

"It's late," Liz interrupted, suddenly afraid of what he might say—or what she might answer. "And we both have early meetings tomorrow."

The repetition of his earlier words created a safe exit, which James accepted with a slight nod. "Of course. I'll see you at the stakeholder review tomorrow."

They gathered their things in silence, the brief moment of whatever-it-had-been carefully packed away with their laptops and portfolios. In the elevator, they stood at opposite sides, professional distance restored. The ride to the lobby passed in silence broken only by the soft chime of passing floors.

Outside the building, the night air carried the first hint of autumn crispness. They paused on the sidewalk, the moment of parting awkward after hours of unexpected connection.

"Goodnight, Elizabeth," James said finally.

"Goodnight, James."

He turned toward the parking garage while she headed for the street to hail a taxi. At the corner, some impulse made Liz glance back. James stood beneath a streetlight, watching her departure with an expression she couldn't decipher from this distance.

For a brief, irrational moment, she considered turning back, continuing their conversation, exploring whatever had sparked between them during those quiet hours in her office. The thought lasted only seconds before reality reasserted itself. She had a husband waiting at home. James had a professional reputation to maintain. They had a building to design, stakeholders to satisfy, boundaries to respect.

Liz raised her hand for an approaching taxi, deliberately turning away from the figure beneath the streetlight. Whatever had happened—or almost happened—in her office belonged to the liminal space of midnight oil and professional dedication, not to the real world of marriages and careers and consequences.

The taxi pulled to the curb. As Liz opened the door, her phone buzzed with a text from Mark: *You coming home tonight?*

The message carried no concern, no affection—just the practical inquiry of a roommate tracking logistics. Liz slid into the taxi, giving her address to the driver before responding: *On my way now. Working late on the project.*

Mark's reply came as the taxi pulled away from the curb: *K. Left your side of the bed turned down.*

Such a small thing—a turned-down sheet—yet it struck Liz as unexpectedly thoughtful. A reminder that whatever intellectual connection she'd felt with James tonight, she had built a life with Mark. Imperfect, perhaps increasingly hollow, but real. Built on fifteen years of shared history, mutual commitment, and the practical, unglamorous business of making a life together.

As the taxi carried her toward that life, Liz refused to look back at the figure she knew still stood beneath the streetlight. Some doors, once opened, couldn't easily be closed again. Tonight, she had glimpsed such a door—and had the wisdom, or perhaps the cowardice, to leave it undisturbed.

For now.

CHAPTER TEN

"Surface Tension"

The Conference Room buzzed with anticipation. Howard Meridian had assembled his executive team for the board presentation review, and the stakes couldn't be higher. Liz arranged her materials with methodical precision, hyperaware of James standing nearby, reviewing his architectural renderings one last time.

They hadn't spoken about their late-night collaboration since it happened three days ago. Their communication had been strictly professional, emails about presentation logistics, text messages confirming slide order. Yet something had shifted between them, an unacknowledged current flowing beneath the surface of their interactions.

"Everyone settled?" Howard asked, taking his position at the head of the table. "Elizabeth, James, you have the floor."

Liz stood, smoothing her charcoal pencil skirt. "Thank you, Howard. Today we're presenting the integrated narrative and architectural approach for the new headquarters entrance sequence."

James stepped forward, activating the first slide. "Our presentation demonstrates how the physical experience of entering Meridian's headquarters will embody the company's 'progressive tradition' philosophy."

What followed surprised everyone in the room—perhaps even Liz and James themselves. Their presentation flowed with remarkable synergy, each picking up seamlessly where the other left off. When Liz described the narrative journey visitors would experience, James illustrated it with architectural specifics. When James explained structural elements, Liz contextualized them within Meridian's brand story.

"The limestone base represents Meridian's foundation in traditional business values," Liz explained, gesturing to James's detailed rendering.

"While the progressive transition to advanced materials as the building rises," James continued without missing a beat, "creates a physical manifestation of evolution and innovation."

Howard leaned forward, clearly captivated. "The material narrative is brilliant. Visitors experience our company values through the building itself."

"Exactly," they responded in unison, then exchanged a quick glance of surprise.

Catherine's eyes narrowed slightly at the exchange, though her expression remained professionally neutral.

As they moved through the presentation, Liz found herself anticipating James's points before he made them, elaborating on concepts they'd developed during their late-night session. The presentation they'd crafted wasn't just a compromise between marketing and architecture—it was a true synthesis, something new and more powerful than either discipline alone could have created.

"The environmental graphics aren't merely decorative," James explained, showing how historical elements would be integrated into the limestone. "They're substantive storytelling moments that enhance the spatial experience without disrupting it."

"Each touchpoint reveals another layer of Meridian's evolution," Liz added. "Creating a journey from established foundation to innovative future."

When they concluded, Howard stood and actually applauded. "This is exactly what I envisioned—architecture that tells our story, marketing that enhances our space. The board will love this."

The CFO nodded appreciatively. "And the phased implementation keeps costs within our quarterly projections. Well done."

"I'm particularly impressed by how seamlessly you've integrated your approaches," Catherine said, her gaze moving between Liz and James. "Given your initial... differences of opinion."

"Professional collaboration at its finest," Liz replied, echoing the phrase she'd used with James that night in her office.

"Creative tension producing superior results," James added with a slight smile.

Howard clapped his hands together. "Let's celebrate this milestone. Coffee in my office—I want to discuss how we present this to the board on Thursday."

As the executives filed out, Catherine lingered behind. "Quite a turnaround from last week's territorial disputes," she murmured to Liz. "You two seem to have found common ground."

"The project benefits from our combined perspectives," Liz replied carefully.

"Mmm." Catherine's expression remained skeptical. "Just remember what I said about personal complications, Elizabeth. This project is too important."

"Everything is strictly professional," Liz assured her, ignoring the slight warmth that rose to her cheeks.

In Howard's office, coffee was served while executives discussed board presentation strategy. Liz stood near the window, half-listening as Howard outlined key talking points. James approached with two cups, offering one to her.

"Black, no sugar," he said quietly. "I noticed that's how you take it."

The small observation—that he'd paid attention to such a detail—created an unexpected flutter in her chest. "Thank you."

"The presentation went well," he continued, his voice low enough that only she could hear. "Better than I expected."

"We make a surprisingly effective team."

"Surprising indeed." His eyes held hers a moment longer than necessary. "Though perhaps it shouldn't be. We always did bring out the best in each other academically. When we weren't busy trying to destroy each other's arguments."

Before she could respond, Howard called them over to discuss the board's potential questions. The moment passed, but Liz remained conscious of James's presence beside her, the slight scent of his cologne, the warmth radiating from his tall frame.

The meeting concluded with enthusiastic support for their approach. As executives dispersed to their respective offices, James caught up with Liz in the hallway.

"Do you have a moment?" he asked. "There's something I'd like to discuss about the material transitions."

"Of course." She led him to her office, closing the door behind them.

Once inside, James's professional demeanor shifted subtly. He set his portfolio on her desk but made no move to open it.

"I didn't actually need to discuss materials," he admitted. "I wanted to ask why you supported my design approach so strongly in there. You could have pushed your digital overlay concept more."

The directness of his question caught her off guard. "Your environmental graphics approach was superior. The integration with architectural elements creates a more cohesive experience."

"That's the professional answer." His eyes held hers. "I'm asking for the real one."

Liz hesitated, weighing her response. "The real answer is that I recognized good design. My job isn't to win arguments but to ensure Meridian gets the best possible headquarters."

"Even if that means conceding points to an old rival?"

"Is that what we still are? Rivals?"

The question hung between them, loaded with implications neither seemed ready to address.

"I don't know what we are, Elizabeth," James finally said, his voice softening. "Colleagues, certainly. Former competitors, definitely. But there's something else happening here that doesn't fit neatly into professional categories."

Her pulse quickened. "We're collaborating on an important project. It's natural to develop mutual respect."

"Is that all it is? Respect?"

"What else would it be?"

James studied her for a long moment. "I respect many people I work with. But I don't find myself thinking about their perspectives at odd hours, or redesigning concepts based on their critiques, or noticing how they take their coffee."

The implication sent a jolt through her system. "James—"

"I'm not suggesting anything inappropriate," he clarified quickly. "I'm simply acknowledging that our professional interaction has an unusual quality to it. A certain... intensity."

"Creative chemistry," Liz offered, grasping for neutral terminology. "It happens in collaborative environments."

"Is that what you call it?" A hint of his old competitive edge returned. "I call it finally meeting someone who challenges me intellectually again. Do you know how rare that is?"

The unexpected honesty disarmed her. "Yes," she admitted quietly. "I do know."

Something shifted in his expression—recognition, perhaps, of shared experience. "Your work on this project has been exceptional, Elizabeth. Not just competent or professional, but genuinely insightful. You see connections others miss. You anticipate problems before they materialize. You push my thinking in directions it wouldn't go otherwise."

The compliment warmed her more than it should have. "Your design vision elevates my marketing approach. The building will be better for our collaboration."

"The building," James repeated with a slight smile. "Always back to the professional."

"That's what this is," Liz insisted, though her tone lacked conviction. "A professional project with professional boundaries."

"Of course." He gathered his portfolio. "I should get back to the studio. Thomas is waiting for direction on the board presentation materials."

At the door, he paused. "For what it's worth, I'm glad it's you representing Meridian on this project. I can't imagine a more formidable or valuable collaborator."

After he left, Liz sat at her desk, trying to process the conversation. James had come dangerously close to acknowledging the undercurrent between them—the intellectual attraction that had nothing to do with architecture or marketing and everything to do with two minds recognizing something rare in each other.

Catherine's warning echoed in her thoughts: *This project is too important for personal complications.* Yet the line between personal and professional had already blurred. Their midnight collaboration, their seamless presentation, the coffee he'd brought her—small moments accumulating into something undefined but increasingly undeniable.

Saturday morning dawned clear and crisp, perfect running weather. Liz laced her shoes at 6:30 AM, her breath visible in the autumn air. Mark hadn't stirred when she slipped from bed—he rarely woke before nine on weekends, especially after Friday night beers with colleagues.

Lakeside Park was three miles from their home, her favorite running spot with its winding trails and water views. The morning solitude allowed her mind to process the week's events, particularly Thursday's successful board presentation. Howard had called it "transformative" and "visionary." The project had official approval now, with groundbreaking scheduled for next month.

Liz set out at a steady pace, following the familiar path around the lake's perimeter. Her thoughts drifted to James and their strange new dynamic—not quite friendship, definitely not romance, but something powerful nonetheless. An intellectual connection that made her feel more alive than she had in years.

She was so absorbed in these thoughts that she almost missed the tall figure approaching from the opposite direction. The recognition hit her mid-stride—James, in running shorts and a technical shirt, his pace matching her own.

He saw her at the same moment, surprise flashing across his features before his expression settled into cautious neutrality. They slowed simultaneously, stopping a few feet apart on the lakeside trail.

"Elizabeth." His voice carried a note of genuine surprise. "I didn't expect to see you here."

"I run this route most weekends," she explained, suddenly conscious of her flushed face and messy ponytail. "You?"

"First time at this park. I usually run the river-front, but they're setting up for a festival." He gestured vaguely toward the water. "The lake seemed like a good alternative."

An awkward silence fell between them, both clearly unsure of proper protocol for running into a professional colleague—particularly one with whom boundaries had become increasingly complicated—during weekend exercise.

"Well," Liz said finally, "enjoy your run."

She moved to continue past him, but James spoke again. "Actually, I was just thinking about the project. The board's questions about sustainability certifications raised some interesting points."

It was the thinnest of professional pretexts, but Liz found herself nodding. "Howard was particularly interested in the water reclamation system."

"Would you mind if I joined you?" James asked. "We could discuss it while running. Unless you prefer solitude."

The sensible answer was yes, she preferred solitude. Running was her time to process, to be alone with her thoughts. Yet she heard herself say, "Not at all. I'm doing the lake loop—about four miles total."

"Perfect."

They fell into step beside each other, finding a compatible pace without discussion. For several minutes they ran in silence, the only sounds their rhythmic footfalls and measured breathing. The morning sun glinted off the lake to their right, ducks skimming the surface in perfect formation.

"The board presentation went well," James said finally. "Howard seems genuinely excited about the design direction."

"He is. It's become his legacy project—the physical embodiment of his business philosophy before retirement."

"No pressure there," James remarked dryly.

Liz laughed, the sound surprising her. "None at all. Just define a man's entire career in architectural form."

Their conversation flowed more easily than she expected, moving from project specifics to broader thoughts on architecture and corporate identity. Running side by side created a different dynamic than their office interactions—more relaxed, less performative. Without the pressure of colleagues watching or deadlines looming, they spoke more freely.

"I've been thinking about our academic rivalry," James said as they rounded the lake's eastern shore. "Why it was so intense."

"Because we were competitive teenagers with something to prove?"

"That's part of it. But it was more than that." He glanced at her profile. "At least for me."

"What do you mean?"

James maintained his steady pace, eyes forward. "Everyone else made it too easy. Teachers were impressed with minimal effort. Other students didn't challenge my thinking." He paused. "You were the only one who ever made me work for it. Really work for it."

The admission hung between them, unexpectedly personal. Liz considered her response carefully.

"I felt the same way," she admitted. "Before Preston, school was effortless. Then suddenly there was someone who matched me thought for thought. It was... unsettling."

"And exhilarating," James added. "Though I wouldn't have admitted that then."

"Nor I." Liz smiled slightly. "I stayed up all night preparing for our debates. Researched until my eyes burned. Rehearsed arguments in the shower."

"I knew it!" James laughed. "I did exactly the same thing. That Hemingway debate? I read six critical analyses and his entire bibliography in one weekend."

"I outlined my rebuttal on index cards and practiced it for my very confused parents."

They both laughed, the shared memory creating un-expected warmth between them. For a moment, they were just two people with a common past, the weight of professional complications temporarily lifted.

"We brought out each other's best work," James observed. "And worst competitiveness."

"A complicated combination."

"Still is, apparently."

The comment shifted the atmosphere, acknowledging their current dynamic. They ran another quarter mile in thoughtful silence before James spoke again.

"Do you ever wonder how things might have been different? If you'd won the Beckman instead of me?"

The question touched a nerve Liz thought long buried. "Sometimes," she admitted. "Though not in the way you might think."

"How then?"

"I don't regret not becoming an architect. That was your passion, not mine." She kept her eyes on the path ahead. "But I do sometimes wonder what would have happened if I'd pursued literary theory. If I'd followed that path instead of the practical one."

"Why didn't you?"

The simple question demanded a complex answer—one involving Mark, their whirlwind courtship senior year, her decision to stay near him rather than accept offers from distant graduate programs. How one choice had led to another until the academic path had closed entirely.

"Life happened," she said finally. "Priorities changed."

"Your husband," James said, the observation neutral but perceptive.

"Partly." Liz felt suddenly exposed. "Mark and I met senior year at Northwestern. Marriage changed my graduate school plans."

"Do you regret it?"

The directness of his question caught her off guard. "That's a very personal inquiry, James."

"You're right. I apologize."

They ran another hundred yards in silence, the tension between them palpable.

"I don't regret marrying Mark," Liz said finally, surprising herself with her candor. "But I sometimes regret losing touch with the part of myself that loved academic challenge. The intellectual engagement. The sense of discovery."

James nodded, his expression thoughtful. "That makes sense. The corporate world doesn't always nurture those qualities."

"No, it doesn't." She hesitated, then added, "This project has been... different. Challenging me in ways my work hasn't for some time."

"I'm glad." His voice carried genuine warmth. "Your mind is too remarkable to waste on ordinary problems."

The compliment created a flutter in her chest that had nothing to do with exertion. "We should probably head back," she said, suddenly conscious of how far they'd strayed from professional territory. "Mark will be wondering where I am."

Something flickered across James's features at the mention of her husband—a subtle tightening around his eyes, quickly masked. "Of course. Family Saturday."

"Something like that."

They turned back toward the parking area, their pace slightly faster than before. The easy camaraderie of minutes earlier had been replaced by a charged awareness, both seemingly conscious of having revealed too much.

"Will Thomas have the material samples ready for Monday's meeting?" Liz asked, deliberately steering them back to safer ground.

"Yes. And Sophia's completed the interior palette options." James matched her professional tone. "We should be able to finalize the atrium specifications by the end of the week."

They discussed project details for the remainder of their run, the conversation carefully contained within work parameters. As they approached the parking lot, Liz spotted her car at the far end.

"That's me," she said, slowing to a walk.

James nodded, also walking now. "Thanks for the company. It made the miles go faster."

"It did." Liz hesitated, then extended her hand in a deliberately professional gesture. "See you Monday."

James took her hand briefly, the contact warm despite the morning chill. "Monday."

As she walked to her car, Liz felt his eyes following her but didn't look back. The encounter had been innocent—two colleagues happening upon each other, sharing a run and conversation. Yet she couldn't shake the feeling that something significant had shifted between them. The personal disclosures, the shared memories, the unexpected connection—all had moved their relationship into undefined territory.

The drive home gave her time to compose herself, to rebuild the mental walls between her professional project with James and her personal life with Mark. By the time she pulled into her driveway, she had convinced herself the morning's encounter was nothing more than friendly collegiality.

The house was silent when she entered. In the living room, she found Mark had made his way downstairs and now sprawled on the couch, still in yesterday's clothes. Empty beer cans littered the coffee table, and the television played a sports highlight show at low volume.

Liz stood in the doorway, observing her husband's sleeping form. His mouth hung slightly open, a day's stubble on his chin, his Northwestern sweatshirt riding up to reveal the softening midsection that had replaced the athletic build she'd fallen for in college. The coffee table told the story of his Friday night—six empty cans, a half-eaten bag of chips, his phone face-down beside a pizza delivery receipt.

The contrast between her morning—the intellectual conversation with James, the shared running rhythm, the sense of connection—and this scene of domestic stagnation created a hollow ache in her chest. When had her marriage become this? When had Mark transformed from the ambitious, engaging man she'd married into this person who spent Friday nights alone with beer and sports while she worked late?

More troubling was her own reaction—not anger or disappointment, but a detached recognition, as if observing a situation that had nothing to do with her. The emotional distance frightened her more than any argument could have.

Mark stirred slightly, his hand reaching for a phantom beer can before settling back into sleep. On the television, athletes celebrated a victory, their joy muted by the low volume. Outside, the morning sun illuminated their carefully maintained front yard, the perfect suburban façade concealing the emptiness within.

Liz turned away, heading upstairs to shower. Water would wash away the evidence of her morning run, the physical exertion, the light sweat that had formed during those miles alongside James. But it couldn't erase the memory of their conversation, the unexpected connection, or the troubling question that had taken root in her mind:

If running four miles with James Calloway made her feel more alive than fifteen years with Mark, what did that say about the life she'd chosen?

CHAPTER ELEVEN

"Foundation Work"

The October morning air carried a hint of winter's approach as Liz surveyed the construction site from behind oversized sunglasses. Meridian executives, board members, and local officials clustered near a temporary stage erected at what would become the main entrance to the new headquarters. Howard Meridian stood at the center, his silver hair catching the sunlight as he chatted animatedly with the mayor. Nearby, a row of gold-painted shovels awaited the ceremonial groundbreaking.

Liz checked her watch—ten minutes until the press arrived. She scanned her tablet, confirming the media advisory had generated confirmations from all major business outlets and local news stations. The press packets were stacked neatly on the registration table, each containing renderings of the completed building, sustainability specifications, and economic impact projections for the neighborhood.

"Everything on schedule?" Catherine appeared beside her, elegant in a charcoal pantsuit despite the dusty surroundings.

"Press arrives at nine, speeches at nine-fifteen, groundbreaking at nine-forty, followed by the reception." Liz gestured toward the refreshment tent. "We're coordinating with the photographer to capture Howard and the mayor mid-shovel for the annual report cover."

Catherine nodded approvingly. "The board is impressed with the media interest. Your press strategy is working."

"The architectural design is the real story. I'm just packaging it effectively."

"Speaking of architecture..." Catherine tilted her head toward the opposite side of the site.

James had arrived with Thomas and several team members, all wearing Calloway Design Group hardhats. Even from this distance, Liz could see the comfortable authority in his posture as he pointed out features of the site to his colleagues. Unlike the executives in their careful business attire, James wore dark jeans and a black button-down with sleeves rolled to expose forearms tanned from site visits. He looked completely in his element amid the dirt and construction equipment.

"I should brief him on the speaking order," Liz said, already moving in his direction.

Catherine's knowing look followed her across the site. Since their weekend encounter at Lakeside Park two weeks ago, Liz had maintained scrupulous professionalism around James. Their communication had been strictly project-focused, their interactions witnessed by others whenever possible. Yet despite these precautions, she remained hyperaware of his presence in any space they shared.

"Elizabeth." James turned as she approached, his expression carefully neutral. "Perfect timing. Thomas was just asking about the media opportunities."

"Local business press, architecture journals, and three television stations." Liz shifted to include Thomas in the conversation. "We're positioning this as both an economic development story and a sustainability breakthrough."

Thomas nodded, his expression serious. "The geothermal system is genuinely innovative for this region. The journalists should understand it's not just marketing hype."

"The press packets include the technical specifications," Liz assured him. "And I've arranged for you to speak with the architecture correspondents during the reception."

"Good." James consulted his watch. "What's our timeline?"

Liz outlined the schedule, maintaining professional distance despite standing close enough to catch the faint scent of his cologne mingling with coffee. As she explained the speaking order, she noticed a smudge of graphite on his thumb—evidence of last-minute sketching. The small detail humanized him, a reminder of the passion behind his polished exterior.

"You're after Howard but before the mayor," she concluded. "Three minutes on the vision for the building, emphasizing how the design embodies Meridian's philosophy."

"I've prepared remarks focusing on the materiality as narrative." James met her eyes briefly. "Similar to what we discussed in our presentation."

The reference to their collaborative breakthrough created a moment of connection despite the professional context. Liz nodded, remembering the night they'd worked late in her office, finding unexpected alignment in their vision.

"That will resonate well with Howard's introduction."

The arrival of media vans interrupted their conversation. Liz excused herself to manage the press check-in, grateful for the distraction of logistical details. For the next half hour, she orchestrated the careful choreography of a corporate milestone event—directing photographers to optimal angles, ensuring executives were positioned prominently, guiding journalists to key visual elements of the site.

From the corner of her eye, she observed James working the crowd with surprising ease for someone she remembered as an intellectually brilliant but socially awkward teenager. He moved comfortably among board members and city officials, explaining architectural concepts in accessible terms without oversimplifying. His passion for the project was evident in his animated gestures as he described features invisible to others but clearly visible in his mind's eye.

The ceremony proceeded according to plan. Howard delivered a stirring speech about Meridian's future, emphasizing the headquarters as physical embodiment of the company's evolution. When James took the podium, his presentation struck the perfect balance between technical expertise and compelling narrative.

"Architecture exists in four dimensions," he explained, his voice carrying across the site. "Three spatial dimensions plus the fourth dimension of time—how people experience the building as they move through it. The Meridian headquarters is designed to tell a story through that movement, from the limestone base representing solid business foundations to the innovative materials as you ascend, literally experiencing 'progressive tradition' through the building itself."

Liz watched the journalists scribbling notes, capturing the sound bite she and James had carefully crafted together. His delivery was flawless, passionate without being theatrical, authoritative without arrogance. The board members nodded appreciatively at the clear connection between architectural vision and corporate philosophy.

After the ceremonial shovelfuls of dirt and obligatory photos, the crowd migrated to the reception tent. Liz circulated among journalists, answering questions and facilitating interviews with key executives. Across the tent, James conducted his own media tour, using a tablet to show detailed renderings to architecture correspondents.

"You two have created quite a compelling narrative," Howard said, appearing at Liz's elbow with a coffee cup. "The material transition concept particularly resonates with our board. It makes the abstract concrete—literally."

"James deserves the credit for translating the philosophy into physical form," Liz replied.

Howard's eyes crinkled. "Don't sell yourself short, Elizabeth. James himself mentioned how your marketing insights shaped the experiential journey through the building." He nodded toward where James stood explaining something to a cluster of journalists. "I've worked with many architects over the years. The brilliant ones are rarely collaborative. They typically present their vision as gospel and expect clients to adapt. James actually incorporates feedback without compromising integrity. That's rare."

"We've found an effective working relationship," Liz acknowledged carefully.

"More than effective—transformative. The design has evolved significantly since your involvement." Howard sipped his coffee. "Creative tension producing superior results, as he put it."

The phrase—James's exact words from their presentation—created an unexpected warmth in her chest. Before she could respond, Catherine summoned Howard to meet a city council member, leaving Liz to consider the implications of James crediting her influence to their CEO.

The reception wound down by eleven, journalists departing with quotes and images for their stories. As the tent emptied, Liz found herself gravitating toward the edge of the foundation area where actual construction work had begun. Concrete footings marked the building's eventual perimeter, with steel reinforcement rods protruding like industrial saplings from the earth.

"Quite different from renderings and models," James said, joining her at the site edge.

"It's so... real." Liz gestured toward the foundation work. "Until now, it's been concepts and drawings. This is actually happening."

"The most satisfying phase for architects," James admitted. "When ideas become physical reality."

They stood in comfortable silence, watching workers position forms for the next concrete pour. The October sun cast long shadows across the site, the day's warmth fading as clouds gathered on the horizon.

"We should review the timeline adjustments," James said eventually. "The foreman mentioned soil composition issues that might affect the foundation schedule."

"I need to update Howard anyway. The project office?"

The temporary structure had been upgraded since their first meeting—proper desks replacing folding tables, architectural plans properly mounted on walls, even a small kitchenette with coffee maker and refrigerator. Still, it retained the frontier quality of a space existing between concept and completion.

Inside, James spread revised timeline charts across the conference table. "The geotechnical report came back with recommendations for deeper footings on the north corner. It adds eight days to the foundation phase."

Liz studied the diagrams, noting the cascading impact on subsequent phases. "Can we recover the time elsewhere?"

"Possibly during structural steel. I've been working with the fabricator on pre-assembly options." James pulled up detailed specifications on his tablet. "The issue is whether Howard will approve the additional cost to accelerate that phase."

"He'll want to maintain the original completion date." Liz ran calculations on projected expenses. "The quarterly earnings announcement is scheduled for the week after target completion. He's been promoting this building as evidence of Meridian's growth trajectory."

"Then we need to compress the schedule elsewhere." James pulled up the master timeline. "If we extend working hours during interior construction and phase the finishing work differently..."

They fell into a familiar pattern, identifying problems and testing solutions with complementary approaches. James focused on technical feasibility while Liz considered stakeholder impacts. The initial tension that had characterized their early interactions had evolved into something more productive—a professional rhythm that leveraged their different perspectives.

Outside, construction equipment rumbled as excavation continued. The afternoon light shifted, shadows lengthening across their workspace. Neither noticed the passing hours as they reconstructed the project schedule, finding creative solutions to maintain the completion target despite the foundation delay.

"If we stage the interior work by quadrant rather than floor," James suggested, sketching rapidly on tracing paper, "we can create this overlapping sequence that shaves twelve days."

Liz leaned closer, examining his drawing. "That affects the furniture installation and technology deployment. I'll need to coordinate with IT on revised server room access."

"We'd need full commitment from the trades to maintain continuous workflow." James added notes to the diagram. "No gaps between drywall and finishing."

"Howard will approve the overtime costs if it maintains the original completion date." Liz made notations in her project file. "I'll draft the request with the full rationale."

The door opened, admitting Thomas and the construction foreman. Both looked surprised to find Liz and James still working as afternoon faded toward evening.

"We thought everyone had left," Thomas said, glancing between them. "We were going to review the excavation progress."

"We're addressing the timeline implications of the soil report," James explained, gesturing to their spread of documents. "Join us—we could use your input on the structural sequence."

For the next hour, the four of them refined the revised schedule, identifying critical path items and contingency options. The conversation remained strictly professional, yet Liz found herself repeatedly drawn to James's hands as he sketched solutions.

When Thomas and the foreman departed to inspect the day's progress, Liz and James remained at the table, finalizing their presentation for Howard. The project office had grown dim as daylight faded, desk lamps creating pools of light in the otherwise shadowed space.

"I think we've mitigated the delay effectively," James said, gathering the drawings they'd created. "The board shouldn't have concerns about the timeline."

"No, we've addressed it thoroughly." Liz closed her laptop, suddenly aware of how long they'd been working. The groundbreaking ceremony felt like days rather than hours ago. "I should get these projections to Howard tonight."

Neither moved to leave. In the quiet office, with darkness gathering outside, the professional buffer cre-

ated by daylight and colleagues had thinned dangerously. Liz found herself noticing details she normally
suppressed—the way James's hair fell across his forehead when he leaned over drawings, the intensity in his
eyes when solving a problem, the slight scar through
his right eyebrow that she'd found herself wondering
about.

"You handled the media well today," she said, retreating to safe professional territory. "The journalists
responded to your material narrative concept."

"Your press strategy was impeccable." James began
organizing the drawings into his portfolio. "The architecture correspondents mentioned how thoroughly
they'd been briefed."

"Collaborative success," Liz offered with a small
smile.

"Indeed." James hesitated, then added, "I meant
what I told Howard about your influence on the design. The experiential journey through the building is
significantly stronger because of your input."

The genuine acknowledgment created warmth that
spread through her chest. "Thank you. That means a
lot coming from you."

"From me specifically?"

The question hung between them, weighted with
implications neither had directly addressed since their

run at Lakeside Park. Liz considered her response carefully.

"Your design standards are exacting. I remember that from Preston—you never gave praise unless it was genuinely earned."

A shadow of something passed across his features. "I was an arrogant teenager with something to prove."

"We both were."

"Some might say we still are." His tone lightened slightly. "Though perhaps we've learned to channel it more productively."

The conversation had drifted from professional to personal without clear demarcation. Liz felt herself on uncertain ground, neither entirely comfortable nor willing to retreat to safer territory.

"Can I ask you something?" she said, surprising herself with the question forming in her mind. "Why architecture? You could have excelled in any field with your analytical abilities."

James leaned back slightly, considering her question with unexpected seriousness. "Architecture combines everything that matters to me—mathematical precision, artistic expression, practical problem-solving, and human experience. It's both deeply technical and fundamentally emotional." He paused. "And there's something profound about creating spaces that shape how people live and work. Long after we're gone, these structures remain as evidence of how we understood the world."

The passion in his voice revealed the person behind the professional façade—someone driven by genuine conviction rather than ambition or competition. Liz found herself wondering what other depths existed beneath his controlled exterior.

"What about you?" James asked. "Marketing seems ... insufficient for your intellectual capabilities."

The observation carried no judgment, only curiosity, yet Liz felt herself bristle slightly. "Marketing at its best is applied psychology, cultural analysis, and strategic communication. It's hardly intellectually unchallenging."

"That's not what I meant," James clarified. "You could have pursued literary theory, academic research, any field requiring deep analytical thinking. You chose corporate application instead. I've always wondered why."

The question probed too close to choices she rarely examined—the gradual surrender of academic ambitions, the compromise of intellectual pursuits for practical career paths. Her relationship with Mark had been only one factor in a complex equation of decisions that had led her here.

"Life happened," she said, echoing her response from their run. "Northwestern offered a dual degree program in marketing and English literature. I excelled at both. The corporate path provided stability and clear advancement."

"And what about now?" James's eyes held hers with uncomfortable perception. "Does it still provide what you need?"

The question crossed an invisible boundary, too personal for their carefully maintained professional relationship. Liz gathered her materials, creating physical distance from the conversation.

"I should call Howard about these timeline adjustments," she said, deflecting rather than answering. "He'll want to inform the board immediately."

James accepted the redirect with a slight nod, though something in his expression suggested he recognized her evasion. "Of course. I'll email the revised drawings tonight."

They packed up in silence, the earlier ease replaced by awareness of how close they'd come to territory neither was prepared to navigate. Outside, the construction site was illuminated by security lights, the excavated foundation a dark void against the earth.

"I'll walk you to your car," James offered as they exited the project office.

"Thank you, but I need to make this call first." Liz held up her phone with forced casualness. "Better reception out here than inside."

"Of course." He hesitated, then added, "Good work today, Elizabeth. On all fronts."

As he walked toward the parking area, Liz watched his retreating figure, struck by the strange mix of professional respect and personal curiosity he consistently evoked in her. She dialed Mark's number first, knowing she'd be late again.

"Hey, it's me," she said when he answered. "The groundbreaking ceremony ran long, and we're dealing with some timeline adjustments. I'll be another hour at least."

"Whatever." Mark's voice competed with sports announcers in the background. "I ordered pizza. Don't worry about dinner."

"Is everything okay? You sound distracted."

"Game's on. Playoffs. We can talk later."

"Right. See you soon."

The call ended without the customary "love you" that had once been automatic. Liz stared at her phone for a moment, the emptiness of the exchange contrasting sharply with the intellectual engagement she'd just experienced. When had her conversations with Mark devolved into logistical updates rather than meaningful exchange?

She dialed Howard next, explaining the timeline adjustments and proposed solutions. His enthusiasm was immediate and genuine.

"This is exactly why I wanted you on this project, Elizabeth. You understand both the business imperatives and the technical constraints." His voice carried real appreciation. "Send me the full proposal tonight and I'll review it before tomorrow's board call."

"I'll have it to you within the hour," Liz promised, already mentally drafting the executive summary.

"Excellent. And please convey my appreciation to James. The way you two have tackled this challenge is exactly the collaborative approach we need."

After the call ended, Liz remained standing at the edge of the foundation, looking out over what would eventually become Meridian's new headquarters. In the harsh security lights, the excavation resembled an archaeological dig, layers of earth exposed, the past removed to make way for future construction.

The metaphor wasn't lost on her. This project had excavated something in her as well, removing layers of professional routine to expose questions she'd long buried. James's simple query, "Does it still provide what you need?" echoed in her mind, demanding an answer she wasn't prepared to articulate.

Her phone chimed with a text from James: *Drawings sent. Also included alternative phasing option worth considering. Let me know your thoughts.*

The message was entirely professional, yet Liz found herself reading it multiple times, searching for subtext that likely didn't exist. She composed an equally professional reply: *Received. Will review tonight and incorporate into Howard's brief. Good work today.*

She hesitated, then added: *Your question earlier, about my career choices. It's more complicated than I indicated. Perhaps another time.*

The response came quickly: *I'd like that. There's more to both our stories than Preston Academy narratives would suggest.*

Liz slipped her phone into her pocket, unwilling to continue a conversation that blurred professional and personal boundaries. Yet as she walked to her car, she couldn't shake the sense that something fundamental had shifted, not in their working relationship, which remained productive and appropriate, but in her understanding of James himself.

The arrogant teenage rival had evolved into a complex adult whose passion for his work matched her own buried intellectual ambitions. His question about her career satisfaction had probed precisely because it echoed doubts she'd suppressed for years. The ease with which they'd collaborated today revealed not just professional compatibility but intellectual resonance rarely found in her corporate life.

Driving home, Liz tried to focus on the project success, the positive media coverage, Howard's approval of their timeline solutions, the tangible progress as

Meridian's future headquarters took physical form. Yet her mind kept returning to James's expression as he'd described why architecture mattered to him—the unguarded passion that had momentarily replaced his usual controlled professionalism.

When had anyone in her life last spoken about their work with such genuine conviction? When had she?

Mark was exactly where she'd expected, sprawled on the couch, empty pizza box on the coffee table, eyes fixed on the basketball game. He acknowledged her arrival with a distracted wave, attention never leaving the screen.

"Important game?" she asked, setting down her briefcase.

"Conference semifinals. Been waiting for this matchup all season."

Liz stood for a moment, watching her husband watch basketball. The distance between them felt suddenly vast, not just physical space but entirely separate mental landscapes with no bridge between them.

"The groundbreaking went well," she offered, unsure why she bothered. "Good media turnout. The building foundation work has started."

"That's nice." Mark reached for his beer without looking away from the television. "There's pizza in the kitchen if you want it."

Liz nodded though he wasn't looking. "I think I'll shower and catch up on some work. We had timeline adjustments to address."

"Mmm-hmm."

In her home office, Liz opened her laptop to draft Howard's brief. The document took shape quickly, clear problem statement, analysis of options, recommended approach with supporting data. Professional, thorough, exactly what Howard needed for the board.

Yet as she worked, part of her mind remained at the construction site, standing with James at the edge of the foundation as he asked why she'd chosen her career path. The question had probed a vulnerability she rarely acknowledged, the gradual surrender of intellectual passion for professional advancement, the growing suspicion that she'd chosen security over fulfillment.

Her phone chimed with an email notification. James had sent additional timeline diagrams with a brief note: *Another approach worth considering. Combines best elements of both options we discussed.*

The solution was elegant, a hybrid approach that minimized disruption while maintaining the original completion target. Liz incorporated it into Howard's brief, noting James's contribution explicitly. Their professional collaboration continued to produce superior results despite, or perhaps because of—the complicated undercurrents between them.

When she finally crawled into bed after midnight, Mark was already asleep, his back turned toward her side. The television downstairs still murmured sports commentary, left on after he'd dozed off. Liz stared at the familiar ceiling crack, listening to her husband's steady breathing and wondering when they had become such strangers sharing the same space.

The contrast between her evening with Mark and her afternoon with James created an uncomfortable clarity. One relationship offered logistical coexistence without meaningful connection; the other provided intellectual engagement that made her feel more alive than she had in years.

It was just a professional project, she reminded herself. Temporary collaboration with a defined endpoint. The intellectual chemistry with James was natural given their shared history and complementary skills. Nothing more.

Yet as sleep finally claimed her, Liz couldn't shake the memory of James's expression as he'd described creating spaces that would outlast them both, evidence of how they understood the world. In that unguarded moment, she'd glimpsed not just the brilliant architect but the person beneath the professional façade.

And that, she realized as consciousness faded, was far more dangerous than any physical attraction could ever be.

CHAPTER TWELVE

"Cracks in the Structure"

Saturday morning sunlight filtered through the bedroom curtains, casting a soft glow across the rumpled sheets. Liz had been awake for an hour already, scrolling through project emails on her phone while Mark's steady breathing filled the room. Three weeks had passed since the groundbreaking ceremony, and the foundation work was progressing faster than scheduled, creating a cascade of decisions requiring her attention.

She slipped out of bed, careful not to disturb Mark, though experience suggested there was no danger of that. In the bathroom, she splashed cold water on her face and studied her reflection. The shadows under her eyes had deepened, evidence of late nights reviewing architectural specifications and revising timeline projections.

Downstairs, the coffee maker gurgled to life under her touch. While it brewed, she spread project documents across the kitchen island—material samples, sustainability metrics, and James's latest sketches for the atrium design. His precise handwriting filled the margins with questions specifically directed to her: *"Elizabeth, does this align with the narrative flow we discussed? See alternative approach on page 3."*

The casual use of her full name in his notes had become familiar, almost intimate in its formality. Not many people called her Elizabeth anymore, not Mark, just a few colleagues, not even her parents. Just James, continuing a pattern established twenty years ago when they'd been academic rivals.

"Seriously? It's not even seven."

Liz looked up to find Mark in the doorway, hair tousled from sleep, expression somewhere between annoyed and incredulous. He gestured at the papers covering the counter.

"I thought weekends were supposed to be, you know, not work."

"Good morning to you too." Liz poured coffee into two mugs, offering one as a peace offering. "I just need to review these before Monday's meeting."

Mark accepted the coffee but not the explanation. "You were at the office until ten last night. And the night before." He leaned against the refrigerator, eyes narrowing. "This building project is taking over your life."

"It's a significant responsibility," Liz replied, keeping her tone neutral. "Howard's counting on me to ensure the marketing integration is seamless."

"Howard, Howard, Howard." Mark rolled his eyes. "And let me guess—James needs these notes immediately too?"

The pointed emphasis on James's name caught her attention. "The architectural team has deadlines, yes."

"The architectural team." Mark's laugh held no humor. "You mean your old high school nemesis who's suddenly the most important person in your life."

Liz set down her coffee, tension building between her shoulder blades. "That's not fair. This is my job, Mark."

"Your job used to be nine to five, with occasional late nights. Now I barely see you." He gestured toward the documents. "When you are home, you're buried in this stuff or on the phone with him."

"With the project team," Liz corrected, though she couldn't deny most of those calls involved James directly.

"Whatever." Mark moved to the pantry, grabbing a box of cereal. "I had to reschedule golf with Kevin twice because you might be free, then weren't. Lisa asked if we're still on for dinner next weekend, and I had no idea what to tell her."

"I'm sorry about the golf," Liz said, genuinely regretful about the canceled plans but also aware she hadn't missed them. "And yes, we can do dinner with the Barnes next weekend."

Mark poured cereal into a bowl, milk sloshing over the edges. "Unless something comes up with the precious building."

"Again, not fair."

"Isn't it?" He turned to face her fully. "You're different lately, Liz. Cold. Distant. Like you're physically here but your mind is somewhere else entirely."

The accusation stung, partly because it contained some truth. She had been distant, though not for the reasons he implied. The Meridian project had awakened something long dormant, intellectual engagement, creative challenge, a sense of genuine impact. The contrast with her emotional disconnection at home had become increasingly stark.

"I'm under a lot of pressure," she said finally. "This project is demanding, but it's temporary. Eighteen months."

"Eighteen months?" Mark's spoon clattered against the bowl. "That's a hell of a long time to put our life on hold."

"I'm not putting our life on hold. I'm doing my job."

"Your job." Mark shook his head. "When did your job become more important than us?"

The question hung between them, loaded with implications neither was prepared to address. Liz looked at her husband, really looked at him, and realized she had no answer that wouldn't lead to a deeper conversation than she was ready to have.

"It's not more important," she said finally. "But it is important."

Mark studied her for a long moment, something shifting in his expression. When he spoke again, his voice had lost its edge, replaced by something that sounded dangerously like indifference.

"You know what? Do whatever you need to do." He grabbed his cereal bowl. "Kevin's watching the game at his place today. I'm going over there."

"Mark—"

"It's fine, Liz. Really." He moved toward the living room, already mentally elsewhere. "You have your building. I have my things. It's fine."

She watched him retreat, struck by how little she felt about his departure. No urge to follow, to explain, to repair. Just a hollow acknowledgment that he was right, they were living parallel lives that occasionally intersected but rarely connected.

The front door closed with a decisive click twenty minutes later. Liz remained at the kitchen island, coffee grown cold beside her, documents untouched. She should feel something more, guilt, regret, determination to fix what was breaking. Instead, she felt a troubling relief at having the house to herself, at not needing to pretend interest in Mark's activities or explain her own.

When had they become such strangers? Had it happened gradually, a slow erosion of connection, or had they always been mismatched in ways youth and passion had temporarily disguised?

The doorbell's chime interrupted her thoughts. Probably Mark, forgotten keys or wallet. She moved to answer it, mentally preparing to restart their conversation with more patience.

Instead, she found her sister Rebecca on the doorstep, weekend bag slung over her shoulder, auburn hair pulled into a messy bun.

"Surprise!" Rebecca grinned, then faltered as she registered Liz's expression. "Or bad timing? You look like someone just ran over your favorite purse."

"Becks." Liz stepped back, genuinely pleased despite her mood. "What are you doing here?"

"My condo's being fumigated this weekend. I texted you yesterday about crashing here." Rebecca stepped inside, eyeing Liz with growing concern. "You didn't respond, but I took silence as consent. Should I not have?"

"No, it's fine, really." Liz closed the door behind her sister. "I've been distracted with work. You're always welcome here."

Rebecca set down her bag, studying Liz with the penetrating gaze that had intimidated her since childhood. At forty-one, Rebecca Mitchell carried herself with the confident ease of a woman who had faced life's disappointments and emerged stronger. Her divorce five years earlier had transformed her from suburban wife to urban professional with an unapologetic approach to life that Liz sometimes envied.

"Where's Mark?" Rebecca asked, glancing toward the silent living room.

"Friend's house. Watching a game." Liz moved toward the kitchen. "Coffee?"

"Already had two, but yes." Rebecca followed, letting out a low whistle at the documents spread across the island. "Damn, sis. This is either work or you're planning a prison break with extraordinary attention to detail."

Despite herself, Liz laughed. "The Meridian headquarters project. I'm the marketing liaison with the
architectural team."

"Right, the big building thing." Rebecca hopped
onto a barstool, rifling through the papers with casual interest. "These are gorgeous renderings. Who's the
architect again?"

Liz busied herself with the coffee maker. "Calloway
Design Group. They specialize in sustainable architecture."

"Calloway?" Rebecca's head snapped up. "Not
James Calloway? Your high school archnemesis?"

"The very same." Liz kept her tone deliberately neutral.

"Holy shit." Rebecca leaned forward, suddenly fas-
cinated. "The guy who beat you for valedictorian? The
Beckman Scholarship guy? That must be awkward as
hell."

"It was at first." Liz handed her sister a fresh mug
of coffee. "We've developed a productive professional
relationship."

Rebecca's eyebrows rose at the careful phrasing.
"Productive professional relationship," she repeated.
"That sounds rehearsed."

"It's accurate." Liz gathered the documents into
a neater pile, suddenly self-conscious about James's

handwritten notes with her name repeated through-out.

Rebecca sipped her coffee, watching Liz over the rim. "So what was the argument about?"

"What argument?"

"The one you and Mark were having before I arrived. The one that has you looking like you haven't decided whether to cry or burn the house down."

Liz sighed, leaning against the counter. "It wasn't really an argument. More like... a statement of facts."

"Which facts?"

"That I'm working too much. That the project is taking over my life." Liz stared into her coffee. "That I'm becoming cold and distant."

"Are you?"

The directness of the question was pure Rebecca. No gentle lead-up, no softening the blow. Just cutting to the heart of the matter with surgical precision.

"I don't know," Liz admitted. "Maybe. Probably. But not for the reasons he thinks."

Rebecca nodded slowly. "Which are?"

"He thinks I'm obsessed with the project. With work."

"And the real reason?"

Liz hesitated, the truth hovering on her lips. How could she explain that the project had awakened her to how deeply unsatisfied she'd been? That working with

James had reminded her of intellectual passions long suppressed? That she'd begun to question not just her marriage but the entire life she'd constructed?

"I think we've been growing apart for years," she said finally. "The project just made it impossible to ignore anymore."

Rebecca nodded, unsurprised. "I wondered when you'd notice."

"What's that supposed to mean?"

"Liz." Rebecca's voice softened. "I love you, but you've been sleepwalking through your marriage for as long as I can remember. Every time I visit, it's like watching two people sharing a house but not a life."

The observation stung precisely because it echoed her own recent thoughts. "We used to be happy."

"Did you? Or were you just younger and better at ignoring the problems?"

Liz moved to the window, gazing out at the perfectly maintained backyard Mark had insisted on installing three years ago, a showcase space neither of them actually used. "When did you get so cynical about marriage?"

"I'm not cynical about marriage," Rebecca corrected. "I'm realistic about compatibility. Some people fit. Some don't. Some fit for a while and then grow in different directions."

"And you think Mark and I..."

"I think you married a guy who peaked in college, and you've spent fifteen years pretending you didn't notice." Rebecca's bluntness was tempered by genuine compassion. "He's not a bad person, Liz. He's just not your person. Not anymore."

The simple assessment hit with unexpected force. Liz sank onto a barstool, something between relief and grief washing over her. "When did you get so wise?"

"Divorce is quite the education." Rebecca reached across the island to squeeze her hand. "Look, I'm not saying you should leave Mark. I'm saying you should be honest with yourself about whether you still want to be with him."

"I don't know," Liz admitted, the words barely audible. "I've been so focused on what I should want, the stable marriage, the nice house, the respectable career. I've lost track of what I actually want."

"And what do you want, Lizzie?" Rebecca's use of her childhood nickname created a safe space for honesty.

"I want to feel alive again." The truth emerged before she could filter it. "I want conversations that challenge me. I want to create something meaningful. I want to stop feeling like I'm playing a role in someone else's life."

Rebecca nodded slowly. "And does Mark fit into that vision?"

Liz's silence was answer enough.

"For what it's worth," Rebecca said gently, "divorce isn't the end of the world. It felt like it at first, but now I can't imagine still being with Richard. My apartment is small, my life is messier, but it's authentically mine."

"I haven't said I want a divorce," Liz protested weakly.

"No, but you're asking the questions that lead there." Rebecca studied her sister with knowing eyes. "Just be honest with yourself about why you're asking them now."

Something in her tone made Liz look up sharply. "What do you mean?"

"I mean," Rebecca said carefully, "that sometimes when we're unhappy in one relationship, we can fixate on someone new as the solution."

"This isn't about anyone else," Liz said too quickly.

Rebecca's gaze flicked meaningfully to the architectural drawings, to James's handwritten notes. "If you say so."

"It's not," Liz insisted, though her warming cheeks betrayed her. "James is a colleague. A challenging, brilliant, occasionally infuriating colleague."

"Mmm-hmm." Rebecca's expression remained skeptical. "The same James who was your intellectual rival? Who pushed all your competitive buttons? Who you used to complain about in every letter from Preston Academy?"

"That was twenty years ago."

"And now you're working closely with him, spending long hours together, sharing a creative vision." Rebecca shrugged. "I'm just saying, be careful about confusing intellectual chemistry with something else."

Liz felt exposed, as if Rebecca had read thoughts she herself had barely acknowledged. Yes, there was something compelling about working with James, the way he challenged her thinking, respected her perspective, made her feel intellectually alive in ways Mark never had. But that was professional admiration, nothing more.

Wasn't it?

"The project is demanding," Liz said carefully. "James and I work well together despite our history. That's all."

Rebecca held up her hands in surrender. "Okay. Just checking." She slid off the barstool. "Now, how about we do something that doesn't involve work or marriage crisis? There's a farmers market in the village. Fresh air might help clear your head."

Grateful for the subject change, Liz agreed. The sisters spent the afternoon wandering through market stalls, talking about everything except the conversation they'd started in the kitchen. Rebecca shared stories about her teenage sons' latest adventures, her dating disasters, her new photography hobby. Liz listened, envying her sister's unapologetic embrace of her reconstituted life.

When they returned home, the house remained empty. Mark had texted, staying for dinner at Kevin's, home later. The brief message contained no affection, no inquiry about her day. Just information, as if reporting to a roommate rather than a wife.

After dinner with Rebecca, Liz found herself in the living room, staring at their wedding photo on the mantel. She barely recognized the beaming young woman in the white dress, or the adoring young man gazing at her. They looked so certain, so connected, so unaware of how time and complacency would transform their relationship.

"Penny for your thoughts," Rebecca said, joining her with a glass of wine.

Liz accepted the offered glass. "Just wondering when we became these people. When Mark stopped looking at me like that. When I stopped wanting him to."

Rebecca studied the photo thoughtfully. "You know, I kept my wedding album for years after the divorce. Used to look at it and wonder the same things. Then one day I realized, those two young people in the pictures? They don't exist anymore. They grew into different people with different needs."

"And that made it easier?"

"It made it clearer." Rebecca sipped her wine. "The question isn't 'what happened to those people?' It's 'do these new people still belong together?'"

Liz traced the edge of her wine glass, considering. "And if the answer is no?"

"Then you have choices to make." Rebecca's voice was gentle but firm. "Hard ones, but less hard than living a lie for another fifteen years."

Later that night, after Rebecca had gone to bed, Liz sat alone in her home office. Mark still hadn't returned, probably fallen asleep on Kevin's couch watching post-game analysis. Once, she would have called to check on him. Tonight, she felt only a distant concern, as if thinking about an acquaintance rather than a husband.

Her phone chimed with an email notification. James, sending revised atrium specifications with a brief note: *These incorporate your narrative flow suggestions. Your insight has transformed this space. Let me know your thoughts when convenient.*

The simple professional acknowledgment shouldn't have created the warm glow that spread through her chest. She shouldn't have reread it three times, analyzing his word choices, wondering if "when convenient" meant he was also working late on Saturday, thinking about the project, about their collaboration.

She set the phone down, Rebecca's warning echoing in her mind. Was she confusing intellectual connection with something else? Was her growing dissatisfaction with Mark influencing her response to James?

The questions had no simple answers. All she knew with certainty was that something fundamental had shifted in her marriage, in her professional life, in her understanding of what she wanted from both.

Liz moved to the window, gazing out at the quiet suburban street. In houses all around them, other couples were living their own versions of compromise and accommodation, of dreams deferred and expectations adjusted. How many were truly happy? How many were simply going through motions established years ago, afraid to acknowledge that the foundations of their relationships had developed hairline cracks that would eventually threaten the entire structure?

Her phone chimed again. Mark this time: *Staying at Kevin's. Too many beers to drive. See you tomorrow.*

No "love you." No "miss you." No acknowledgment of their morning argument. Just logistics between two people who shared an address but increasingly little else.

Liz set the phone down without replying and returned to the living room. She picked up the wedding photo, studying the young couple with their bright smiles and bright futures. She tried to remember how it felt to be that woman, to believe that Mark was her perfect match, to envision their life unfolding exactly as planned.

The memory felt distant, like recalling a movie she'd seen long ago rather than her own experience. Perhaps Rebecca was right. Those two young people no longer existed. They had evolved into different people with different needs, different dreams, different understandings of what made life meaningful.

The question was whether those new people still belonged together. And as Liz carefully returned the photo to the mantel, she realized she already knew the answer, had known it for longer than she'd been willing to admit.

The real question was what she intended to do about it.

CHAPTER THIRTEEN

"Paper Cuts"

The Calloway Design Group studio hummed with focused energy as Liz made her way past workstations where architects bent over drawings or stared intently at computer screens. Four months into the Meridian project, she navigated the space with familiar ease, nodding to team members who recognized her as a regular presence rather than an outside client.

The conference room had been transformed into a design war room, walls covered with renderings, material samples arranged on a side table, and a scale model of the emerging headquarters dominating the center. Thomas Chen was already there, organizing presentation boards with meticulous precision.

"Morning, Ms. Donovan," he said, glancing up briefly. "James is just finishing a call. The sustainability consultant had questions about the geothermal specifications."

"No rush. I'm early." Liz set her portfolio on the table and moved to examine the model. In the four months since groundbreaking, the project had evolved from foundation work to the beginnings of structural steel. The model reflected these changes, updated weekly to match construction progress.

She ran her finger along the miniature facade, tracing the material transition from traditional limestone base to innovative composites. The physical manifestation of Meridian's "progressive tradition" philosophy was taking shape, not just in drawings but in actual steel and concrete rising from the earth.

"Admiring our progress?" James's voice came from behind her.

Liz turned to find him leaning against the doorframe, coffee in hand. Today he wore charcoal trousers and a navy button-down with sleeves rolled up. The silver at his temples caught the light, creating a distinguished contrast with his dark hair.

"It's becoming real," she said, gesturing to the model. "Not just plans anymore."

"The most satisfying phase," James agreed, entering the room fully. "When ideas transform into physical reality."

Thomas cleared his throat. "I've arranged the material samples as requested and updated the sustainability metrics based on the latest consultant report."

"Perfect timing," James said as Sophia Rodriguez breezed in, arms full of interior finish boards.

"Sorry I'm late," Sophia announced, dropping her materials onto a side table. "Traffic was apocalyptic. Oh good, you brought actual food, not just those sad protein bars Thomas calls lunch."

She gestured to a tray of sandwiches Liz hadn't noticed James carrying. The casual inclusion of lunch suggested this meeting would run longer than the scheduled hour.

"I thought we might work through," James explained, setting down the tray. "The atrium design needs resolution today if we're going to maintain the structural timeline."

For the next two hours, they reviewed progress across all aspects of the design. The professional tension that had characterized early meetings had evolved into something more productive, a collaborative rhythm where each contributed from their area of expertise without territorial disputes.

"The integrated environmental graphics are working beautifully," Sophia noted, indicating where brand elements merged with architectural features. "Much more cohesive than separate systems would have been."

"Elizabeth's insight about narrative flow transformed the approach," James said, pulling up detailed renderings on his tablet. "The visitor experience now tells Meridian's story through a deliberate progression rather than isolated moments."

The casual credit surprised Liz. Early in their collaboration, James had defended his design concepts with territorial vigor. Now he acknowledged her contributions without prompting or apparent calculation.

"The marketing team is impressed with how the brand integration avoids corporate clichés," Liz responded. "Howard specifically mentioned the material narrative as 'sophisticated without being pretentious.'"

"High praise from Howard," Thomas remarked. "He's not easily impressed by design concepts."

"He's impressed by results," James corrected. "And this approach delivers measurable outcomes, visitor engagement, employee satisfaction, operational efficiency. It's not just aesthetically pleasing; it's functionally superior."

As they worked through technical details, Liz found herself watching James's hands as he sketched modifications to address engineering concerns. His fingers moved with precise confidence, the pencil an extension of his thought process. He drew with remarkable speed, translating complex ideas into clear visual form without hesitation.

"The curtain wall connection needs refinement," Thomas pointed out, indicating a junction where materials met. "The thermal break is creating a detail challenge."

James sketched three alternative solutions in quick succession. "Option one maintains visual continuity but complicates the weather seal. Option two simplifies construction but creates a visible joint. Option three splits the difference with this transitional element."

"Option three," Liz said immediately. "It turns a technical necessity into a design feature that reinforces the progressive tradition narrative."

James nodded, adding detail to the third sketch. "Agreed. Thomas, can you develop this for engineering review?"

"Already on it," Thomas said, photographing the sketch with his tablet.

By one o'clock, they had resolved most critical design issues. Sophia suggested they break for the lunch James had provided, spreading sandwiches and drinks across the conference table. The conversation shifted to project logistics as they ate.

"The construction manager is concerned about material delivery schedules," Thomas said between bites. "The limestone quarry reported potential delays."

"I've already contacted an alternative supplier," James replied. "Slightly higher cost but more reliable timeline. Howard approved the contingency budget yesterday."

"Speaking of timelines," Sophia interjected, "the interior installation schedule is getting compressed. We need to finalize finish selections next week."

"I've blocked Thursday for that," Liz said, checking her calendar. "Catherine wants to review options before final decisions."

The working lunch continued with easy professionalism, each team member addressing their area of responsibility without the territorial disputes that had characterized early meetings. Liz found herself relaxing into the collaborative atmosphere, genuinely enjoying the problem-solving process with this team.

As they discussed sustainability features, James mentioned the geothermal system's expected lifespan. "The technology is designed for seventy-year operation with minimal maintenance. Most buildings don't survive that long, but we design assuming permanence."

"Quite different from your experience with the Thomas Building," Thomas commented. "Wasn't there discussion of retrofitting after just five years?"

A shadow crossed James's face. "That was a unique situation. The client changed ownership mid-construction, and the new management had different priorities."

"It's challenging when long-term vision collides with short-term thinking," Liz observed. "Like relationships that look sustainable on paper but fail under real-world conditions."

The personal comment slipped out before she could filter it. James gave her a curious look.

"An apt comparison," he said after a moment. "My divorce taught me that lesson rather definitively. Eight years of marriage collapsed in three months when priorities diverged."

The casual mention of his divorce created a sudden shift in the room's atmosphere. Thomas and Sophia exchanged quick glances, clearly surprised by the personal disclosure.

"I'm sorry," Liz said, genuinely caught off guard. "I didn't mean to—"

"It's fine," James cut her off with a dismissive wave. "Ancient history. My ex-wife and I had different definitions of commitment, professionally and personally. She saw our firm's design principles as negotiable when client demands conflicted. I didn't."

The brief explanation revealed more than James likely intended. Liz had researched his career extensively but found no mentions of his divorce. Now pieces clicked into place, his occasional wariness, his intense commitment to design integrity, his reluctance to compromise on principles.

"Architectural philosophy as relationship deal-breaker," Sophia mused. "That's actually refreshingly principled compared to most divorce stories I hear."

"It wasn't just professional," James admitted, surprising them further. "She had an affair with a client who preferred her more... flexible approach to design. They started their own firm afterward."

The personal revelation hung in the air. Thomas looked distinctly uncomfortable, while Sophia watched with undisguised fascination. Liz felt an unexpected surge of sympathy for James, the betrayal explained his occasional defensiveness about design decisions and his intense commitment to integrity.

"That must have been difficult," she said quietly.

James met her eyes briefly. "It clarified what matters. Both in design and in life."

The moment stretched between them, a flash of genuine connection amid professional collaboration. Then James straightened, visibly shifting back to project leader.

"The limestone samples need review," he said briskly. "Thomas, can you bring the new options?"

As Thomas left to retrieve the samples, Sophia gathered the lunch debris, shooting Liz a meaningful glance that clearly communicated her interest in the unexpected personal turn.

James spread specification sheets across the table, his manner entirely professional again. "These alternative suppliers offer comparable quality with better delivery guarantees."

Liz leaned forward to examine the documents, reaching for a material sample at the same moment James slid it toward her. The heavy stone sample caught her finger between it and the table edge.

"Ouch!" She pulled back, a thin line of blood appearing along her index finger.

"Let me see," James said, taking her hand before she could protest. He examined the cut with clinical focus. "Not deep, but paper cuts bleed disproportionately to their size."

His fingers were warm against hers, the casual contact sending an unexpected current up her arm. Liz found herself acutely aware of his proximity, the slight scent of his cologne, the gentle pressure of his thumb near the small wound.

"First aid kit in my office," he said, releasing her hand. "Come on."

Liz followed him across the studio to his glass-walled office, conscious of Sophia watching their departure with undisguised interest. Inside, James retrieved a small medical kit from his desk drawer.

"Hazard of the profession," he explained, opening an antiseptic wipe. "Architectural models create more injuries than you'd expect. Paper, chipboard, metal edges, we keep bandages in stock."

He took her hand again, gently cleaning the cut. The antiseptic stung, but Liz found herself more distracted by the careful way he held her fingers, the clinical efficiency of his movements contrasting with the intimacy of the gesture.

"You don't need to do this," she said, her voice sounding strange to her own ears. "It's just a paper cut."

"Infected cuts delay projects," James replied, selecting a bandage. "Can't have our marketing liaison sidelined by sepsis."

His attempt at humor didn't quite mask the unusual tension that had developed between them. As he wrapped the bandage around her finger, his thumb brushed across her palm, a touch that might have been accidental but didn't feel that way.

Liz looked up to find him watching her, his professional mask momentarily slipping to reveal something more complicated. For a heartbeat, neither moved, caught in an unexpected moment of awareness.

Then James released her hand and stepped back, the moment breaking as quickly as it had formed.

"Should be fine now," he said, his voice deliberately casual. "Sophia's probably wondering if we've abandoned the limestone discussion."

"Right." Liz flexed her bandaged finger, struggling to recalibrate. "We should get back."

In the doorway, she paused. "Thank you. For the first aid."

"Professional courtesy," James replied with a careful smile that didn't quite reach his eyes.

The remainder of the meeting proceeded with heightened awareness on both sides. They maintained scrupulous professionalism, focusing entirely on technical details and project timelines. If Thomas and Sophia noticed the subtle shift in dynamics, neither commented.

By four o'clock, they had resolved all critical design issues and established the next steps. As the meeting concluded, James assigned follow-up tasks with his usual efficiency.

"Thomas, develop the curtain wall detail for engineering review. Sophia, prepare the interior finish presentation for Thursday. Elizabeth, can you confirm Howard's availability for the quarterly progress review next week?"

The use of her full name, always his preference, now carried a weight it hadn't before. Liz nodded, gathering her materials with deliberate focus.

"I'll coordinate with his assistant today," she said, not quite meeting his eyes.

As they dispersed, Sophia fell into step beside Liz. "Well, that was unexpectedly revealing," she murmured. "I've worked with James for three years and never heard him mention his divorce."

"It came up organically," Liz replied, keeping her tone neutral. "Professional relationships sometimes include personal context."

Sophia's knowing smile suggested she wasn't convinced by the explanation. "Your dynamic with him has certainly evolved since those first contentious meetings. You've found a productive rhythm."

"The project benefits from our combined perspectives," Liz said, echoing words she'd used with Catherine months earlier.

"Mmm-hmm." Sophia's expression remained skeptical. "Well, whatever it is, keep it up. The design is better for it."

At the elevator, Liz glanced back toward the conference room. Through the glass walls, she could see James still at the table, pencil moving rapidly across tracing paper. He was sketching something new, his focus complete, the outside world temporarily forgotten.

Even from this distance, she recognized the intensity that characterized his creative process, the same focused attention he'd given her small injury moments earlier. The memory of his fingers against hers lingered, creating a confusion she wasn't prepared to examine.

The elevator arrived, and Liz stepped inside, deliberately turning away from the sight of James working. The bandage on her finger seemed to pulse with each heartbeat, a physical reminder of a moment that should have been insignificant but somehow wasn't.

The Calloway Design studio was silent except for the soft scratch of pencil on paper. Most of the team had departed hours ago, leaving James alone with the design problem that had occupied him since the afternoon meeting.

The atrium space had evolved significantly from his original concept, incorporating elements of Liz's narrative approach in ways he hadn't initially envisioned. Her insight about visitor experience had transformed what might have been merely beautiful architecture into something more profound, a space that told a story through its very structure.

His pencil moved quickly, developing the curtain wall detail they'd discussed. The technical solution was straightforward, but he found himself adding elements that explicitly referenced marketing concepts Liz had proposed, the material transition becoming more pronounced, the junction between old and new more deliberately articulated.

He paused, studying what he'd drawn. The design now incorporated her thinking so thoroughly that he could no longer separate his architectural vision from her marketing narrative. They had become intertwined, each strengthening the other.

James flexed his hand, remembering the unexpected jolt he'd felt when taking her injured finger. The moment had caught him off guard, a simple first aid gesture suddenly charged with awareness he hadn't anticipated.

He'd noticed her, of course. Her intelligence, her quick analytical mind, her capacity to challenge his thinking in ways few others could. But today something had shifted, a brief, unguarded moment when professional appreciation had transformed into something more personal.

The realization was unwelcome. James had maintained careful boundaries since his divorce, focusing entirely on his firm's success. Complications with a client representative, particularly one with Liz's connection to his past, were exactly what he didn't need.

Yet as he returned to his drawing, he found himself incorporating another element she had suggested during their discussion, a lighting detail that would highlight the material transition at different times of day. It was her idea, but it enhanced his architectural concept perfectly.

Their collaboration had evolved from competitive tension to genuine synergy. The project was better for it. That was all this was, professional respect, creative chemistry, the satisfaction of working with someone who kept pace with his thinking.

Nothing more.

James continued sketching late into the night, developing the design they had discussed together, each line on the paper reflecting both his architectural vision and her marketing insight, separate disciplines merging into something neither could have created alone.

CHAPTER FOURTEEN

"Structural Integrity"

The ballroom of the Grand Plaza Hotel glittered with corporate success. Crystal chandeliers cast flattering light over round tables draped in cream linens, each centered with modest floral arrangements in Pharmco's signature blue and silver. A banner stretched across the stage: "Annual Sales Excellence Awards."

Liz smoothed the skirt of her navy cocktail dress, observing the room with anthropological detachment. After fifteen years of marriage to Mark, she'd attended countless corporate functions just like this one, events where spouses served as accessories, proof that successful salespeople could close the deal in their personal lives too.

"There's my beautiful wife." Mark appeared with two glasses of wine, momentarily attentive in a way he rarely was at home. His charcoal suit fit better than usual, he'd actually taken it to the tailor at her suggestion. "You remember Bill Thompson and his wife Janet?"

"Of course." Liz smiled, accepting both the wine and her role for the evening. "Congratulations on your promotion, Bill. Mark mentioned you're heading the Midwest division now."

Bill, red-faced, slightly too loud, launched into a detailed account of his recent triumph while his wife stood silently beside him, practiced smile never wavering. Liz recognized the expression from countless bathroom mirrors at similar events.

"And how about you, Liz?" Bill finally asked. "Mark says you're involved with some big building project?"

"I'm the marketing liaison for Meridian's new headquarters development. We're integrating brand narrative into the architectural experience to create a—"

"She's making sure the fancy architect doesn't blow the budget on useless pretty stuff," Mark interrupted with a chuckle. "My practical girl keeps everyone's feet on the ground."

Liz felt the familiar sting of his casual dismissal but maintained her smile. "Something like that."

As conversation shifted to golf handicaps, she took the opportunity to scan the room. Couples clustered in predictable formations, men in dark suits forming the center, wives orbiting their perimeter like moons around planets. She'd never noticed the pattern so starkly before.

At a nearby table, Kevin Barnes caught her eye and waved. Lisa sat beside him, looking elegant if slightly bored in a black sheath dress. Liz excused herself and navigated through the crowd toward them.

"Escaped already?" Lisa asked with knowing sympathy. "I timed Kevin earlier, seventeen minutes of sales talk before he remembered I exist."

"Fifteen for Mark," Liz replied, settling into an empty chair. "But who's counting?"

"All of us wives, apparently." Lisa sipped her martini. "Twenty years of marriage and these events never change. Though I've gotten better at looking interested while mentally redecorating my kitchen."

Liz studied her neighbor with new curiosity. "Does it bother you? Being relegated to 'Kevin's wife' at these things?"

"Sometimes." Lisa shrugged. "But it's just one night. And he's good to me the rest of the time. Marriage is about compromise, right? He attends my charity galas; I pretend to care about pharmaceutical sales targets."

"Right." Liz nodded, though something in Lisa's easy acceptance unsettled her. "Compromise."

The evening progressed with mechanical predictability, dinner, speeches from executives, recognition of top performers. Mark remained attentive in the performative way reserved for public settings, his hand occasionally resting on her knee, refilling her wine without being asked. If anyone observed them, they'd appear the perfect couple, successful, attractive, comfortable.

When dinner concluded, the regional director took the stage to present the annual awards. Mark sat straighter, adjusting his tie. He'd won top sales representative three years running, and tonight would likely make it four.

"You've got this," Liz whispered, squeezing his hand. Despite their growing distance, she still wanted him to succeed.

"And this year's Northeast Regional Sales Excellence Award goes to... Mark Donovan!"

The table erupted in applause. Mark kissed her cheek before striding to the stage, accepting the crystal trophy with practiced humility. He adjusted the microphone, his salesman's smile firmly in place.

"Wow, four years running. I'm honored." He launched into his speech, thanking his team, his mentors, the company leadership. The words flowed with rehearsed precision, Mark had always excelled at public speaking, his natural charm magnified under spotlights.

Liz's phone vibrated in her clutch. She ignored it initially, not wanting to appear disengaged during her husband's moment. But when it vibrated again thirty seconds later, she discreetly checked the screen.

An email from James: *Urgent design issue with atrium connection. Structural engineer flagged potential integrity problem. Need your input on marketing impact if we modify as attached. Time-sensitive.*

A detailed rendering followed, showing two possible solutions to what appeared to be a significant structural challenge. The issue involved the dramatic glass atrium that served as the headquarters' centerpiece, a space Liz had fought for as essential to the visitor experience.

She glanced up at Mark, who was now recounting an amusing client anecdote that had the audience laughing appreciatively. His moment wouldn't end soon; his speeches typically ran long, especially after two glasses of wine.

Liz studied the renderings more carefully. The engineer's preferred solution significantly altered the visitor flow through the space, disrupting the narrative progression she'd carefully designed with James. The alternative preserved the experience but required more expensive materials and additional support columns.

"...and of course, I couldn't have done it without my beautiful wife, Liz."

Her head snapped up at the mention of her name. Mark was gesturing toward her table, and suddenly all eyes turned her way. She smiled and gave a small wave, the perfect supportive spouse.

"Fifteen years of marriage, and she still puts up with my crazy schedule and late nights," Mark continued. "And she only occasionally reminds me that she graduated with higher honors from Northwestern."

Polite laughter rippled through the room. Liz maintained her smile while her mind raced through the structural problem in James's email. The solution seemed obvious, they needed to preserve the experiential flow even if it meant additional cost. Howard would back her on this; he understood the atrium's importance to the brand story.

As Mark concluded to enthusiastic applause, Liz quickly typed a response: *Option B maintains narrative integrity. Essential to preserve visitor experience. Will convince Howard re: budget adjustment tomorrow. Can you hold engineer until then?*

Mark returned to the table, trophy in hand, accepting congratulations from colleagues. He slid into his chair beside Liz, flushed with success and champagne.

"Great speech," she said automatically.

"Thanks, babe." He placed the trophy in front of her. "Another one for the shelf. Did you see Thompson's face? He was sure he had it this year."

"Mmm-hmm." Her phone vibrated again.

James had responded: *Agreed on Option B. Engineering meeting tomorrow 9am. Detailed cost analysis attached. Appreciate quick response.*

"Is that work?" Mark's voice had cooled noticeably. "Seriously? During my award ceremony?"

Liz slipped her phone back into her clutch. "Sorry. Just a quick question about tomorrow's meeting."

"From the architect?" Mark's tone carried an edge she rarely heard in public. "What's his name again? James?"

"It's a team project, Mark. Not just James."

"Right." He took a long swallow of champagne. "Seems like you're always available for that team. Even during your husband's big night."

A few heads turned at nearby tables. Liz placed her hand on Mark's arm, lowering her voice. "Let's not do this here. It was thirty seconds of my attention during a three-hour event."

Mark shrugged off her touch, but managed a tight smile as the company president approached to congratulate him. The moment passed, social masks firmly back in place.

The remainder of the evening unfolded with practiced politeness. They circulated among Mark's colleagues, accepted congratulations, participated in the expected rituals of corporate celebration. Liz played her role flawlessly while her mind repeatedly drifted to the atrium problem, mentally refining arguments to present to Howard about preserving the design integrity.

As the event wound down, she found herself cornered by Janet Thompson near the ladies' room.

"Thirty-two years," Janet said without preamble, straightening her lipstick in the mirror.

"I'm sorry?"

"Bill and I. Thirty-two years of marriage next month." Janet turned to face her directly. "I saw what happened at your table. The phone, Mark's reaction."

Liz tensed. "It was nothing. Just a minor work issue."

"Of course." Janet's smile held surprising compassion. "But take it from someone who's been doing this a long time, these corporate marriages require maintenance. My first priority has always been supporting Bill's career, being available when he needs to shine."

"That's... admirable," Liz managed, though the words felt wrong in her mouth.

"It's practical." Janet patted her arm. "Men like our husbands need to be the center sometimes. Small sacrifices keep the foundation strong."

Liz studied the older woman, wondering if this was her future, dispensing wisdom about subordinating her own interests to maintain a marriage that increasingly felt like a performance rather than a partnership.

"I should find Mark," she said, unwilling to continue the conversation. "Thank you for the advice."

The drive home unfolded in tense silence. Mark stared straight ahead, his earlier public warmth completely evaporated. His trophy sat on the back seat, momentarily forgotten.

Liz watched the city lights blur past her window, mentally calculating what she'd need to prepare for tomorrow's meeting. The structural issue with the atrium wasn't just a technical problem, it represented the intersection of physical integrity and experiential authenticity. The solution they chose would reveal their true priorities for the building.

"You couldn't give me one night," Mark finally said, breaking the silence as they turned onto the highway. "One night without checking your phone, without thinking about that fucking project."

"It was an emergency situation that needed immediate input," Liz replied, keeping her voice even. "I gave you my full attention for the entire evening otherwise."

"Right." His laugh held no humor. "Your body was there, but your mind was somewhere else entirely. With him."

The accusation hung between them. Liz turned to study her husband's profile, his jaw tight with resentment.

"This isn't about James," she said carefully. "It's about a professional responsibility I take seriously."

"Is it? Because you never checked your phone during dinner at my company events before this project started."

"That's not fair. I've always been dedicated to my work."

"Not like this." Mark's knuckles whitened on the steering wheel. "Not where you light up talking about 'design integrity' and 'narrative flow' and whatever other bullshit you two discuss until all hours."

The car felt suddenly too small, the air between them charged with unspoken tensions. Liz looked out the window again, watching familiar landmarks pass, the grocery store where they shopped every Sunday, the park where they occasionally walked when weather permitted, the gas station where Mark always filled up on Tuesdays. The geography of their shared life, mapped in routine and habit rather than passion or purpose.

"I don't want to fight," she said finally. "You won your award. It's a significant achievement. Let's focus on that."

Mark's shoulders slumped slightly, anger deflating into something closer to resignation. "Sure. The award. Another trophy for the shelf no one sees except us."

The remainder of the drive passed in silence. At home, Mark headed straight upstairs while Liz lingered in the kitchen, pouring herself a glass of water. The house felt cavernous and still, their footsteps echoing in separate rhythms through the carefully decorated rooms.

She moved to her home office, closing the door softly behind her. The space had become her sanctuary, the one room in the house that truly reflected her rather than their joint compromise or, more accurately, Mark's preferences accommodated by her acquiescence.

Liz opened her laptop, reviewing James's email more thoroughly now. The structural issue was more significant than she'd initially realized. The atrium's glass ceiling junction required additional support that would either alter the visitor path or require substantial reinforcement columns that weren't in the original design.

She studied both options carefully. Option A preserved the budget but compromised the experience, visitors would no longer flow naturally from Meridian's historical displays into the innovation showcase, breaking the narrative thread she'd carefully constructed with James. Option B maintained that flow but required expensive modifications and would delay construction by at least two weeks.

The choice seemed obvious from a marketing perspective, but she needed to understand the engineering constraints better before meeting with Howard. She began drafting notes, outlining the experiential impact of each option, developing arguments for preserving the narrative integrity even at additional cost.

As she worked, Liz found herself relaxing into the familiar rhythm of professional problem-solving. Here, in this space, things made sense. Problems had solutions. Decisions could be evaluated against objective criteria. Unlike her marriage, where the problems remained nameless and the criteria for success shifted constantly beneath her feet.

Without consciously deciding to, she began composing an email to James:

Re: Atrium Structural Issue

After reviewing both options more thoroughly, I'm even more convinced Option B is the only viable solution from a brand experience perspective. The atrium represents the heart of the headquarters, the space where Meridian's past and future visibly connect. Disrupting that flow undermines the entire narrative structure we've built.

I understand the engineering concerns, but I believe we can make a compelling case to Howard that the additional investment preserves essential design integrity. The columns could actually enhance the experience if we integrate them thoughtfully, perhaps as timeline markers or innovation milestones?

I've attached some initial thoughts on how we might position this to the board. The language about "structural integrity reflecting brand integrity" might be particularly effective with Howard.

Let me know your thoughts before tomorrow's meeting. I think we can turn this challenge into an opportunity to strengthen both the physical structure and the experiential narrative.

Elizabeth

She paused before sending, struck by how much more open and passionate her communication with James had become compared to conversations with her husband. With James, she didn't filter her enthusiasm or temper her intellectual engagement. She didn't worry about appearing too invested or too analytical.

The realization was uncomfortable but undeniable. Somewhere along the way, she had started compartmentalizing herself, the professional Liz who engaged fully with challenges and spoke her mind without hesitation, and the wife Liz who carefully modulated her responses to maintain an increasingly fragile peace.

Tonight, those compartments had collided in the ballroom when James's email arrived during Mark's speech. The resulting tension revealed more than just scheduling conflicts or professional priorities, it exposed the growing disconnect between the person she was becoming through her work and the person she pretended to be in her marriage.

Liz sent the email, then leaned back in her chair, listening to the sounds of the house. Upstairs, water ran briefly as Mark prepared for bed. The furnace hummed, cycling on against the autumn chill. A car passed on their quiet street. Normal sounds of a normal night in a normal marriage.

Except it wasn't normal anymore. Perhaps it never had been.

Her phone chimed with a response from James:

Elizabeth,

Your insights are exactly what I needed. The narrative integrity argument is compelling, and your suggestion about integrating the columns as timeline elements is brilliant, solving both engineering and experiential requirements simultaneously.

I've asked Thomas to mock up visualizations incorpo-
rating your concept. We'll have them ready for tomor-
row's meeting with Howard.

This is why our collaboration works, you see possi-
bilities where others see only constraints. I'll have coffee
waiting when you arrive tomorrow.

James

The simple professional acknowledgment shouldn't
have created the warm glow that spread through her
chest. It was just colleagues solving problems together, appreciating each other's contributions. Nothing
more.

Yet as Liz finally headed upstairs to the bedroom she
shared with Mark, she couldn't help comparing his dismissive comment at dinner, "making sure the fancy architect doesn't blow the budget on useless pretty stuff."
with James's genuine appreciation of her perspective.

Mark was already in bed, his back turned toward her
side, breathing not quite regular enough to be asleep.
She changed quietly in the bathroom, removing her
makeup and jewelry, transforming from corporate wife
back to herself.

When she slipped between the sheets, Mark didn't
stir. The distance between them, barely eighteen inches
of mattress, might as well have been miles. Liz stared at
the ceiling, the familiar crack now a well-worn friend,
and allowed herself to imagine a different life.

A life where her intellectual passions weren't treated as inconvenient distractions. Where her professional insights were valued rather than diminished. Where she didn't have to make herself smaller to maintain someone else's comfort.

A life where structural integrity, in buildings and relationships, wasn't compromised for appearance or convenience.

The thought followed her into uneasy dreams of glass atriums and support columns, of foundations cracking under pressure, of structures beautiful but fundamentally unsound.

CHAPTER FIFTEEN

"Sleepless Design"

T he bedroom was dark except for a sliver of moonlight cutting through the partially closed curtains. Mark's snoring filled the space with a rumbling cadence that once seemed endearing but now felt like the soundtrack to her discontent.

Liz lay motionless beside him, staring at the familiar ceiling crack. Sleep refused to come despite her exhaustion. The contrast between her husband's indifference and James's professional appreciation created a dissonance she couldn't reconcile. One man barely acknowledged her existence while another valued her perspective enough to email at night about structural decisions.

With a quiet sigh, she slipped from bed and padded down the hallway to her home office. Perhaps reviewing the atrium specifications would quiet her racing mind.

The room welcomed her with its ordered calm—the one space in their house that truly reflected her sensibilities rather than Mark's sports memorabilia or their mutual compromises. She settled at her desk and opened her laptop, the blue light illuminating stacks of project materials.

James had sent detailed renderings of the atrium modifications they'd discussed earlier. His precise notes filled the margins, each addressing her concerns about narrative flow and visitor experience. Unlike Mark's dismissive characterization of her work, James had incorporated her marketing concepts so thoroughly they'd become inseparable from the architectural vision.

Liz studied the drawings, losing herself in the elegant solution they'd developed together. The supporting columns they'd initially viewed as problematic now served as timeline markers in Meridian's corporate history, each one showcasing a milestone in the company's evolution. What had been a structural necessity had transformed into a central narrative element.

Her eyes grew heavy as she reviewed the specifications. The technical details blurred as fatigue finally overtook her. She rested her head on her arms, just for a moment...

She was walking through the Meridian construction site, but not as it currently existed. The foundation had progressed to structural steel—a skeleton of beams and columns rising from the earth, outlining spaces that didn't yet exist. Moonlight silvered the metal framework, creating dramatic shadows across the bare concrete floor.

"I thought I might find you here."

James emerged from between steel columns, his white shirt almost luminous in the darkness. He moved with familiar confidence through the unfinished space.

"The columns work better than we expected," he said, gesturing to where the atrium would eventually stand. "Your timeline concept transformed a structural compromise into a design feature."

"That's what good design does," Liz heard herself respond. "Turns constraints into opportunities."

He smiled, the expression softening his features. "We've always pushed each other that way. Finding possibilities others miss."

They walked together through the skeletal building, their footsteps echoing on concrete. James pointed out features as if they already existed—the limestone base transitioning to innovative materials, the environmental graphics integrated into structural elements, the dramatic glass ceiling that would eventually crown the atrium.

"It's beautiful," Liz said, looking up through the empty steel frame to stars beyond.

"It's honest," James corrected, stopping beside her. "The structure doesn't pretend to be something it's not. Every element serves both function and narrative."

Their shoulders nearly touched as they stood within the outlined atrium. Without the walls that would eventually define the space, the night air moved freely around them, carrying the scent of earth and steel and something distinctly James—his cologne mingled with drafting paper and coffee.

"Unlike some structures," Liz found herself saying, "that maintain perfect external appearances while the foundation crumbles."

James turned to face her, suddenly closer than professional boundaries allowed. "You're not talking about buildings anymore."

"No."

His hand rose to her face, fingers tracing her cheekbone with architect's precision. "Some structures can't be saved. They were built on flawed assumptions from the beginning."

"And others?" Her voice sounded strange to her own ears, breathless and uncertain.

"Others can be transformed. Repurposed. Given new life."

The steel beams around them seemed to pulse with possibility—the ghost of a building not yet realized but vividly imagined. James's hand moved to the nape of her neck, his touch sending electricity down her spine.

"We shouldn't," she whispered, even as she leaned into his touch.

"I know." His voice had dropped to match hers. "But we've been building toward this since Preston Academy."

When his lips met hers, the kiss held none of the hesitation she might have expected. It was decisive, confident—like his architectural drawings with their bold, assured lines. His hands framed her face with the same care he showed handling delicate models, as if she were something precious and precisely made.

Liz responded with a hunger that surprised her, fingers tangling in his hair, body pressing against his with urgent need. The professional boundaries they'd maintained dissolved like scaffolding removed from a completed structure, revealing the true form beneath.

They sank to the concrete floor, the building's skeleton rising around them like a cathedral of steel and possibility. His hands moved with deliberate purpose, unfastening buttons, tracing curves, learning her body with the same focused attention he gave to his designs.

"I've imagined this," he murmured against her throat, "since that day in my studio. Your questions challenging my assumptions. Your mind keeping pace with mine."

Her own hands explored the lean muscles of his back, the surprising strength in his shoulders. "This is madness," she gasped as his mouth found sensitive skin below her ear.

"No," he corrected, pulling back to meet her eyes. "This is the most logical conclusion to our particular equation."

When they came together, it was with the perfect synthesis they'd found in their professional collaboration, each anticipating the other's movements, responding to unspoken cues, building toward a shared vision. The steel framework surrounding them seemed to vibrate with the energy they generated, as if the building itself approved of their union.

James watched her face with unwavering focus as they moved together, his blue eyes reflecting moonlight and something deeper, more complex than mere desire. The intensity of his gaze made her feel truly seen for the first time in years—not as a wife, not as a marketing director, but as Elizabeth Mitchell, the brilliant, passionate woman who had once been his only worthy competitor.

"Elizabeth," he whispered, her full name on his lips an intimacy more profound than their physical connection.

The pleasure built with architectural precision, each sensation supporting the next, creating a structure of experience that rose toward an inevitable conclusion. When it crested, Liz cried out, the sound echoing through the skeletal building like a benediction...

Liz jerked awake, heart pounding, body flushed with lingering arousal. For a disorienting moment, she couldn't place herself, the steel framework and moonlight replaced by her darkened home office, James's presence a phantom sensation still tingling on her skin.

A dream. Just a dream.

But the vivid details refused to fade like normal dreams. She could still feel the cool concrete beneath her, the warm pressure of his hands, the intensity of his gaze as he moved above her. The physical response had been no less real than if it had actually happened.

She pressed shaking fingers to her lips, half-expecting them to feel bruised from kisses that had never actually occurred. The clock on her desk showed 3:17 AM. Mark would still be asleep, oblivious to her absence, oblivious to the fact that his wife had just experienced the most intense erotic dream of her life—about another man.

Guilt and confusion warred within her. The dream wasn't just about physical attraction; it had been about being truly seen, truly understood. Dream-James had valued her mind as much as her body, had seen her as an equal partner in creation rather than an accessory to his life.

Liz closed the laptop, plunging the office into darkness. She sat motionless, waiting for her heartbeat to steady, for the flush to fade from her skin. What did it mean that her subconscious had constructed such a detailed fantasy? That it had placed their encounter in the very building they were creating together, a physical manifestation of their intellectual collaboration?

More troubling was how right it had felt. Not just the physical pleasure, but the sense of connection, of finally being with someone who challenged and appreciated her mind.

She made her way back to the bedroom on unsteady legs. Mark hadn't moved, his breathing still deep and regular, one arm flung across what had been her side of the bed. Liz stood in the doorway, studying her husband in the dim light. Once, she had loved him with the uncomplicated passion of youth. Once, his attention had made her feel special, chosen, adored.

When had that changed? When had they become strangers sharing a house, a name, a tax return—but not a life?

The question had no simple answer. Their disconnection hadn't happened in a single moment but through a thousand small surrenders, a gradual erosion of intimacy and understanding until they merely occupied the same space without truly seeing each other.

Liz slipped back into bed, careful not to disturb Mark. The physical distance between them felt unbridgeable now. She turned away from his sleeping form, curling into herself at the edge of the bed.

The dream lingered in her consciousness, refusing to fade with wakefulness. Not just the physical encounter, but the conversation that preceded it. James saying some structures couldn't be saved, that they were built on flawed assumptions from the beginning. The uncomfortable parallel to her marriage was impossible to ignore.

Sleep remained elusive as her mind cycled between guilt, confusion, and the lingering sensations from her dream. By the time dawn lightened the bedroom curtains, Liz had reached no conclusions except one: something fundamental had shifted inside her, and there would be no returning to the careful equilibrium she'd maintained before.

Morning arrived with painful brightness. Liz moved through her routine with mechanical precision, showering longer than necessary as if water might wash away the lingering effects of her dream. Mark stumbled into the kitchen as she prepared coffee, his hair rumpled from sleep, apparently having forgotten their argument from the previous evening.

"Morning," he mumbled, reaching for the mug she'd prepared. "You're up early."

"Couldn't sleep," Liz replied, avoiding his eyes. "Thinking about the project."

Mark grunted, attention already shifting to his phone. "What time will you be home tonight?"

"Not sure. We have a structural issue to resolve."

"Of course you do." His tone carried a hint of yesterday's resentment, but he seemed too tired to revive the argument. "I'll probably grab dinner with Kevin then."

Liz nodded, relieved at the prospect of an empty house. "That's fine."

They moved around each other with practiced choreography, neither acknowledging the growing distance between them. Mark prepared cereal while scrolling through sports highlights. Liz gathered project materials into her portfolio, mentally rehearsing arguments for the atrium design meeting.

"I should go," she said finally, desperate to escape the suffocating normality of their morning routine. "Howard wants an update before the team meeting."

Mark looked up briefly. "Sure. Have a good day."

No kiss goodbye. No meaningful eye contact. Just the perfunctory exchange of two people managing shared logistics rather than sharing a life.

In her car, Liz sat motionless for several minutes, hands gripping the steering wheel. The dream images resurfaced with cinematic clarity, James's hands on her skin, his voice murmuring her name, the steel framework rising around them like a cathedral to possibility.

What terrified her wasn't the dream itself, but how desperately she wished it had been real.

She started the engine, forcing her thoughts toward the day's meetings, the structural challenges, the professional obligations awaiting her at Meridian. But as she navigated familiar streets toward the office, one truth remained inescapable, she could no longer pretend that her interest in James Calloway was purely professional, nor that her marriage was merely going through a temporary rough patch.

Both structures showed significant cracks in their foundations. The question was which, if either, could be saved, and whether she had the courage to make that determination honestly.

CHAPTER SIXTEEN

"Precipitation"

G ray clouds had been gathering all morning, darkening the sky over the Meridian construction site. Liz checked her weather app again as she pulled into the parking area, the storm warning had intensified, but she needed these site photos for tomorrow's executive presentation. The foundation work was progressing faster than expected, and Howard wanted visual documentation to accompany the timeline updates.

She stepped from her car, zipping her light jacket against the unseasonably cool air. The site hummed with activity despite the threatening weather, workers securing loose materials, equipment operators covering machinery, foremen consulting clipboards with concerned expressions. The steel framework for the first floor had begun to rise from the concrete foundation, skeletal but already suggesting the building's eventual form.

"Ms. Donovan!" A construction supervisor waved from near the site trailer. "We're battening down for the storm. Not the best day for a visit."

"I just need some progress photos," she called back, holding up her tablet. "Ten minutes, tops."

He nodded reluctantly. "Stay within the marked visitor path. We're pulling crews off the high steel with this lightning risk."

Liz followed the designated route, stopping occasionally to photograph key progress points. The limestone base was taking shape along the eastern edge, while steel columns rose from the western foundation. Even in this early stage, the material transition that formed the core of their design narrative was becoming visible, tradition giving way to innovation, just as they'd envisioned.

The first fat raindrops began to fall as she reached the center of what would eventually become the atrium. She quickened her pace, capturing several angles of the steel framework rising toward the sky. The drops became a steady patter, then a sudden deluge as the storm front arrived with startling speed.

Liz tucked her tablet inside her jacket and turned toward the exit path, but the rain had already transformed the site into a maze of puddles and mud. Her heels, impractical for construction but necessary for the client meeting she'd attended earlier, sank into the softening ground with each step.

The sky flashed with lightning, followed almost immediately by a crack of thunder that vibrated through her chest. The storm had arrived in earnest, far faster than predicted. Rain pounded down, instantly soaking through her light jacket and blouse. She quickened her pace, squinting through the downpour toward the distant trailer.

"Elizabeth!"

She turned at the sound of her name and saw James jogging toward her, an oversized black umbrella held against the wind. He wore work boots and a weatherproof jacket, clearly better prepared for the conditions.

"What are you doing out here?" he called over the drumming rain.

"Progress photos for Howard," she shouted back, gesturing to her tablet. "I didn't expect the storm to hit so quickly."

He reached her side, extending the umbrella to cover them both. The sudden shelter from the rain created an intimate space amid the deluge, forcing them to stand closer than they had since their encounter in his office during the paper cut incident.

"The weather service upgraded it to severe thunderstorm status ten minutes ago," he said, his voice closer to her ear than strictly necessary. "The site manager is clearing all non-essential personnel."

Another lightning flash illuminated his face, concern in his eyes, raindrops clinging to his dark hair where it had escaped the umbrella's protection. The thunder followed almost immediately, indicating the storm was directly overhead.

"We should get to the trailer," James said, his hand finding the small of her back to guide her. The casual touch sent an electric current up her spine that had nothing to do with the lightning.

They moved awkwardly under the shared umbrella, the wind occasionally catching its edge and threatening to turn it inside out. James adjusted his stride to match hers, his body occasionally brushing against her side as they navigated the increasingly muddy path.

"Your shoes are completely impractical for this," he observed, glancing down at her heels sinking into the muck.

"I came from a client meeting," she explained, grimacing as cold water seeped through the expensive leather. "I didn't plan on hiking through a monsoon."

James chuckled, the sound warm despite the surrounding chaos. "Next time check the radar before your site visits."

"I'll add meteorology to my marketing skill set," she replied dryly.

They reached the trailer just as another lightning bolt split the sky, followed by a thunderclap that seemed to shake the very ground. James held the door as Liz stepped inside, both of them dripping onto the industrial mat in the entryway.

The trailer was empty, the construction team had apparently sought shelter elsewhere or left the site entirely. The sudden silence after the storm's roar created an unexpected intimacy. Rain drummed against the metal roof, and the windows had fogged from the temperature difference between the humid outside air and the air-conditioned interior.

Liz became acutely aware of her appearance, her silk blouse clinging to her skin, her hair plastered to her face, mascara likely smudged beneath her eyes. She crossed her arms self-consciously, feeling exposed in more ways than one.

"You're soaked through," James observed, setting his umbrella in a stand by the door. He shrugged off his jacket and hung it on a wall hook, revealing a simple gray t-shirt beneath. "Let me find you a towel."

He disappeared into the small kitchenette area while Liz remained in the entryway, a puddle forming around her ruined shoes. Through the window, she could see the rain coming down in sheets, the construction site transformed into a landscape of mud and standing water. They wouldn't be leaving anytime soon.

"Here." James returned with a reasonably clean towel and a Calloway Design Group sweatshirt. "It's not exactly high fashion, but it's dry."

Liz accepted both gratefully. "Thank you. I'm freezing."

"The bathroom's through there," he said, nodding toward a door at the end of the trailer. "I'll make coffee."

In the small bathroom, Liz assessed the damage. Her blouse had become nearly transparent, her skirt was spattered with mud, and her carefully styled hair hung in wet strands around her face. She toweled off as best she could, then slipped off the sodden blouse and replaced it with James's sweatshirt. The dark gray fabric bore his firm's logo over the left breast and smelled faintly of his cologne—a scent she'd become uncomfortably familiar with during their close work sessions.

The sweatshirt was comically large on her frame, the sleeves extending well past her fingertips, but the dry fabric was an immediate relief against her chilled skin. She rolled the sleeves back and attempted to repair her makeup with dampened paper towels, managing to remove the worst of the mascara smudges.

When she emerged, James had set two steaming mugs on the conference table. He'd changed into a dry shirt himself—apparently he kept spare clothes at the site—and had toweled his hair, leaving it charmingly disheveled.

"Better?" he asked, looking up from his laptop.

"Much. Thank you for the rescue." She gestured to the oversized sweatshirt. "I'll get this back to you cleaned."

"Keep it. It looks better on you anyway." The casual compliment hung in the air a moment too long before he cleared his throat and gestured to the coffee. "Black, no sugar. That's how you take it, right?"

The fact that he'd noticed and remembered such a detail created a warmth that had nothing to do with the coffee. "Yes. Thank you."

Liz settled into a chair across from him, cradling the mug between her palms. Outside, the storm showed no signs of abating. Lightning flashed at regular intervals, followed by rolling thunder that rattled the trailer windows.

"The weather service says it'll pass through in about an hour," James said, glancing at his laptop screen. "The site manager has suspended operations for the day."

"I should let Howard know I'll be delayed." Liz reached for her phone, relieved to find it had survived the downpour in her jacket's inner pocket.

While she texted Howard, James busied himself with something on his laptop, the silence between them broken only by the drumming rain and occasional thunder. The strange intimacy of their situation—alone together, Liz wearing his clothing, trapped by circumstances beyond their control—created a tension neither seemed willing to acknowledge.

After sending her message, Liz set down her phone and took a sip of coffee. "At least I got most of the photos Howard needed before the deluge hit."

"The foundation work is progressing ahead of schedule," James observed, clearly grateful for the safe topic. "The structural steel delivery arrived early, which should accelerate the next phase."

"That's good news. Howard will be pleased."

Conversation lapsed again, the professional discussion feeling oddly forced in their current circumstances. Liz found herself studying James when he glanced down at his computer—the slight silver at his temples, the faint lines at the corners of his eyes that appeared when he concentrated, the lean strength in his forearms as he typed. Her dream suddenly flashed unbidden through her mind, bringing a flush to her cheeks that she hoped he would attribute to the hot coffee.

"So," James said suddenly, closing his laptop. "Since we're stuck here, we might as well use the time productively."

"What did you have in mind?" The question came out more suggestively than she'd intended, and she quickly added, "For the project, I mean."

A smile touched his lips, suggesting he'd caught her unintentional innuendo. "I thought we might finally discuss the Preston Academy elephant that's been following us around for months."

The unexpected pivot to their shared past caught her off guard. "That's your idea of productive use of time?"

"Clearing the air seems productive," he replied, leaning back in his chair. "We've been dancing around it since that first presentation. Might as well address it directly while we're trapped by acts of nature."

Liz considered deflecting, returning to safe professional territory, but something in his direct gaze challenged her. Perhaps it was time to lance this particular boil.

"Fine," she said, setting down her mug. "Where would you like to start? The debate team rivalry? The class ranking competition? The Beckman Scholarship?"

"Let's start with the scholarship," he suggested, his tone surprisingly gentle. "You know, I only won that by fractions of a point."

The admission caught her off guard. For twenty years, she'd imagined his victory as decisive, his superiority clearly established by the judges' decision.

"What?"

"Three-tenths of a point separated our final scores," James continued, watching her reaction carefully. "The foundation president told me afterward it was the closest decision in the scholarship's history."

Liz absorbed this information, unsure how to respond. The Beckman had represented such a pivotal moment in her life—the loss that had altered her trajectory, steering her away from academic ambitions toward practical career paths.

"I didn't know that," she finally said.

"Would it have made a difference if you had?"

She considered the question honestly. "I don't know. Maybe. I built it up in my mind as this definitive judgment—you were better, more deserving. Knowing it was that close..." She shook her head. "It might have changed how I viewed myself afterward."

James nodded slowly. "I wondered about that. You disappeared after graduation. Didn't attend any alumni events. Changed your academic focus entirely."

"You noticed that?" The idea that he'd tracked her movements after high school was unexpected.

"Of course I noticed." Something flickered in his eyes—a vulnerability she rarely glimpsed beneath his professional confidence. "You were the only person at Preston who ever truly challenged me. When you suddenly weren't there to compete against, it felt like losing a worthy opponent."

The admission created a strange ache in her chest. All these years, she'd defined their relationship through the lens of her own defeat, never considering he might have valued their rivalry differently.

"I needed distance," she explained, surprising herself with her candor. "Preston Academy Elizabeth was defined by academic achievement. When I lost the Beckman, it felt like losing my identity. Northwestern was a chance to become someone new."

"Someone who didn't measure herself against James Calloway," he suggested, his perception uncomfortably accurate.

"Something like that." She offered a small smile. "Though apparently I wasn't entirely successful, given how quickly we fell back into old patterns when you walked into that presentation."

James laughed softly. "Some dynamics are too fundamental to change, I suppose."

The storm continued its assault outside, rain lashing against the windows, but inside the atmosphere had shifted subtly. The acknowledgment of their shared history had somehow eased the tension rather than heightening it.

"Did you ever wonder what would have happened if you'd won?" James asked, his gaze direct.

"The scholarship? Of course. For years." Liz traced the rim of her coffee mug with one finger. "I imagined this alternate life where I became an academic, wrote brilliant literary criticism, never met Mark..."

"Never married," James finished for her.

"Probably not to Mark, no." The admission felt dangerous, too close to her current marital dissatisfaction. "But that's the butterfly effect, isn't it? Change one decision, and everything downstream changes too."

James nodded thoughtfully. "I used to wonder what would have happened if we'd acknowledged the other thing between us back then."

Liz's heart skipped a beat. "What other thing?"

His eyes met hers steadily. "The reason our competition was so intense. It wasn't just academic rivalry, Elizabeth. At least, not for me."

The implication hung in the air between them, charged as the atmosphere outside. Had there been something more beneath their teenage competition? A sublimated attraction neither had been mature enough to recognize or acknowledge?

"We were different people then," she said carefully.

"Were we? Or just unfinished versions of who we are now?"

The question struck uncomfortably close to thoughts she'd been having since their reconnection—about paths not taken, choices that had shaped her into someone she sometimes barely recognized.

Before she could formulate a response, lightning struck somewhere very close, the flash immediately followed by a deafening crack of thunder. The trailer lights flickered once, twice, then went out, plunging them into gray semi-darkness broken only by the glow from James's laptop screen.

"Perfect timing," he murmured, the dim light casting shadows across his features. "The universe apparently thinks we're getting too close to dangerous territory."

The power outage had reset the boundaries of their conversation, offering an escape from the precipice they'd been approaching. Liz seized it gratefully.

"Does the trailer have a generator?"

"Should kick in automatically for essential systems," James replied, standing to check the electrical panel near the door. "Though I'm not sure the lights qualify as essential."

As if on cue, emergency lighting activated along the baseboards, casting an eerie glow through the trailer. The rain continued its assault, seeming even louder in the relative darkness.

"I've been following your career, you know," James said suddenly, his back still turned as he examined the panel. "Since Preston."

The admission surprised her. "You have?"

He nodded, turning to face her. The emergency lighting illuminated him from below, highlighting the strong line of his jaw. "Your marketing campaigns for Meridian have won industry recognition. The experiential retail concept you developed three years ago was particularly innovative."

"You researched me." She wasn't sure whether to be flattered or unsettled.

"I kept tabs on most of our graduating class," he said with a casual shrug that didn't quite convince. "Professional curiosity."

"Did you keep tabs on everyone's coffee preferences too?" The question slipped out before she could stop it, more teasing than she'd intended.

James smiled, the expression transforming his serious features. "Only the ones who made an impression."

The moment stretched between them, charged with something neither seemed willing to name. Outside, the storm raged on, lightning illuminating the trailer in brief, stark flashes, thunder rolling continuously overhead. Inside, a different kind of storm was brewing—one Liz had been trying to ignore since that vivid dream in her office.

James moved back to the table, closing his laptop to conserve battery. The action dimmed the space further, leaving them in the soft glow of emergency lighting. He seemed suddenly closer than before, though neither had physically moved.

"We should probably talk about something safer," he suggested, his voice lower than it had been. "The atrium specifications, perhaps. Or the limestone sourcing challenges."

"Probably," Liz agreed, though neither made any move to change the subject.

The rain drummed against the roof, creating a cocoon of white noise that seemed to insulate them from the outside world. In this strange liminal space, not quite professional, not quite personal, the boundaries they'd carefully maintained seemed suddenly permeable.

"I dreamed about you," Liz heard herself say, immediately regretting the admission. "About the project, I mean. The other night."

James went very still. "Did you?"

She should stop talking, redirect to safer territory, but something about the storm's isolation loosened her usual restraint. "It was about the building. The frame-work. Standing in the space before the walls existed."

"I have those dreams too," he said quietly. "Occupy-ing spaces that only exist in blueprints. It's an archi-tect's hazard."

Their eyes met across the table, and Liz knew he understood she wasn't just talking about architecture. The attraction between them, intellectual, profession-al, and increasingly physical, had become a presence as tangible as the storm surrounding them.

A particularly violent gust of wind rattled the trailer, breaking the moment. James cleared his throat and stood, moving to the window to assess the conditions outside.

"The worst seems to be passing," he observed, his back to her. "Rain's lightening up."

Liz felt simultaneously relieved and disappointed. Their forced proximity was ending, along with what-ever truth they'd been approaching in the storm's strange intimacy.

"I should check in with Howard," she said, reaching for her phone with a steadiness she didn't feel.

For several minutes, they occupied the same space without speaking, each retreating to professional tasks, Liz responding to emails, James reviewing something on his tablet. The rain gradually diminished from downpour to steady shower, the thunder moving off into the distance.

When the trailer lights suddenly flickered back on, both blinked in the unexpected brightness, the spell of semi-darkness broken completely.

"Power's back," James stated unnecessarily. "Storm must be moving on."

Liz nodded, gathering her things. Her blouse was still damp, but she could wear her jacket zipped over James's sweatshirt for the drive back to the office. "Thank you for the shelter. And the coffee. And the..." she gestured to the sweatshirt, "emergency fashion intervention."

"Anytime," he replied with a small smile. "Though perhaps check the weather forecast before your next site visit."

The return to light banter felt like safe harbor after the dangerous waters they'd been navigating. Liz moved toward the door, peering out at the now-gentle rain. "I think I can make it to my car without drowning now."

James reached past her for his umbrella, his arm briefly brushing hers. The casual contact shouldn't have affected her, but after their charged conversation, even this slight touch sent awareness skittering across her skin.

"I'll walk you," he said, opening the umbrella as they stepped outside.

The construction site glistened in the aftermath of the storm, puddles reflecting the emerging sunlight as clouds began to break. They walked in silence, the umbrella creating that same intimate space it had earlier, though now the proximity felt more dangerous than protective.

At her car, Liz turned to face him. "I should return your sweatshirt."

"Keep it," James said again. "Consider it emergency site visit equipment."

She nodded, suddenly reluctant to leave despite the awkwardness between them. Something significant had shifted during their storm-enforced isolation, acknowledgments made, truths approached if not fully articulated.

"About what you said," she began, unsure how to continue. "About our rivalry having other dimension s..."

"We don't need to discuss it," James interrupted gently. "It was a long time ago. We're different people now, with different responsibilities and commitments."

The diplomatic retreat should have been a relief. Instead, it felt like a door closing on a room they'd only just discovered.

"Right," Liz agreed, forcing a professional smile. "Ancient history."

She held out her hand for the umbrella, but as James passed it to her, their fingers brushed. The contact lasted barely a second, yet Liz felt it like an electric current, awareness shooting up her arm and spreading through her body with alarming intensity.

James's sharp intake of breath suggested he'd felt it too, his eyes darkening momentarily before he stepped back, creating deliberate distance between them.

"I'll see you at tomorrow's planning meeting," he said, his voice carefully neutral. "Drive safely."

"Thank you again," Liz replied with equal professionalism, slipping into her car before she could say or do anything she might regret.

As she drove away, she caught a glimpse of him in her rearview mirror, still standing in the rain, watching her departure. The image struck her with uncomfortable familiarity, echoing her dream where they'd stood together in the skeletal framework of the building they were creating.

The sweatshirt she wore carried his scent, a tangible reminder of their strange interlude. Tomorrow they would return to their professional roles, maintaining the careful boundaries their situation demanded. But something had changed during those storm-trapped hours, truths acknowledged, possibilities glimpsed.

Like the foundation emerging from the construction site, something was taking shape between them, something neither had planned for, neither had sought, yet neither could entirely deny. The question was whether they would continue building on that foundation or deliberately demolish it before the structure became too substantial to easily dismantle.

As Liz turned onto the highway, she realized she already knew the answer, had known it since that vivid dream in her office. The only real question was how long they could maintain the pretense that what existed between them was merely professional respect between former rivals.

The storm had passed, but its effects lingered, much like the revelations it had precipitated.

CHAPTER SEVENTEEN

"Structural Failure"

The aroma of garlic and roasting chicken filled the kitchen as Liz stirred the risotto, adding another ladleful of stock to the simmering rice. She'd left work early, a rarity these days, to prepare Mark's favorite meal. The dining table was already set with their wedding china, candles waiting to be lit, a bottle of the Cabernet they'd discovered on their tenth anniversary trip to Napa chilling nearby.

A peace offering. An attempt to bridge the growing chasm between them. After the storm-trapped conversation with James and the lingering confusion it had created, Liz had spent the weekend in a state of uncomfortable self-examination. Whatever was happening with James, the intellectual connection, the charged moments, the dream that still haunted her, didn't change the fact that she had made vows to Mark. Fifteen years of shared history deserved more than a gradual, silent dissolution.

She checked her watch. Mark should have been home twenty minutes ago. She'd texted him earlier about dinner, though he hadn't responded. Not unusual these days, their communication had devolved into logistical updates rather than meaningful exchanges.

The risotto was reaching the perfect consistency, creamy but still with slight resistance to the bite. Liz reduced the heat, added a final pat of butter and a sprinkle of parmesan. The chicken would need to rest before carving. She'd timed everything for Mark's usual arrival, but now the meal threatened to pass its peak.

She poured herself a small glass of wine and leaned against the counter, surveying her efforts. The domestic scene should have felt natural after fifteen years of marriage, but instead it struck her as a performance, a carefully constructed tableau of marital harmony that bore little resemblance to their reality.

Her phone chimed with a text. Mark, finally.

Running late. Drinks with Simmons after meeting. Don't wait up.

No mention of the dinner she'd told him about. No apology for the lack of notice. Just information delivered with the casual disregard of someone who expected accommodation without question.

Liz set down her wine glass with deliberate care, fighting the urge to throw it against the wall. The carefully prepared meal, the wedding china, the anniversary wine, all now seemed like props in an absurd play where she was the only one who had bothered to learn the lines.

She picked up her phone, typing and deleting several responses before settling on one that matched his tone in its detachment: *Dinner is ready now. Will put yours in the fridge.*

The kitchen suddenly felt too warm, the domestic aromas cloying rather than comforting. Liz moved to the dining room and blew out the candles she hadn't yet lit. The small action felt symbolic, extinguishing the last flickering hope that they could recapture whatever had once existed between them.

She ate alone at the kitchen island, not bothering with the dining room tableau she'd created. The food tasted like ashes despite its technical perfection. She'd put Mark's portion in the refrigerator, though she suspected it would remain untouched, eventually discarded like so many other attempts at connection.

After cleaning the kitchen, Liz retreated to her home office. Work had become her refuge, the one place where her efforts were acknowledged, her insights valued. She opened the latest architectural renderings James had sent, losing herself in the clean lines and elegant solutions they'd developed together.

The front door opened shortly after ten, Mark's arrival announced by the jingle of keys and the thud of his briefcase hitting the entryway table. Liz remained in her office, listening to his movements through the house, the refrigerator opening and closing, the television coming to life in the living room, the familiar pattern of a husband returning to a wife he barely seemed to notice anymore.

After twenty minutes, his footsteps approached her office door. Liz closed the architectural renderings, switching to a marketing spreadsheet before he appeared in the doorway.

"Hey," Mark said, leaning against the frame. His tie was loosened, his eyes slightly glassy from what was clearly more than one after-work drink. "Saw the food in the fridge. Wasn't hungry."

"It was supposed to be dinner together," Liz replied, keeping her voice even. "I mentioned it in my text this morning."

Mark frowned slightly, as if trying to recall. "Must have missed that. Simmons wanted to discuss the Johnson account over drinks. Couldn't say no."

"You could have texted earlier."

"I did text." His tone carried a hint of defensiveness. "As soon as I knew I'd be late."

"After I'd already cooked everything." Liz turned in her chair to face him fully. "It was a special dinner, Mark. I left work early to prepare it."

"How was I supposed to know it was special? You're always working late these days. How is tonight different from any other night?"

The question hung between them, loaded with more truth than perhaps he intended. How was tonight different? In her attempt to reconnect, she'd created an occasion out of thin air, without context or communication. They had become so disconnected that even her efforts at reconciliation were unrecognizable to him.

"I wanted us to talk," she said finally. "About us. About what's happening between us."

Mark's posture stiffened. "What's that supposed to mean?"

"It means we barely speak anymore. We occupy the same house but live separate lives. When was the last time we had a real conversation about anything that matters?"

"Is this about the project again? Because I'm trying to be supportive, Liz, but it's taking over everything."

"It's not about the project." She stood, needing to be on equal footing for this conversation. "It's about us. About how we've been drifting apart for years, and neither of us has been willing to acknowledge it."

Mark ran a hand through his hair, a gesture of frustration she recognized from countless minor disagreements. But this wasn't minor, and his reflexive dismissal only confirmed what she was trying to articulate.

"We're fine," he said. "Every marriage goes through phases. You're busy with work, I'm busy with clients. It's temporary."

"Is it? Because it feels like we've been living parallel lives for years now. You with your sports and friends, me with my career. When did we stop sharing anything meaningful?"

Mark's expression hardened. "What brought this on? You've been different since that project started. Cold. Distant."

"I've been different because the project made me realize how disconnected I've been, from my work, from myself, from what I want in life."

"And what do you want, Liz? Because it sure as hell doesn't seem to include me anymore."

The blunt question caught her off guard. What did she want? The answer was complicated by thoughts she wasn't ready to examine fully, thoughts that featured James Calloway and intellectual connection and feeling truly seen in ways Mark hadn't managed in years.

"I want a partnership," she said carefully. "Not just coexistence. I want conversations that go deeper than shopping lists and schedules. I want to feel like my husband is actually interested in my thoughts, my work, my life."

"C'mon." Mark's voice rose slightly. "I ask about your day all the time."

"You ask if I'll be home for dinner. You don't ask about what I'm creating, what challenges me, what excites me intellectually."

"Excites you intellectually?" He repeated the phrase with an edge of mockery. "Listen to yourself. You sound like you're in some college seminar, not a marriage."

"That's exactly my point. You don't value that part of me. You never have."

The words hung between them, too honest to retract. Mark stared at her as if seeing a stranger.

"So this is my fault?" he asked finally. "I'm not intellectual enough for you?"

"It's not about fault. It's about compatibility. About whether we still want the same things."

Mark stepped further into the office, his gaze falling on her computer screen where the marketing spreadsheet failed to completely hide the architectural rendering beneath it. His jaw tightened.

"This is about him, isn't it? The architect. James."

The accusation sent a jolt through her system. "This is about our marriage, Mark. About us."

"Right." His laugh held no humor. "That's why you're working on his designs at ten o'clock at night instead of watching TV with your husband."

"I'm working because it's my job. Because the project matters to Howard and to my career."

"And the fact that you light up whenever you talk about 'the project'—that has nothing to do with working closely with your old high school rival?"

The question cut too close to truths she wasn't ready to confront. Liz felt heat rising to her cheeks, anger and guilt creating a volatile mixture.

"James is a colleague," she said, the words sounding hollow even to her own ears. "The project is professionally challenging and creatively fulfilling. That's all."

"Is it? Because you've changed since he came back into your life. The late nights, the distraction, the sudden dissatisfaction with our marriage, it all started with that project."

"You're wrong." Liz's voice strengthened with the conviction of at least partial truth. "The problems in our marriage existed long before James or the project. I've just finally stopped ignoring them."

Mark studied her face, searching for something, confirmation or denial, she wasn't sure. Whatever he saw caused his expression to shift from anger to something closer to resignation.

"Do you want him?" The question was direct, stripped of pretense.

"This isn't about James," Liz insisted, evading rather than lying outright. "This is about us. About whether we still have a marriage worth saving."

"That's not an answer."

"It's the only answer that matters right now."

They stood in tense silence, the gulf between them suddenly visible in a way it hadn't been before. All the unspoken disappointments, the accumulated compromises, the gradual surrender of expectations, everything that had eroded their connection over fifteen years now stood exposed in the harsh light of honest confrontation.

Mark broke the silence first. "I'm going to watch the game highlights. We can talk about this when you're ready to be honest, with me and with yourself."

He turned and walked out, leaving Liz standing alone in her office, surrounded by the evidence of her professional life and the absence of her personal one. The sound of the television rose from the living room, sportscasters' voices creating the familiar background noise of their domestic divide.

Liz sank back into her chair, emotions churning. Mark's accusation about James had struck uncomfortably close to the truth, though not in the way he imagined. It wasn't a simple physical attraction or emotional affair. It was the recognition of intellectual compatibility she'd never experienced with Mark, the exhilaration of being challenged, understood, valued for her mind as much as any other quality.

But was that James specifically, or what he represented? The road not taken, the self not developed, the potential unfulfilled?

The questions had no simple answers. All she knew with certainty was that her marriage had been failing long before James reappeared in her life. His presence had simply illuminated the cracks that had been forming for years.

Hours later, Liz made her way upstairs. Mark had fallen asleep on the couch, the television still playing to an unconscious audience. She covered him with a throw blanket, a gesture of care that felt more habitual than heartfelt.

In their bedroom, she prepared for sleep with mechanical efficiency. The bed seemed vast and empty without Mark's solid presence, though she'd grown accustomed to sleeping beside his unconscious form without true intimacy.

As she lay in the darkness, staring at the familiar ceiling crack, Liz found herself mentally comparing the mechanical sex with Mark to her vivid dream of

James. Even in fantasy, the connection with James had felt more authentic, more engaging, more alive than anything she'd experienced with Mark in years.

The realization brought tears to her eyes, not for the marriage that was clearly ending, but for the years she'd spent convincing herself that emotional and intellectual disconnection was a normal evolution of long-term relationships. That passion naturally faded into companionship. That wanting more was somehow immature or unrealistic.

The tears flowed silently, dampening her pillow. Mark wouldn't notice her red eyes in the morning. He barely looked at her anymore, seeing only the space she occupied in his life rather than the woman she had become.

Liz reached for her phone, scrolling through contacts until she found Rebecca's number. Her sister would understand, would offer perspective without judgment, would help her navigate the complicated terrain ahead. Her finger hovered over the call button, then retreated.

Not tonight. Tonight was for acknowledging the truth she'd been avoiding for too long: the foundation of her marriage had developed structural flaws that no amount of surface renovation could repair. Like a building constructed on unstable ground, the cracks had been spreading for years, compromising the integrity of the entire structure.

The architectural metaphor wasn't lost on her. In her professional collaboration with James, they insisted on addressing foundational issues before they became catastrophic failures. They refused to compromise structural integrity for cosmetic appeal or convenience.

Perhaps it was time to apply those same standards to her personal life, to acknowledge that some structures couldn't be saved, that the most honest course of action was to recognize the failure and begin again with better understanding of what created true stability.

Liz set her phone on the nightstand, decision unmade but direction clear. Whatever happened with James, or didn't happen, the conversation with Mark had revealed truths that couldn't be unseen. Their marriage had failed not because of external temptation but because it had been built on insufficient foundation from the beginning, youthful passion mistaken for lasting compatibility, physical attraction confused with deeper connection.

The realization brought a strange combination of grief and relief. Grief for the years invested, the shared history, the genuine affection that had existed despite the fundamental mismatch. Relief at finally acknowledging what she had known subconsciously for years:

she and Mark had been growing in different directions for so long that they now occupied entirely different landscapes.

As sleep finally claimed her, Liz's last conscious thought was not of James or Mark or the uncertain future ahead, but of the liberating power of honesty, with others and, more importantly, with herself.

CHAPTER EIGHTEEN

"Design Flaw"

The fluorescent lights of Meridian's executive floor seemed unusually harsh as Liz arranged her presentation materials with mechanical precision. The quarterly review meeting would begin in fifteen minutes, and she'd spent the entire weekend perfecting her slides, analyzing budget projections, documenting construction milestones, and crafting the narrative of progress that Howard expected.

Catherine entered the Conference Room, her silver bob immaculate as always, tablet tucked under one arm. She studied Liz with that penetrating gaze that made junior executives quake.

"You look exhausted," she observed, setting her tablet on the table. "Late night?"

"Just finalizing the presentation." Liz straightened an already perfectly aligned stack of handouts. "The foundation phase metrics needed recalculation after the soil composition adjustments."

Catherine nodded, though her eyes remained shrewd. "Howard's particularly interested in timeline projections today. The board is questioning whether the additional investment in Option B for the atrium was necessary."

"The structural integrity would have been compromised otherwise," Liz replied automatically. "The narrative flow through that space is essential to the visitor experience."

"I'm aware." Catherine's tone carried a hint of something Liz couldn't quite identify. "Just be prepared to defend the decision thoroughly."

The room gradually filled with Meridian executives, each carrying coffee and expectations. Howard arrived last, his confident stride and firm handshake moving methodically around the table before he took his position at the head.

"Let's begin with the headquarters update," he announced once everyone settled. "Elizabeth?"

Liz stood, hyperaware of every eye on her. She launched into her presentation with practiced ease, the words flowing automatically while part of her mind remained distracted by thoughts she couldn't entirely suppress. It had been days since her vivid dream about James, days of avoiding direct eye contact during project meetings, days of analyzing what it meant that her subconscious had constructed such an elaborate fantasy.

"The structural steel phase is proceeding ahead of schedule," she explained, advancing to a slide showing the skeletal framework rising from the foundation. "We've recovered the eight days lost during the soil composition adjustments."

Howard nodded approvingly. "And the budget implications?"

"Within projected parameters." Liz moved to the financial summary. "The additional expenditure for the atrium supports was offset by efficiencies in the material supply chain that James, that Calloway Design Group negotiated."

She stumbled slightly over his name, a momentary lapse that Catherine seemed to notice, her eyebrows rising fractionally. Liz continued smoothly, discussing sustainability metrics and energy efficiency projections, but she felt Catherine's gaze lingering on her with uncomfortable perception.

The presentation concluded with enthusiastic support from Howard. "This is exactly what I envisioned when we selected Calloway," he declared, looking around the table. "A building that embodies our philosophy while pushing boundaries in sustainable design."

"The design is certainly innovative," the CFO acknowledged. "Though I remain concerned about the construction timeline compression Elizabeth mentioned. Accelerated schedules typically mean premium costs."

"James has assured me the schedule adjustments won't impact the budget," Liz replied, the use of his first name slipping out again before she could catch herself. "The phased interior approach actually creates efficiencies in trade scheduling."

"You seem to have developed quite a rapport with Mr. Calloway," Catherine observed, her tone neutral but her eyes sharp. "His team has been remarkably responsive to our requirements."

"Professional collaboration at its finest," Liz responded, echoing words she'd used before.

Howard stood, signaling the meeting's conclusion. "I'm pleased with the progress. The board presentation is next week, Catherine, can you coordinate with Elizabeth to refine the materials?"

"Of course."

As executives filtered out, Catherine remained seated, her tablet untouched before her. "Elizabeth, do you have a moment?"

Liz nodded, though internal alarms immediately sounded. She gathered her presentation materials with deliberate calm, waiting until the last executive departed before sitting across from Catherine.

"Your presentation was thorough," Catherine began, "but your delivery lacked your usual focus."

"I'm sorry if it seemed that way. I've been working long hours on the timeline adjustments."

"It's not just today." Catherine leaned forward slightly. "You've seemed distracted for weeks. Particularly when discussing aspects of the project that involve direct collaboration with James Calloway."

The direct mention of James sent a jolt through Liz's system. "The project is demanding," she said carefully. "We're working closely to resolve complex integration challenges."

"How closely?"

The question hung between them, loaded with implication. Liz met Catherine's gaze steadily, though she felt heat rising to her cheeks.

"We maintain professional boundaries," she replied, the words sounding hollow even to her own ears. "The project benefits from our combined perspectives."

Catherine studied her for a long moment. "When I first noticed the tension between you two, I assumed it was your old academic rivalry resurfacing. Now I'm seeing something different."

"I'm not sure what you mean."

"I think you do." Catherine's voice softened slightly. "Elizabeth, I've mentored you for five years because I recognize your potential. You're too valuable to Meridian to jeopardize your career over personal complications."

"There are no personal complications," Liz insisted, though the dream images flashed quickly through her mind.

"Perhaps not yet." Catherine stood, gathering her tablet. "But I've been in corporate leadership long enough to recognize the signs. Whatever is developing between you and James Calloway, and something clearly is, remember that this project is too important to both your careers to risk with unprofessional entanglements."

After Catherine departed, Liz remained seated, her heart pounding unnaturally fast. Had she been so transparent? She'd maintained scrupulous professionalism in all their interactions since the storm-trapped conversation. Yes, there had been moments of connection that transcended typical colleague relationships, but nothing that crossed actual boundaries.

Except in her dreams. Except in her thoughts. Except in the way her pulse quickened whenever he entered a room.

Liz returned to her office, closing the door before allowing herself a moment of genuine reaction. Catherine's warning had struck uncomfortably close to truths she'd been avoiding. The intellectual connection with James had evolved into something more complex, a recognition of possibilities, an awareness of what genuine partnership might feel like, a window into a life where she was valued for her mind as much as any other quality.

Her computer chimed with an email notification. James had sent revised drawings for the executive floor layout with a brief note: *These incorporate your suggestions about flow between departments. Your insight about transitional spaces transformed the approach. Available to discuss tomorrow morning?*

It was a simple professional communication but it made her heart flutter. She stared at his message, analyzing each word for subtext that likely didn't exist. The phrase "your insight transformed the approach" echoed Catherine's concerns about their relationship, was there more behind his consistent acknowledgment of her contributions than professional courtesy?

Liz began composing a reply, writing and deleting several versions before settling on careful professionalism: *Drawings received. Approach looks promising. Available at 9am tomorrow at your studio.*

She hesitated before sending, then added: *The quarterly review went well. Howard remains enthusiastic about our collaborative vision.*

Our collaborative vision. The phrase carried weight she hadn't intended. She deleted it, replacing it with the more neutral "the project direction."

As afternoon faded into evening, Liz remained at her desk, buried in project specifications that failed to distract her from Catherine's warning. The executive floor emptied gradually, conversations and footsteps fading until only the soft hum of air conditioning remained.

Her phone chimed with a text from Mark: *Working late again? Leftover pizza in fridge.*

The message carried no affection, no inquiry about her day, just information delivered with the casual disregard that had become their standard mode of communication. Liz replied with equal detachment: *Budget projections to finish. Don't wait up.*

She set down her phone and turned back to her computer, but the architectural renderings blurred before her eyes. What was she doing? Her marriage was clearly failing, yet instead of addressing it directly, she was working late and dreaming about a man who represented everything her relationship with Mark lacked, intellectual challenge, mutual respect, genuine interest in her thoughts.

Was she developing feelings for James, or was he simply a convenient contrast that highlighted her marital dissatisfaction? The question had no simple answer. Their connection was undeniably powerful, but it had developed in the context of professional collaboration during a period of personal vulnerability. How much was genuine and how much was circumstantial?

By nine o'clock, Liz had made no progress on either the budget projections or her emotional confusion. She gathered her things and headed for the elevator, the empty hallways echoing with her solitary footsteps.

In the executive bathroom, she paused to assess her reflection. The woman who stared back looked exhausted, shadows beneath her eyes, tension in the set of her mouth, a brittleness to her professional composure that hadn't been there six months ago.

"Get it together," she whispered to her reflection, straightening her shoulders and arranging her features into a mask of confident control. The expression felt false, a performance she was growing tired of maintaining.

Tomorrow she would see James again. They would discuss executive floor layouts and transitional spaces and departmental flow patterns. They would maintain professional boundaries and pretend that the air between them wasn't charged with unacknowledged awareness.

And she would return home to Mark, to their parallel lives and growing silence, to a marriage that existed more in memory than in present reality.

Liz practiced another expression in the mirror, professional interest, pleasant but not too warm, engaged but not too personal. The face that would greet James tomorrow morning. The face that would reveal nothing of her dreams or Catherine's warnings or her increasing certainty that something fundamental was breaking apart in her carefully constructed life.

The mask held for several seconds before crumbling at the edges, revealing the truth beneath, a woman standing at a crossroads, uncertain which path led to authentic happiness and which to deeper regret.

CHAPTER NINETEEN

"Pressure Test"

The Blueprint Gallery occupied the ground floor of a renovated architectural firm from the 1920s, its interior a sophisticated blend of historic preservation and contemporary design. Blueprint-themed wallpaper lined the private dining alcoves, while drafting tables from the original firm had been repurposed as host stations. Vintage architectural drawings hung in gilded frames alongside modern renderings of the city's most iconic buildings.

Liz arrived ten minutes early, sliding into a corner booth with good sight lines to both the entrance and kitchen. The urgent text from James—*Structural issue with atrium connection. Need to review options before tomorrow's engineering meeting*, had prompted this last-minute dinner. A professional necessity, she told herself, ignoring the flutter in her stomach as she checked her reflection in the polished brass sconce beside the table.

She smoothed her silk blouse, a deep emerald that brought out the green in her hazel eyes. The choice had been deliberate, professional but flattering. She'd reapplied her lipstick before leaving the office, a detail that made her uncomfortably aware of her own self-deception. This was work, nothing more. The fact that she'd texted Mark she'd be late without specifying why was merely an efficiency, not evasion.

James arrived precisely on time, navigating between tables with confident grace. He wore what she recognized as his client meeting attire, charcoal trousers and a navy button-down, no tie, sleeves rolled to expose his tanned forearms . He carried his leather portfolio like an extension of himself.

"Elizabeth." He slid into the seat across from her, his expression carefully neutral. "Thank you for making time on short notice."

"The atrium connection is critical path. We can't afford delays." She gestured to the portfolio. "What's the structural issue?"

James extracted several detailed drawings, spreading them across the table. "The steel subcontractor identified a potential stress point where the glass ceiling meets the limestone elements. The engineer is concerned about thermal expansion differentials."

For the next twenty minutes, they maintained scrupulous professionalism, discussing load-bearing requirements and material tolerances with focused intensity. The waiter approached twice before they finally paused to order, James choosing the duck confit without glancing at the menu, Liz opting for sea bass.

"Option two seems structurally sound but compromises the visual lightness," Liz observed, tracing the alternative connection detail with her finger. "The whole point of the atrium is creating that floating sensation as visitors move from traditional materials to innovative ones."

"Exactly my concern." James leaned forward slightly. "The engineer is pushing for the heavier connection, but I think we can achieve both structural integrity and aesthetic lightness with this modified approach."

He sketched rapidly on tracing paper, his hand moving with confident precision. Liz found herself watching his fingers rather than the drawing itself, the way they manipulated the pencil with practiced ease, the slight callus on his middle finger where writing instruments habitually rested.

"What do you think?" James turned the sketch toward her.

Liz pulled her attention back to the design problem, studying his solution with professional focus. "It maintains the visual transition while addressing the stress concerns. Howard will appreciate preserving the experiential narrative."

"That's what I thought." A hint of a smile touched his lips. "You've made him quite the architectural narrative enthusiast."

"He was always receptive to good design. He just needed the vocabulary to articulate what he responds to instinctively."

Their wine arrived, a Willamette Valley Pinot Noir James had selected with casual confidence. The waiter poured with practiced flourish, leaving them alone again in their private alcove.

James raised his glass slightly. "To structural solutions that don't compromise design integrity."

"A worthy toast." Liz sipped the wine, rich notes of cherry and spice blooming across her palate. "This is excellent."

"I thought you'd like it. It has complexity without being showy about it."

The comment carried a personal undertone that created a moment of awareness between them. Liz redirected to safer ground.

"The foundation work is progressing ahead of schedule," she noted. "Howard mentioned the board is impressed with the timeline management."

"Thomas deserves credit for that. He's coordinating with the contractors daily to prevent sequencing issues."

The conversation maintained its professional veneer through the arrival of their appetizers, architectural terms and project milestones providing safe territory. Yet beneath this surface discourse, Liz felt an undercurrent of awareness, a hyperconscious recognition of James's every gesture, his occasional glances, the careful distance he maintained.

As their entrées arrived, the discussion gradually shifted from immediate structural concerns to broader design philosophy. The wine softened their usual competitive edge, creating space for more reflective exchange.

"The challenge with sustainable design is balancing innovation against proven performance," James said, gesturing with his fork for emphasis. "Clients want cutting-edge solutions but panic at the first sign of uncertainty."

"That's not unique to architecture," Liz replied. "Marketing faces the same tension, push boundaries but don't alienate traditional customers. It's why

Meridian's 'progressive tradition' philosophy resonates so well with the design approach."

"It's rare to find clients who genuinely understand that tension." James refilled their wine glasses. "Most want either safe mediocrity or impossible innovation with no tolerance for the development process."

"Howard's different. He sees the building as a physical manifestation of his business philosophy, not just a corporate headquarters."

"Because you framed it that way for him." James's eyes held hers with unexpected intensity. "Your narrative approach transformed how he views the entire project."

The genuine compliment created warmth that spread through her chest. "We did that together. Your design vision gave the narrative physical form."

"True collaboration." James's expression softened. "Something I've rarely experienced in my career."

The admission hung between them, weighted with implications neither seemed ready to address. Liz took another sip of wine, using the moment to recalibrate.

"Speaking of collaboration," she said, "Thomas mentioned you're considering the Hayes Museum renovation. That's a prestigious project."

"We're in early discussions. The building has significant historical constraints that make it particularly challenging." James studied her over the rim of his glass. "You seem surprised I'd be interested."

"Not surprised. It's just a departure from your usual forward-looking projects. The Hayes is decidedly traditional."

"Perhaps I'm developing my own appreciation for 'progressive tradition.'" A smile played at the corners of his mouth. "Besides, preservation can be radical in its own way—honoring history while creating space for contemporary function."

"Now who's talking about narrative integration?" Liz laughed, the sound surprising her with its genuine warmth.

James's smile broadened in response, transforming his features. "I've learned from the best."

The moment of shared amusement created an unexpected bridge between their professional and personal selves. For a heartbeat, they weren't project collaborators with complicated history but simply two people enjoying each other's company.

Their shared laughter drew curious glances from nearby diners, the sound incongruous with their otherwise professional demeanor. Liz felt something tight within her chest loosen, a knot of old resentment unraveling in the face of shared experiences.

"Elizabeth? James? Is that really you two together without arguing?"

The voice startled them both. Liz looked up to find an elegant older woman with silver hair and penetrating eyes standing beside their table.

"Mrs. Abernathy!" Recognition dawned immediately. Their former English teacher looked remarkably unchanged, perhaps a few more lines around her eyes, her hair fully silver now, but the same erect posture and shrewd expression that had intimidated generations of Preston Academy students.

"I thought it was you." Mrs. Abernathy's gaze moved between them with undisguised curiosity. "What a surprising reunion. The Mitchell-Calloway academic rivalry was legendary in faculty circles."

James recovered first, standing to pull out a chair. "Would you join us for a moment? It's wonderful to see you."

"Just briefly. My husband is waiting at the bar." Mrs. Abernathy settled into the offered seat with regal precision. "So, what brings my two most competitive students together after all these years? Last I heard, Elizabeth, you were in marketing at Meridian, and James, your firm designed that controversial building downtown, the Thomas, wasn't it?"

"We're actually working together," Liz explained, acutely aware of how this dinner might appear to their former teacher. "James's firm is designing Meridian's new headquarters. I'm the marketing liaison."

"How fascinating." Mrs. Abernathy's eyes sparkled with amusement. "And you're managing to collaborate without turning it into a competition? That shows remarkable growth."

James smiled diplomatically. "We've found our different perspectives create stronger outcomes together than separately."

"I always thought you two brought out the best in each other academically, though neither of you would have admitted it then." Mrs. Abernathy glanced between them with the perceptiveness that had once uncovered plagiarism from the slightest textual anomaly. "Your debates in my class raised the level of discourse for everyone."

"Elizabeth's literary analysis was always incisive," James acknowledged, surprising Liz with the candid praise. "She saw connections others missed."

"And James had an irritating talent for finding the perfect supporting evidence for his arguments," Liz added, her tone warmer than she'd intended.

Mrs. Abernathy smiled knowingly. "The Beckman Scholarship competition was the closest in the foundation's history, you know. The committee was divided for weeks."

Liz felt a familiar twist in her chest at the mention of the scholarship that had altered her trajectory. "James mentioned it was a close decision."

"Three-tenths of a point," Mrs. Abernathy confirmed. "So close...the margin was negligible. Either one of you could have won. Actually, I think both of you were winners."

The observation hung in the air, laden with implications about paths not taken and lives that might have unfolded differently. Liz found herself unable to meet James's eyes, suddenly aware of the wine warming her cheeks and the intimate atmosphere of their secluded booth.

"Well, I should return to my husband." Mrs. Abernathy stood, adjusting her elegant shawl. "It's wonderful to see you both. And I must say, it's refreshing to see you finally getting along after all these years."

After she departed, a charged silence fell between them. The casual reminiscence that had flowed so naturally minutes before now felt dangerous, loaded with unacknowledged undercurrents.

"She always did have impeccable timing," James finally said, his attempt at lightness not quite landing.

"And perception," Liz added. "Nothing escaped her notice in class."

"Including our mutual antagonism." James studied his wine glass. "Though she apparently saw something we didn't."

"What do you mean?"

"That we brought out the best in each other." His eyes met hers. "Perhaps she was right."

The statement created a shift in the atmosphere, acknowledging something that had been building since their first reconnection months ago. Their server chose that moment to appear, offering dessert menus that both declined.

James settled the bill despite Liz's protest that they should split it as a business expense. "Consider it an apology for the last-minute meeting request," he insisted.

Outside, the evening had turned cool, a light breeze carrying the first hints of autumn. The restaurant's entrance was set back from the street, creating a shadowed alcove illuminated only by subtle architectural lighting that highlighted the building's historic façade.

"Where are you parked?" James asked as they stepped into the night air.

"The garage around the corner." Liz gestured vaguely to the right. "You?"

"Street parking, the opposite direction." He hesitated, clearly reluctant to end the evening. "I can walk you to your car."

"That's not necessary." She remained rooted in place, equally unwilling to separate. "Thank you for dinner. And for the structural solution. I think Howard will approve the modified approach."

"It was your insight about maintaining the experiential narrative that made the solution work," James countered. "Another example of our perspectives creating something better together."

They stood in the shadowed doorway, professional pretense growing thinner by the moment. The wine, the reminiscence, Mrs. Abernathy's knowing observations—everything had conspired to weaken the careful boundaries they'd maintained.

"Elizabeth," James said, his voice lower than it had been inside. "There's something happening here that goes beyond professional collaboration."

The direct acknowledgment sent a jolt through her system. "James—"

"I know," he continued, stepping slightly closer. "It's complicated. Your marriage, our professional relationship, the project stakes. Every rational consideration argues against pursuing whatever this is."

"Then we should be rational," Liz said, though she made no move to increase the distance between them.

"Rationality has its limits." His eyes held hers with an intensity that made her breath catch. "At some point, we have to acknowledge what's actually happening rather than what should be happening."

"And what is happening?" The question emerged barely above a whisper.

Instead of answering, James moved closer still, his hand rising to her face with the same architect's precision she'd observed earlier. His fingers traced her cheekbone in a gesture so gentle it made her heart ache.

The moment stretched between them, possibility humming in the narrow space separating their bodies. Liz found herself leaning forward almost imperceptibly, drawn by a force that overwhelmed professional caution and marital obligation alike.

Their lips were inches apart when James suddenly stepped back, his expression shifting from desire to regret.

"This is a complication neither of us needs," he said, his voice rough with suppressed emotion. "The project is too important to risk with personal entanglements."

The echo of Catherine's warning created a cold clarity that broke the moment's spell. Liz straightened, smoothing her blouse in a gesture of composure she didn't feel.

"You're right," she agreed, relieved her voice sounded steadier than she felt. "We have professional responsibilities that take priority over... whatever this is."

"Whatever this is," James repeated softly. "A question for another time, perhaps."

"Perhaps." Liz took a deliberate step toward the street. "I should go. Mark will be wondering where I am."

The mention of her husband created further distance between them, restoring the boundaries that had momentarily dissolved.

"Of course." James nodded, his professional mask sliding back into place. "I'll email the revised structural details tomorrow morning."

"I'll review them before the engineering meeting." Liz matched his tone, grateful for the return to safe territory. "Goodnight, James."

"Goodnight, Elizabeth."

They parted ways at the sidewalk, walking in opposite directions without looking back. Liz maintained her composed stride until reaching her car, where she sank into the driver's seat and released a shaking breath.

For several minutes, she sat motionless, hands gripping the steering wheel, mind replaying the almost-kiss in excruciating detail. What would have happened if James hadn't pulled back? If Mrs. Abernathy hadn't appeared earlier? If they'd ordered another bottle of wine?

Across the parking lot, she spotted James sitting similarly frozen in his own vehicle. Even at this distance, she could see his white-knuckled grip on the steering wheel, the rigid set of his shoulders. He was experiencing the same turbulent emotions that churned through her, desire, regret, confusion, relief.

Eventually, both cars started and pulled away in different directions, carrying them back to their separate lives and responsibilities. But something had fundamentally shifted between them, a line not quite crossed but certainly approached, a possibility acknowledged if not acted upon.

The pressure test had revealed structural weaknesses in their carefully maintained professional boundaries. The only question now was whether those boundaries would hold under increasing strain, or whether they would ultimately fail, bringing down the entire carefully constructed edifice of their collaboration.

CHAPTER TWENTY

"Crisis Point"

The fluorescent lights of the Meridian conference room cast harsh shadows across the architectural drawings spread across the table. Outside, rain pelted against the windows, the Saturday afternoon storm matching the tension that had been building all day. The structural issue with the atrium connection had blindsided everyone, what had seemed a minor engineering concern yesterday had revealed itself as a fundamental flaw requiring significant redesign.

"The entire load-bearing system needs recalculation," Thomas explained, pointing to the detailed diagrams. "The stress points are concentrating here and here, creating potential failure points during thermal expansion."

Howard had left an hour ago after authorizing whatever resources were needed to solve the problem. Catherine had departed shortly after, her parting glance at Liz carrying a clear warning about maintaining professional focus. The remaining team members, engineers, project managers, and design specialists, had spent the last six hours developing alternative approaches.

Liz massaged her temples, fighting the headache that had been building since morning. "The timeline implications are significant. We're looking at a minimum two-week delay unless we find a way to parallel-track the redesign with ongoing construction."

"Three weeks," James corrected, his voice tight with frustration. "The steel fabrication can't proceed until we resolve the load distribution. Everything downstream is affected."

Sophia yawned, checking her watch. "It's nearly seven. I've got dinner plans I can't break. Can we reconvene tomorrow?"

"Go," James nodded. "Thomas, take the team home. Elizabeth and I will finalize the approach tonight and circulate it for review in the morning."

The room gradually emptied, team members gathering drawings and laptops with the weary movements of people who'd been problem-solving for too many hours. Derek lingered by the door, eyeing Liz with concern.

"Want me to stay? I can cancel my plans."

"No need," Liz assured him, summoning a professional smile. "We just need to synthesize the options and prepare Howard's brief. Go enjoy your Saturday night."

After the door closed behind Derek, silence descended on the conference room. Liz became acutely aware of being alone with James for the first time since their almost-kiss outside The Blueprint Gallery three nights ago. They'd maintained careful distance since then, interacting only in group settings with deliberately neutral courtesy.

James moved to the whiteboard, erasing their earlier diagrams with sharp, aggressive strokes. "The engineering team's approach is too conservative. We'd lose the visual lightness that makes the atrium concept work."

"And your approach prioritizes aesthetics over structural integrity," Liz countered, gathering scattered documents into organized piles. "We need a solution that addresses both."

"There's always a solution that doesn't require compromise." James turned, his frustration evident in the tightness around his eyes. "You're still playing it safe, just like you did at Preston."

The personal jab caught her off guard. "Excuse me?"

"Your debate strategy. Always the pragmatic approach, never the truly innovative one." He gestured toward her notes. "You're looking for the easiest path to approval rather than the best design solution."

"And you're still letting ego override practicality," Liz shot back, professional restraint fraying. "The building needs to function, not just win design awards for James Calloway."

"This isn't about my ego." He moved closer, pointing to her marked-up drawings. "This is about your unwillingness to push beyond comfortable solutions. You did the same thing with your literary analysis senior year—technically correct but lacking courage."

"You don't get to criticize my work based on who I was twenty years ago." Liz stood, meeting his gaze directly. "And if we're revisiting ancient history, let's remember your 'innovative' approaches often missed the practical implications. Like your Hemingway analysis that completely ignored historical context."

"At least I took risks." James stepped closer, the conference table no longer between them. "You've always calculated every move, Elizabeth. Even now—playing it safe in your marketing career, in your marriage—"

"Don't." Her voice dropped dangerously. "My marriage is off-limits."

"Is it? Because it seems to be affecting your willingness to consider bold approaches to this design problem."

"That's absurd." Liz moved around him toward the whiteboard, needing physical distance from his intensity. "My professional judgment has nothing to do with my personal life."

"Doesn't it?" James followed, his voice lowering. "You're compartmentalizing. Keeping everything in neat, separate boxes. The problem is, design doesn't work that way. Life doesn't work that way."

"This isn't about life philosophy. It's about a structural engineering problem with a deadline." She grabbed a marker, sketching a modified connection detail with quick, angry strokes. "This approach maintains visual lightness while addressing the stress points."

James studied her drawing for a moment, then reached past her to add his own modifications, his arm brushing against hers. "The connection needs to articulate here, creating flexibility during thermal expansion."

The slight contact sent an electric current through her system. Liz stepped sideways, maintaining professional focus despite her accelerating pulse. "That could work if we reinforce the secondary supports."

"Exactly." His voice had softened, the earlier antagonism replaced by collaborative energy. He sketched rapidly, building on her concept. "Like this."

They worked side by side at the whiteboard, the solution evolving through their combined perspectives. The earlier tension transformed into creative synergy, each building on the other's ideas with increasing animation. Their hands occasionally brushed as they added details to the emerging design, each contact creating a jolt of awareness neither acknowledged.

"It's working," Liz said finally, stepping back to assess their creation. "The articulated joint maintains visual lightness while distributing the load across these secondary supports."

"And preserves the narrative flow through the space," James added, his eyes bright with the satisfaction of solving a complex problem. "This is exactly why we—"

He stopped abruptly, their gazes locking. Something shifted in the atmosphere, the professional enthusiasm suddenly charged with a different energy entirely.

"Why we what?" Liz asked, her voice barely above a whisper.

"Why we're effective together." James remained motionless, his expression intensifying. "We see different aspects of the same problem. Always have."

They stood too close, the whiteboard at Liz's back preventing retreat. The room seemed to contract around them, the storm outside fading to background noise as awareness crystallized between them.

"James," she began, unsure what would follow his name.

"I know," he said quietly. "We agreed this was a complication neither of us needs."

"We did."

"And nothing has changed."

"Nothing," she echoed, though everything had.

His eyes dropped to her lips for the briefest moment before returning to meet her gaze. The air between them seemed to vibrate with possibility and restraint, professional boundaries straining against something more powerful.

"We should finalize the drawings," Liz said, her voice not entirely steady.

"We should."

Neither moved. Rain lashed against the windows, punctuating the silence between heartbeats. Later, Liz wouldn't be able to say who moved first—whether she leaned forward or he closed the final distance—only that the tension between them finally, inevitably broke.

His lips met hers with surprising gentleness that quickly deepened into urgency. Her hands found his shoulders as his slid around her waist, drawing her closer. The kiss held none of the hesitation of their almost-moment outside the restaurant, this was decisive, certain, a dam breaking after months of building pressure.

Liz felt herself responding with a hunger that shocked her, fingers threading through his hair, body pressing against his with urgent need. The whiteboard markers clattered to the floor, forgotten as the professional pretense they'd maintained dissolved completely.

The kiss seemed to exist outside time—could have been seconds or minutes—before reality crashed back with jarring force. They broke apart simultaneously, both stepping back as if burned.

"That was—" James began.

"A mistake," Liz finished, touching her fingers to her lips in disbelief. "We can't—this is—"

"I know." He ran a hand through his hair, visibly struggling to recalibrate. "The project—our professional relationship—"

"My marriage," she added, the word hanging between them like a physical barrier.

James nodded, his expression shifting from desire to regret with painful clarity. "I should go. We both need... distance."

"Yes." Liz couldn't manage more than the single syllable, her mind reeling between shock and lingering desire.

He gathered his things with mechanical efficiency, not meeting her eyes. "I'll finalize the drawings at home and email them to you. For Howard's brief."

"Thank you."

At the door, he paused, his back to her. "Elizabeth, I—"

"Don't," she interrupted. "Please."

James nodded once, then left without looking back, the door closing with quiet finality behind him.

Liz sank into a chair, legs suddenly unsteady. The conference room felt cavernous in his absence, the whiteboard covered with their collaborative solution a stark reminder of what they'd created together—and what they'd just jeopardized.

She pressed her fingers to her lips again, still feeling the imprint of his mouth, the unexpected softness followed by demanding pressure. In fifteen years of marriage, she couldn't remember feeling so completely consumed by a single kiss, so utterly present in a moment of connection.

The door opened without warning. Liz straightened abruptly, smoothing her blouse with shaking hands.

"Forgot my umbrella," Derek said, stepping inside. He paused, taking in her flushed face and disheveled appearance. "Everything okay? You look..."

"Fine," she said too quickly. "Just tired. Long day of problem-solving."

Derek's gaze moved to the scattered markers on the floor, then back to her face. His expression shifted from curiosity to dawning comprehension. "Where's James?"

"He left. We... finished the redesign approach." She gestured vaguely toward the whiteboard, unable to meet his eyes.

"I see." Derek retrieved his umbrella from beside the door, his usual playfulness replaced by careful neutrality. "Did you reach a satisfactory solution?"

The double meaning wasn't lost on her. "We developed an approach for Howard's approval. The articulated joint preserves both structural integrity and design vision."

"That's not what I asked, Liz."

She finally met his gaze, finding concern rather than judgment. "Derek, I can't—"

"You don't need to explain." He moved toward the door, then paused. "Just be careful. Whatever's happening... there's a lot at stake."

After he left, Liz remained motionless, the reality of what had just occurred settling over her like a physical weight. She had kissed James Calloway. In the Meridian conference room. During a project crisis. While still married to Mark.

The professional implications alone were devastating, potential conflict of interest, compromised judgment, risk to the project that defined both their careers. The personal implications were even more complex, what it meant for her already-troubled marriage, for her self-image as someone who honored commitments, for the carefully constructed narrative of her life.

Yet beneath the shock and guilt, she couldn't deny the exhilaration that still coursed through her veins. For those brief moments, she had felt more alive, more authentically herself, than she had in years. The intellectual connection that had been building between them had finally found physical expression, and the resulting chemistry had been undeniable.

Liz began gathering her things, moving with the deliberate focus of someone navigating treacherous ground. She needed to think, to process, to understand what had happened and what it meant. Not here, surrounded by evidence of their collaboration and momentary surrender.

In her office, she closed the door and leaned against it, finally allowing herself to acknowledge the truth she'd been avoiding for months: her feelings for James had evolved far beyond professional respect or even friendship. The kiss hadn't created something new; it had merely revealed what already existed beneath their careful professional façade.

She touched her lips once more, the gesture becoming a tangible connection to a moment that had changed everything. Guilt and exhilaration warred within her, neither fully conquering the other. Whatever happened next, with the project, with James, with her marriage, nothing would be the same after crossing this line.

The rain continued its assault on the windows, matching the storm that had broken loose within her. Like the structural issue they'd spent the day addressing, this crisis point demanded resolution, not just a temporary patch, but a fundamental reconsideration of the entire design.

CHAPTER TWENTY-ONE

"Damage Control"

The windshield wipers slashed frantically against the rain, struggling to keep pace with the downpour that had started minutes after Liz left Meridian. The rhythmic swishing matched her racing heartbeat as she gripped the steering wheel with white knuckles. Traffic crawled along the rain-slicked streets, each red light an opportunity for unwanted reflection.

She had kissed James Calloway. Or he had kissed her. The distinction seemed meaningless now, they had crossed a line that couldn't be uncrossed. Her lips still tingled with the memory, the pressure and heat of his mouth against hers replaying in vivid detail despite her attempts to focus on the road.

What had she been thinking? Fifteen years of marriage thrown into jeopardy for a moment of weakness. A professional relationship jeopardized for what, the thrill of intellectual connection translated into physical chemistry?

"It was a mistake," she said aloud to the empty car. "A momentary lapse in judgment during a stressful situation."

The rationalization sounded hollow. The kiss hadn't materialized from nowhere, it had been building for months, through charged conversations and shared insights, through accidental touches and lingering glances. The storm-trapped conversation in the trailer, the almost-moment outside The Blueprint Gallery, the vivid dream that still haunted her, all stepping stones to this inevitable crossing.

A horn blared behind her, startling Liz from her thoughts. The light had turned green. She accelerated through the intersection, wiping condensation from the inside of the windshield with her sleeve.

Her phone chimed with a text notification. She ignored it, though her heart leapt with the possibility it might be James. What would he say? What could either of them say that would make sense of what had happened?

The suburbs gradually replaced downtown buildings, familiar landmarks signaling her approach home.

Home, the word felt strange now, as if it belonged to someone else's life. The colonial house with its perfect landscaping and hollow rooms awaited her, along with a husband who had become a stranger long before James Calloway reappeared in her life.

That was the truth she needed to face. Whatever had happened with James, whatever might happen, wasn't the cause of her marital problems. It was merely the catalyst that had forced her to acknowledge what she'd been avoiding for years: her marriage had been failing long before that kiss.

The driveway was empty when she pulled in. Mark had texted earlier about watching the game at Kevin's, another evening spent apart that neither would acknowledge as significant. She sat in the car for several minutes after turning off the engine, rain drumming on the roof, gathering the strength to enter a house that no longer felt like hers.

Inside, the silence was oppressive. Liz moved through the rooms turning on lights, creating the illusion of life in the carefully decorated space. In the kitchen, she poured a glass of wine with shaking hands, then abandoned it on the counter, untouched.

Her phone chimed again. This time she checked it, bracing herself.

It wasn't James. Mark: *Kevin ordered pizza. Staying for the post-game. Don't wait up.*

The casual message, devoid of affection or inquiry about her day, created a hollow ache in her chest. When had they stopped asking about each other's lives? When had they stopped caring about the answers?

Liz typed a response, deleted it, typed again: *Having a quiet night at home. See you later.*

She hesitated, then added: *Love you.*

The words felt foreign, a phrase from a language she'd once spoken fluently but had gradually forgotten. She sent it anyway, a desperate attempt to reconnect with the woman she'd been before, the one who had loved Mark without reservation, who had believed in their shared future, who hadn't known what it felt like to be truly seen by someone like James.

The phone remained silent. No immediate response, not even the typing indicator. Liz set it down and moved to the living room, sinking onto the couch. Rain continued to pelt the windows, matching her turbulent thoughts.

What would happen Monday? How could she face James across a conference table, discussing architectural specifications and marketing narratives as if nothing had changed? How could she face Catherine, whose warning about "personal complications" now seemed prophetic?

More importantly, how could she face Mark, carrying the weight of what had happened? The guilt was substantial, but not crushing, and that realization brought its own kind of pain. Shouldn't she feel more remorse for betraying her marriage vows? Shouldn't the thought of hurting Mark be unbearable?

Instead, she felt something closer to resignation, as if the kiss had merely confirmed what she'd already known but hadn't been ready to acknowledge: her marriage existed now more in memory than in present reality.

Liz moved to her home office, seeking refuge in the one space that truly reflected her rather than their joint compromise. She opened her laptop, intending to lose herself in work, but found herself staring at James's most recent email about the atrium specifications. His precise notes filled the margins, each addressing her concerns about narrative flow and visitor experience with a thoroughness that revealed how completely he'd absorbed her perspective.

Mark had never understood her work that way, had never tried to. "Making sure the fancy architect doesn't blow the budget on useless pretty stuff," he'd said at his company dinner, reducing her professional contribution to a punchline.

James, by contrast, had integrated her marketing concepts so thoroughly they'd become inseparable from his architectural vision. He valued her mind, challenged her thinking, saw her as an intellectual equal rather than an accessory to his life.

The sound of the garage door opening jolted her from these dangerous comparisons. Mark was home, hours earlier than she'd expected. Liz closed the laptop quickly, as if he might somehow see her thoughts displayed on the screen.

She moved to the kitchen, composing her features into neutral welcome. Mark stumbled slightly as he entered, the distinctive flush on his face indicating several beers beyond his usual limit.

"You're home early," she said, leaning against the counter. "I thought you were staying for post-game analysis."

"Game sucked." Mark dropped his keys on the counter with a clatter. "Kevin's wife started complaining about the noise." He opened the refrigerator, pulling out another beer. "You eat?"

"Not hungry." Liz watched him pop the tab, wondering if he'd notice anything different about her, if the kiss had somehow marked her in ways visible to someone who knew her intimately.

But Mark merely nodded, his attention already shifting to his phone. "Reynolds texted about the Johnson account. Gotta review the numbers before Monday."

"Mark," she began, not sure what would follow his name but needing to establish some kind of meaningful connection. "Can we talk?"

He looked up, surprise flickering across his features. "About what?"

The question hung between them, loaded with fifteen years of accumulated silence. Where would she even begin? With her growing dissatisfaction? With the intellectual connection she'd found with James? With the kiss that had changed everything and nothing simultaneously?

"About us," she said finally. "About where we're going."

Mark's expression closed, wariness replacing surprise. "It's been a long day, Liz. Can this wait?"

"That's the problem. It always waits." The words emerged with unexpected force. "We're always too tired, too busy, too distracted to have real conversations anymore."

"What's brought this on?" He set down his beer, eyes narrowing. "Did something happen at work?"

The direct question sent a jolt through her system. Did he suspect? Could he somehow sense the shift that had occurred? But his expression held only confusion, not suspicion.

"Nothing specific," she lied, guilt flaring briefly. "Just... thinking about where we are. As a couple."

Mark sighed, running a hand through his hair. "Look, I know I've been distracted with the Johnson account. And you've been buried in that building project. We're both busy. It happens."

"It's more than being busy, Mark. We're living separate lives. When was the last time we had a real conversation? When was the last time you asked about my work and actually listened to the answer?"

"Is that what this is about? Your work?" His tone sharpened. "Because I've been trying to be supportive of these crazy hours, but it's not exactly easy when your wife is never home."

"This isn't about hours or schedules." Liz struggled to articulate the emptiness that had been growing between them long before the Meridian project. "It's about connection. About seeing each other. About wanting to share our lives instead of just occupying the same space."

Mark stared at her as if she were speaking a foreign language. "We're married, Liz. We share a house, a name, a life. What more do you want?"

The question struck at the heart of her confusion. What did she want? The answer was complicated by thoughts of James—his intellectual challenge, his genuine interest in her perspective, the electricity of his kiss. But those feelings had emerged because something fundamental was already missing in her marriage.

"I want to feel like my husband actually knows me," she said quietly. "Like he's interested in my thoughts, my work, my dreams. Like we're partners in more than just mortgage payments and grocery lists."

Mark's expression shifted from confusion to hurt. "That's not fair Liz. I've always supported your career. I've never complained about your late nights or weekend work sessions."

"Support isn't the same as engagement, Mark. You tolerate my career. You don't actually care about it."

"And you care about mine?" he challenged. "When's the last time you asked about my sales targets or client meetings?"

The question landed with uncomfortable accuracy. She had become as disengaged from his professional life as he was from hers. The realization didn't negate her point but complicated it, their disconnection wasn't one-sided.

"You're right," she acknowledged. "We've both stopped sharing those parts of our lives. That's exactly my point. We've drifted so far apart we don't even notice the distance anymore."

Mark took a long swallow of beer, his expression hardening. "So what are you saying? That our marriage is in trouble because we don't chat about work enough?"

"It's not just work. It's everything." Liz felt suddenly exhausted, the emotional weight of the day, the kiss, the guilt, this confrontation, crashing down at once. "When did we stop talking about books, ideas, dreams? When did we stop being curious about each other's inner lives?"

"Jesus, Liz. Listen to yourself." Mark's laugh held no humor. "'Inner lives'? This isn't some college philosophy class. This is real life. People grow up, settle down, focus on practical things."

"And stop connecting on any meaningful level?" She shook her head. "That's not growing up, Mark. That's giving up."

Silence fell between them, heavy with unspoken truths. Mark finished his beer, the empty can joining others in the recycling bin with a hollow clang.

"I'm going to bed," he said finally. "We can talk about this when you're not... whatever this is."

"Mark—"

"Not tonight, Liz." His voice left no room for argument. "I've had a few beers, you're clearly worked up about something. This isn't the time."

She watched him walk away, shoulders rigid with defensive anger. The conversation had accomplished nothing except confirming what she already knew: they were speaking different languages, valuing different things, living different lives despite sharing the same address.

Upstairs, she heard the shower running, then the familiar sounds of Mark preparing for bed. She remained in the kitchen, that peculiar transitional realm where difficult conversations often began but rarely concluded. The house felt suddenly confining, the careful décor and matching furniture sets like a stage set for a play she'd been performing without realizing the audience had left.

When she finally climbed the stairs, Mark was already in bed, his back turned toward her side, breathing not quite regular enough to be asleep. Liz gathered pajamas and retreated to the guest bathroom, unwilling to share the intimate space of their en-suite after the failed conversation.

The face that greeted her in the mirror looked strange, flushed cheeks, bright eyes, lips slightly swollen from James's kiss hours earlier. She touched her mouth gently, the memory flooding back with visceral clarity. The contrast between that moment of connection and the hollow exchange with Mark created a schism she couldn't reconcile.

After showering, Liz hesitated outside the bedroom door. The thought of lying beside Mark, pretending nothing had changed when everything had, seemed suddenly unbearable.

She turned toward the guest room instead, settling into the rarely-used bed with a sense of both guilt and relief. If Mark noticed her absence, he didn't come looking for her. The silence stretched between their separate rooms, physical distance merely reflecting the emotional reality they'd been avoiding for years.

Sleep refused to come despite her exhaustion. The day's events replayed in an endless loop, the structural crisis, the heated argument with James, the moment when professional boundaries had dissolved completely. The kiss that had changed everything and nothing simultaneously.

What would happen now? The project still needed completion, their professional collaboration couldn't simply end because of one moment of weakness. Howard was counting on them, careers and reputations hung in the balance. Somehow, they would need to find a way forward that protected the project while acknowledging what had happened between them.

As for her marriage, that question loomed larger and more complex. The kiss with James hadn't created problems with Mark; it had merely illuminated issues that had been developing for years. The emotional disconnect, the parallel lives, the gradual surrender of expectations, everything that had eroded their connection existed independent of James Calloway.

Yet he had become the catalyst for confronting truths she'd been avoiding. In the intellectual challenge he provided, the genuine interest he showed in her thoughts, the respect he demonstrated for her perspective, James had reminded her of what partnership could feel like, what it should feel like.

The guest room clock glowed 3:47 AM when Liz finally drifted into uneasy sleep, questions still circling without resolution. Morning arrived too soon, gray light filtering through unfamiliar curtains. She reached for her phone, finding a text from Mark sent hours earlier: *Why are you in guest room?*

No concern, no attempt to check on her during the night. Just a question delivered with the same detachment that characterized most of their communication now.

She typed a response: *You were snoring. Didn't want to wake you.*

A plausible excuse that avoided the more complicated truth: she couldn't bear to lie beside him carrying the weight of what had happened with James.

As she scrolled through other notifications, a new message appeared that made her heart stutter:

James Calloway: We need to discuss professional boundaries before tomorrow's meeting. Coffee at Riverside Café, 2pm?

The neutral language couldn't disguise the urgency behind the request. They needed damage control, a strategy for moving forward that protected both the project and their careers. The kiss couldn't be undone, but its consequences might still be managed.

Liz stared at the message, thumb hovering over the reply button. Whatever happened next would shape not just the project's future but her own. The carefully constructed narrative of her life had reached a plot twist she hadn't anticipated, one that demanded choices she wasn't sure she was ready to make.

With a deep breath, she typed her response: *I'll be there.*

CHAPTER TWENTY-TWO

"Containment Strategies"

The Riverside Café occupied a quiet corner overlooking the water, its Sunday afternoon crowd sparse enough to offer privacy without the awkward intimacy of complete isolation. Liz chose a table near the back window, visible from the entrance but removed from neighboring conversations. She arrived fifteen minutes early, ordering black coffee that arrived in a white ceramic mug she now gripped like a lifeline.

James entered precisely at two, his usual confident stride slightly hesitant as he scanned the room. He wore dark jeans and a gray button-down, casual weekend attire that still managed to look impeccably tailored.

Their eyes met across the café, a moment of electric connection before professional masks slid into place.

"Elizabeth." He settled into the chair across from her, placing his portfolio on the table between them like a physical barrier. "Thank you for meeting."

"Of course." She kept her voice steady despite the rapid acceleration of her pulse. "The structural issue needs resolution before tomorrow's engineering meeting."

The pretense that this was purely a work discussion hung between them, transparent but necessary. James signaled for coffee, using the moment to gather himself.

"About yesterday—" he began once the server departed.

"It was a mistake," Liz interrupted, the rehearsed line emerging with practiced calm. "We were under extreme pressure with the design crisis. It was... a momentary lapse in judgment."

James studied her face, searching for something beneath the professional veneer. "Is that what you really think?"

The direct question undermined her carefully constructed explanation. Liz dropped her gaze to her coffee, finding refuge in the dark liquid rather than the intensity of his eyes.

"What I think doesn't matter," she replied finally. "What matters is the project, our professional reputations, and the commitments we've made to others."

"Always the pragmatist." A ghost of a smile touched his lips, though it didn't reach his eyes. "But you're right, of course. We have too much invested professionally to complicate this with... whatever happened yesterday."

"Exactly." The word tasted bitter despite its rational truth. "Howard is counting on us. The entire team is counting on us. We can't jeopardize the project because of one moment of weakness."

James's coffee arrived, providing a brief reprieve from the tension. He added a single packet of sugar, stirring methodically before setting the spoon aside with deliberate precision.

"So we establish boundaries," he said, his architect's mind already structuring the problem. "Professional interaction only. No private meetings without clear project purpose. No discussions of personal matters."

"No unnecessary physical proximity," Liz added, remembering the electric current that had passed between them whenever they stood too close. "And we should probably copy team members on communications when possible."

"Reasonable precautions." James nodded, his expression carefully neutral. "Though it might raise

questions if our working dynamic changes too abruptly."

"We'll maintain professional collaboration," Liz
clarified. "Just with... safeguards."

James reached for his portfolio, extracting several
drawings of the atrium connection that had precipitated yesterday's crisis. He spread them across the table,
creating a neutral territory of architectural specifications.

"I've developed three potential solutions for the
structural issue," he explained, his voice shifting to its
professional register. "Each addresses the load distribution problem while maintaining visual lightness."

Liz leaned forward to examine the drawings, grateful
for the solid ground of project details. As she reached
for one sketch, her fingers accidentally brushed against
his. Both withdrew instantly, the brief contact sending a jolt through her system that belied their rational
agreement moments before.

"Sorry," she murmured, tucking her hand safely into
her lap.

James cleared his throat. "Option three preserves the
narrative flow you emphasized while addressing the
engineering concerns."

They spent the next thirty minutes discussing technical specifications, material tolerances, and timeline
implications. The familiar rhythm of professional ex-

change gradually eased the tension, allowing them to settle into the collaborative pattern they'd developed over months. If their gazes occasionally held a moment too long, if they were hyperaware of each other's smallest movements, neither acknowledged it.

"We should review the actual site," James suggested as they finished their second cups of coffee. "The physical context might reveal options we're missing on paper."

The proposal made perfect sense professionally while creating exactly the private scenario they'd just agreed to avoid. Yet refusing would only highlight the awkwardness they were trying to minimize.

"That's a good idea," Liz agreed, gathering her notes. "The concrete pour for that section is scheduled for Tuesday."

The construction site was eerily quiet on Sunday afternoon, the usual cacophony of equipment and workers replaced by stillness. Their footsteps echoed on temporary walkways as James led the way toward the atrium foundation. The skeletal framework of steel beams rose from concrete footings, outlining spaces that didn't yet exist except in their shared vision.

"The problem area is here," James indicated the junction where the glass ceiling would eventually meet the limestone elements. "The stress concentrates at this connection point during thermal expansion."

Liz studied the space, mentally overlaying the architectural renderings onto the raw structure before them. "What if we modify the transition sequence? Create a more graduated connection between materials?"

"That could work." James moved closer to the junction point, sketching in the air with his hands. "If we articulate the joint here, allowing for movement while maintaining visual continuity..."

They fell into the familiar pattern of collaborative problem-solving, each building on the other's ideas. For several minutes, the complexity of the design challenge superseded the personal tension between them. James sketched rapidly on his tablet as Liz pointed out narrative implications of each modification.

"This approach preserves the visitor experience while addressing the structural concerns," she observed, examining his revised drawing. "The articulated connection actually enhances the transition story from traditional to innovative materials."

"Exactly." James's expression brightened with the satisfaction of solving a complex problem. "The necessity becomes a feature rather than a compromise."

Their eyes met in shared understanding, the intellectual connection that had drawn them together from the beginning momentarily eclipsing the complications of their personal situation. For a heartbeat,

Liz forgot their careful boundaries, responding to the genuine pleasure of minds working in harmony.

The moment stretched between them, charged with awareness. James was the first to step back, creating deliberate distance.

"We should walk the perimeter," he suggested, his voice carefully professional again. "Check if there are other areas that might benefit from similar articulation."

They circled the foundation, maintaining several feet between them as they discussed technical details. The physical space helped reinforce the boundaries they'd established, allowing professional collaboration without dangerous proximity.

As they completed the circuit, returning to where they'd begun, James paused at the edge of what would become the main entrance.

"I think we have a viable solution," he said, closing his tablet. "I'll have Thomas prepare detailed drawings for tomorrow's engineering meeting."

"I'll draft the narrative justification for Howard," Liz added. "He'll want to understand how this modification enhances rather than compromises the visitor experience."

The professional discussion concluded, they stood awkwardly at the site boundary, neither quite ready to end the meeting yet uncertain how to navigate the departure.

"Elizabeth," James began, his formal use of her name creating emotional distance. "I want to be clear about something. Yesterday wasn't just... stress or proximity or momentary weakness."

The candid statement caught her off guard. "James—"

"Let me finish." His expression was serious, his eyes holding hers with uncomfortable directness. "I respect the boundaries we've established. They're necessary and appropriate given our professional obligations and your personal situation. But I won't pretend that what happened was meaningless or purely circumstantial."

Liz felt her carefully constructed rationalizations wavering under his honest assessment. "What are you saying?"

"I'm saying that we have an intellectual and personal connection that transcends professional collaboration. I'm saying that ignoring it won't make it disappear." He maintained careful physical distance despite the intensity of his words. "But I'm also saying that I respect you, and myself, too much to pursue it under the current circumstances."

The truth of his statement resonated uncomfortably. Their connection wasn't just physical attraction or momentary weakness, it was a recognition of something rare and valuable that had been building since their first contentious meeting months ago.

"We have too much invested professionally to complicate this," she repeated their earlier agreement, though the words felt inadequate against the honesty of his assessment.

"Yes." James nodded, a sad smile touching his lips. "So we focus on the project. We create something extraordinary together professionally. And we acknowledge that timing and circumstances aren't in our favor for anything else."

The pragmatic conclusion should have felt like relief. Instead, it carried the weight of paths not taken, possibilities acknowledged but deliberately set aside.

"I should go," Liz said, gathering her portfolio. "I'll email you the narrative justification tonight."

"I'll have the drawings to you by morning."

They walked to the parking area in silence, the professional detente established but the underlying awareness undiminished. At Liz's car, they paused for a final moment.

"Thank you for meeting today," James said, extending his hand in a deliberately professional gesture. "I think we have a strong solution for tomorrow."

Liz accepted the handshake, the formal contact somehow more intimate than it should have been. His fingers were warm against hers, the simple touch sending awareness across her skin despite their rational agreement.

The handshake lasted a fraction too long, neither quite willing to break the connection. When they finally separated, Liz felt the absence of his touch like a physical loss.

"See you tomorrow," she said, her voice steadier than she felt.

"Tomorrow," he echoed, stepping back to allow her to open her car door.

As she drove away, Liz glanced in the rearview mirror to see James still standing in the parking lot, watching her departure. The image reminded her painfully of their encounter during the storm, of other partings where professional facades had barely contained the current running beneath.

Their containment strategy was logical, necessary, appropriate. The boundaries they'd established would protect the project, their careers, and her marriage, already fragile before James had re-entered her life.

Yet as the construction site receded in her mirror, Liz couldn't shake the feeling that they were attempting to contain something that had already escaped their control, something that had been building since two competitive teenagers had first recognized worthy opponents in each other twenty years ago at Preston Academy.

Some connections, once acknowledged, couldn't simply be resealed behind professional boundaries. The only question was whether those boundaries would hold under the increasing pressure of proximity and collaboration, or whether they would eventually give way, transforming both the project and their lives in ways neither could fully anticipate.

CHAPTER TWENTY-THREE

"Fault Lines"

The morning light spilled through the bedroom curtains, casting a soft glow across the rumpled sheets. Liz had been awake for an hour already, pretending to read a novel while Mark's steady breathing filled the room. Days had passed since her coffee shop meeting with James, where they'd established careful boundaries to contain whatever had sparked between them. The professional detente was holding, but beneath it, the awareness remained, a constant hum of electricity she couldn't quite silence.

She slipped out of bed, padding downstairs to start the coffee. Saturday stretched before her, empty hours she once would have filled with errands and household management. Today she craved that mindless routine, anything to distract from the thoughts that had kept her tossing through the night.

The kitchen gleamed with unused perfection. Liz measured coffee beans with methodical precision, the familiar motions grounding her in normalcy. She'd barely started the grinder when Mark appeared in the doorway, his presence unexpected at this early hour.

"Morning," he said, voice still rough with sleep. "Thought I'd join you for breakfast."

Liz nodded, surprised. "Coffee will be ready in a minute."

Mark settled at the island, watching her move through the kitchen with unusual attentiveness. Something in his expression made her uneasy, a determined focus she hadn't seen directed her way in months.

"I was thinking," he began, accepting the mug she offered, "maybe we should start trying."

"Trying what?" Liz asked, though a cold certainty was already forming in her stomach.

"For a baby." Mark's eyes held hers, searching for a reaction. "We're not getting any younger, and we've always said 'someday.' Maybe someday should be now."

The mug nearly slipped from Liz's fingers. She set it down carefully, buying time as her mind raced. Of all the moments for Mark to resurrect this particular topic, one they hadn't seriously discussed in years, why now?

"That's... quite a suggestion for seven thirty on a Saturday morning," she managed, her voice impressively steady.

"Is it?" Mark frowned. "We've talked about it before. We even set up that room upstairs years ago."

"As a 'someday' nursery," Liz countered. "A theoretical possibility, not an immediate plan."

"Well, maybe I'm tired of theoretical." Mark's tone sharpened. "Maybe I want something real in this marriage besides mortgage payments and passing each other in the hallway."

The accusation stung precisely because it echoed her own thoughts. But children—that was a different matter entirely. The visceral rejection she felt at his suggestion revealed a truth she'd been avoiding for years.

"Mark, we can't just have a baby to fix whatever's happening between us."

"So you admit something's happening?" He leaned forward, coffee forgotten. "Because you've been different for months, Liz. Distant. Distracted. Coming home late, working weekends, barely present even when you're here."

"And your solution is to add a child to that dynamic?" Liz fought to keep her voice level. "That's not fair to anyone, especially not a baby."

"Then what is your solution?" Mark pushed back from the counter, frustration evident in every line of his body. "Because from where I'm standing, you've checked out of this marriage. You're going through motions, but you're not really here."

The accuracy of his assessment left her momentarily speechless. When had Mark become so perceptive about their relationship? Or had he always known and simply chosen not to acknowledge it until now?

"I'm trying to figure things out," she said finally. "But a baby isn't the answer, Mark. That's a lifetime commitment, not a marriage Band-Aid."

"Maybe it would give us something to focus on besides ourselves. Something that matters more than your precious building project."

And there it was, the undercurrent of resentment that had been building since the Meridian headquarters began. The project had become a convenient target for Mark's frustration, easier to blame than addressing the deeper issues between them.

"This isn't about the project," Liz said, though the image of James flashed unbidden through her mind. "It's about us. About how we've been drifting apart for years, not just months."

"Drifting apart?" Mark's laugh held no humor. "Is that what we're calling it? Because it feels more like you've set sail for another continent while I'm still standing on the shore."

"Not fair Mark."

"Isn't it? When was the last time you initiated a conversation that wasn't about schedules or groceries? When was the last time you actually wanted to be home instead of at the office?"

Each question landed like a physical blow, not because they were unfair but because they contained kernels of truth she couldn't deny. She had been withdrawing long before James reappeared in her life, retreating into work, into the safety of routine, away from the growing emptiness of their connection.

"I could ask you the same questions," she countered. "When was the last time you asked about my day and actually listened to the answer? When was the last time you chose me over a game or drinks with Kevin?"

Mark's expression hardened. "So this is my fault?"

"It's not about fault." Liz pressed her palms against the cool countertop, anchoring herself. "It's about recognizing that we've been moving in different directions for a long time. Adding a child to that equation would be irresponsible."

"Or it might remind us why we got married in the first place."

"Did we get married to have children?" Liz asked, genuinely curious about his perspective. "Because I don't remember that being our primary motivation."

Mark ran a hand through his hair, frustration evident. "We got married because we loved each other and wanted to build a life together. Children were supposed to be part of that life."

"Were they? Or was that just an assumption we never really examined?" The questions tumbled out before she could filter them. "Have you ever asked yourself if you actually want children, Mark? Or is it just what comes next in the life script we're supposed to follow?"

His eyes narrowed. "Now you don't want kids at all? Since when?"

The direct question forced Liz to confront a truth she'd been avoiding for years. She took a deep breath, commitment to honesty overriding her instinct to smooth things over.

"I don't know if I ever did," she admitted quietly. "I think I accepted the idea because it was expected. Because that's what married couples do. But when I really examine what I want..."

"What do you want, Liz?" Mark's voice had dropped, something like fear creeping into his expression. "Because it's starting to seem like it's not this life. Or me."

The moment stretched between them, weighted with fifteen years of shared history and growing distance. Liz struggled to articulate feelings she was only beginning to understand herself.

"I want purpose," she said finally. "Intellectual challenge. Creative fulfillment. Connection that goes beyond sharing an address and a tax return."

"And you don't find that with me." It wasn't a question.

"We stopped trying to connect on that level years ago, Mark. Both of us."

He stared at her as if seeing a stranger. "This is about him, isn't it? The architect. James."

The accusation sent a jolt through her system. "This is about us, Mark. About the fact that we've been growing apart for years before any project or... anyone else entered the picture."

"Right." His bitter laugh held no humor. "You light up talking about 'narrative integration' and 'experiential design' with him, but when I mention starting a family, you look like I suggested jumping off a cliff."

"Mark, that's not true—"

"Isn't it?" Mark pushed away from the counter. "I'm not blind, Liz. Something changed when that project started. When he came back into your life."

The proximity to truth made her defensive. "James is a colleague. The project is professionally challenging and creatively fulfilling. That's all."

"If that's what you need to tell yourself." Mark grabbed his keys from the counter. "I'm going to Kevin's. At least there I won't have to pretend everything's fine while my wife mentally checks out of the conversation."

"Mark—"

"Save it." He moved toward the door, shoulders rigid with anger. "When you're ready to have an honest conversation about what's really happening here, let me know."

The front door slammed with decisive finality, leaving Liz alone in the kitchen, surrounded by the trappings of domestic life that suddenly felt like props in a play she'd been performing without conviction.

She sank onto a barstool, hands shaking slightly as she reached for her abandoned coffee. Mark's accusation about James had cut too close for comfort, though not in the way he imagined. It wasn't a simple physical attraction or emotional affair. It was the recognition of intellectual compatibility she'd never experienced with Mark, the exhilaration of being challenged, understood, valued for her mind.

But that wasn't James specifically, was it? It was what he represented, the road not taken, the self not developed, the potential unfulfilled. The fact that she found those qualities in him was circumstantial, not causal. The problems in her marriage existed independent of James Calloway.

Didn't they?

Her phone chimed with a text, breaking the spiral of her thoughts. Rebecca: *Free for lunch? Need sister therapy after teenager drama.*

The timing couldn't have been more perfect. Liz texted back immediately: *Please come. Mark and I just had major fight. Need advice.*

Rebecca's response came quickly: *On my way. Wine or whiskey level problem?*

Somewhere in between. Bring both.

An hour later, Rebecca's distinctive knock echoed through the silent house. Liz opened the door to find her sister balancing a bottle of wine, a smaller paper bag that presumably contained whiskey, and a bakery box.

"I brought reinforcements," Rebecca announced, sweeping inside. "Alcohol and chocolate croissants—the foundation of all good crisis management."

Despite everything, Liz smiled. At forty-one, Rebecca Mitchell carried herself with the confident ease of a woman who had faced life's disappointments and emerged stronger. Her divorce five years earlier had transformed her from suburban wife to urban professional with an unapologetic approach to life that Liz sometimes envied.

"The kitchen's this way," Liz said, leading her through the immaculate living room.

Rebecca whistled softly. "This place is spotless. Bad sign. You only clean like this when you're avoiding something."

"Or someone," Liz admitted, retrieving wine glasses from the cabinet.

Rebecca set her provisions on the counter and studied her sister with penetrating eyes. "Okay, spill. What happened with Mark?"

Liz poured wine for both of them before answering. "He ambushed me this morning with the suggestion we should start trying for a baby."

"Wow." Rebecca's eyebrows rose. "Talk about a Hail Mary pass."

"What do you mean?"

"Come on, Liz." Rebecca took a sip of wine. "Even I can see your marriage has been on life support for years. Mark's not stupid—he must sense it too. A baby is the classic last-ditch effort to save a failing relationship."

The blunt assessment was pure Rebecca—no gentle lead-up, no softening the blow. Just cutting to the heart of the matter with surgical precision.

"We've had the theoretical someday-nursery for years," Liz said, gesturing vaguely upstairs. "But we've never seriously discussed timing."

"Why now, then?"

"He says we're not getting any younger." Liz traced the rim of her wine glass. "But the subtext was pretty clear—he thinks I've 'checked out' of the marriage."

"Have you?"

The directness of the question demanded equal honesty. "Maybe. Probably. But not for the reasons he thinks."

Rebecca studied her sister over the rim of her glass. "Which are?"

"He's convinced it's because of the Meridian project. Or more specifically, because of James."

"Ah." Rebecca's expression shifted to one of understanding. "The high school rival turned colleague. You've mentioned him a few times. More than a few, actually."

Liz felt heat rise to her cheeks. "It's a significant project with complex challenges."

"Mmm-hmm." Rebecca's skepticism was evident. "And James, he's just a colleague? Nothing more?"

The question hung in the air, weighted with implications Liz wasn't ready to fully examine. The kiss in the conference room flashed through her mind, along with their careful boundary-setting afterward.

"It's complicated," she admitted finally. "We have a connection that goes beyond professional collaboration. An intellectual chemistry I've never experienced with Mark."

"Intellectual chemistry," Rebecca repeated, her tone making it clear she suspected there was more to the story. "Is that what the kids are calling it these days?"

"I'm serious, Becks. It's not just physical attraction. It's the way he challenges my thinking, values my perspective, sees me as an intellectual equal." Liz set down her glass, frustrated by her inability to articulate the complex dynamic. "With Mark, I've spent years making myself smaller, dumbing down my interests, pretending to care about fantasy sports statistics while he's never once asked about the creative aspects of my work."

Rebecca nodded slowly. "I remember that from my marriage too. That gradual erasure of self. The parts Richard found inconvenient or uninteresting just.. . disappeared over time."

"Exactly." Liz felt a rush of relief at being understood. "It's not that Mark is a bad person. He's just... never been interested in the parts of me that matter most."

"And James is?"

"He sees me," Liz said simply. "The real me, not just the good little wife."

Rebecca studied her sister for a long moment. "Have you crossed any lines with him?"

The direct question deserved honesty, but Liz found herself hesitating. "There was a moment. During a project crisis. We... kissed. Once. It was a mistake."

"Was it?"

"Of course it was. I'm married."

"A marriage you just admitted isn't working," Rebecca pointed out. "Look, I'm not condoning affairs. But I am suggesting that your reaction to this James person might be a symptom, not the disease."

Liz considered this perspective. "What do you mean?"

"I mean that if your marriage was fulfilling, if Mark truly saw and appreciated you, would you be so affected by someone else's attention?" Rebecca reached for a croissant, breaking it in half. "Maybe your response to James isn't about him specifically, but about what he represents, recognition you've been starving for."

The insight struck uncomfortably close to Liz's own thoughts earlier. "So what do I do? Mark's right about one thing, I have been different since the project started. Since James came back into my life."

"The question isn't what you do about James," Rebecca said, handing half the croissant to Liz. "It's what you do about your marriage. Do you want to save it? Can it be saved? Is it worth saving?"

"I don't know," Liz admitted, the words barely audible. "Fifteen years is a long time to just walk away from."

"It's also a long time to be unhappy." Rebecca's voice softened. "And an even longer time to raise a child in a marriage held together by obligation rather than love."

The mention of children brought Liz back to the morning's argument. "When Mark suggested trying for a baby, my first reaction was absolute panic. Not excitement or even ambivalence, pure, visceral rejection."

"That seems pretty telling."

"It is, isn't it?" Liz stared into her wine glass. "I've been going through the motions for so long, I never stopped to ask myself if I actually wanted the life I was living. If I wanted children at all, or if that was just another box I was supposed to check."

"And now that you're asking?"

"I think I've known the answer for a while," Liz said quietly. "I never really wanted children. I accepted the idea because it was expected, because Mark assumed it would happen eventually. But whenever I try to imagine myself as a mother, it feels... wrong. Like trying on someone else's life."

Rebecca nodded, unsurprised. "I always suspected as much. You've never shown the interest in my kids that most women planning families do. You're a wonderful aunt, but I've never seen you look at them with envy or longing."

"Why didn't you say something?"

"Not my place," Rebecca shrugged. "Some realizations you have to come to on your own."

They sat in comfortable silence for a moment, the weight of the morning's revelations settling between them. Outside, a neighbor's lawn mower droned, the ordinary sound at odds with the life-altering conversation taking place in the kitchen.

"So what now?" Rebecca asked finally. "Mark wants a baby. You don't. That's not exactly a compromise situation."

"No, it's not." Liz took a deep breath, the path forward suddenly clearer than it had been in years. "I think I need to consider a trial separation."

The words hung in the air, both terrifying and liberating in their concreteness. Rebecca studied her sister carefully, searching for hesitation.

"Are you sure that's what you want? Not just a reaction to this morning's fight?"

"I'm sure it's what I need," Liz clarified. "Mark and I have been avoiding the truth for years. We've grown so far apart I'm not sure we even recognize each other anymore. Staying together out of habit or fear of change isn't fair to either of us."

Rebecca reached across the counter to squeeze her hand. "For what it's worth, I think you're right. And speaking from experience, as scary as it is to leave, it's nowhere near as soul-crushing as staying in a relationship that's stopped feeding your soul."

"What about James?" Liz asked, the question slipping out before she could stop it.

"What about him?" Rebecca's expression remained carefully neutral. "Are you asking my permission to pursue something there?"

"No. Maybe. I don't know." Liz shook her head in frustration. "We've agreed to maintain professional boundaries. The project is too important to both our careers to risk with romantic complications ."

"Smart," Rebecca nodded. "And completely unsustainable if the chemistry is as strong as you're implying."

"We can make it work," Liz insisted, though her conviction wavered. "We're adults with self-control and professional responsibilities."

"Sure," Rebecca's smile held gentle skepticism. "Just remember, whatever you decide about your marriage should be independent of James. Leave Mark because your relationship has run its course, not because someone new is waiting in the wings."

"I know." Liz toyed with a croissant crumb on the counter. "I just never imagined my life taking this turn. Fifteen years of marriage ending, career in flux, feelings I don't fully understand for someone I once considered my greatest rival."

"Life rarely follows the blueprints we draft for it," Rebecca said, reaching for the whiskey bottle. "Sometimes the most beautiful structures emerge from unexpected revisions."

The architectural metaphor wasn't lost on Liz. "Now you sound like James."

"I'll take that as a compliment, given how you light up when you mention him." Rebecca poured a small measure of whiskey into each of their glasses. "To clarity, even when it comes with complications."

They clinked glasses, the gesture sealing something significant. Liz felt a strange combination of grief and relief washing over her, grief for the years invested, the shared history, the genuine affection that had existed despite the fundamental mismatch. Relief at finally acknowledging what she had known subconsciously for years: she and Mark had been growing in different directions for so long that they now occupied entirely different landscapes.

"I should probably start figuring out logistics," Liz said, reality beginning to assert itself. "Where to stay, how to broach the subject with Mark when he returns..."

"One step at a time," Rebecca advised. "You can stay with me if needed. The guest room is small, but it's yours for as long as you want."

"Thank you." Liz felt tears threatening for the first time. "For everything. For seeing me clearly when I couldn't see myself."

"That's what sisters are for." Rebecca squeezed her hand again. "Now, let's make a plan. Practical steps always help in emotional chaos."

As they began discussing details, Liz felt a curious lightness despite the gravity of her decision. Something fundamental had shifted, not just in her understanding of her marriage, but in her vision of herself and what she wanted from life.

Later, after Rebecca left with promises to prepare the guest room, Liz found herself drawn to the room at the end of the upstairs hallway. She hesitated at the door, hand on the knob, before pushing it open.

The "someday nursery" was a study in neutral expectation, cream walls, a bookshelf filled with classic children's literature, a rocking chair positioned by the window. The room had been prepared years ago, during a home renovation when Mark had insisted they designate the space for its eventual purpose.

Liz stood in the doorway, studying the carefully curated emptiness. The room contained no actual baby items, no crib, no changing table, nothing that would make the theoretical future too concrete. Just the shell of a possibility they had maintained without ever fully committing to it.

How had she never recognized the symbolism? A room prepared but never completed. A future discussed but never embraced. A marriage that existed in form but had gradually emptied of substance.

She moved to the window, looking out at the perfectly maintained backyard where no children had ever played. The garden beds she'd designed for visual appeal rather than hardiness against little hands. The patio furniture arranged for adult conversation rather than family gatherings.

Their entire home suddenly revealed itself as a stage set, a convincing facade of domestic perfection that had never quite translated into lived reality. She had been performing the role of wife without inhabiting it fully, going through motions that looked right from the outside while feeling increasingly hollow within.

The realization brought not sadness but clarity. She didn't want this life, had never truly wanted it. Not the carefully neutral nursery, not the showcase house in the suburbs, not the marriage that existed more out of habit than passion.

What she wanted was purpose. Challenge. Connection that engaged her mind as much as her heart. The freedom to discover who she might become when not defined primarily as Mark's wife or a potential mother.

As Liz closed the door on the empty nursery, she recognized she was also closing the door on a version of herself that had never quite fit, a self constructed from external expectations rather than authentic desire. Whatever came next, with her marriage, with her career, with James or without him, would be built on a foundation of honesty about who she truly was and what she actually wanted.

For the first time in years, that prospect felt not frightening but exhilarating, a design challenge more compelling than any project, with herself as both architect and client.

CHAPTER TWENTY-FOUR

"Seismic Activity"

The Meridian Hotel stood thirty-eight stories above the city, its sleek glass exterior reflecting clouds and sky like a vertical mirror. Inside, the modernist lobby bustled with business travelers and tourists, their voices creating a constant hum beneath soaring ceilings. Liz checked her watch as she crossed the polished marble floor toward the elevators. She was early for the 7:00 PM meeting with James to review their findings from today's site visits, a deliberate choice to ensure she'd be settled and composed when he arrived.

The business trip to Westridge had been Howard's idea, sending his marketing liaison and architect to study a similar corporate headquarters project that had successfully integrated sustainability features with brand narrative. "Bring back concrete ideas we can implement," he'd instructed before approving the overnight stay.

The elevator whisked her to the fourteenth floor where the hotel had arranged a small conference room for their evening work session. Liz arranged her materials with methodical precision, site photos, competitor analysis notes, sustainability metrics, creating a professional buffer against the awareness that had hummed between them all day.

Since their coffee shop meeting and establishment of careful boundaries, they'd maintained scrupulous professionalism. Today had been no different, visiting three architectural sites, taking separate notes, discussing technical details with appropriate distance. If their gazes occasionally held a moment too long, if they were hyperaware of accidental proximity in crowded spaces, neither acknowledged it.

The conference room door opened precisely at seven. James entered with his leather portfolio tucked under one arm, his expression carefully neutral.

"Sorry if I kept you waiting," he said, though they both knew he was exactly on time.

"Just got here myself," Liz replied, the small lie creating comfortable space between them. "I've organized the site documentation by implementation phase."

They settled into work with practiced efficiency, reviewing the day's findings and comparing observations. The Westridge headquarters had indeed offered valuable insights, particularly their innovative approach to environmental graphics integrated with architectural elements.

"The material transition narrative was more sophisticated than I expected," James noted, spreading photographs across the table. "See how they've incorporated historical timeline elements into the actual structural components? That's similar to what we've been developing for Meridian."

"The execution wasn't as elegant as your design," Liz countered, pointing to a particular junction. "Their narrative flow breaks here, creating a disjointed visitor experience. Your approach maintains continuity through these transition points."

James looked up, surprise flickering across his features. "That's generous coming from you."

"It's accurate," Liz said simply. "Your design is superior."

A small smile touched his lips before he redirected to safer ground. "The solar integration was worth studying, though. Their roof design captures 30% more energy than conventional panels."

They continued working through their observations, the conversation flowing with professional ease.

Outside the windows, darkness gradually claimed the city, lights blinking on in surrounding buildings like stars appearing in an urban sky. Neither mentioned the time as they moved from technical specifications to implementation strategies to budget implications.

By nine-thirty, they had compiled a comprehensive report for Howard. Liz stretched subtly, her shoulders tight from hours hunched over the table.

"I think we've covered everything," she said, gathering her notes into a neat stack. "The Westridge approach validates many of our design decisions while highlighting areas we can refine."

James nodded, closing his portfolio. "We should have the final recommendations ready for Howard by Monday."

An awkward silence fell as they realized the professional pretext for their meeting had concluded. The evening stretched before them, separate hotel rooms on the same floor, a city neither knew well, the weight of boundaries they'd established hanging between them.

"It's earlier than I expected," James said finally. "Would you like to continue this discussion over dinner? The hotel restaurant is supposed to be excellent."

The invitation was carefully phrased, professional, appropriate, nothing that crossed their established lines. Yet Liz felt the dangerous potential humming beneath the surface.

"The restaurant kitchen closes at ten," she replied, checking her watch. "We might not make it."

"The bar on the top floor serves food until midnight," James suggested. "Altitude, I think it's called. And the view is supposedly spectacular."

Another moment where professional courtesy battled with self-preservation. Dinner in a public space to discuss project findings, completely appropriate. Yet something in his eyes suggested they both recognized the risk of extending their time together.

"That sounds reasonable," Liz heard herself say. "We should document the sustainability applications while they're fresh in our minds."

The elevator carried them to the top floor in silence, the small space amplifying their awareness of each other. Altitude occupied the entire top level, its glass walls offering panoramic views of the city lights spread below like a circuit board of illumination. A pianist played something low and jazzy in the corner, the music floating above the murmur of conversations.

They were seated at a corner table beside floor-to-ceiling windows, the spectacular view creating an immediate topic of safe conversation.

"The architectural integration with the landscape is impressive," James observed, gesturing toward the cityscape. "The building follows the natural topography rather than imposing upon it."

"Is that your approach to all design?" Liz asked, genuinely curious. "Working with existing conditions rather than overriding them?"

"The best architecture responds to context," he replied, his expression thoughtful. "Whether that's physical landscape, cultural environment, or historical framework. Ignoring what exists creates buildings that feel alien to their surroundings."

A server appeared with menus and took their drink orders—a gin and tonic for James, a glass of cabernet for Liz. The interruption reset their conversation to safer professional territory as they discussed implementation timelines for the Meridian atrium.

Their drinks arrived, followed by orders for small plates to share. The alcohol loosened the careful distance they'd maintained all day, conversation gradually shifting from project specifics to broader architectural philosophy to personal reflections on creative process.

"The most challenging aspect of design isn't technical," James said, gesturing with his second drink. "It's communicating vision to people who can't see what doesn't yet exist. Making them trust the blueprint represents something worth building."

"That's not so different from marketing," Liz replied, swirling the remains of her wine. "We're selling possibilities, potential futures. The product is just the physical manifestation of that promise."

James studied her across the table, the city lights reflected in his eyes. "You would have made an exceptional architect."

"And you would have been a formidable literary critic," she countered with a small smile. "Your analysis of structural narrative in built environments isn't so different from textual interpretation."

"The roads not taken," he murmured, raising his glass slightly. "To parallel lives we might have lived."

The toast carried them into dangerous territory—acknowledging the divergent paths that had followed their academic rivalry. Liz took a sip of wine, buying time before responding.

"Do you ever regret it?" she asked. "The architecture path?"

"Never," James replied without hesitation. "It's my purpose, not just my profession. But I do occasionally wonder about the literature path—who I might have become with that focus."

"I wonder about the academic path," Liz admitted. "What my life would look like if I'd pursued literary theory instead of corporate marketing."

"Why didn't you?" The direct question carried no judgment, only genuine curiosity.

Liz considered deflecting but found herself answering honestly. "Many reasons. Practical concerns about career stability. My parents' subtle pressure toward 'real world' application of my education. And then meeting Mark, who was so certain about his future that I started adjusting mine to align with his vision."

"And now?"

"Now I realize I've spent fifteen years becoming someone I'm not entirely sure I recognize." The admission emerged before she could filter it, the combination of wine and James's attentive presence loosening her usual restraint.

He nodded slowly. "My divorce taught me something similar. I'd constructed an identity partially built around Vanessa's expectations. When that collapsed, I had to rediscover which parts were authentically me and which were performance."

"Was it terrifying?" Liz asked, thinking of her growing certainty about her own marriage's inevitable end.

"Terrifying and liberating simultaneously." James signaled for another round of drinks. "There's profound freedom in acknowledging when something isn't working, even when that acknowledgment carries pain."

Their fresh drinks arrived, the alcohol creating a warm glow that softened the edges of professional caution. The bar had gradually emptied, leaving their corner increasingly private. Outside the windows, the city sparkled below them, a constellation of lights mapping human activity in the darkness.

"Do you ever wonder what would have happened if I hadn't won that scholarship?" James asked suddenly, his voice dropping to a more intimate register.

The question struck at the heart of their shared history—the pivotal moment when their paths had diverged. Liz felt the weight of twenty years of what-ifs compressed into those few words.

"I've measured every achievement against you for fifteen years," she admitted, the truth slipping out before she could reconsider. "Not consciously, not constantly, but that moment—losing to you by decimal points—became a reference point for everything that followed."

James's expression shifted to surprise, then understanding. "I didn't know."

"How could you? We didn't speak after graduation."

"I looked for you at Northwestern once," he confessed. "During my second year at Rice. I was in Chicago for a student architecture conference and took the train to Evanston."

"You did?" Liz set down her glass, genuinely startled. "Why?"

"To apologize, I think. Or to explain." He shook his head slightly. "I'd had this revelation that our competition had been the most intellectually stimulating experience of my life. That no one at Rice challenged me the way you had at Preston."

"What happened?"

"I couldn't find you. The English department said you'd switched your focus to marketing. I left a note with your advisor, but I guess you never got it."

Liz stared at him, recalibrating their history with this new information. "I never knew."

"Would it have mattered?" James asked, his eyes holding hers across the table.

"I don't know," she answered honestly. "I was already dating Mark by then. Already shifting toward the life I thought I was supposed to want."

"The safe path," James observed, the comment carrying no judgment but striking a nerve nonetheless.

"Is that how you see it?" Liz felt a flare of defensiveness. "My life as the safe choice?"

"I see someone who compromised her intellectual passions for practical stability," he replied, his directness amplified by alcohol. "Someone who calibrated her ambitions to match her husband's limited vision."

"That's unfair," Liz countered, heat rising to her cheeks. "You don't know what my marriage is like."

"I know you light up discussing architectural theory but go quiet when your husband calls. I know you work late rather than rush home. I know you've never once mentioned him with the animation you show discussing your work."

The accuracy of his assessment felt like a physical blow. "And you're so emotionally available? You, who buries yourself in work and maintains such careful distance from everyone?"

"I never claimed to be a model of psychological health," James replied with unexpected candor. "My divorce left me wary of entanglements. I protect myself through professional focus."

"At least you're honest about your emotional unavailability," Liz said, the alcohol fueling her directness. "You hide behind architectural brilliance and arrogant certainty."

"While you hide behind perfect professionalism and a marriage that's clearly failing." The words hung between them, too honest to retract.

Liz stared at him, anger and recognition warring within her. "We shouldn't be having this conversation."

"Probably not," James agreed, though he made no move to end it. "But it may be the most honest exchange either of us has had in months."

The truth of his statement deflated her anger. They sat in charged silence, the pianist's music filling the space between them as they regarded each other across the small table.

"I apologize," James said finally. "I have no right to comment on your marriage."

"No, you don't," Liz agreed. "But you're not entirely wrong, either."

Another silence, this one weighted with mutual recognition. The server appeared to ask about dessert, breaking the tension momentarily. Both declined, though neither suggested ending the evening.

"It's getting late," James observed, though he remained seated. "We should probably call it a night."

"Probably," Liz agreed, making no move to leave.

The check arrived. James insisted on paying despite Liz's protest that they should split it as a business expense. "Consider it an apology for overstepping," he said, his signature decisive on the bill.

They rode the elevator in silence, the small space charged with awareness after their unusually candid exchange. When they reached their floor, they walked the long hallway toward their rooms, footsteps muffled by thick carpet.

Liz's room came first. She stopped outside her door, key card in hand, suddenly uncertain how to conclude the evening after such uncharacteristic honesty.

"Thank you for dinner," she said finally, the formality absurd after their intimate conversation.

"Thank you for your insights today," James replied, equally formal. "The report for Howard will be stronger for our combined perspectives."

They stood facing each other in the quiet hallway, professional pretense wearing increasingly thin. James took a step back, creating deliberate distance.

"Goodnight, Elizabeth."

"Goodnight, James."

She slipped her key card into the lock, the green light flashing as the mechanism released. As she pushed the door open, James spoke again, his voice lower than before.

"For what it's worth, I think you're extraordinary. Not despite your choices, but because of how you've navigated them while maintaining your intellectual integrity. I've never met anyone who challenges me the way you do."

Before she could respond, he turned and continued down the hallway toward his own room. Liz entered her room and closed the door, leaning against it as his words echoed in her mind. No one had spoken to her that way in years, acknowledging her intellect, recognizing her compromises without judgment, seeing her complexity rather than just her function.

The hotel room felt suddenly claustrophobic despite its generous proportions. She moved to the window, gazing out at the unfamiliar city below. The conversation in the bar had shifted something fundamental between them, breaking through carefully constructed professional boundaries to something more honest, more dangerous.

A knock at the door startled her from these thoughts. She knew who it was before opening it.

James stood in the hallway, his expression a complex mixture of determination and uncertainty. "I shouldn't be here."

"No, you shouldn't," Liz agreed, yet found herself stepping back, creating space for him to enter.

He remained in the doorway, tension evident in every line of his body. "We established boundaries for good reasons. The project, our careers, your marriage—"

"I know." She met his gaze directly. "All valid reasons to say goodnight and mean it."

"Then why am I still standing here?"

"For the same reason I haven't closed the door."

The admission hung between them, acknowledgment of what had been building since their first contentious meeting months ago. James took a single step forward, crossing the threshold but stopping just inside the room.

"If I stay," he said quietly, "we can't pretend it's a momentary lapse or project stress or alcohol. It would be a deliberate choice."

"I know." Liz closed the door behind him, the soft click sealing them into private space. "I'm tired of pretending."

"Pretending what?"

"That I don't think about you constantly. That our connection is purely professional. That my marriage isn't already over in every way that matters."

The honesty stripped away the last pretense between them. James moved toward her with deliberate intent, stopping just short of touching her.

"I've wanted to kiss you again since that moment in the conference room," he admitted. "Even knowing all the reasons I shouldn't."

"Then stop thinking about why you shouldn't," Liz whispered, closing the remaining distance between them.

Their lips met with none of the hesitation of their first kiss—this was decisive, certain, a choice made with full awareness of its implications. James's hands framed her face with the same precision he showed in his architectural drawings, as if mapping territory he intended to know thoroughly.

Liz responded with a hunger that surprised her, fingers threading through his hair, body pressing against his with urgent need. The intellectual tension that had characterized their relationship from the beginning transformed into physical chemistry that felt both shocking and inevitable.

They moved deeper into the room, neither willing to break contact. James's jacket fell to the floor, followed by Liz's blazer. Each layer removed felt like shedding pretense, revealing truth beneath professional facades.

"Are you certain?" James asked as they paused beside the bed, his voice rough with desire but eyes searching hers for confirmation.

"More certain than I've been about anything in years," Liz replied, reaching for the buttons of his shirt with steady hands.

What followed was nothing like her dream in the office, nothing like her mechanical encounters with Mark, nothing like she could have imagined. James approached her body with the same focused attention he gave to his designs—learning her responses, discovering what made her gasp, building sensations with architectural precision.

"You're so beautiful," he murmured against her skin, the words carrying weight beyond physical appreciation. "Your mind, your spirit, everything about you."

Liz felt herself responding with abandoned freedom she'd forgotten was possible. With Mark, sex had become performative, going through expected motions while her mind drifted elsewhere. With James, she found herself intensely present, every nerve ending alive to his touch, every moment demanding her complete attention.

Where Mark rushed toward completion with predictable efficiency, James took his time, exploring, discovering, building pleasure with deliberate patience. His hands moved over her body with careful precision, filled with a desire she hadn't experienced in years, finding sensitive places she hadn't known existed, creating responses she'd forgotten were possible.

"I've imagined this," he admitted between kisses that traveled down her body. "Not just physically. Being with someone who truly sees me. Who challenges me. Who keeps pace with my thinking."

The words resonated deeply, articulating what made their connection so powerful. It wasn't just physical attraction but recognition, two minds finding rare compatibility, two people seeing each other with unusual clarity.

When they finally came together, Liz felt a sense of rightness that transcended physical pleasure. James watched her face with unwavering focus as they moved together, his blue eyes reflecting moonlight from the window and something deeper, more complex than mere desire.

"Elizabeth," he whispered, her full name on his lips an intimacy more profound than their physical connection.

The pleasure built, each sensation supporting the next, creating a structure of experience that rose toward an inevitable conclusion. When it crested, Liz cried out, the sound muffled against his shoulder as waves of sensation washed through her.

Afterward, they lay in charged silence, the magnitude of what had happened settling over them. James traced patterns on her skin with gentle fingers, his expression thoughtful in the dim light.

"That wasn't just..." he began, searching for words.

"I know," Liz finished for him. "It wasn't just physical."

"No." His hand stilled on her shoulder. "It was recognition."

The simple assessment captured what had made the experience so profound. Not just bodies finding pleasure, but souls recognizing a compatible frequency, an intellectual and emotional resonance as powerful as the physical connection.

"What happens now?" Liz asked, the question encompassing far more than the immediate aftermath.

"I don't know," James admitted, his honesty refreshing after years of Mark's facile assurances. "I know what should happen, we should maintain professional boundaries, complete the project, make rational decisions. But I'm not sure I can pretend this didn't change everything."

"It didn't change everything," Liz corrected gently. "It just revealed what was already changing. My marriage has been failing for years. This, you, just made it impossible to keep ignoring that reality."

James brushed hair from her face with tender affection. "I don't want to be the reason your marriage ends."

"You're not. You're the catalyst that made me finally acknowledge what I've known for a long time." She traced the line of his jaw with her fingertips. "But that doesn't make this any less complicated."

"No," he agreed. "The project, our professional reputations, the timing, everything argues against this making sense."

"Yet here we are."

"Here we are," he echoed, pulling her closer against him.

They talked for hours, bodies entwined as conversation moved from professional complications to personal histories to possible futures neither was ready to fully articulate. The intellectual connection that had drawn them together from the beginning deepened through honest exchange, creating intimacy beyond the physical.

As dawn lightened the sky outside the hotel windows, James finally disentangled himself from Liz's embrace. "I should go back to my room. We have the final site visit this morning."

She nodded, though her expression revealed reluctance. "The professional world awaits."

He gathered his clothes, dressing with deliberate movements while Liz watched from the bed. The night's intimacy made the simple act of buttoning his shirt feel strangely vulnerable.

"I don't regret this," she said, needing to articulate the certainty amid all the complications.

"Neither do I," James replied. "Though I suspect we'll both have moments of panic about the implications."

"Undoubtedly." Liz smiled slightly as she slipped out from the sheets. "But right now, I just feel... awake. More myself than I have in years."

James pulled on boxers before crossing to where she stood. He cupped her face in his hands, studying her with an intensity that made her breath catch.

"Whatever happens next," he said quietly, "know that this wasn't casual for me. You...weren't casual for me."

"I know." She leaned into his touch. "For me either."

Their final kiss held tenderness rather than urgency—acknowledgment of something significant rather than mere physical desire. Then Liz stepped back, creating necessary distance.

"See you at breakfast," she said, the mundane words carrying new weight. "Professional faces firmly in place."

"Of course," James agreed. "Though I can't promise I won't remember you exactly as you were an hour ago."

The comment brought heat to her cheeks despite their intimacy. James moved to the door, pausing with his hand on the knob as Liz called out. "James?"

"Yes?"

"Thank you for seeing me. The real me, not just the role I've been playing."

His smile transformed his features, softening the usual intensity. "Thank you for the same gift in return."

The hallway was empty as James made his way back to his room, the early morning quiet broken only by distant sounds of the hotel awakening.

Inside her own room, Liz moved directly to the shower, letting hot water sluice over her body as if it might wash away the complexity of what had just happened.

But the water couldn't erase the memory of James's touch, the things he'd whispered against her skin, the way he'd looked at her with complete recognition. Nor could it diminish the certainty that had crystallized during their night together, her marriage was over, had been over long before James Calloway reappeared in her life.

The realization brought not guilt but clarity. Whatever happened with James, whether this night was an isolated moment or the beginning of something more substantial, she could no longer pretend her marriage had a future. The contrast between mechanical routine with Mark and profound connection with James had illuminated the emptiness she'd been trying to ignore.

As Liz dressed for the day ahead, she studied her reflection in the bathroom mirror. She looked different somehow, more vivid, more present, her eyes brighter despite the lack of sleep. The woman who gazed back at her wasn't the carefully controlled marketing director or the dutiful wife, but someone more authentic, the Elizabeth Mitchell who had once challenged James Calloway thought for thought, the woman who had temporarily disappeared beneath years of compromise and accommodation.

In a few hours, they would return to their professional roles, the architect and marketing liaison collaborating on Meridian's headquarters. They would maintain appropriate distance, discuss technical specifications, present united findings to Howard. The night's intimacy would be carefully concealed beneath professional facades.

But something fundamental had shifted, not just in their relationship but in Liz's understanding of herself and what she wanted from life. Like a seismic event that permanently alters the landscape, their night together had created fault lines that couldn't be repaired, revealing structural weaknesses in her marriage that had existed long before the tremors began.

The only question now was whether she had the courage to build something new on ground that had been so thoroughly shaken.

CHAPTER TWENTY-FIVE

"Aftershocks"

T he plane shuddered through mild turbulence as Liz stared at the safety card in the seat pocket, pretending to read its illustrated instructions. In reality, her mind replayed scenes from the previous night in an endless loop, James's hands on her skin, his voice murmuring her name, the way he'd looked at her with complete recognition that had nothing to do with physical pleasure and everything to do with seeing her, truly seeing her, perhaps for the first time in her adult life.

Three rows ahead, James sat reviewing architectural documents, his dark head occasionally visible when he shifted position. They'd arrived at the airport separately that morning, exchanged professional nods in the departure lounge, and boarded with deliberate distance between them. Now, suspended thirty thousand feet above the earth, the physical space seemed necessary yet insufficient protection against the gravity of what had happened.

"More coffee, ma'am?" The flight attendant's voice startled her.

"No, thank you." Liz managed a polite smile, though her hands trembled slightly as she straightened her tray table.

The cabin felt simultaneously too warm and too cold. She'd chosen clothing with careful precision that morning, a high-necked blouse that concealed the mark James had left on her collarbone, a structured blazer that created professional armor. Yet beneath these protective layers, her skin still hummed with the memory of his touch.

What had she done? The question circled like the plane in a holding pattern. The technical answer was simple: she'd slept with a colleague while still married. But the emotional reality was far more complex. Last night hadn't been a mere physical indiscretion. It had been a seismic event, revealing fault lines in her marriage that began long ago.

The pilot announced their initial descent. Liz watched James gather his materials, his movements precise and controlled. Not once did he glance back toward her seat, maintaining the professional fiction they'd silently agreed upon that morning. At the hotel, they'd barely spoken as he'd slipped from her room at dawn, both understanding the necessary compartmentalization required to face the day ahead.

When the plane touched down, Liz remained seated while other passengers retrieved luggage, creating deliberate delay. James deplaned quickly, his tall figure disappearing up the jetway without a backward glance. The choreographed avoidance should have felt reassuring, evidence they could maintain professional boundaries despite what had happened. Instead, it created a hollow ache beneath her ribs.

In the terminal, they moved through separate security lines, nodded brief acknowledgments when paths unavoidably crossed, and headed to different parking areas. The careful dance might have appeared natural to observers, but Liz felt every calculated step like a physical strain.

Her car provided the first true privacy since leaving the hotel. Liz sat motionless behind the wheel, hands gripping the leather with unnecessary force. The professional mask she'd maintained for hours cracked, allowing suppressed emotions to surface. Not regret exactly, she couldn't bring herself to regret something that had felt so profoundly right, but a complicated tangle of guilt, exhilaration, confusion, and clarity that defied simple categorization.

The drive home stretched before her like a countdown to confrontation, though Mark wouldn't know what had happened. He wouldn't see the invisible transformation that had occurred, wouldn't recognize that his wife had returned fundamentally altered from who she'd been two days ago.

Traffic moved sluggishly through afternoon congestion, giving Liz unwanted time to rehearse various scenarios. Should she maintain normalcy? Initiate the conversation about separation she'd been contemplating since her talk with Rebecca? Confess what had happened with James?

The last option created immediate resistance. Whatever happened with her marriage needed to be about the fundamental disconnect between her and Mark, not about James. Using the affair as catalyst or justification would only obscure the deeper truth, that she and Mark had been growing apart for years, becoming strangers who shared an address but little else.

As she turned onto their suburban street, Liz felt the familiar constriction in her chest that had become associated with coming home. The perfectly maintained colonial with its manicured lawn had once represented achievement, tangible evidence of their success. Now it felt like an elaborate stage set where she performed a role that no longer fit.

Mark's car sat in the driveway, unexpected at this hour. Liz checked her watch, only four-thirty. He rarely returned before six, often later. The anomaly created immediate tension as she pulled alongside his vehicle.

She gathered her overnight bag and briefcase, taking a moment to compose herself before entering. The house smelled of pizza, not homemade but delivery from the chain Mark preferred. She found him in the living room, feet propped on the coffee table, beer in hand, watching basketball highlights.

"You're home early," she observed, setting down her bags.

Mark looked up, his expression neutral. "Meeting got canceled. Figured I'd beat traffic." He gestured toward the kitchen. "Got pizza if you're hungry."

The casual normality of the scene created cognitive dissonance against the emotional upheaval of the past twenty-four hours. Liz felt like she'd stepped into a parallel universe where nothing had changed, where she hadn't experienced a profound connection with James, where her marriage wasn't crumbling beneath the weight of accumulated disconnection.

"How was the trip?" Mark asked, attention already drifting back to the television. "See any cool buildings?"

The reductive question exemplified everything wrong with their communication. Her complex professional experience distilled to "cool buildings," asked without genuine interest in her answer.

"It was productive," she replied, the understatement almost making her laugh. "We visited three sites with innovative sustainability features that we might incorporate into the Meridian design."

"That's nice." Mark took another swig of beer. "The Hornets traded Mitchell. Terrible decision—he was their best shooter."

The conversational whiplash was so familiar Liz almost found it comforting. This was their pattern—her attempting meaningful exchange, Mark redirecting to sports, both pretending this constituted actual communication.

"I'm going to unpack," she said, gathering her bags again.

Mark nodded absently, already absorbed in player statistics scrolling across the screen.

Upstairs, Liz closed the bedroom door and leaned against it, exhaling slowly. The room looked exactly as she'd left it—bed neatly made, her nightstand organized, Mark's side cluttered with sports magazines and empty water glasses. Yet it felt like a museum exhibit of someone else's life—recognizable but no longer relevant to who she'd become.

She unpacked methodically, sorting clothes for laundry, arranging toiletries in their designated places. The routine actions created illusion of normalcy while her mind continued processing the previous night.

James had touched her with such focused attention, as if mapping territory he intended to know thoroughly. His hands had moved with architect's precision, learning her responses, building sensations with deliberate patience. Where Mark rushed toward completion with predictable efficiency, James had taken his time, exploring, discovering, creating pleasure that built like a well-designed structure, each element supporting the next.

The comparison was both unfair and unavoidable. It wasn't just the physical differences but the profound contrast in connection. With Mark, sex had become performative, going through expected motions while her mind drifted elsewhere. With James, she'd been intensely present, every nerve ending alive to his touch, every moment demanding complete attention.

"Hey." Mark appeared in the doorway, another beer in hand. "Want to watch the game tonight? Lakers versus Bulls. Should be good."

Liz looked up from folding laundry, the mundane question highlighting the chasm between them. Did he really not sense the shift in her? Could he not feel the earthquake that had occurred?

"I have some work to finish," she replied. "The Westridge findings need to be compiled before tomorrow's meeting."

"Always working." Mark shook his head with familiar disapproval. "That building is taking over your life."

The irony wasn't lost on her—how accurately he identified the project's importance while completely missing its true significance. The Meridian headquarters had become more than a professional assignment; it represented her intellectual reawakening, her creative fulfillment, her recognition that she deserved more than the comfortable mediocrity her marriage had become.

"It's an important project," she said simply.

Mark studied her for a moment longer than usual, his expression shifting subtly. "You look different."

The observation sent a jolt of panic through her system. Could he somehow see evidence of James on her skin? Did guilt manifest in visible symptoms?

"Probably just tired from the trip," she managed, turning back to the laundry.

"No, it's something else." His eyes narrowed slightly. "You seem... I don't know. Different."

For a heartbeat, Liz thought he might actually see her—truly see the woman she'd become rather than the dutiful wife she been portraying. But his next words shattered that illusion.

"You should take some vitamins or something. You're working too hard."

The moment passed, his perception skimming the surface without penetrating to deeper truth. Liz felt simultaneous relief and disappointment—relief that her secret remained undiscovered, disappointment that her transformation was invisible to the man who should know her best.

"I'll think about it," she said, the noncommittal response satisfying him enough to retreat downstairs.

Alone again, Liz moved to the bathroom, studying her reflection in the mirror. Did she look different? The woman who gazed back had the same features as always, hazel eyes, chestnut hair, the small freckle near her left eyebrow. Yet something had shifted in her expression, a certain intensity or awareness that hadn't been there before.

James had awakened something she'd forgotten existed, not just physical desire but intellectual passion, creative energy, the exhilaration of being fully seen and valued. The contrast with her marriage created clarity that couldn't be undone.

She showered, water beading over skin that still carried the memory of James's touch. Despite the heat, she couldn't wash away the fundamental shift that had occurred, the recognition that she deserved more than what her marriage had become.

Downstairs, Mark had settled into his evening routine, pizza box open on the coffee table, basketball game at volume that precluded conversation, phone in hand for checking fantasy sports statistics during commercial breaks. The scene was so familiar it felt like watching a rerun of a show she'd seen too many times.

"I'll be in my office," she said, though she doubted he heard over the announcer's excited commentary.

In her sanctuary, Liz opened her laptop, intending to compile the Westridge findings as promised. Instead, she found herself staring at a blank document, mind returning repeatedly to the hotel room, to James's voice murmuring against her skin, to the way he'd looked at her afterward, not with guilt or triumph but with wonder, as if discovering something precious and unexpected.

The physical encounter had been profound, but the conversation that followed had transformed it from mere affair to something more significant. They'd talked for hours, bodies entwined as discussion moved from professional complications to personal histories to possible futures neither were entirely sure of.

"I've never experienced this kind of connection," James had admitted in the pre-dawn darkness. "The intellectual challenge matched with physical chemistry. It's like finding a missing piece I didn't know was absent."

The sentiment had resonated deeply, articulating what made their relationship so powerful. It wasn't just attraction but recognition, two minds finding rare compatibility, two people seeing each other with unusual clarity.

Her phone chimed with a text notification, startling her from remembrance. Her heart leapt, expecting James, but it was Derek: *How was Westridge? Bringing coffee tomorrow for full report.*

The mundane professional check-in created unexpected guilt. How would she face her colleagues tomorrow? Could they somehow sense what had happened? Would Catherine's perceptive gaze identify the shift that Mark had noticed but misinterpreted?

Liz forced herself to open the site documentation, focusing on architectural specifications and sustainability metrics. The professional task gradually absorbed her attention, providing temporary escape from emotional complexity. She worked steadily for hours, compiling findings and preparing recommendations as if nothing had changed.

When she finally emerged from her office, the house had fallen silent. Mark had apparently gone to bed without interrupting her work—another symptom of their disconnection. Once, he would have checked on her, brought her tea, tried to coax her away from late-night projects. Now they orbited separate planets, their gravitational fields no longer strong enough to affect each other's trajectories.

In their bedroom, Mark was already asleep, sprawled across two-thirds of the mattress. Liz changed quietly in the bathroom, the routine motions feeling increasingly performative. She slipped into bed, maintaining careful distance from his sleeping form.

The contrast between lying beside Mark and the intimacy she'd shared with James created physical discomfort. Not just the obvious comparison between lovers, but the profound difference in connection. With James, she'd felt truly seen—her mind valued as much as her body, her thoughts as welcome as her touch. With Mark, she'd become furniture—present but unnoticed, useful but unremarkable.

Sleep refused to come despite her exhaustion. The ceiling crack had grown since she'd last studied it, the hairline fracture extending further across the smooth surface. Like her marriage, the damage had been developing gradually, imperceptibly, until suddenly it couldn't be ignored.

Mark's breathing maintained its steady rhythm, untroubled by the seismic shifts occurring inches away. How had they reached this point? When had they stopped seeing each other, stopped caring about each other's inner lives, stopped being partners rather than roommates?

The questions had no simple answers. Their disconnection hadn't happened in a single moment but through a thousand small surrenders, a gradual erosion of intimacy and understanding until they merely occupied the same space without truly sharing it.

Her phone glowed softly on the nightstand, tempting her with potential connection to the one person who would understand her current turmoil. Would James be lying awake too? Processing the implications of what had happened between them? Questioning professional boundaries and personal ethics?

The desire to reach out was nearly overwhelming. Not for arrangements or assignations, but for acknowledgment that something profound had occurred, something that couldn't be dismissed as momentary weakness or project stress or alcohol-induced poor judgment.

Liz slipped from bed, taking her phone to the bathroom where soft light wouldn't disturb Mark's sleep. She stared at the blank message screen, fingers hovering over the keyboard. What could she possibly say that would capture the complexity of her feelings without creating professional complications or personal expectations?

After several false starts, she typed a single word: *Regrets?*

The question encompassed everything she needed to know, whether he viewed their night as mistake or revelation, whether professional concerns outweighed personal connection, whether the earthquake they'd experienced had altered his landscape as profoundly as it had changed hers.

Her thumb hovered over the send button, the simple action weighted with implications. Sending the message would acknowledge that something significant had happened, something that transcended professional collaboration. It would open communication channels that proper boundaries would keep firmly closed.

Mark's snoring continued from the bedroom, the familiar sound suddenly unbearable in its representation of all she'd settled for. The contrast between mechanical routine with him and profound connection with James had illuminated the emptiness she'd been trying to ignore.

Liz pressed send, watching the message bubble transform from blue to delivered. No immediate response appeared, no typing indicator. Just silence that might represent sleep, consideration, or deliberate distance.

She returned to bed, placing the phone face-down on her nightstand. Whatever James's answer, if he answered at all, wouldn't change the fundamental truth she'd been avoiding: her marriage had reached its natural conclusion long before James Calloway reappeared in her life.

The realization brought strange comfort as she finally drifted toward sleep. The aftershocks of their encounter would continue reverberating through her personal and professional landscape, but the initial quake had merely revealed structural weaknesses that had existed all along.

Her last conscious thought wasn't of James or Mark or the uncertain future ahead, but of the liberating power of honesty, with others and, more importantly, with herself.

CHAPTER TWENTY-SIX

"Blueprints and Boundaries"

T he glass walls of Calloway Design Group's studio caught the morning light, transforming the space into a kaleidoscope of architectural shadows. Liz stepped off the elevator, her heart hammering against her ribs despite the carefully composed expression she'd practiced in her car mirror. Three days had passed since their night at the Meridian Hotel, three days of avoiding direct contact, communicating only through necessary emails about the project, three days of waiting for James's response to her single-word text: *Regrets?*

His reply had arrived yesterday morning: *We need to discuss. My office, 9am tomorrow. Design review as cover.*

Now she navigated between drafting tables where architects bent over drawings or stared at computer screens, nodding professionally to those who looked up. The normalcy of the scene felt surreal against the storm of emotions she'd been battling since returning from their business trip.

James's office door stood open. He sat at his desk, reviewing drawings with Thomas, his expression neutral and professional, betraying nothing of what had transpired between them. He looked up as she approached, his eyes meeting hers for a fraction of a second before shifting back to the documents.

"Elizabeth. Right on time." His voice carried none of the intimacy she'd heard in the hotel room. "Thomas and I were just finalizing the structural modifications for the atrium connection."

Thomas glanced between them, his perceptive eyes narrowing slightly. "The stress distribution calculations look promising. The articulated joint should maintain visual lightness while addressing the thermal expansion concerns."

Liz set her portfolio on the conference table, grateful for the technical discussion that required no emotional engagement. "Howard was pleased with our solution.

The board has approved the additional expense for the specialized materials."

"Excellent." James gathered the drawings, handing them to Thomas. "Can you review these with the engineering team? I need to discuss the narrative integration with Elizabeth."

Thomas hesitated, his gaze moving between them again with unmistakable awareness. "Of course. I'll be in the main studio if you need anything... specific."

The emphasis on his final word wasn't subtle. As he left, Thomas closed the glass door behind him, an unusual action in the typically open office environment. The soft click of the latch felt deafening in the sudden silence.

James remained standing, maintaining the width of his desk between them. "I think Thomas suspects something."

"He's observant." Liz stayed near the conference table, equally unwilling to reduce the physical distance. "He's not the only one. Derek noticed immediately after our... incident in the conference room."

"And Catherine has been watching us like a hawk since the Blueprint Gallery dinner." James ran a hand through his hair, the first crack in his professional facade. "This is exactly what we were trying to avoid."

The reference to their earlier boundaries, the careful limits they'd established after that first kiss, hung between them. Boundaries that had shattered completely in the Meridian Hotel.

"Your text," James said after a moment. "You asked if I had regrets."

Liz met his gaze directly. "Do you?"

"About timing, not about the act itself." He moved around the desk but stopped short of approaching her. "What happened between us was... inevitable, in retrospect. But the circumstances couldn't be worse."

"Professional collaboration, married status, project implications." Liz ticked off the complications on her fingers. "Yes, I'm well aware of the problematic timing."

"That doesn't answer whether YOU regret it."

The directness of his question demanded equal honesty. Liz took a deep breath.

"No. I don't regret what happened. But I do recognize it complicates an already complex situation."

James nodded slowly. "That's where I am as well. No regret for the connection, significant concern about the complications."

They stood in charged silence, the glass walls of his office suddenly feeling too transparent despite the privacy they technically provided. Anyone walking past could see them, though their conversation remained private.

"We need to establish clearer boundaries," Liz said finally. "What happened at the hotel can't happen again."

"Agreed." James's quick response carried both relief and something that might have been disappointment. "The project is too important to both our careers to risk with personal entanglements."

"And my marriage," Liz began, then stopped herself. The word felt hollow after what had happened between them, after the clarity their connection had brought to her long-deteriorating relationship with Mark.

"Your marriage," James repeated carefully. "Is that still a primary consideration for you?"

The question probed directly at the heart of her confusion. Liz moved to the window, needing physical distance from his perceptive gaze.

"My marriage was failing long before you reappeared in my life," she admitted, the truth feeling both liberating and terrifying. "What happened between us didn't create problems with Mark; it just made it impossible to keep ignoring them."

James took a step toward her, then stopped himself. "I don't want to be the reason your marriage ends."

"You're not." Liz turned to face him. "You're the catalyst that forced me to acknowledge what I've known subconsciously for years. Mark and I have been growing apart for so long we barely recognize each other anymore."

"Still, the timing creates... implications."

"It does." Liz sighed, returning to the conference table and spreading her hands on its smooth surface. "Which is why we need to be extremely careful professionally while I sort out my personal situation."

James nodded, moving to the opposite side of the table, close enough for conversation but with a clear barrier between them. "So we maintain professional collaboration, nothing more."

"Nothing more," Liz agreed, ignoring the hollow feeling the words created. "We focus on the project, keep interactions witnessed when possible, and acknowledge that whatever happened at the hotel was—"

"A momentary lapse in judgment?" James suggested, though his expression suggested he didn't believe it.

"A complication neither of us needs," Liz corrected, echoing his words from outside the Blueprint Gallery.

Something shifted in James's eyes, recognition, perhaps, of how their careful dance had been building toward that hotel room despite their best intentions.

"The problem," he said quietly, "is that I can't stop thinking about you. Not just... physically. Your mind, your perspective, the way you challenge my thinking, it's become essential to how I approach this project."

The admission sent warmth spreading through her chest. "I know. I feel the same way. Our intellectual connection is unlike anything I've experienced before."

"Which makes 'nothing more than professional collaboration' particularly challenging to maintain."

"Challenging but necessary." Liz straightened, gathering her professional resolve. "We have responsibilities, to Howard, to our teams, to the project itself."

"And you have decisions to make about your marriage independent of... this." James gestured between them.

"Yes." The simple acknowledgment carried the weight of fifteen years, of accumulated compromises and growing distance, of the life-altering choices that loomed before her. "Whatever happens with Mark needs to be about Mark and me, not about you."

James nodded, his expression softening with understanding. "For what it's worth, I think that's the right approach. Clean lines, clear boundaries."

"The architect's perspective," Liz noted with a small smile.

"Structural integrity matters in relationships as much as buildings." James returned the smile, though his eyes remained serious. "Compromise the foundation, and the entire structure becomes unstable."

The metaphor wasn't lost on her. Their shared language of design and structure had become a way of understanding personal dynamics as well.

"So we establish boundaries," Liz said, returning to practical matters. "Professional interaction only. No private meetings without clear project purpose."

"No discussions of personal matters," James added. "And we maintain appropriate physical distance."

"Exactly." Liz gestured to the table between them. "Like this. Clear delineation of space."

"With transparent walls to ensure accountability." James nodded toward the glass office.

The architectural metaphors continued, each of them finding comfort in the familiar professional terminology to address deeply personal matters. As they spoke, Liz felt the tension gradually easing, replaced by the intellectual connection that had drawn them together from the beginning.

"We should probably review the actual atrium modifications," she suggested after they'd established their new parameters. "In case Thomas or anyone else asks what we discussed."

"Good thinking." James retrieved the drawings from his desk, spreading them across the table. "I've been considering how the articulated joint might enhance the narrative flow rather than disrupt it."

They bent over the drawings together, careful to maintain appropriate distance while examining the detailed specifications. As James explained the modified connection points, Liz found herself responding to the elegance of his solution, their shared enthusiasm for the design temporarily overshadowing the complicated emotions beneath.

"The transition elements actually strengthen the brand story," she observed, indicating where material changes aligned with Meridian's evolution timeline. "The necessity becomes a feature rather than a compromise."

"Exactly." James's eyes lit with genuine pleasure at her understanding. "The structural requirement creates a more nuanced narrative transition than our original concept."

For the next hour, they worked through the design modifications with growing animation, each building on the other's ideas.

Thomas returned as they were finalizing notes on the visitor experience, pausing in the doorway to observe their interaction. If he noticed anything unusual in their dynamic, his expression revealed nothing.

"The engineering team approved the modified approach," he announced, entering with additional drawings. "They've requested some minor adjustments to the load distribution here and here."

The technical discussion continued with Thomas's presence creating a buffer that allowed both Liz and James to relax slightly. The three of them worked through the engineering concerns, developing solutions that addressed both structural requirements and experiential objectives.

As their meeting concluded, Thomas gathered the marked-up drawings. "I'll prepare the revised specifications for tomorrow's construction meeting."

"Thank you, Thomas." James's tone was purely professional. "Elizabeth, does this approach align with the narrative requirements Howard emphasized?"

"Completely," she confirmed, matching his formal tone. "The structural modifications actually enhance the visitor journey rather than compromising it."

Thomas glanced between them again, his perceptive eyes narrowing slightly. "Your collaborative approach has evolved significantly since those first contentious meetings."

"Professional respect develops through successful problem-solving," James replied smoothly. "Elizabeth's marketing insights have transformed how I approach the spatial narrative."

"And James's architectural vision has expanded my understanding of how physical space shapes experience," Liz added, the praise genuine despite its strategic purpose.

Thomas nodded, seemingly satisfied with their explanation. "I'll leave you to finalize the presentation for Howard."

After he departed, Liz and James exchanged glances, both recognizing how their carefully constructed professional explanation mirrored the personal boundaries they'd just established.

"This can work," James said quietly. "The professional collaboration, I mean."

"It has to," Liz replied. "Too much depends on it."

She gathered her notes, maintaining deliberate focus on the task rather than the man across from her. "I should get back to Meridian. Catherine has questions about the timeline adjustments."

"Of course." James moved toward the door, maintaining appropriate distance. "I'll email the revised renderings this afternoon."

At the door, they paused, the moment of departure suddenly weighted with unspoken awareness. For a heartbeat, Liz allowed herself to remember the hotel room, James's hands on her skin, his voice murmuring her name, the profound connection that had transcended physical pleasure.

"This is the right decision," she said, as much to convince herself as him.

"I know." His eyes held hers with understanding that went beyond words. "Clear boundaries create sound structures."

"And sound structures last," Liz finished, the architectural metaphor providing safe expression for complicated emotions.

As she walked through the studio toward the elevator, Liz felt Thomas watching her departure. The weight of their secret created hyperawareness of every movement, every expression that might betray what had happened between them.

In the elevator, she finally allowed her professional mask to slip, releasing a shaky breath as the doors closed. The boundaries they'd established were necessary, appropriate, and entirely insufficient to address the connection that had formed between them.

Like architectural drawings that could never fully capture the experience of occupying the actual space, their careful rules and professional parameters couldn't contain the reality of what had happened. The blueprints for their boundaries looked solid on paper, but Liz suspected the actual construction would prove far more challenging than either of them had acknowledged.

The elevator reached the ground floor, doors opening to release her back into the world beyond James Calloway's orbit. As she stepped into the sunlight, Liz straightened her shoulders and reconstructed her professional composure. The day ahead required her complete attention, project timelines, marketing strategies, and the growing certainty that her marriage had reached its natural conclusion.

Whatever happened with James, or didn't happen, would need to wait until she addressed the structural failure in her own life. Like any sound architectural approach, she needed to shore up the foundation before considering new construction.

CHAPTER TWENTY-SEVEN

"Foundation Inspection"

The waiting room of Dr. Eleanor Farmer's practice exuded carefully designed tranquility, neutral tones, abstract watercolors, and strategically placed plants creating an atmosphere of restrained calm. Liz checked her watch for the third time in five minutes. The emergency appointment she'd scheduled yesterday felt simultaneously urgent and terrifying.

A discreet door opened, revealing a woman in her late fifties with silver-streaked black hair and observant eyes behind stylish frames. "Elizabeth? I'm Dr. Farmer. Please come in."

Liz followed her into a comfortable office where two armchairs faced each other across a small table rather than the stereotypical couch she'd half-expected. The room smelled faintly of jasmine, the walls lined with bookshelves containing psychology texts and what appeared to be literary classics.

"Thank you for fitting me in," Liz said, settling into the offered chair. "I don't usually... I mean, I've never done therapy before."

"Many people find their first session the most challenging," Dr. Farmer replied, her voice carrying a gentle authority. "Why don't we start with what brought you here today?"

Liz had rehearsed this moment during her sleepless night, carefully editing the narrative to exclude certain complications. "I'm having marriage problems. Significant ones. After fifteen years, I think it might be ending."

Dr. Farmer nodded, her expression neutral. "That's certainly a profound challenge. Can you tell me more about what's happening in your relationship?"

"We've grown apart," Liz began, the practiced words flowing easily. "My husband Mark and I have been drifting in different directions for years. We barely communicate beyond logistics. We have separate interests, separate friends. We're essentially roommates at this point."

"When did you first notice this disconnection?"

"That's the thing," Liz leaned forward slightly. "I can't pinpoint when it started. It was so gradual, a missed conversation here, an ignored interest there. Then suddenly I realized we'd been living parallel lives for years."

"What made you realize it now, specifically?"

The question probed dangerously close to James. Liz chose her words with precision. "A work project has been... intellectually stimulating in a way I haven't experienced in years. It made me recognize how much I've been missing, meaningful conversation, creative challenge, feeling truly seen and valued for my mind."

"And Mark doesn't provide that intellectual stimulation?"

"He never really has," Liz admitted. "We connected differently in college, physical chemistry, shared social activities. He was a business major, basketball player. I was studying literature and marketing. Our worlds overlapped enough then, but they've diverged completely now."

Dr. Farmer made a brief note. "You mentioned feeling 'truly seen.' That's a powerful phrase. Can you elaborate?"

Liz felt heat rising to her cheeks. This territory was dangerously close to James again. "Mark doesn't really see me anymore, not the real me. He sees me as his wife, and that's about it. My thoughts, my work, my creative passions, they're background noise to him."

"And this work project has made that contrast more apparent?"

"Yes." Liz exhaled slowly. "It's shown me what it feels like when someone actually values my perspective, challenges my thinking, sees me as an intellectual equal."

Dr. Farmer's expression remained carefully neutral. "Is there a specific colleague who provides this intellectual recognition?"

The direct question created immediate tension. Liz had promised herself she wouldn't mention James, wouldn't complicate her marital issues with the affair. Yet Dr. Farmer had homed in on precisely the element she was trying to avoid.

"The project team is collaborative," Liz replied, the evasion feeling transparent even to her own ears. "It's the nature of the work itself that's stimulating."

Dr. Farmer let the answer stand without challenge, though something in her eyes suggested she recognized the deflection. "Let's talk about what you want from your marriage. What would need to change for the relationship to feel fulfilling again?"

The question created unexpected clarity. "I don't think it can change," Liz said, the realization solidifying as she spoke. "The foundation was never strong enough. We built a relationship on physical attraction and youthful optimism, not on genuine compatibility or shared values."

"That's quite an insight," Dr. Farmer observed. "Many people struggle to recognize when a relationship's basic structure is fundamentally unsound versus just needing maintenance."

"I'm working on a building project," Liz smiled faintly. "Architectural metaphors come naturally these days."

"Tell me about this project that's been so intellectually stimulating."

For the next several minutes, Liz described the Meridian headquarters—the sustainability features, the narrative integration, the material transition concept. As she spoke, her voice grew animated, her hands gesturing to illustrate spatial concepts.

"You come alive when discussing this work," Dr. Farmer noted when she paused. "It clearly engages parts of yourself that have been dormant."

"It does," Liz acknowledged. "It's reminded me who I was before I started compromising myself to fit into my marriage. I used to have intellectual passions, creative ambitions. Somewhere along the way, I surrendered those to become the person Mark could be comfortable with."

"That's a significant sacrifice."

"One I made so gradually I barely noticed until recently."

Dr. Farmer set down her notepad. "Elizabeth, I'm hearing someone who has already done considerable self-reflection. You seem to have clarity about your marriage's limitations. What specifically are you hoping to gain from therapy?"

Liz considered the question carefully. "Confirmation that I'm not just running away from a difficult situation? Assurance that ending a fifteen-year marriage isn't just impulsive self-destruction?"

"Do you believe it's impulsive?"

"No," Liz admitted. "It feels like the culmination of years of growing awareness. But..."

"But there's something complicating your decision," Dr. Farmer supplied when she hesitated. "Something you're not mentioning."

The perception was uncomfortably accurate. Liz studied her hands, weighing how much to reveal. "There is... someone. A colleague on the project. We've developed a connection that goes beyond professional collaboration."

"I see," Dr. Farmer's tone remained neutral. "Has this connection become physical?"

"Yes." The single word emerged barely above a whisper. "It wasn't planned. We tried to maintain professional boundaries, but..."

"These situations rarely are planned," Dr. Farmer observed without judgment. "How do you understand this relationship in the context of your marital dissatisfaction?"

Liz looked up, meeting the therapist's eyes directly. "That's why I'm here. I need to separate my feelings about James from my decision about my marriage. I don't want to leave Mark because of James. I need to know I'm leaving because the marriage itself has failed."

"That's an important distinction," Dr. Farmer nodded. "Many people use new relationships as escape routes from existing ones, only to realize later they've brought old patterns with them."

"Exactly. I don't want James to be an escape. I want any decision about my marriage to stand independently."

"Let me ask you this," Dr. Farmer leaned forward slightly. "If James weren't in the picture at all, if this connection had never developed, would you still be questioning your marriage?"

The question created immediate clarity. "Yes," Liz said without hesitation. "I'd still recognize the fundamental disconnect between Mark and me. I might not have had the courage to face it so directly, but the problems would still exist."

"That's significant insight," Dr. Farmer observed. "What is it about your connection with James that feels different from your relationship with Mark?"

Liz chose her words carefully. "With James, I feel intellectually alive. He challenges me, values my perspective, sees complexity in me that Mark never has. We connect on multiple levels, mind, values, creative vision."

"So it's not just physical attraction or the excitement of something new?"

"No. The physical aspect came after months of intellectual connection. It's almost... secondary to the recognition I feel with him."

Dr. Farmer made a brief note. "You mentioned that you and Mark connected differently in college, physical chemistry, shared activities. It sounds like your relationship with James reverses that pattern, intellectual connection first, physical attraction following."

The observation struck Liz with unexpected force. "I never thought of it that way, but yes. Exactly."

"Many people discover in midlife that what attracted them to their partners in youth no longer sustains them as they evolve," Dr. Farmer said. "The qualities that seem important at twenty-two often differ dramatically from what nourishes us at forty."

"Mark and I haven't evolved together," Liz acknowledged. "We've grown in completely different directions."

"And with James, you feel a connection to aspects of yourself that have been undervalued in your marriage?"

"Yes. The intellectual parts, the creative parts. The ambitious, passionate self I used to be before I started making myself smaller to maintain Mark's comfort."

Dr. Farmer set down her pen. "Elizabeth, I can't tell you whether to end your marriage. That decision belongs to you alone. But I can observe that you're approaching this with remarkable self-awareness. You're asking the right questions about your motivations."

"So I'm not just having a midlife crisis or running from commitment?"

"Those are simplistic explanations for complex human experiences," Dr. Farmer smiled gently. "What I'm hearing is someone recognizing that a relationship formed in youth may no longer serve the person she's become. That's not a crisis, it's growth."

Liz felt unexpected tears forming. "I've been so afraid I'm just being selfish or impulsive."

"There's a difference between selfish and self-aware," Dr. Farmer replied. "Recognizing your needs isn't selfish, it's necessary for authentic living. The question is how you honor those needs while treating others with compassion."

Their session continued for another twenty minutes, exploring practical considerations about separation and the emotional challenges ahead. As it concluded, Dr. Farmer offered a final observation.

"Remember that ending your marriage and pursuing a relationship with James are separate decisions. Give yourself permission to address them sequentially rather than simultaneously."

Liz nodded, gathering her purse. "Thank you. That distinction helps enormously."

"Would you like to schedule another session?"

"Yes," Liz said without hesitation. "I think I'll need support navigating whatever comes next."

The coffee shop near Meridian's offices buzzed with midday energy—laptops open, business conversations humming, baristas calling out elaborate drink orders. Liz spotted Derek at their usual corner table, two steaming mugs already waiting.

"You're a lifesaver," she said, sliding into the seat across from him. "I desperately needed caffeine after my morning."

"Rough executive meeting?" Derek pushed her latte closer.

"Something like that." Liz wasn't ready to mention therapy, even to Derek.

"You look..." he studied her face, "different. Not bad, just intense. Like you're about to make a major decision or detonate something."

She laughed despite herself. "Your perception is terrifying sometimes."

"It's my superpower. That and coordinating patterns that shouldn't work together." He gestured to his boldly patterned shirt beneath a striped blazer that somehow looked perfectly harmonious.

They chatted about office politics and the upcoming marketing campaign launch, the familiar professional territory creating comfortable distance from her morning revelations. Derek filled her in on department gossip, his commentary providing welcome distraction.

"So," he said finally, stirring his second cappuccino, "are we going to talk about what's really going on, or continue this pleasant fiction that everything's normal?"

Liz set down her mug. "What do you mean?"

"Please." Derek's expression shifted from playful to concerned. "I've known you for five years, Liz. You've been different for weeks—distracted, emotional, occasionally looking like you've seen a ghost. Something's happening, and I'm guessing it's not just project stress."

The direct confrontation created momentary panic. How much did he suspect? How much could she safely reveal?

"My marriage is in trouble," she admitted, the truth feeling both terrifying and liberating. "Serious trouble."

Derek's expression softened immediately. "I'm so sorry. Though I can't say I'm entirely surprised."

"You're not?"

"You and Mark have seemed... disconnected for as long as I've known you," he said carefully. "The few times I've seen you together at company events, it's like watching two people sharing space but not really seeing each other."

The observation stung with its accuracy. "That obvious, huh?"

"Only to someone paying attention." Derek reached across the table to squeeze her hand briefly. "What happened? Or was it a gradual thing?"

"Glacially gradual," Liz sighed. "Years of drifting apart until we barely recognize each other anymore. We want completely different things from life. Always have, probably, but it's impossible to ignore now."

Derek nodded, his expression thoughtful. "Sometimes relationships have expiration dates we don't recognize until we've passed them."

"That's exactly it," Liz felt a rush of gratitude for his understanding. "We should have ended years ago, but we just kept going through motions because it was easier than admitting failure."

"So what now? Counseling? Separation?"

"I'm considering a trial separation," Liz admitted. "I need space to figure out what I actually want, not just what I've settled for."

Derek studied her face for a moment, something shifting in his expression. "And does what you want include James Calloway?"

The question hit hard. Liz felt heat rising to her cheeks, her carefully constructed narrative crumbling. "Why would you ask that?"

"Because I'm not blind," Derek said gently. "I've seen how you are around him. How you light up discussing his designs. How you defend his vision to Howard. How you both look at each other when you think no one's watching."

"It's a professional collaboration," Liz protested weakly.

"Sure." Derek's skepticism was evident. "And I'm secretly dating the Royal Ballet's principal dancer."

Liz stared into her coffee, weighing how much to reveal. Derek was her closest workplace confidant, but admitting the affair carried professional risks for both of them.

"There's... something," she acknowledged finally. "A connection I wasn't expecting. But that's not why my marriage is ending. Mark and I have been broken for years."

"I believe you," Derek said, his voice softening. "But be careful, Liz. Office relationships are complicated enough without adding divorce and high-profile projects to the mix."

"I know." She met his gaze directly. "Trust me, I'm acutely aware of the complications."

"Catherine suspects, you know." Derek lowered his voice. "She mentioned your 'interesting dynamic' with James in our last department meeting."

Fresh anxiety bloomed. "What exactly did she say?"

"Nothing explicit. Just that the marketing-architecture collaboration was 'unusually synergistic' with a look that could have frozen Mercury." Derek shrugged. "She values your work too much to interfere unless it affects the project."

"It won't," Liz insisted. "We're professionals first. The project remains our priority."

Derek studied her for a moment longer. "Can I share something personal?"

"Of course."

"Before Jacob, I was with someone for eight years. Ryan." Derek rarely mentioned his past relationships.

"We had the apartment, the friends, the routines. Everything looked perfect from outside."

"What happened?"

"I woke up one day and realized I'd been performing a relationship rather than living one." His eyes held a distant pain. "We'd been going through motions for years, both afraid to admit we'd grown into different people with different dreams."

"How did it end?"

"Messily at first. I stayed too long out of fear and guilt. By the time I finally left, we both resented each other for the wasted years." Derek refocused on her. "Don't make my mistake, Liz. Don't stay out of habit or obligation when you know it's already over."

His candor created a lump in her throat. "I'm afraid of hurting Mark. He doesn't deserve pain just because we're incompatible."

"Continuing a marriage that's already emotionally over hurts both of you more in the long run," Derek said gently. "The kindest thing might be the hardest thing, being honest about what you really want, even if that doesn't include him."

"When did you get so wise?" Liz attempted a smile.

"Therapy. Lots and lots of therapy." Derek grinned. "Highly recommend it. Changed my life."

"I actually saw someone this morning," Liz admitted. "First session."

"Good for you." Derek's approval was genuine. "It helps to have someone objective guiding you through the emotional minefield."

They finished their coffees, conversation shifting to safer topics. As they prepared to return to the office, Derek paused.

"Whatever happens with your marriage, with James, just be honest with yourself about what you truly want," he said. "Not what you think you should want, or what would make things easier, but what would make your life authentic."

"I'm trying," Liz promised. "For the first time in years, I'm really trying."

Rebecca's loft was quiet except for the distant hum of traffic fourteen floors below. Liz sat cross-legged on the guest bed, yellow legal pad balanced on her knee, pen hovering over the blank page. Dr. Farmer had suggested an exercise, listing what she truly wanted in life without filtering for practicality or obligation.

"Not what you should want," the therapist had explained. "Not what would please others or match external expectations. What would make your life feel authentic and fulfilling."

The simple instruction had paralyzed her for twenty minutes. After years of accommodating Mark's preferences, adjusting her ambitions to fit their shared life, and gradually surrendering parts of herself to maintain marital peace, identifying her genuine desires felt like archaeology, digging through layers of compromise to find original foundations.

Finally, she pressed pen to paper and wrote: .

What I Want:

1. Intellectual challenge and stimulation

2. Creative fulfillment through meaningful work

3. Genuine connection with someone who values my mind

4. Freedom to pursue interests without justification

5. Professional recognition for substantive contribution

6. Living space that reflects my aesthetic, not compromise

7. Relationships where I don't make myself smaller

8. Travel focused on cultural/architectural exploration

9. Time for reading without feeling guilty

10. Financial independence and security

She stared at the completed list, struck by what was missing. No children. No suburban lifestyle. Nothing about maintaining her marriage or saving the relationship with Mark. The absence felt simultaneously terrifying and liberating, confirmation that her authentic desires had diverged completely from the life she'd constructed.

Liz turned to a fresh page and wrote a second heading:

What I Don't Want:

1. Pretending interest in sports to maintain connection

2. Suppressing intellectual enthusiasm to avoid making others uncomfortable

3. Sunday afternoons wasted watching games I don't care about

4. Vacations planned around sporting events

5. Dinner conversations limited to schedules and logistics

6. Being "Mark's wife" as primary identity

7. Feeling intellectually isolated in my own home

8. Mechanical physical intimacy without emotional connection

9. Dreading weekends because they mean more time in uncomfortable silence

10. Living someone else's version of success

The second list flowed more easily, years of accumulated frustrations finding concrete expression. Looking at both pages side by side created painful clarity, her marriage to Mark contradicted nearly everything she genuinely wanted while reinforcing everything she didn't.

Liz set down the pen, emotions washing through her in alternating waves of grief and relief. Grief for the years invested, the genuine affection that had existed despite the fundamental mismatch, the shared history that couldn't be erased. Relief at finally acknowledging what she had known subconsciously for years: she and Mark had been growing in different directions for so long that they now occupied entirely different landscapes.

The revelation wasn't about James, though his presence in her life had certainly accelerated her recognition. The fundamental incompatibility with Mark existed independently, would have existed even if James Calloway had never reappeared in her life.

Her phone chimed with a text from Mark: *Working late again? Leftovers in fridge.*

The message carried no affection, no inquiry about her day, just information delivered with the casual disregard that had become their standard mode of communication. Liz replied with equal detachment: *At Rebecca's. Staying here tonight. Talk tomorrow.*

She set down the phone and returned to her lists, adding one final item to "What I Want":

11. A relationship where "I love you" isn't just habit but genuine recognition

The addition crystallized everything. Whatever happened with James, whether their connection developed into something lasting or remained a catalyst for necessary change, she deserved more than what her marriage had become. Mark deserved more too, though he might not recognize it yet.

Liz closed the notebook, decision solidifying into certainty. The foundation inspection was complete, the structural assessment undeniable. Her marriage hadn't failed suddenly; it had been built on insufficient understanding of who they both were and who they would become. The cracks weren't recent developments but inevitable consequences of that original misalignment.

She would have to begin the difficult conversation with Mark. Not about James, that complication would only distract from the fundamental truth. About the growing recognition that they had become strangers sharing an address, going through motions of a relationship that existed more in memory than present reality.

The path ahead would be painful, messy, complicated by professional entanglements and emotional history. But for the first time in years, it would be authentic, aligned with who she truly was rather than who she had pretended to be.

As Liz prepared for bed in Rebecca's guest room, she felt the strange combination of grief and liberation that accompanies difficult truth. The life she had constructed was ending, but the life she actually wanted might finally be possible.

CHAPTER TWENTY-EIGHT

"Structural Weakness"

The Calloway Design Group studio stood eerily quiet in the late evening hours, most of the staff having departed hours ago. Only the soft hum of the climate control system and the occasional distant ping of the elevator broke the silence. Pools of light from scattered desk lamps created islands in the darkness, illuminating abandoned drafting tables and dormant computer screens.

Liz stood before the large windows in the conference room, staring at the illuminated construction site in the distance. The skeletal framework of Meridian's future headquarters rose from concrete foundations, steel beams silhouetted against the night sky like an architect's dream taking physical form. Six months into the project, the building had progressed from concept to reality, each beam and column a manifestation of designs she and James had developed together.

Behind her, blueprints and material samples covered the conference table where they'd been working for the past three hours. What had begun as a legitimate review of construction progress had gradually shifted as the evening deepened and the office emptied, leaving them alone in a space that suddenly felt dangerous in its privacy.

"The limestone integration is proceeding ahead of schedule," James said, his voice closer than she expected.

She turned to find him standing just a few feet away, his jacket discarded hours ago, sleeves rolled to expose his forearms. In the soft light, the silver at his temples caught the glow from the desk lamp, creating a distinguished contrast with his dark hair.

"The transition elements look exactly as we envisioned," she replied, forcing her attention back to professional matters. "The material narrative is clearly legible even at this early stage."

James nodded, moving to stand beside her at the window. "The articulated joints are working beautifully. The engineering team was skeptical, but the execution is validating our approach."

They stood in silence, both staring at the distant construction site while acutely aware of each other's proximity. Since their night at the Meridian Hotel, they'd maintained careful professional boundaries, no private meetings, no personal conversations, no unnecessary physical contact. The rules they'd established had preserved their working relationship while creating a constant undercurrent of longing and desire that seemed to intensify rather than diminish with time.

"We should finalize the executive floor modifications," Liz said, returning to the table and the safety of blueprints. "Howard wants to review them tomorrow."

James remained at the window a moment longer before joining her. As they bent over the drawings, their hands nearly touched reaching for the same document. Both withdrew instantly, the brief almost-contact sending electricity through the space between them.

"The flow between departments needs refinement," James observed, his voice deliberately professional. "The transitional spaces feel abrupt rather than intuitive."

Liz studied the floorplan, grateful for the technical distraction. "What if we create intermediate zones here and here?" She sketched quickly on tracing paper laid over the blueprint. "Spaces that serve both departments while maintaining necessary boundaries."

"Boundaries that connect rather than separate," James murmured, watching her draw. "That could work."

The word "boundaries" hung between them, loaded with meaning beyond architectural divisions. Liz continued sketching, adding details to her concept while hyperaware of James beside her, his breathing, his scent, the energy radiating from him that seemed to create a magnetic field she struggled to resist.

"The narrative flow would be enhanced," she continued, her voice sounding strained even to her own ears. "Departments maintain identity while encouraging collaboration."

"Like separate entities finding connection points," James observed, the architectural discussion taking on unmistakable subtext. "Maintaining integrity while acknowledging relationship."

Liz set down her pencil, unable to maintain the pretense any longer. "James, we're not really talking about floorplans anymore, are we?"

He met her gaze directly, professional mask slipping. "No. We're not."

The honesty created a shift in the atmosphere, as if a pressure valve had been released. Liz took a deliberate step back, creating physical distance she desperately needed to think clearly.

"We established boundaries for good reasons," she said. "The project, our professional reputations—"

"Your marriage," James added, though his tone carried a question.

"My separation," Liz corrected. "I'm going to be... taking some time apart. I'm going to be staying at my sister Rebecca's place for awhile, until I can sort things out."

James's expression shifted, surprise and something else, hope, perhaps, flickering across his features before he carefully controlled his reaction. "I didn't know. When did this happen?"

"I made the decision days ago. After I made that list of what I truly want." Liz moved back to the window, needing space from both James and the blueprints with their metaphorical resonance. "It wasn't because of you. Or not primarily because of you. I just need to tell Mark."

"I understand." James remained by the table, respecting her need for distance. "The hotel was a catalyst, not a cause."

"Exactly." She turned to face him. "My marriage has been failing for years. What happened between us just made it impossible to keep ignoring that reality."

James nodded slowly. "I've thought about you every day since the hotel," he admitted, his voice dropping to a lower register. "Tried to focus on work, on the project, on maintaining professional boundaries. But I can't stop thinking about you."

The confession sent warmth spreading through her chest despite her resolve to maintain control. "I've had the same experience," she acknowledged. "Despite my best intentions."

"So where does that leave us?" James took a step toward her, then stopped himself. "The boundaries we established were necessary, but they don't change what happened. Or what's still happening between us."

"It's complicated," Liz sighed. "I'm in the middle of a separation that will likely become divorce. You're my primary professional collaborator on the most important project of my career. The timing couldn't be worse."

"I know." James ran a hand through his hair, frustration evident. "Logically, we should maintain distance until your situation resolves and the project reaches completion. That would be the sensible approach."

"But?" Liz prompted, hearing the unspoken contradiction.

"But I've never felt this kind of connection before." His eyes held hers with uncomfortable directness. "The intellectual challenge matched with something more.

It's like finding that final missing piece in huge jigsaw puzzle."

The sentiment resonated so deeply that Liz felt momentarily breathless. "I know exactly what you mean," she said quietly. "It's not just physical attraction or emotional response. It's recognition on multiple levels."

"So what do we do?" James moved closer, the distance between them narrowing. "Ignore it because the timing is inconvenient? Pretend it doesn't exist because it complicates our professional lives?"

"We can't act on it," Liz insisted, though her body seemed to sway toward him of its own accord. "There's too much at stake professionally. And I need to resolve my marriage situation cleanly, not clouded by... this."

"This," James repeated, now standing close enough that she could feel the heat radiating from him. "This connection that's stronger than anything I've experienced in my adult life. This understanding that goes beyond words. This chemistry that makes it almost impossible to stand this close to you without touching you."

His words created a physical response she couldn't control, pulse quickening, breath shortening, skin suddenly hypersensitive. The professional boundaries they'd established seemed to dissolve in the face of this undeniable reality between them.

"James," she whispered, his name both warning and invitation.

"Tell me to step back," he said, his voice rough with restraint. "Tell me our professional relationship matters more than exploring this connection, and I'll respect that. I'll maintain whatever distance you need."

The choice crystallized before her, the safe professional path versus the unknown territory of whatever existed between them. She should tell him to step back. She should reinforce their boundaries. She should prioritize the project and her separation process and all the rational considerations that argued against complication.

Instead, she closed the final distance between them, her hand rising to touch his face with a gentleness that surprised them both.

"I can't tell you that," she admitted. "Because I don't believe it's true."

The confession hung in the air for a heartbeat before James's control finally broke. His mouth found hers with an urgency that matched her own, the kiss deeper and more deliberate than their first frantic encounter in the Meridian conference room. His hands cradled her face.

Liz responded with equal intensity, fingers threading through his hair, body pressing against his with undeniable need. The professional tension that had characterized their relationship from the beginning transformed into physical chemistry that felt both shocking and inevitable.

They moved backward until Liz felt the edge of the table behind her. James lifted her easily, setting her on its surface, architectural drawings crinkling beneath her. Material samples scattered as his hands moved to her waist, thumbs tracing the curve of her ribs through her silk blouse.

"We shouldn't," she gasped as his mouth found the sensitive spot below her ear.

"I know," he murmured against her skin. "Tell me to stop."

But she couldn't form the words, her body betraying her rational mind as his touch awakened sensations she'd forgotten were possible. Her hands moved to the buttons of his shirt, fingers trembling slightly as she exposed tanned skin and lean muscle beneath.

James watched her face with unwavering focus as she explored him, his breathing uneven but his restraint evident. "Elizabeth," he whispered, her full name on his lips an intimacy that transcended their physical connection.

The sound of her name broke something loose inside her, the last hesitation, the final reservation. This wasn't a mistake or momentary weakness or project stress. This was deliberate choice, entered with full awareness of both its complications and its potential.

"I want this," she said, meeting his gaze directly. "I want you."

The simple declaration transformed something between them. James's expression shifted from desire to something deeper, more complex. He kissed her again, this time with exquisite slowness, as if they had all the time in the world rather than stolen moments in an empty office.

His hands moved to the buttons of her blouse with the same deliberate patience, each one undone with careful attention. When he finally slipped the silk from her shoulders, his sharp intake of breath at the sight of her created a rush of confidence that swept away lingering self-consciousness.

"You're perfect," he murmured, hands skimming over her breasts with reverent precision. "Everything about you."

Unlike their hotel encounter, fueled by alcohol and argument and years of suppressed tension, this moment unfolded with deliberate awareness. Each touch, each discovery, each response acknowledged and savored. The architectural models surrounding them seemed fitting witnesses, physical manifestations of their collaborative vision watching as they built something new between them.

When clothing became too much of a barrier, they helped each other discard pieces until nothing remained between them but shared breath and racing hearts. James lifted her again, moving them to the leather sofa in the corner, his strength both surprising and arousing.

"Is this real?" he asked as they settled together, his weight balanced above her. "Or another moment of weakness we'll regret tomorrow?"

"It's real," Liz assured him, hands tracing the muscles of his back. "But we'll probably regret it anyway."

His laugh was unexpected, the sound transforming his serious features. "Worth it," he decided, lowering his mouth to hers again.

When their bodies joined, Liz felt a sense of recognition that transcended physical pleasure. James watched her face with unwavering focus as they moved together, his blue eyes reflecting the city lights and something deeper, more complex than mere desire.

Unlike Mark's predictable efficiency or even their own passionate but frantic hotel encounter, this connection built like a well-designed structure, each element supporting the next, creating an experience that rose toward an inevitable conclusion.

"Elizabeth," James whispered as tension built between them, her name a prayer and promise simultaneously.

The pleasure crested with unexpected intensity, waves of sensation washing through her as James followed moments later, his control finally surrendering to shared completion. They remained entwined afterward, neither willing to break the connection that felt simultaneously fragile and unbreakable.

"I've never experienced this," James admitted in the quiet aftermath, his fingers tracing patterns on her skin. "This level of connection. Physical, intellectual, emotional, all aligned."

"Neither have I," Liz confessed, the honesty easier in this moment of vulnerability. "Even in the early days with Mark, it was different. More physical than intellectual. We never had this kind of... connection."

James propped himself on one elbow, studying her face with that focused attention that made her feel truly seen. "You know what's strange? I think it started at Preston, this connection. Even when we were competing, there was recognition. You were the only person who matched me thought for thought."

"You challenged me in ways no one else ever had," Liz acknowledged. "I measured myself against you for years afterward."

"Against me?" Surprise flickered across his features. "But you were brilliant. Your literary analysis was more insightful than half our teachers'."

"Not according to the Beckman committee." The old pain surfaced unexpectedly. "Losing that scholarship to you by decimal points shaped my entire trajectory. I abandoned literary theory, chose Northwestern instead of Rice, met Mark, followed a completely different path."

James's expression shifted to genuine regret. "I never knew it affected you that deeply. The Beckman was so close they actually reconvened twice to break the deadlock. It could have gone either way."

"Really?" The revelation created a strange ache in her chest. "All these years, I imagined your victory as decisive. As confirmation you were simply better."

"God, no." James shook his head. "I was terrified of you, Elizabeth. Your mind worked in ways mine didn't. You saw connections I missed, challenged assumptions I didn't even realize I was making. Winning felt almost accidental, and hollow, because you disappeared afterward. No alumni events, no academic conferences where I might have encountered you again."

They lay in comfortable silence, the intimacy of their conversation creating connection as profound as their physical joining had been. Outside the windows, the city continued its nighttime rhythm—lights blinking in distant buildings, occasional sirens wailing, the constant hum of urban existence.

Eventually, practical reality reasserted itself. They were still in the office, still surrounded by project materials, still bound by professional obligations that wouldn't disappear because of what had happened between them.

"We should probably get dressed," Liz said reluctantly, though she made no move to disentangle herself from his embrace.

"Probably," James agreed, equally motionless. "Though I'm finding it difficult to care about...should at the moment."

His hand continued its gentle exploration of her skin, tracing the curve of her shoulder, the line of her collarbone, the sensitive spot at the base of her throat that made her breath catch. The touch wasn't demanding but appreciative, an architect studying beloved design.

"What happens now?" Liz asked, the question encompassing far more than the immediate aftermath.

James sighed, his breath warm against her hair. "The sensible answer is that we acknowledge this happened, recognize it can't happen again until your situation resolves and the project completes, and return to our professional boundaries."

"And the non-sensible answer?"

"That we've spent twenty years denying this connection, and I'm not sure I have the strength to deny it any longer." His arms tightened slightly around her. "That whatever is happening between us feels too significant to dismiss for the sake of convenient timing."

The honesty created both comfort and complication. Liz sat up, reluctantly separating from his warmth as she reached for her scattered clothing.

"My marriage was over long before you showed up," she said, slipping into her bra with a self-consciousness that seemed absurd given their recent intimacy. "But I do need to resolve it cleanly, honestly. Not clouded by... this."

"This," James repeated, watching her dress with undisguised appreciation. "You keep using that word for whatever exists between us."

"Because I don't have a better one," Liz admitted, buttoning her blouse. "Affair seems sordid. Relationship seems presumptuous. Connection doesn't capture the complexity."

"How about recognition?" James suggested, pulling on his own clothes with efficient movements. "Finding someone who sees you completely and values what they see."

The definition resonated deeply. "Recognition," she repeated, testing the word. "Yes, that fits."

Fully dressed again, they moved to the window overlooking the construction site. The Meridian headquarters skeleton stood illuminated by security lights, steel beams outlining spaces that didn't yet exist except in their shared vision.

CHAPTER TWENTY-NINE

"Exposed Elements"

Morning light streamed through the floor-to-ceiling windows of Meridian's Conference Room, casting dramatic shadows across the polished table where Liz had meticulously arranged presentation materials. The quarterly executive review was scheduled to begin in fifteen minutes, and she'd spent the entire weekend perfecting her slides, analyzing construction progress, documenting budget adherence, and crafting the narrative of achievement that Howard expected.

Despite her professional focus, her mind kept drifting to James and their encounter in his office three nights ago. The memory remained vivid, his hands on her skin, his undeniable hunger as his lips explored every inch of her body, the profound connection that had transcended physical pleasure. They'd maintained careful distance since then, communicating only through necessary emails about the project, both hyperaware of the professional risks they were taking.

Catherine entered, her silver bob catching the morning light as she surveyed the room with shrewd efficiency. "Everything ready for the presentation?"

"Yes," Liz nodded, straightening an already perfectly aligned stack of handouts. "Construction progress is exceeding projections despite the atrium connection modifications."

Catherine studied her with that penetrating gaze that she had mastered over years in charge. "And you've included the sustainability metrics Howard requested?"

"Page twelve, with comparative analysis against industry benchmarks." Liz tapped the relevant section in her presentation notes.

"Good." Catherine settled into a chair, her expression unreadable. "James will be joining us?"

"For the architectural portion, yes." Liz kept her voice carefully neutral. "He's bringing updated renderings of the completed sections."

Something in Catherine's eyes sharpened at the mention of James, but before she could respond, other executives began filtering into the room. Howard finally making his way to head of the table.

"Let's begin with the headquarters update," he announced once everyone settled. "Elizabeth?"

Liz stood, hyperaware of every eye on her. She launched into her presentation with practiced ease, the words flowing automatically while part of her mind remained vigilantly on guard against any hint of her personal complications. The door opened quietly as she discussed timeline adherence, and James slipped in, nodding apologetically to Howard before taking a seat directly across from her.

Their eyes met briefly, a moment of electric connection before both returned to strict professionalism. James wore a charcoal suit that emphasized the breadth of his shoulders, his expression revealing nothing of what had transpired between them. To anyone watching, they were merely project collaborators with a well-established working relationship.

"The structural steel phase completed two weeks ahead of schedule," Liz continued, advancing to a slide showing the building's impressive framework. "This acceleration creates positive downstream effects for the interior phases."

"And budget implications?" Howard inquired.

"Within projected parameters." Liz moved to the financial summary. "The additional expenditure for the atrium supports was offset by efficiencies in material procurement that James, that Calloway Design Group negotiated."

She stumbled slightly over his name, a momentary lapse that Catherine seemed to notice, her eyebrows rising fractionally. Liz continued smoothly, discussing sustainability metrics and energy efficiency projections, but she felt Catherine's gaze lingering on her with uncomfortable perception.

When James took over to present the architectural updates, Liz maintained a composed expression despite her hyperawareness of his every movement. He discussed material integration and construction challenges with professional detachment, his deep voice filling the room with confident authority.

"The limestone elements are being installed according to the narrative sequence we developed," he explained, gesturing to detailed photographs. "The material transition from traditional to innovative components physically embodies Meridian's progressive tradition philosophy."

"Elizabeth's marketing concept brought to life in stone and glass," Howard observed with approval. "This is exactly the integration I envisioned."

James nodded, his expression revealing nothing beyond professional agreement. "Her narrative approach transformed the visitor experience. The architecture simply gives it physical form."

The casual credit sent warmth spreading through Liz's chest despite her efforts to maintain emotional distance. Throughout their collaboration, James had consistently acknowledged her contributions, integrating her marketing concepts so thoroughly they'd become inseparable from his architectural vision.

As the presentation continued, Liz noticed Catherine watching them with increasing scrutiny, not their slides or data, but their interaction. The way James referred to concepts they'd developed together. The seamless handoffs between marketing and architectural elements. The occasional glance they exchanged when discussing particularly challenging aspects of the project.

The meeting concluded with enthusiastic support from Howard. "The board will be pleased with this progress. The timeline acceleration is particularly impressive given the structural challenges we faced."

As executives filtered out, Catherine remained seated, her tablet untouched before her. "Elizabeth, do you have a moment?"

Liz nodded, though internal alarms immediately sounded. She gathered her presentation materials with deliberate calm, waiting until the last executive departed before sitting across from Catherine. James had left with Howard, discussing something about material sourcing as they walked toward the executive offices.

"Your presentation was thorough," Catherine began, "but I couldn't help noticing something concerning."

"Oh?" Liz kept her expression neutral despite her accelerating pulse.

"The dynamic between you and James has... evolved." Catherine leaned forward slightly. "There's an obvious chemistry that goes beyond professional collaboration."

The direct observation sent a jolt through Liz's system. "We've developed an effective working relationship," she said carefully. "Creative tension producing superior results, as Howard likes to say."

"Elizabeth." Catherine's voice dropped, her tone shifting from professional to personal. "I've been in corporate leadership for twenty years. I recognize the signs when I see them."

"I'm not sure what you're implying," Liz replied, though heat rose to her cheeks.

"I'm not implying anything. I'm stating directly that whatever is happening between you and James Calloway has moved beyond professional boundaries." Catherine's expression held no judgment, only concern. "The way you look at each other when you think no one is watching. The non-verbal communication during presentations. The tension that fills any room you both occupy."

Liz felt momentarily speechless, her carefully constructed professional facade crumbling under Catherine's perceptive assessment.

"Your personal life is your business," Catherine continued. "But when it intersects with a hundred-million-dollar project that represents Meridian's future, it becomes my concern."

"The project remains our absolute priority," Liz insisted, finding her voice. "Nothing has compromised our professional judgment or the quality of our work."

"Not yet," Catherine acknowledged. "But entanglements like this have a way of becoming... complicated, messy. Particularly when they inevitably end."

The implication that what existed between her and James was temporary stung more than Liz expected. "You're making assumptions based on limited observations," she said, her tone cooler than intended.

"Am I wrong?" Catherine challenged, her gaze unflinching.

Liz held her mentor's eyes for a long moment before looking away. "The situation is more complex than it appears."

"It always is." Catherine's voice softened slightly. "I'm not here to judge you, Elizabeth. I've mentored you for years because I recognize your exceptional tal-

ent. But talent isn't enough when personal complications interfere with professional obligations."

"I would never allow that to happen," Liz said firmly.

"We rarely intend for our personal lives to derail our
professional ones," Catherine observed. "Yet it happens
with remarkable frequency." She gathered her tablet,
preparing to leave. "Create some distance, Elizabeth.
For the project's sake, if not your own."

After Catherine departed, Liz remained seated, her
heart pounding unnaturally fast. Had they been so
transparent? She'd thought their careful boundaries
and professional interactions had concealed the reality
of what existed between them. Yet Catherine had seen
through their performance with unsettling accuracy.

The conference room suddenly felt exposed, its glass
walls allowing anyone passing to observe her distress.
Liz gathered her materials and retreated to her office,
closing the door before allowing herself a moment
of genuine reaction. Catherine's warning had struck
uncomfortably close to truths she'd been avoiding,
that her connection with James created professional
risks neither could afford, that the project could suffer
if their personal relationship became complicated or
ended badly.

Her computer chimed with an email notification.
James had sent revised drawings for the executive floor
layout with a brief note: *Need to discuss these modifi-*

cations before submitting to engineering. Available this afternoon?

The simple professional request shouldn't have created the flutter in her chest, but it did. She stared at his message, wondering if others would read subtext into such ordinary communication. Had their relationship already compromised their professional judgment, as Catherine feared? Were they putting the project at risk through their inability to maintain appropriate boundaries?

Liz began composing a reply, writing and deleting several versions before settling on careful professionalism: *Drawings received. Available at 2pm in the small conference room.*

She hesitated before sending, then added: *We should include Thomas and Derek for comprehensive review.*

The addition of team members would ensure their meeting remained strictly professional, no opportunity for private conversation or moments of unguarded connection. It was the right decision for the project, for their careers, for maintaining the boundaries Catherine had just emphasized.

Yet as she sent the email, Liz felt a hollow ache beneath her ribs. The connection she'd found with James, intellectual, emotional, physical, had awakened parts of herself long dormant in her marriage. The thought of deliberately distancing herself from that recognition created a sense of loss that surprised her with its intensity.

The conference room remained empty after Thomas and Derek departed, leaving Liz gathering presentation materials while James collected his architectural drawings. The meeting had proceeded with perfect professionalism, technical discussions of structural requirements and material specifications, team input on timeline adjustments, collaborative problem-solving without a hint of the personal connection that hummed beneath the surface.

"You added Thomas and Derek to what should have been a simple review," James observed quietly, rolling blueprints with methodical precision. "Any particular reason?"

Liz glanced toward the glass walls, ensuring no one was within earshot. "Catherine noticed something between us during this morning's presentation."

James stilled, his expression tightening. "What exactly did she say?"

"That our 'obvious chemistry' goes beyond professional collaboration." Liz kept her voice low despite the empty room. "She warned me about personal complications interfering with project obligations."

"I see." James resumed rolling the blueprint, his movements more controlled than before. "Did you confirm her suspicions?"

"Not explicitly. But I didn't convince her they were unfounded either." Liz gathered her laptop, needing something to do with her hands. "She's perceptive, James. She sees the way we interact."

"So we need to be more careful," he concluded, securing the blueprint with an elastic band. "Maintain stricter boundaries in public settings."

"I think we need to create actual distance," Liz said, the words feeling like stones in her mouth. "Not just performance for others, but real separation."

James looked up, his eyes meeting hers with sudden intensity. "What exactly are you suggesting?"

"That we minimize direct contact. Communicate through team members when possible. No private meetings without clear project necessity."

"You want to end what's happening between us." His voice remained neutral, though something flickered in his eyes, hurt, perhaps, or resignation.

"I want to protect the project," Liz clarified, though the distinction felt meaningless. "And our professional reputations. Catherine's right, this kind of complication rarely ends well for anyone involved."

James was silent for a long moment, studying her with that focused attention that had always made her feel truly seen. "Is that what you really want, Elizabeth? Or what you think you should want?"

The question probed uncomfortably close to her confusion. "What I want doesn't matter," she replied finally. "We have responsibilities to Howard, to our teams, to this building that will define both our careers."

"What you want always matters," James countered, his voice softening. "At least to me."

The simple statement created an ache in her chest. How long had it been since anyone had prioritized her desires? Mark certainly hadn't for years, treating her needs as inconvenient afterthoughts to his own preferences.

"James—" she began.

The door opened, cutting off whatever she might have said. Sophia Rodriguez entered with an armful of material samples, her expressive face registering surprise at finding them alone.

"Sorry to interrupt," she said, glancing between them with undisguised curiosity. "I thought everyone had left. I needed to check something in the conference materials."

"We were just finishing," James replied smoothly, gathering his portfolio. "Elizabeth had questions about the executive floor modifications."

"Of course." Sophia's tone suggested she wasn't entirely convinced by the explanation. "The limestone integration looks beautiful in the entrance sequence, by the way. Your narrative approach transformed everything."

"Thank you," Liz managed, grateful for the professional redirect. "The material transition is more elegant than I'd anticipated."

An awkward silence fell, the three of them caught in the strange tension of interrupted conversation. James broke it first, moving toward the door with deliberate purpose.

"I should get these revisions to engineering," he said, his professional mask firmly in place. "Elizabeth, let me know if you have additional questions about the modifications."

"I will," she replied, matching his formal tone. "Thank you for the clarification."

After he left, Sophia set down her materials, studying Liz with uncomfortably perceptive eyes. "Everything okay? That felt... tense."

"Just project pressure," Liz deflected, gathering her laptop and notes. "The board presentation is next week, and Howard expects perfection."

"Mmm-hmm." Sophia's skepticism was evident in her raised eyebrow. "And that's why you two looked like you were having a deeply personal conversation when I walked in?"

"We were discussing professional boundaries," Liz said, the truth emerging before she could filter it.

"I bet you were." Sophia's expression softened from curiosity to compassion. "Look, I've worked with James for three years. I've never seen him connect with anyone the way he does with you, professionally or otherwise."

The observation created both warmth and anxiety. "That's exactly the problem," Liz admitted. "The connection is complicating our professional relationship."

"Complications aren't always negative," Sophia observed, arranging her material samples on the conference table. "Some of the most beautiful designs emerge from unexpected constraints."

"This isn't about design aesthetics. It's about project integrity and professional reputations." Liz moved toward the door, needing to escape this conversation before she revealed too much. "I should go. I have a meeting with Howard in twenty minutes."

"Elizabeth." Sophia's voice stopped her at the threshold. "For what it's worth, I've never seen James as engaged or alive as he's been since this project started. Whatever's happening between you has made him better at what he does, not worse."

The observation lingered as Liz walked toward her office, creating uncomfortable questions about Catherine's warning. Was distance truly necessary to protect the project? Or was their connection actually enhancing their professional collaboration rather than compromising it?

Before she could resolve this contradiction, she spotted James in the hallway ahead, speaking with a junior engineer. He looked up as she approached, their eyes meeting briefly before both carefully looked away. The deliberate avoidance felt like physical pain, a denial of the recognition that had formed the core of their connection.

As she passed, maintaining professional distance, James continued his conversation without interruption. Only the slight tension in his shoulders revealed any awareness of her presence. The performance was perfect, colleagues acknowledging each other with appropriate courtesy and nothing more.

Liz continued to the ladies room, closing the door behind her before leaning against it, suddenly struggling to breathe. The walls seemed to close in, the space feeling like a prison rather than a sanctuary. She moved to the sink, splashing cold water on her face.

A panic attack. She recognized the symptoms from the rare episodes she'd experienced during particularly stressful periods in college. The racing heart, constricted breathing, sensation of impending doom, all physiological responses to emotional overwhelm.

Liz forced herself to inhale slowly, counting to four, holding, then exhaling to a count of six. The controlled breathing gradually calmed her racing pulse, though the emotional turmoil remained undiminished.

What was happening to her? She'd always prided herself on emotional control, on rational decision-making, on professional focus that transcended personal complications. Yet here she was, having a panic attack in an office bathroom because she'd walked past James without acknowledging their connection.

The truth she'd been avoiding crystallized with painful clarity: she was falling in love with James Calloway. Not just physical attraction or intellectual stimulation or emotional response, but something that encompassed all three, a recognition of compatibility so profound it had shaken the foundations of her carefully constructed life.

And now she faced an impossible choice. Create distance from the person who made her feel truly alive, or risk the project that represented both their professional futures. Protect her awakening heart, or protect her hard-earned career. Choose personal fulfillment or professional responsibility.

The bathroom mirror reflected a woman she barely recognized, flushed cheeks, bright eyes despite the shadows beneath them, an intensity of expression that had been absent for years. She splashed more cold water on her face, attempting to restore her professional composure.

"Get it together," she whispered to her reflection. "The project comes first. It has to."

But as she dried her hands and straightened her blouse, Liz couldn't silence the voice asking whether she was making the right choice for the right reasons. Was she creating distance to protect the project, as she claimed? Or was she retreating from the vulnerability James evoked, from the terrifying prospect of being truly seen and known after years of emotional isolation?

Catherine was right about one thing, personal complications rarely ended well in professional contexts. What she and James had discovered together was too precious, too profound to risk destroying through hasty entanglements amid project pressures and her unresolved marriage.

Yet as she returned to her office, Liz couldn't shake the sense that in choosing professional responsibility over personal connection, she might be sacrificing something irreplaceable. The recognition James offered, seeing her completely and valuing what he saw, had awakened her to possibilities she'd forgotten existed.

Could she truly walk away from that recognition now that she'd experienced it? And if she did, would she ever find it again?

The questions had no easy answers. Like the exposed structural elements in architectural design, the truth of her situation was now visible, impossible to conceal behind professional facades or rationalization. Whatever choice she made would shape not just the project but the woman she was becoming, the Elizabeth Mitchell who had begun to emerge from beneath years of compromise and accommodation.

All she knew with certainty was that the path ahead would require courage she wasn't sure she possessed, courage to either deny her awakening heart for professional obligation, or to risk everything for a connection that had no guarantees beyond its present power.

CHAPTER THIRTY

"Breaking Point"

The dining room table gleamed under soft candlelight, a bottle of Cabernet, their wedding vintage, breathing beside carefully arranged place settings. Liz adjusted the roses in their crystal vase, smoothing invisible wrinkles from the tablecloth as she waited for Mark to return from changing his clothes. Fifteen years of marriage culminating in this carefully orchestrated anniversary dinner that felt more like a wake than a celebration.

She'd spent the afternoon cooking his favorite meal, beef Wellington, roasted potatoes, haricots verts with almonds, dishes that required attention and precision. The activity had given her something to focus on besides the conversation that loomed ahead. Now, with everything prepared and the stage set, nervous energy thrummed through her veins.

Mark appeared in the doorway, freshly showered and wearing the blue button-down she'd given him for Christmas. He'd made an effort, at least with his appearance. His eyes widened slightly at the formal table setting.

"Wow. You went all out." He approached, dropping a perfunctory kiss on her cheek before settling into his usual chair. "Smells great."

Liz poured wine for both of them, taking a steadying sip before serving the food. "I thought we should mark the occasion properly."

Mark nodded, already cutting into his Wellington. "Fifteen years. Pretty major milestone."

The silence that followed felt leaden. Once, they would have reminisced about their wedding day, shared memories of early adventures, perhaps even made plans for future celebrations. Now they sat like polite strangers at a dinner party neither had particularly wanted to attend.

"This is delicious," Mark offered after several bites. "You outdid yourself."

"Thank you." Liz pushed food around her plate, appetite vanishing despite hours of preparation. "I found the recipe in that cookbook from our Napa trip."

"The anniversary trip." Mark nodded, remembering. "That was a good vacation."

"It was five years ago," Liz said quietly. "Our tenth anniversary."

Mark looked up, confusion flickering across his features. "Was it that long ago? Seems more recent."

"Time blurs together when every day feels the same." The words emerged more sharply than she'd intended.

Mark set down his fork, wariness replacing confusion. "Okay. What's that supposed to mean?"

Liz took another sip of wine, gathering courage. "When was the last time we really talked, Mark? Not about schedules or groceries or fantasy sports scores. Actually connected about something that matters?"

"We're talking now," he said defensively. "I'm complimenting your cooking, discussing our anniversary. What more do you want?"

The question hung between them, so perfectly encapsulating their disconnect that Liz almost laughed. What did she want? Everything he couldn't give her, intellectual challenge, genuine interest in her thoughts, recognition of who she truly was rather than her sole identity as 'Marks wife'.

"I want to feel like my husband actually sees me," she said finally. "Knows me. Cares about what I think and feel beyond how it affects his dinner plans."

Mark's expression hardened. "C'mon, you know that's not fair. I've always supported you."

"Support isn't the same as engagement, Mark." Liz set down her wine glass carefully. "When was the last time you asked about my work and actually listened to the answer? When was the last time we had a conversation about ideas or dreams or anything beyond our daily routine?"

"Is this about the project again?" Mark's voice rose slightly. "Because I've been trying to be supportive of these crazy hours, but it's not exactly easy when you're never home."

"This isn't about hours or schedules." Liz struggled to articulate the emptiness that had been growing between them long before the Meridian project. "It's about connection. About seeing each other. About wanting to share our lives instead of just living together."

Mark stared at her as if she were speaking a foreign language. "We're married, Liz. We share a house, a name, a life. What more do you want?"

The question struck at the heart of her confusion. What did she want? The answer was complicated by thoughts of James, his intellectual challenge, his genuine interest in her perspective, the electricity of their connection. But those feelings had emerged because something fundamental was already missing in her marriage.

"I want to feel alive again," she admitted. "To have conversations that challenge me. To create something meaningful. To be seen for who I really am, not just what I can provide."

Mark's expression shifted from confusion to hurt. "So I'm not enough for you anymore? I don't make you feel 'alive'?" He made air quotes around the word, mockery edging his tone.

"That's not what I said." Liz took a deep breath, trying to steer the conversation away from defensiveness. "I'm talking about us, about how we've grown apart. When was the last time we felt truly connected to each other?"

Mark opened his mouth to respond, then closed it again. His brow furrowed as he actually considered the question. "Things were good in Napa," he offered finally. "The anniversary trip."

"Five years ago," Liz repeated softly. "And even then, we spent half the time doing separate activities. You golfed while I visited wineries. We met up for dinner and talked about... what? The weather? Golf scores?"

"You're making it sound worse than it was."

"Am I? What did we talk about at dinner last night?"

Mark's silence was answer enough.

"You don't know because we didn't have dinner together last night," Liz continued. "Or the night before. When we do eat together, you watch sports highlights on your phone. We haven't had a real conversation in months. Maybe years."

Mark pushed his plate away, appetite apparently gone. "So this anniversary dinner is what? Some kind of test I'm failing?"

"It's not a test, Mark. It's an opportunity to be honest with each other." Liz reached for the card he'd given her earlier, a generic anniversary message with a hasty signature, no personal note. Beside it sat the small wrapped package containing a gift certificate to a department store. "Do you even know what I like anymore? What interests me? What I dream about?"

"You're being dramatic." Mark's voice hardened further. "Every marriage goes through phases. We're busy people with demanding careers."

"It's more than a phase." Liz met his gaze directly. "We've become strangers who share a house. We don't talk, we don't connect, we don't even seem to like each other very much anymore."

"Jesus, Liz." Mark ran a hand through his hair in frustration. "Where is this coming from? We were fine last month."

"Were we? Or were we just going through motions because it was easier than acknowledging the truth?"

Mark studied her face, something shifting in his expression. "You've changed," he said slowly. "The past few months, you've been different. Distant. Critical. Like you're measuring me against some standard I don't even know about."

The observation was uncomfortably perceptive. Had she been comparing him to James? The intellectual stimulation, the genuine interest in her thoughts, the feeling of being truly seen—all things she'd experienced with James that had been missing from her marriage for years.

"I've changed because I've remembered who I used to be," Liz said carefully. "The person with thoughts and dreams and ambitions beyond keeping this household running smoothly."

"And I'm what? The anchor dragging you down?" Mark's voice took on a bitter edge. "The boring husband who can't keep up with the brilliant marketing director?"

"That's not what I'm saying." Liz felt the conversation slipping away from her, deteriorating into accusation rather than understanding. "I'm trying to be honest about where we are. About the disconnect that's been growing between us for years. Mark, when was the last time we made love? I mean truly made love, not mounting me after a ballgame and then rolling over and falling asleep. I'm not trying to be mean...but I haven't felt desired in a very long time."

Mark was silent for a long moment, staring into his wine glass. When he looked up, his expression had shifted from defensive to suspicious.

"Is there someone else?"

The direct question sent a jolt through her system. "This is about us, Mark. About our marriage."

"That's not an answer." His eyes narrowed. "You start talking about feeling 'alive' and 'seen' right around the time you began working crazy hours on this building project. It doesn't take a genius to connect those dots."

Heat rose to Liz's cheeks, guilt and indignation warring within her. "The problems in our marriage existed long before the Meridian project," she said, technically truthful while avoiding direct denial. "I've just finally stopped ignoring them."

"Because someone else is making you feel 'alive'?" Mark's emphasis dripped with accusation. "That architect guy? James?"

The proximity to truth made her defensive. "This isn't about James. It's about us. About the fact that we've been growing apart for years, and neither of us has been willing to acknowledge it."

"Right." Mark's bitter laugh held no humor. "You just suddenly decided our fifteen-year marriage is empty on the exact same timeline you started working closely with your old high school rival. Pure coincidence."

"It's not sudden," Liz countered, clinging to this undeniable truth. "It's been building for years. The project just gave me perspective I was missing, reminded me what it feels like to be intellectually engaged, to have my thoughts valued, to create something meaningful."

"So I don't value your thoughts? I don't engage you intellectually?" Mark's voice rose with each question. "I'm just the dumb jock who can't keep up with your brilliant mind?"

"I never said that." Liz struggled to steer the conversation back to productive ground. "But when was the last time you asked about my work and actually listened? When was the last time we discussed a book or a film or an idea that challenged either of us?"

Mark stared at her, anger gradually giving way to something that looked almost like fear. "I don't know what you want from me, Liz. I've been the same person since the day we met."

"That's exactly the problem," she said quietly. "We're not the same people we were fifteen years ago. At least, I'm not. I've changed, grown, evolved. But our relationship has stayed frozen in patterns that don't fit who I've become."

"And who have you become? Someone too good for her husband? Someone who needs fancy architects to feel 'intellectually engaged'?" The mockery in his voice couldn't quite mask the hurt beneath.

"Someone who wants more than going through the motions," Liz replied, refusing to be baited into anger. "Someone who's tired of pretending everything's fine when we both know it isn't."

Mark pushed back from the table abruptly, chair legs scraping against hardwood. He paced to the window and back, agitation evident in every movement. When he turned to face her again, his expression had transformed from anger to something closer to pleading.

"I can change," he said suddenly. "I can be more attentive, ask about your work, read those marketing books you're always talking about. We could do couples therapy. People fix marriages all the time."

The unexpected pivot caught Liz off guard. She'd prepared for anger, defensiveness, even accusations, but not this desperate bargaining from a man who'd shown no interest in their emotional connection for years.

"Mark—"

"We've been together fifteen years," he continued, returning to the table and reaching for her hand. "That's worth fighting for. We can make this work. I'll try harder."

His fingers felt foreign against hers, the gesture of connection too little, too late. Liz gently withdrew her hand.

"I think we're past that point," she said softly. "The issues between us aren't things that can be fixed with therapy or sudden interest in my work. We've grown in fundamentally different directions."

"You're not even willing to try?" Disbelief colored his voice. "Fifteen years and you're just... done?"

"I've been trying for years," Liz replied, the truth of this statement resonating deeply. "Making myself smaller, suppressing my interests, pretending to care about things that bore me. I can't do it anymore."

"Because you've found someone who makes you feel 'alive'?" The accusation returned, sharper than before.

"Because I've remembered what it feels like to be authentic," Liz corrected. "To not perform a role every minute I'm home. To be valued for my mind as much as any other quality."

Mark stared at her, realization dawning in his eyes. "You're having an affair."

"This isn't about anyone else," Liz insisted, though the flush spreading across her cheeks betrayed her. "It's about us. About the fundamental disconnect that's been growing for years."

"You are," Mark said, certainty replacing suspicion. "It's written all over your face. Jesus, Liz. After everything we've built together?"

"What have we built, Mark?" The question emerged with unexpected force. "A house we occupy like separate tenants? A marriage that exists on paper but not in reality? We haven't had a meaningful conversation in years. We haven't made love—really made love, not just gone through the motions—in longer than I can remember."

"So you found someone else to fill those gaps," Mark concluded, his voice flat. "Instead of talking to me about problems, you just replaced me."

"That's not what happened." Liz struggled to make him understand. "My unhappiness in our marriage isn't because of anyone else. It existed long before... complications arose."

"Complications." Mark repeated the word with bitter emphasis. "Nice euphemism for cheating on your husband."

The accusation stung, not because it was entirely false but because it oversimplified a complex situation. "I'm not proud of every choice I've made," Liz acknowledged. "But my decision about our marriage stands independently. We've been going through motions for years, Mark. Both of us."

"And now you want out." It wasn't a question.

"I think we need space to figure out what we truly want," Liz said carefully. "A separation to gain perspective without this daily performance."

"A separation." Mark laughed without humor. "Just say what you mean, Liz. You want a divorce so you can be with him."

"I want to be honest about where we are," she countered. "About the fact that our marriage has been empty for years. About the reality that we've become different people with different needs and dreams."

"And your dream doesn't include me anymore." Mark's voice had gone dangerously quiet.

"My dream includes being authentic," Liz replied. "Living honestly instead of performing a role that doesn't fit. Don't you want that too? To be with someone who truly sees and appreciates who you are, not just what you provide?"

"What I want," Mark said slowly, "is the wife I married. The woman who used to look at me like I mattered. Who didn't measure me against some intellectual standard I can never meet."

"That woman doesn't exist anymore," Liz said gently. "And I don't think you've seen the real me for a very long time."

Silence fell between them, the anniversary dinner cooling on plates neither would finish. Outside, a neighbor's dog barked, the ordinary sound at odds with the life-altering conversation taking place across their dining table.

"I think we should separate," Liz said finally, the words feeling both terrifying and liberating. "Give ourselves space to figure out what we truly want."

Mark stared at her for a long moment, something crumbling behind his eyes. When he spoke, his voice was eerily calm. "You've already decided. This whole dinner was just... what? A courtesy notification, A fuck you...I'm done. I've found someone else. Oh, by the way, happy anniversary?"

"An attempt at honest conversation," Liz corrected. "Something we haven't had in years."

"Well, you've said your piece." Mark stood abruptly. "I hope he's worth it."

"This isn't about anyone else," Liz insisted, though the protest sounded hollow even to her own ears. "It's about us. About what we've become."

"What you've become," Mark corrected bitterly. "Someone who throws away fifteen years for... what? Intellectual stimulation? Feeling 'alive'?"

"For authenticity," Liz said quietly. "For the chance to live honestly instead of performing a role that doesn't fit anymore."

Mark shook his head, a mixture of hurt and disgust crossing his features. "I don't even know who you are anymore."

"That's exactly the problem," Liz replied. "Neither of us really knows the other. We've been living with ghosts of who we were fifteen years ago."

He stared at her a moment longer, as if memorizing the face of someone he might never see again. Then he turned and walked out of the dining room. Seconds later, the front door slammed with decisive finality, leaving Liz alone with cooling food and undrunk wine.

The sound echoed through the house, their house, filled with carefully selected furniture and framed vacation photos and all the trappings of a shared life that had gradually emptied of substance. Fifteen years of marriage ending not with dramatic revelation but with the quiet acknowledgment of a truth they'd both been avoiding: they had become strangers sharing an address, going through motions of a relationship that existed more in memory than present reality.

Liz remained at the table, emotions washing through her in alternating waves. Grief for the years invested, the genuine affection that had existed despite the fundamental mismatch, the shared history that couldn't be erased. Relief at finally acknowledging what she had known subconsciously for years: she and Mark had been growing in different directions for so long that they now occupied entirely different landscapes.

The anniversary dinner sat untouched before her, a fitting metaphor for their marriage, carefully prepared, beautifully presented, and ultimately unsatisfying. Like the relationship itself, it had been constructed with more attention to appearance than substance.

Outside, she heard Mark's car start and pull away, tires squealing slightly as he accelerated down their quiet street. She made no move to follow or call after him. Some departures were necessary, some endings inevitable despite best intentions.

The candles burned lower, wax dripping onto the tablecloth she'd so carefully ironed hours earlier. Liz finally stood, gathering plates to carry to the kitchen. The simple act of cleaning up felt strangely appropriate, the first step in dismantling the life they'd constructed together, sorting what to keep from what to discard.

Whatever happened next, with her marriage, with James, with the life she was only beginning to envision, would be built on honesty rather than performance. The foundation had been inspected, the structural assessment completed. Now came the harder work of determining what could be salvaged and what needed to be torn down completely.

The breaking point had arrived, not in dramatic collapse but in quiet recognition of a truth too fundamental to ignore: some structures couldn't be saved, no matter how impressive their facades appeared to passing observers. The integrity had been compromised long ago, hairline cracks spreading gradually until the entire foundation was threatened.

As Liz wrapped leftover food that neither would eat, she felt the strange combination of grief and liberation that accompanies difficult truth. The life she had constructed was ending, but the life she actually wanted might finally be possible.

CHAPTER THIRTY-ONE

"Demolition"

The weekend arrived with oppressive inevitability. Liz stood in the master bedroom, surrounded by open suitcases and cardboard boxes, methodically sorting through the artifacts of fifteen years shared with Mark. Each item required a decision, keep, leave, discard, that felt both mundane and monumental.

Mark moved through the house like a ghost, appearing in doorways to watch her pack before retreating without speaking. The silence between them had calcified into something almost tangible, broken only by the occasional necessary question about household logistics or shared possessions.

"I'm taking the blue suitcase," Liz said when he appeared in the bedroom doorway for the third time that morning. "Unless you need it."

Mark shrugged, leaning against the doorframe. "Take whatever you want." His voice carried the dull edge of resentment that had characterized their interactions since the anniversary dinner three nights earlier.

Liz continued folding clothes into neat stacks, the practiced efficiency masking her internal turmoil. She'd expected anger, recrimination, perhaps even tearful pleas to reconsider. Instead, Mark had retreated into cold silence punctuated by occasional bitter comments, a response that somehow felt worse than outright hostility.

"I'm not taking much," she said, gesturing to the modest pile of clothing and personal items. "Just what I need until... things are settled."

"Until the divorce, you mean." Mark's flat statement hung in the air between them. "Might as well say it."

Liz set down the sweater she'd been folding, meeting his gaze directly. "Yes. Until the divorce."

Something flickered in Mark's eyes, pain, perhaps, or resignation, before his expression hardened again. "Fifteen years. Thrown away like it meant nothing."

"It meant something," Liz replied, struggling to maintain her composure. "But meaning something and working aren't the same thing. We've been unhappy for years, Mark. Both of us."

"Speak for yourself." He pushed away from the doorframe, hands jammed in his pockets. "I was fine until you decided I wasn't enough anymore."

The accusation stung precisely because it contained a kernel of truth. She had changed, had awakened to possibilities beyond their comfortable but hollow existence. But the awakening had merely illuminated what was already broken, not created the fractures.

"Do you really believe that?" she asked quietly. "That we were truly happy? That our marriage was fulfilling for either of us?"

Mark looked away, his jaw tightening. "We had a life together. A good one. Maybe not perfect, but what is?"

"We had routines," Liz corrected gently. "Schedules. Logistics. But connection? Real partnership? When was the last time we had that?"

He had no answer, which was answer enough.

A memory surfaced unexpectedly, their first apartment, barely six hundred square feet with a kitchenette that could barely fit one person. How happy they had been even without luxury.

The contrast between those early days and what they'd become created an ache in her chest, not for what she was losing now, but for what had slipped away so gradually neither had noticed until it was gone.

"Remember our first place?" she asked softly. "That tiny apartment with the leaky faucet and the neighbor who played saxophone at midnight?"

A ghost of a smile touched Mark's lips. "The one with the bathroom door that wouldn't close all the way. You used to sing in the shower so loud Mrs. Peterson would bang on the ceiling."

"We were happy then," Liz acknowledged. "Young and in love and excited about everything."

"What happened to us?" The question emerged with unexpected vulnerability, Mark's defensive anger momentarily replaced by genuine confusion.

Liz considered her answer carefully. "Life happened. Careers. Routines. We started going through the motions instead of really seeing each other. And somewhere along the way, we became different people with different needs."

"Different people," Mark repeated, bitterness returning. "You mean you became different. Too good for your basketball-playing husband with his boring sales job and fantasy leagues."

"That's not fair," Liz countered, though she couldn't entirely deny the evolution he described. "We both changed. The difference is that I finally acknowledged it instead of pretending everything was fine."

Mark studied her face, something shifting in his expression. "You really believe that? That we've been broken for years?"

"I do." Liz held his gaze steadily. "And I think part of you knows it too. Otherwise, you'd be fighting harder to save this."

The doorbell's chime interrupted whatever response Mark might have made. He turned away without another word, footsteps heavy on the stairs as he went to answer it.

Liz released a shaky breath, returning to her methodical packing. Each item carried memories, the cashmere sweater from their Napa trip, the silk scarf he'd given her for their tenth anniversary, the worn Northwestern t-shirt she'd stolen from him during their first year dating. She sorted them with careful deliberation, separating necessities from nostalgia.

"Your sister's here," Mark announced from the doorway, his tone making it clear he considered Rebecca an interloper in their private drama.

"I asked her to help," Liz explained, closing the suitcase. "And to give me a ride to her place."

Mark's expression hardened. "So you're staying with her. Not even a hotel. You've had this planned."

"I called her after our conversation," Liz corrected. "I needed somewhere to go while we figure things out."

"While you figure things out, you mean." Mark's voice dropped to a dangerous quiet. "I'm pretty clear on where things stand."

Before Liz could respond, Rebecca appeared behind him, her practical energy immediately changing the atmosphere. Rebecca Mitchell carried herself with a no nonsense confidence, a woman who had navigated her own divorce years before and emerged stronger for the experience.

"Hey, sis," she said, squeezing past Mark with deliberate cheerfulness. "Making progress?"

"Almost done with the essentials," Liz replied, grateful for the buffer. "Just need to grab a few things from the bathroom."

"I'll start taking these down," Rebecca said, hefting the suitcase with surprising strength. She turned to Mark with professional politeness. "Good to see you, Mark. I'm sorry about the circumstances."

Mark nodded stiffly, retreating downstairs without response. Rebecca raised an eyebrow at Liz once he was out of earshot.

"Icy reception," she murmured. "How's it been?"

"About what you'd expect," Liz sighed, gathering toiletries from the master bathroom. "Alternating between angry silence and bitter comments, with occasional glimpses of the hurt underneath."

"Classic first stage," Rebecca nodded knowingly. "Richard went through the same pattern. It'll evolve to bargaining soon, then depression, then eventually acceptance. The divorce grief cycle is surprisingly predictable."

Liz paused, toothbrush in hand. "You make it sound so clinical."

"It helps to see patterns sometimes," Rebecca shrugged. "Makes the emotional chaos feel less personal, more universal." She picked up a framed photo from the dresser, Liz and Mark on their honeymoon, young and beaming. "Are you taking any of these?"

"Not now," Liz said, turning away from the visual reminder of what they'd once been. "Maybe later, when it doesn't feel so..."

"Raw," Rebecca supplied. "I get it. I kept our wedding album in a box for three years before I could look at it without crying."

They worked in companionable silence, Rebecca helping sort remaining essentials while Liz made final decisions about what to take. The process felt strangely like archeology, excavating layers of a shared life, determining which artifacts still held meaning and which had become mere relics of a past no longer relevant.

Downstairs, they found Mark in the kitchen, staring out the window toward the carefully maintained backyard he'd spent countless weekends perfecting. He turned as they entered, his expression unreadable.

"Is that everything?" he asked, gesturing to the bags Rebecca carried.

"For now," Liz replied, setting down her tote. "I'll need to come back for more once I find a permanent place."

"No rush," Mark said, the words contradicting his tense posture. "Not like I'm going anywhere."

Rebecca glanced between them, then tactfully announced, "I'll put these in the car. Take your time."

After she left, the kitchen fell into uncomfortable silence. Liz looked around at the space they'd renovated together three years ago, custom cabinets, quartz countertops, the expensive refrigerator Mark had insisted on for its sports drink dispenser. Like everything in their home, it was beautiful, functional, and ultimately hollow, a showcase rather than a heart.

"I never wanted this," Mark said suddenly, his voice rough with emotion. "I thought we were fine. Building a life together."

"I know you did," Liz acknowledged, the simple truth creating unexpected compassion. "And part of me wanted to believe that too. It was easier than admitting how far apart we'd grown."

"We could fix this," he said, a desperate edge entering his voice. "Couples therapy. Date nights. Whatever it takes. I can change, Liz."

The bargaining stage, right on cue. Rebecca's prediction materializing with painful accuracy.

"It's not about changing, Mark," Liz said gently. "It's about recognizing that we want fundamentally different things from life. You deserve someone who shares your interests, your vision for the future. So do I."

"Someone like your architect?" The bitter question carried all the accusations he hadn't directly voiced.

Liz met his gaze steadily. "This isn't about James or anyone else. It's about us. About the fact that we've been sleep walking through this marriage for years without really seeing each other."

"But there is someone else," Mark pressed, his expression hardening. "Don't insult me by denying it."

"There are... complications," Liz admitted carefully. "But they're not why our marriage is ending. They're a symptom of what was already broken between us."

Mark turned away, hands gripping the edge of the counter until his knuckles whitened. "Fifteen years, Liz. Fifteen fucking years, and you're walking away for some guy you reconnected with months ago."

"I'm walking away because staying means continuing to pretend," Liz countered, maintaining her calm despite his escalating anger. "Because we both deserve more than living a lie for another fifteen years."

"What I deserve is a wife who honors her vows," Mark shot back. "Who works on problems instead of running away."

"Is that what you think I'm doing? Running away?" Liz felt her own anger rising to match his. "I've been trying to connect with you for years, Mark. Initiating conversations you dismiss. Sharing thoughts you ignore. Suggesting activities you reject for sports or fantasy leagues or whatever game is on that night."

"So this is my fault?" Mark's voice rose. "I'm the bad guy because I like sports and don't want to discuss marketing strategies over dinner?"

"It's not about fault," Liz said, forcing her voice to remain steady. "It's about compatibility. About whether we still want the same things, if we ever did."

Mark stared at her, anger gradually giving way to something that looked almost like fear. "What do you want from me, Liz? Just tell me what you want, and I'll do it."

The desperate plea struck at her heart, not because it tempted her to reconsider but because it revealed how little he understood the fundamental problem. He still believed this was a negotiation, a set of behaviors he could modify to restore the status quo.

"I want you to be happy, Mark," she said quietly. "With someone who loves sports and fantasy leagues and lazy Sundays watching games. Someone who shares your vision for life instead of pretending to for the sake of peace."

"And I want my wife back," he countered, voice breaking slightly. "The woman I married. The one who used to look at me like I mattered."

"That woman doesn't exist anymore," Liz said gently. "And I don't think she has for a very long time."

The front door opened and closed, Rebecca's deliberate noise announcing her return without intruding. Mark straightened, composing his features into a mask of indifference that didn't quite conceal the pain beneath.

"Your ride's waiting," he said flatly. "Wouldn't want to keep her."

Liz picked up her tote, hesitating in the kitchen doorway. "I'll call about coming back for more things. And we should talk about practical matters, bills, the house, legal next steps."

"Whatever." Mark turned back to the window, shoulders rigid with tension. "Do what you need to do."

The dismissal stung despite its predictability. Liz lingered a moment longer, searching for words that might ease the transition, might honor what they'd once meant to each other without pretending it could be salvaged.

"For what it's worth," she said finally, "I did love you, Mark. Very much. And part of me always will."

He didn't respond, didn't turn, gave no indication he'd even heard her. Liz sighed and walked away, each step both burden and liberation. In the foyer, Rebecca waited with car keys in hand, her expression sympathetic but mercifully free of judgment.

"Ready?" she asked simply.

Liz nodded, unable to trust her voice. As they walked to the car, she resisted the urge to look back at the house, the perfect colonial with its manicured lawn and welcoming facade that had concealed the emptiness within. Like her marriage, it had been beautiful on the surface but ultimately hollow, a stage set rather than a home.

Rebecca drove in thoughtful silence, allowing Liz space to process the morning's emotions. The familiar neighborhoods gave way to city streets as they headed toward Rebecca's downtown loft, physical distance mirroring the emotional journey Liz had begun.

"He'll be okay, you know," Rebecca said finally as they waited at a red light. "It doesn't feel like it now, but Mark will adjust. Find his way forward."

"I hope so," Liz replied, watching raindrops begin to speckle the windshield. "I never wanted to hurt him."

"Divorce always hurts," Rebecca said matter-of-factly. "But sometimes staying hurts more in the long run. For both people."

The simple truth resonated deeply. Whatever pain their separation caused now, continuing the performance would have created deeper damage over time, resentment calcifying into bitterness, disappointment hardening into contempt.

Rebecca's loft welcomed them with its open floor plan and eclectic furnishings, a space that reflected its owner's personality rather than following design trends. Art from local painters covered the walls, vintage furniture mixed with modern pieces, books stacked on every available surface. The contrast with the carefully coordinated aesthetic of the house Liz had just left couldn't have been more striking.

"Guest room's all set up," Rebecca announced, setting down Liz's suitcase. "Bathroom's stocked with towels and those fancy products you like. And I've cleared a shelf in the medicine cabinet for your stuff."

The thoughtful preparations brought unexpected tears to Liz's eyes. "Thank you," she managed. "For everything."

Rebecca squeezed her shoulder. "That's what sisters are for. Now, unpack what you need while I open wine. This day definitely requires alcohol."

An hour later, they sat on Rebecca's balcony overlooking the city, wine glasses in hand, Liz's essentials arranged in the guest room that would be her temporary home. The rain had stopped, leaving behind the fresh scent of wet concrete and that peculiar clarity of air that follows a storm.

"So," Rebecca said after they'd settled, "we've discussed Mark. We've discussed logistics. We've discussed divorce attorneys. But we haven't discussed the architect in the room."

Liz nearly choked on her wine. "That's not subtle, Becks."

"Subtlety is overrated," Rebecca shrugged. "And you've been carefully avoiding the topic since you called about staying here. Which means there's definitely something to discuss."

Liz stared into her wine glass, weighing how much to reveal. Her relationship with James remained complicated, professional collaboration tangled with personal connection, intellectual compatibility deepened by physical attraction. How could she explain something she barely understood herself?

"It's complex," she said finally. "James and I have a connection that goes beyond professional collaboration. An intellectual chemistry I never experienced with Mark."

"Intellectual chemistry," Rebecca repeated, her skepticism evident. "So he's smokin' hot?"

"I'm serious," Liz insisted. "It's not just physical attraction. It's the way he challenges my thinking, values my perspective, sees me as an intellectual equal."

"And I'm sure he's absolutely hideous to look at," Rebecca teased. "Just a troll with a brilliant mind."

Despite everything, Liz laughed. "Fine. He's attractive. But that's not the foundation of what's happening between us."

"So something is definitely happening," Rebecca pounced on the admission. "Details, please. Preferably juicy ones."

Liz hesitated, then decided her sister deserved honesty. "We've been... involved. Physically. It started during a business trip, after months of professional collaboration and growing awareness."

"While you were still with Mark," Rebecca clarified, her tone shifting from teasing to serious.

"Yes." Liz met her sister's gaze directly. "I'm not proud of that part. But my marriage was over long before anything happened with James. We were just going through the motions, both of us."

Rebecca studied her for a long moment. "I believe you. But be careful about the narrative you're creating, Liz. It's easy to rewrite history to justify present actions."

"I'm not rewriting anything," Liz protested. "Mark and I have been disconnected for years. You've seen it yourself."

"I have," Rebecca acknowledged. "Your marriage has been on life support for as long as I can remember. But timing matters in these situations. Starting something new before ending something old creates... complications."

"Trust me, I'm aware of the complications," Liz sighed, refilling her wine glass. "Professional, personal, ethical—it's a minefield."

"And yet you stepped into it anyway," Rebecca observed. "Which tells me this connection with James must be pretty significant."

Liz considered this perspective. "It is. He sees me in ways Mark never did, never could, maybe. We connect on multiple levels, mind, values, creative vision."

"And I'm guessing the sex doesn't hurt either," Rebecca said dryly.

Heat rose to Liz's cheeks. "That part is... different too."

"Different good or different weird? Because some architects have very strange ideas about structural integrity, if you know what I mean."

"Rebecca!" Liz laughed despite herself. "You're impossible."

"Just trying to lighten the mood," Rebecca grinned. "But seriously, I'm glad you've found someone who values your mind. That's rarer than it should be."

They sat in silence, watching the city lights emerge as dusk descended. The day's emotional weight began to lift slightly, perspective emerging with physical and temporal distance from the morning's difficult scenes.

"What happens now?" Rebecca asked finally. "With James, I mean. Now that you're officially separated."

"I honestly have no friggin' clue," Liz admitted. "We still have the project to complete. Professional boundaries to maintain. And I need time to process the end of my marriage before jumping into something new."

"Wise approach," Rebecca nodded approvingly. "Though timing is rarely convenient when it comes to matters of the heart."

"Or matters of architectural deadlines," Liz added ruefully. "The Meridian project enters a critical phase next month. James and I will be working even more closely together."

"While maintaining professional boundaries," Rebecca said skeptically. "Good luck with that."

"We're adults with self-control," Liz protested, though her conviction wavered. "The project has to come first."

"Mmm-hmm." Rebecca's expression remained doubtful. "Just remember—whatever you decide about James should be independent of your divorce. Leave Mark because your relationship has run its course, not because there's someone new in your life."

"I know," Liz nodded, the advice echoing her therapist's guidance. "That's why I need time. To make sure any decision comes from clarity, not reaction."

They finished their wine as night fell completely, the city transformed into a constellation of lights mapping human activity in the darkness. Inside the loft, Liz's phone chimed with a text notification. She checked it reflexively, expecting Mark with practical questions or angry accusations.

Instead, it was James: *Sophia mentioned you weren't at the office today. Everything okay?*

The simple inquiry created a warmth that spread through her chest. No demands, no expectations, just genuine concern. Liz considered her response carefully, aware of Rebecca watching her with knowing eyes.

Taking a personal day. Mark and I are separating. I've moved to Rebecca's temporarily.

She hesitated, then added: *Will explain more later. At office Monday.*

The reply came almost immediately: *I'm sorry about the difficult situation. Here if you need anything. Not because of me, I hope.*

The last sentence carried all the complexity of their entanglement, his awareness of potential influence, his concern about being the catalyst rather than the cause, his genuine care for her wellbeing regardless of what it meant for them.

Liz typed her response with careful honesty: *Because of us—Mark and me. A long time coming. But thank you for caring.*

She set down the phone, meeting Rebecca's questioning gaze. "James," she explained simply. "Checking if I'm okay."

"And are you?" Rebecca asked. "Okay, I mean. It's been a hell of a day."

Liz considered the question seriously. The morning's painful conversations with Mark, the symbolic weight of packing essential items, the finality of walking away from fifteen years of shared history, all created genuine grief that couldn't be dismissed. Yet beneath that grief ran a current of something that felt surprisingly like relief, the liberation of honesty after years of pretense.

"I'm sad," she acknowledged. "About what we lost. About hurting Mark. About the life we tried to build together."

"But?" Rebecca prompted, hearing the unspoken qualification.

"But I also feel... lighter. Like I've set down a burden I've been carrying for years." Liz gazed out at the city lights. "Is that terrible? To feel relief alongside the grief?"

"It's human," Rebecca said simply. "And it's honest. Two things you haven't allowed yourself to be for a very long time."

The observation struck with unexpected force. How long had she been performing rather than living? Accommodating rather than expressing? Shrinking to fit the space allocated rather than expanding into her full self?

"I don't even know who I am without Mark," Liz confessed. "We've been together since college. My adult identity formed around being his wife."

"Then maybe this is your chance to find out," Rebecca suggested. "To rediscover Elizabeth Mitchell beneath the layers of Elizabeth Donovan."

The prospect was simultaneously terrifying and exhilarating, a blank canvas after years of painting by numbers. Whatever came next, with her divorce, with James, with her career and life, would emerge from authentic choice rather than obligation or expectation.

As they cleared their wine glasses and moved inside, Liz felt the strange combination of grief and possibility that accompanies major life transitions. The demolition had begun, the necessary dismantling of a structure that no longer served its purpose. What would be built in its place remained uncertain, the blueprints still forming.

But for the first time in years, she felt genuinely present in her own life, architect rather than occupant, creator rather than curator. The foundation inspection had revealed structural weaknesses too significant to ignore. Now came the harder, more important work of building something new on ground that had been thoroughly cleared.

CHAPTER THIRTY-TWO

"Project Setback"

T he steel beams of the Meridian construction site gleamed in the afternoon sunlight, a skeletal framework promising the building to come. Liz stood at the edge of the excavation, watching workers swarm like ants around a massive concrete pour that had gone terribly wrong. The foreman gestured frantically at blueprints spread across a makeshift table while Howard Meridian's face grew increasingly flushed with each passing minute.

"How bad is it?" she asked James, who had just emerged from an intense conversation with the structural engineer.

"Bad enough." His voice was tight, professional mask firmly in place despite the tension radiating from him. "The concrete mixture was improperly formulated. The foundation section we poured yesterday won't cure correctly—the entire east wing connection point will need to be demolished and rebuilt."

Liz winced. "Timeline impact?"

"Three weeks minimum. Possibly five." James ran a hand through his hair, the only visible crack in his composure. "I need to tell Howard."

They both glanced toward the CEO, who was already stalking in their direction, his normally affable expression replaced by thunderous irritation.

"Please tell me there's a solution that doesn't involve starting over," Howard said without preamble.

James straightened, meeting the challenge directly. "I wish I could. The mixture had insufficient Portland cement and excessive water content. It won't achieve structural integrity within the acceptable parameters."

"In English, James." Howard's tone sharpened.

"It's too weak to support the building safely," Liz translated. "We have to remove it and start again."

Howard's eyes closed briefly, a man calculating costs against timelines against board expectations. "How long?"

"Three to five weeks," James replied. "Depending on how quickly we can source replacement materials and coordinate the specialty contractors."

"Unacceptable." Howard shook his head. "The board presentation is in six weeks. I promised them we'd be ahead of schedule, not falling behind."

"We can't compromise on structural integrity," James insisted. "This is literally the foundation of the entire project."

Howard paced a tight circle, mind clearly racing. "What about parallel tracking other elements? Can we accelerate something else to offset this delay?"

"Possibly," James nodded. "We could begin fabricating the curtain wall components while the foundation issue is being addressed. It's risky—we'd be committing to measurements before the foundation is complete—but it could save two weeks on the backend."

"Do it," Howard commanded. "And I want daily updates, not weekly. This project cannot fall behind schedule." He turned to Liz. "I need you to craft the messaging for the board. Position this as a quality control success, not a construction failure."

"I'll prepare a communication strategy," she assured him.

"Good." Howard checked his watch. "I have to get back for the investor call. Fix this." The last command encompassed them both before he strode toward his waiting car.

As Howard's vehicle pulled away, the site seemed to exhale collectively. The foreman approached, looking grim.

"We'll need to bring in the demolition equipment tomorrow," he said. "And I'll need approval for the overtime costs."

"You'll have it within the hour," James promised. "Start making the calls. I want everything ready to go at first light."

The foreman nodded and retreated, leaving Liz and James standing at the edge of what had suddenly become a massive problem rather than progress.

"I should get back to the office," Liz said. "Start working on the board communication."

"I'll be here late," James replied. "The engineers need to revise the pour specifications, and I want to personally verify the new mixture formulation."

Their eyes met briefly, the first direct contact since her text about the separation three days earlier. James's expression softened momentarily, professional distance giving way to personal concern.

"How are you doing?" he asked, voice dropping. "With everything."

The simple question created an unexpected lump in her throat. After days of Mark's cold silence and logistical negotiations, the genuine inquiry felt like water in a desert.

"I'm managing," she replied. "Rebecca's been amazing. Having space to think clearly has been... necessary."

James nodded, understanding in his eyes. "If you need anything—"

"Thank you." She cut him off gently, aware of the construction team watching from a distance. "But we should focus on the crisis at hand."

"Of course." His professional mask slid back into place. "I'll email the revised specifications once the engineers complete them."

"I'll be at the office late," Liz said. "Preparing Howard's brief."

The conversation felt strained, artificial, both of them hyperaware of maintaining appropriate boundaries while standing amid dozens of workers. James nodded once more before turning back toward the site office, his posture rigid with controlled tension.

Liz watched him go, the distance between them feeling both necessary and painful. Whatever existed between them, the intellectual connection, the physical attraction, the sense of recognition neither had experienced elsewhere, had to remain contained until the project was secure. Howard's reaction to today's setback only reinforced the professional stakes.

The Meridian offices stood eerily quiet at nine-thirty that evening. Liz sat alone in the conference room, surrounded by timeline projections and contingency plans. She'd spent hours crafting Howard's board communication, transforming a construction disaster into a narrative about quality control excellence and proactive problem-solving.

Her phone chimed with an email notification. James had sent the revised foundation specifications with a brief note: *Engineers have approved these modifications. Will increase structural integrity beyond original specifications, giving us a stronger foundation despite the delay.*

The update was like an oasis in a desert. A lifeline she could work with to reframe the latest disaster. She studied the technical drawings, admiring the elegant solution he'd developed under pressure. Where most architects might have simply replicated the original design, James had used the setback as opportunity to enhance the foundation's load-bearing capacity.

A soft knock at the conference room door startled her. James stood in the doorway, his tall frame silhouetted against the dim hallway lighting.

"I thought you were still at the site," Liz said, surprise making her voice higher than intended.

"Finished about twenty minutes ago." He remained in the doorway, maintaining a careful distance. "Saw your light on when I was driving past. Thought you might want to discuss the revised approach before tomorrow's emergency meeting."

The professional pretext was transparent but necessary. Liz gestured to the chair across from her, establishing a safe physical boundary between them.

"Howard's going to push for a more aggressive timeline compression," she said as James settled into the seat. "He's already concerned about the board's reaction."

"We can't compromise structural integrity," James replied, fatigue evident in the shadows beneath his eyes. "But I've been working on some alternative sequencing that might recover some time."

He spread additional drawings across the table, explaining his approach with the focused intensity that always characterized his work. As they discussed technical details and timeline implications, the initial awkwardness gradually dissolved, replaced by the familiar rhythm of collaborative problem-solving.

"If we stage the interior work by quadrant rather than floor," James explained, sketching rapidly on tracing paper, "we can create this overlapping sequence that shaves twelve days."

They continued working through the crisis management plan, each building on the other's ideas with the intellectual synergy that had characterized their best collaborations. For over an hour, professional focus superseded personal awareness, the project's needs creating safe territory for their interaction.

As they finalized the presentation for tomorrow's emergency meeting, a comfortable silence fell between them. The late hour and empty building created a bubble of privacy that made the carefully maintained professional distance more difficult to sustain.

James was the first to break the silence. "About your separation."

Liz looked up, meeting his eyes directly for the first time that evening. "I should have done it sooner."

"You had a lot to process." His voice carried no judgment, only concern. "Are you okay?"

The simple question again created that unexpected tightness in her throat. "It was the right decision," she said carefully. "Necessary. But still difficult."

James nodded, understanding in his eyes. "Ending a relationship always is, even when it's clearly the right choice."

"Mark thinks it's because of you," Liz admitted. "That you're the reason I left."

"Am I?" The direct question carried no defensiveness, only a desire for truth.

Liz considered her answer carefully. "No," she said finally. "What happened between us forced me to acknowledge what was already broken in my marriage. But those problems existed long before you showed up in my life."

Relief flickered across James's features. "I wouldn't want to be the reason your marriage ended."

"You're not," Liz assured him. "You're the reason I finally found the courage to face what I've known subconsciously for years: Mark and I grew in completely different directions. We want fundamentally different things from life."

James was silent for a moment, absorbing her words. "I had a similar realization during my divorce," he said finally. "Vanessa and I looked perfect on paper, two ambitious architects with shared professional interests. But we wanted different things at a fundamental level. I was building for legacy; she was building for recognition. I never saw it until I came home one night and found a colleague mounting my wife and grunting furiously. That was the wake up call."

"Jesus, I'm sorry, how long did it take you?" Liz asked. "To feel... normal again?"

"To stop feeling like I'd failed?" James clarified with surprising perception. "About a year. To rediscover who I was without her? Longer." He leaned forward slightly. "The hardest part was recognizing that ending a relationship isn't failure. Sometimes it's the most honest choice two people can make. Honestly, I look back now and can't recognize the person I was with her. It may sound...strange but I think it was the best thing that ever happened to me. I'm a new man...I'm me."

The insight resonated deeply, articulating what Liz had been struggling to explain to herself. "That's exactly it," she said quietly. "Staying would have been dishonest, to Mark, to myself, to what marriage should be."

"It takes courage to choose authenticity over comfort," James observed. "Most people never do."

Their eyes held across the table, the conversation creating connection that transcended physical proximity. For a moment, the professional boundaries they'd so carefully established seemed to dissolve, leaving only two people sharing honest recognition of each other.

"I've missed this," Liz admitted, gesturing between them. "The ability to discuss complex ideas without filtering or simplifying. To be understood without having to explain every thought."

"I've missed you," James replied simply. "Not just intellectually. All of you."

The candid admission sent warmth spreading through her chest. "James—"

"I know," he interrupted gently. "The timing is complicated. The project is at a critical juncture. You're just beginning...separated. Everything argues against pursuing whatever this is between us."

"But?" Liz prompted, hearing the unspoken contradiction.

"But I can't stop thinking about you," James admitted, his voice dropping to a lower register. "About the connection we've found. About the possibility of exploring it without the complications that existed before."

Liz felt herself leaning toward him, drawn by the honesty in his expression. "I've thought about you too," she confessed. "More than is probably wise given everything else happening."

The conference table between them suddenly felt like an unnecessary barrier. James stood, moving around to her side but stopping short of actual contact, maintaining a small but crucial distance.

"I don't want to pressure you," he said quietly. "You need time to process your separation, to rediscover who you are outside your marriage. I respect that completely."

"Thank you," Liz replied, genuinely touched by his consideration. "But I've been thinking about who I am apart from Mark for longer than you might realize. The separation is just making official what's been emotionally true for months, maybe years."

James took a step closer, close enough that she could see the flecks of darker blue in his eyes, the slight shadow of stubble along his jaw. "Elizabeth, whatever happens between us, or doesn't happen, I want you to know that I see you. Not just as a brilliant marketing director or a challenging collaborator, but as yourself."

The simple declaration struck at the heart of what had been missing in her marriage for so long, the feeling of being truly seen, valued for her mind as much as any other quality. Without conscious thought, Liz found herself rising from her chair, eliminating the remaining distance between them.

Their lips were inches apart when a sharp knock echoed through the conference room. They stepped apart instantly as the night security guard appeared in the doorway.

"Sorry to interrupt," he said, clearly embarrassed. "Just checking who was still in the building. System shows the alarm was never set for this floor."

"We're working late on a project crisis," Liz explained, her voice remarkably steady despite her racing heart. "Should be wrapping up shortly."

"No problem, ma'am. Just doing my rounds." The guard nodded and retreated, closing the door behind him.

The interruption had effectively shattered the moment's intimacy. James stepped back, creating deliberate professional distance once more.

"We should finish the presentation for tomorrow," he said, voice returning to its professional register.

"You're right," Liz agreed, grateful for the redirect despite the lingering warmth in her chest. "Howard will want the complete recovery plan first thing."

They returned to the architectural drawings, the conversation shifting back to safe technical territory. For another thirty minutes, they finalized timeline adjustments and contingency scenarios, the personal connection carefully contained beneath professional focus.

When they finally packed up their materials, the office remained empty and silent around them. James walked Liz to her car, maintaining appropriate distance as they crossed the parking garage.

"Thank you for your help tonight," he said as they reached her vehicle. "The presentation is stronger for our combined perspective."

"That's always been true," Liz replied, the simple observation carrying deeper meaning. "We create better work together than either of us could alone."

James nodded, his expression softening in the dim garage lighting. "Get some rest. Tomorrow will be challenging."

"For both of us," Liz acknowledged, unlocking her car door. "Goodnight, James."

"Goodnight, Elizabeth."

As she drove toward Rebecca's loft, Liz replayed their conversation in her mind. The almost-moment in the conference room, interrupted by the security guard, had crystallized something she'd been avoiding acknowledging: whatever existed between her and James couldn't be contained indefinitely by professional boundaries or rational considerations.

Like the foundation issue at the construction site, they had discovered a structural weakness that couldn't be ignored. The only question was whether they would demolish and rebuild something stronger, or attempt temporary patches that would inevitably fail under pressure.

The project setback had created professional crisis requiring their complete attention. But it had also provided unexpected opportunity for honest connection, a reminder that some structures were worth rebuilding from the ground up, even when the process was messy, expensive, and time-consuming.

The foundation of her marriage had proved insufficient for the life she wanted to build. Now she faced the challenging but necessary work of clearing away what had failed and establishing something new, something designed with clear understanding of her authentic needs rather than external expectations.

Whether that new foundation would include James remained uncertain. But for the first time in years, Liz felt genuinely hopeful about the possibilities ahead, not just professionally, but personally as well.

CHAPTER THIRTY-THREE

"Redesign Process"

T he morning light filtered through Rebecca's loft windows, casting geometric patterns across the hardwood floors. Liz sat cross-legged on the guest bed, yellow legal pad balanced on her knee, coffee cooling on the nightstand beside her. A week had passed since she'd moved out of the house she'd shared with Mark, a week of emotional recalibration in this temporary sanctuary her sister had created.

She studied the list she'd been working on: *Activities I Used to Love*. The page filled gradually with items she'd abandoned over the years: art gallery visits, literary discussions, architecture tours, sketching, foreign films, poetry readings. Each entry represented a piece of herself surrendered in the slow erosion of her marriage, interests deemed too intellectual, too esoteric, too disconnected from Mark's world of sports statistics and fantasy leagues.

"Planning your renaissance?" Rebecca appeared in the doorway, her own coffee mug in hand, hair still damp from her shower.

"Something like that." Liz smiled, setting down the pad. "Dr. Farmer suggested I reconnect with abandoned interests, rediscover who I am outside my marriage."

Rebecca settled at the foot of the bed, peering at the list. "Poetry readings? You never mentioned being into poetry."

"I minored in it at Northwestern. Used to write some, too." Liz shrugged, a hint of embarrassment coloring her admission. "Mark thought it was pretentious, so I stopped mentioning it. Then stopped going. Then stopped writing."

"That's the saddest thing I've heard all week." Rebecca squeezed her sister's foot through the blanket. "How many other parts of yourself did you pack away?"

"Too many to count," Liz admitted. "It happened so gradually I barely noticed. A skipped gallery opening here, an abandoned book there. Easier to watch basketball than argue about why contemporary literature mattered."

"And now?"

"Now I'm excavating." Liz gestured to the growing list. "Trying to remember who Elizabeth Mitchell was before she became Elizabeth Donovan."

Rebecca nodded approvingly. "That's exactly what I did after my divorce. Rediscovered photography, started taking those cooking classes Richard thought were a waste of money." She paused, studying her sister. "How's the project going? The concrete issue resolved?"

"Getting there." Liz sipped her coffee. "We've redesigned the foundation approach. Should only lose three weeks instead of five."

"We?" Rebecca's eyebrow arched knowingly. "You and the brilliant architect, you mean."

Liz felt heat rise to her cheeks. "James and the entire team. It's a collaborative effort."

"Mmm-hmm." Rebecca's skepticism was evident. "And how's that collaboration going? Still maintaining those professional boundaries you mentioned?"

"Strictly professional," Liz insisted, though the almost-kiss in the conference room flashed vividly in her memory. "The project is too important to both our careers to risk with complications."

"Noble," Rebecca commented, clearly unconvinced. "And completely unrealistic given what you've told me about your connection."

Before Liz could respond, her phone chimed with a text message. She glanced at the screen, her heart accelerating despite her best intentions.

James: *Need to discuss atrium modifications before engineering meeting. Coffee at Riverside Park café, 2pm?*

Rebecca, reading the message upside down, grinned triumphantly. "Strictly professional, huh?"

"It is," Liz protested. "The atrium design is critical to the visitor experience narrative."

"Of course it is." Rebecca stood, heading for the door. "Just remember what your therapist said about distinguishing between escape and growth. Make sure whatever happens with James is about moving forward, not just running away from Mark."

The advice lingered as Liz typed her response: *See you at 2. Bringing the narrative integration notes.*

The Riverside Park café bustled with activity, weekend visitors strolling along the shore or paddling rental boats across the water. Liz arrived early, selecting a table on the outdoor patio where architectural drawings could be spread without crowding other patrons.

She arranged her materials with methodical precision, narrative flow diagrams, visitor experience metrics, brand integration concepts, creating a professional buffer against the awareness that had hummed between them since their almost-moment in the conference room.

James arrived precisely at two, his casual weekend attire, dark jeans and a navy button-down with his sleeves rolled up, somehow more disconcerting than his usual professional armor.

"Elizabeth." He settled into the chair across from her, placing his portfolio on the table. "Thank you for meeting on a weekend."

"The engineering deadline doesn't respect weekends," she replied, maintaining professional distance despite the warmth spreading through her at his presence. "I've reviewed the structural modifications. The impact on narrative flow is minimal if we adjust these transition points."

They fell into work with practiced efficiency, discussing technical details and design implications. For nearly an hour, professional focus superseded personal awareness, the project's demands creating safe territory for their interaction.

"The material transition works better with this approach," James observed, indicating where limestone elements met more innovative components. "The visitor literally experiences progressive tradition through physical movement."

"Exactly." Liz leaned forward, enthusiasm momentarily overriding caution. "The journey becomes embodied narrative rather than intellectual concept."

Their eyes met across the table, shared understanding creating a moment of connection that transcended the architectural discussion. James was the first to break contact, his gaze returning to the drawings with deliberate focus.

"How are you?" he asked quietly, the personal question emerging after an hour of professional conversation. "With everything. The separation."

The simple inquiry created that familiar tightness in her throat. After a week of practical negotiations and emotional processing, the genuine concern in his voice touched something raw and vulnerable.

"Better than expected," she admitted. "Reconnecting with myself after years of... not doing that."

"What does that look like?" James asked, genuine curiosity in his expression.

"Small things. Reading poetry again. Visiting galleries. Sketching." Liz gestured to the notebook peeking from her bag. "Remembering interests I abandoned because they didn't fit into Mark's world."

"You sketch?" Surprise and pleasure mingled in his voice.

"Used to. Architectural details, mostly. Interesting facades, structural elements." She felt suddenly self-conscious. "Nothing professional, just personal observation."

"I'd love to see them sometime," James said, then immediately added, "if you're comfortable sharing, of course."

The request created unexpected warmth. When had anyone last expressed interest in her creative pursuits? Mark had viewed her sketching as a peculiar hobby, something to be tolerated rather than encouraged.

"Maybe someday," she replied, neither promising nor refusing. "What about you? How did you recalibrate after your divorce?"

James considered the question thoughtfully. "Immersed myself in work initially, classic avoidance strategy. Then gradually rediscovered things Vanessa had dismissed. Jazz concerts. Rowing on the river. Cooking elaborate meals for no one but myself."

"Cooking?" Liz couldn't hide her surprise. "You never mentioned that."

"Another data point in our ongoing discovery," he said with a small smile. "We've known each other since we were seventeen, yet there's so much we're still learning."

The observation hung between them, weighted with implication. Their shared history created both connection and complication, former rivals who had become collaborators and now stood at the threshold of something neither could fully define.

"I've been thinking about us," James said finally, his voice dropping to ensure privacy despite the open-air setting. "About what's happening between us."

Liz felt her pulse quicken. "James—"

"Let me finish," he interrupted gently. "I've never met anyone who excites me the way you do. In every way imaginable. It's... rare. Something I'd given up hoping to find."

The candid admission created a flutter beneath her ribs. "I feel the same way," she acknowledged. "The connection we have, it's unlike anything I've experienced before."

"Which makes our situation particularly complicated," James continued. "Your separation is fresh. The project is at a critical juncture. Everything argues for caution."

"But?" Liz prompted, hearing the unspoken qualification.

"But I can't stop thinking about..." he admitted, his eyes holding hers with uncomfortable directness. "About what might be possible between us under different circumstances."

The honesty demanded equal vulnerability in return. "I think about you too," Liz confessed. "More than is probably wise given the chaos that is my life at the moment."

James reached across the table, his hand stopping just short of touching hers. "I think we should pause the physical aspect of our relationship until your situation resolves," he said carefully. "Not because I don't want you, I do, more than I can express, but because whatever is developing between us deserves a clean foundation."

The suggestion created both disappointment and respect. "That's... surprisingly traditional," Liz observed with a small smile.

"I prefer 'ethical,'" James countered, returning her smile. "Or maybe just 'strategic.' Rushing physical intimacy while emotional complexities remain unresolved rarely ends well. I've made that mistake before."

"With Vanessa?"

"With several relationships," he admitted. "Physical chemistry masking fundamental incompatibilities. It took my divorce to recognize the pattern."

Liz nodded slowly, understanding dawning. "So you're suggesting..."

"That we explore this connection carefully. Get to know each other beyond project collaboration and physical attraction. Build something with structural integrity rather than just an appealing façade."

The architectural metaphor wasn't lost on her. "Foundations before finishes," she said, the professional terminology offering safe expression for complicated emotions.

"Exactly." James's expression softened. "I believe what's happening between us has potential beyond temporary comfort or convenient timing. I'd like to discover what that might be without all these complications."

The thoughtfulness of his approach touched her deeply. How different from Mark's simplistic view of relationships, the assumption that physical attraction and shared space constituted a sufficient foundation for a partnership.

"I'd like that too," she said finally. "To discover what's possible without rushing or creating unnecessary complications."

Relief flickered across James's features. "Good. Then we'll proceed with appropriate caution. Professional collaboration continues while we explore personal connection at a pace that respects your circumstances."

"And the project," Liz added. "Which still has to be our priority."

"Of course." James nodded, professional focus returning. "Speaking of which, the engineering meeting Monday will require consensus on these atrium modifications."

They returned to the architectural drawings, the conversation shifting back to technical details and design implications. Yet something had changed, a mutual acknowledgment of possibility that transformed their interaction from cautious avoidance to deliberate exploration.

As afternoon shadows lengthened across the patio, their discussion evolved from project specifications to broader architectural philosophy to personal reflections on creative process. The intellectual connection that had drawn them together from the beginning deepened through honest exchange, creating intimacy beyond the physical encounters they'd agreed to pause.

"I should go," Liz said finally, gathering her materials as the café began filling with dinner patrons. "Rebecca's expecting me for movie night."

"Of course." James collected his portfolio. "I'll walk you to your car."

They moved through the park in comfortable silence, maintaining appropriate distance while acutely aware of each other's presence. At her car, they paused, the moment of parting suddenly weighted with unspoken awareness.

"Thank you for today," Liz said, keys in hand but making no move to leave. "For your perspective on the atrium. And... everything else."

"Thank you for your honesty," James replied, his eyes holding hers with that focused attention that always made her feel truly seen. "About your separation, about us. It's refreshing after years of professional masks and social performances."

The observation resonated deeply. How long had she been performing rather than living? Accommodating rather than expressing? Shrinking to fit the space allocated rather than expanding into her full self?

"I should go," she repeated, though she remained motionless.

"You should," James agreed, equally still.

The tension between them built in the small space separating their bodies. All the rational considerations they'd just discussed, appropriate timing, emotional clarity, professional priorities, seemed suddenly less compelling than the magnetic awareness humming between them.

"This is where we demonstrate that self-control we discussed," James said, his voice roughening slightly.

"Absolutely," Liz agreed, her body swaying imperceptibly toward his despite her words.

Neither moved for a heartbeat, then both stepped back simultaneously, creating deliberate distance.

"I'll see you Monday," James said, his professional mask sliding back into place. "Nine AM engineering meeting."

"Nine AM," Liz confirmed, opening her car door with relief and regret tangled together. "Bring coffee. It's going to be a long one."

As she drove away, Liz glanced in her rearview mirror to see James still standing in the parking lot, watching her departure. The image struck her with uncomfortable familiarity, echoing their previous partings where professional facades had barely contained the current running beneath.

Rebecca's loft was empty when Liz returned, a note on the kitchen counter explaining her sister had been called to her ex-husband's to deal with "teenage drama" involving her older son. *Back late. Don't wait up. Wine in fridge if needed!*

The unexpected solitude felt like both gift and challenge. After a week of Rebecca's constant supportive presence, the quiet space offered opportunity for deeper reflection, or dangerous rumination, depending on how she used it.

Liz poured a glass of wine and moved to the balcony, watching twilight settle over the city. Her conversation with James replayed in her mind, his suggestion to pause physical intimacy while exploring their connection more deliberately.

The approach made rational sense. Her separation from Mark was barely a week old. The divorce process hadn't even officially begun. The project remained at a critical juncture requiring their complete professional focus. Everything argued for caution, for careful consideration rather than impulsive action.

Yet beneath this logical assessment ran a current of something less rational, the powerful recognition she'd experienced with James, the sense of being truly seen and valued for her mind as much as any other quality. How long had she yearned for that connection without even knowing what she was missing?

Her phone chimed with a text message. James again: *Home safely? Forgot to mention the engineer wants material samples Monday. Bringing limestone and composite options.*

She typed a response: *Home safe. Will prepare narrative justifications for each option. Thanks for today's perspective, on everything.*

His reply came quickly: *The perspective is mutual. Your insight transforms both design and designer.*

Liz stared at the message, reading layers of meaning beneath the professional compliment. The acknowledgment of mutual transformation felt profoundly intimate despite its restrained expression.

She set down the phone without responding, unwilling to continue a conversation that blurred professional and personal boundaries despite their earlier agreement. Instead, she retrieved her sketchbook from her bag, a purchase from yesterday's art supply expedition, her first in years.

The blank page invited exploration. Liz began drawing without conscious intention, her hand remembering rhythms long neglected. Lines emerged gradually, suggesting architectural elements, the curve of an archway, the intersection of beams, the transition between materials.

As the sketch developed, she recognized what her subconscious had chosen: the atrium space they'd been discussing earlier, the critical junction where traditional limestone elements met innovative materials. Her pencil moved with increasing confidence, adding details that existed only in shared vision, not yet constructed in physical reality.

CHAPTER THIRTY-FOUR

"Material Strength"

The law office of Meredith Campbell occupied the twenty-second floor of a sleek downtown building, its reception area designed to convey both success and discretion. Tasteful abstract paintings hung on muted walls, comfortable seating arranged to prevent awkward encounters between clients who might be dismantling different marriages in adjacent conference rooms.

Liz arrived early, her leather portfolio clutched like a shield. The receptionist greeted her with practiced warmth, offering water she declined. Sitting in the corner chair that afforded the most privacy, Liz reviewed her meticulously prepared documents, financial statements, property assessments, the timeline of separation she'd constructed with her therapist's guidance.

"Ms. Donovan?" A woman in her fifties appeared in the doorway, silver-streaked dark hair framing an expression of competent compassion. "I'm Meredith Campbell. Please come in."

Liz followed her into a corner office where floor-to-ceiling windows offered panoramic views of the city. Unlike the deliberately calming reception area, this space projected quiet authority, law degrees and professional certifications displayed alongside photographs of what appeared to be completed marathons.

"Thank you for fitting me in," Liz said, settling into the chair across from Meredith's substantial desk.

"Your situation sounded time-sensitive on the phone." Meredith opened a leather folder, pen poised. "You mentioned you're separated but haven't filed formal paperwork yet?"

"That's correct. I moved out three weeks ago. We've had minimal contact since then, mostly texts about household stuff."

"And how long were you married?"

"Fifteen years. No children."

Meredith nodded, making notes. "That simplifies things considerably. What prompted the separation?"

Liz had rehearsed this answer with Dr. Farmer, crafting a response that was honest without being unnecessarily revealing. "We've been growing apart for years. Different interests, different goals, different visions for the future. We essentially became roommates sharing a house rather than partners sharing a life."

"I see." Meredith's neutral tone suggested she'd heard similar stories countless times. "And has your husband indicated his position on divorce proceedings?"

"He's angry but not surprised. I think he's known things weren't working for a long time too." Liz hesitated, then added, "He believes there's someone else involved."

Meredith's pen paused. "Is there?"

The direct question deserved honesty. "There are... complications. A colleague with whom I've developed a connection. But that relationship isn't why my marriage ended, it simply made it impossible to keep ignoring problems that already existed."

"I appreciate your candor." Meredith set down her pen. "This is a no-fault state, so legally speaking, the reason for your divorce doesn't impact proceedings. However, if your husband believes infidelity was involved, it could affect his approach to negotiations."

"I understand."

"What are your priorities in this process, Ms. Donovan? Property division? Financial settlement? A quick resolution?"

Liz considered the question carefully. "Fairness and closure. I don't want a protracted battle. Mark and I built a life together, even if it ultimately wasn't the right one for either of us. I want to honor that history while moving forward cleanly."

Meredith nodded approvingly. "That's refreshingly mature. Many clients come in seeking vengeance rather than resolution." She opened a drawer, retrieving several documents. "Let me outline the process for you."

For the next hour, they discussed legal requirements, timelines, and strategic considerations. Liz presented her financial documentation, Meredith explaining how property would likely be divided given their equal financial contributions throughout the marriage. The conversation remained practical and focused, the emotional weight of dismantling fifteen years temporarily contained within procedural frameworks.

"Assuming your husband is amenable to mediation rather than litigation, we could complete this process in three to four months," Meredith concluded, assembling the documents into a folder. "I'll prepare the initial paperwork based on what you've provided today."

"Thank you." Liz gathered her portfolio, a strange mixture of grief and relief washing over her. The con-

crete steps toward divorce made her decision irrevocable in ways that simply moving out hadn't.

At the door, Meredith paused. "One last thing, Ms.
Donovan. While your personal life is your business, I'd
advise discretion regarding any new relationship until
your divorce is finalized. It can unnecessarily complicate negotiations."

"I understand," Liz replied, the advice aligning with
her own instincts about proceeding carefully with
James.

Outside the building, Liz checked her phone to find
a text from James: *Materials arrived for atrium junction. Need your input on narrative integration. At studio
this afternoon if you're available.*

After their park conversation and subsequent agreement to explore their connection deliberately while
pausing physical intimacy, they'd maintained careful
professional boundaries. Yet beneath every architectural discussion and project decision ran an undercurrent of awareness neither could fully suppress.

Liz typed her response: *Just finished lawyer appointment. Can be at studio by 2pm.*

His reply came immediately: *Perfect. Thomas will be
here reviewing engineering specs. See you then.*

The mention of Thomas's presence created both
disappointment and relief. Their agreement to proceed cautiously was wise, necessary—and increasingly

difficult to maintain. Having Thomas as buffer would ensure their interaction remained appropriately professional.

The Calloway Design Group studio hummed with midday energy when Liz arrived. Thomas spotted her first, waving from the conference room where material samples covered the large table.

"Ms. Donovan," he called, his typically serious expression brightening. "James is grabbing the revised junction models from the fabrication lab."

"How are the engineering specifications looking?" Liz asked, setting down her bag and examining the limestone samples arranged by shade gradation.

"Promising. The structural modifications are actually enhancing the narrative flow rather than compromising it." Thomas indicated a series of technical drawings. "The load distribution issue created an opportunity to articulate the material transition more deliberately."

"Necessity becoming feature," Liz observed, the phrase they'd used repeatedly throughout the project when challenges transformed into design opportunities.

"Exactly." James's voice came from the doorway, his tall frame balancing several architectural models. "The structural requirement is creating a more nuanced narrative transition than our original concept."

He set the models on the conference table, his professional mask firmly in place despite the quick glance that assessed her condition. How did he always know when she'd had a difficult day? The lawyer appointment had left her emotionally drained, yet nothing in her appearance or demeanor should have revealed that.

"These are the revised junction models," James explained, indicating where traditional limestone elements met innovative materials. "We've articulated the connection points to address both structural requirements and narrative flow."

For the next hour, they reviewed the modifications with Thomas, the conversation remaining focused on technical specifications and visitor experience. The collaboration flowed with familiar ease, James explaining architectural concepts, Liz identifying narrative implications, Thomas addressing engineering constraints. Their professional synergy had only strengthened in recent weeks, as if their personal connection enhanced rather than compromised their working relationship.

"The transition elements actually strengthen the brand story," Liz noted.

"That's exactly what I was aiming for," James replied, the brief flash of pleasure in his eyes revealing genuine appreciation of her understanding.

Thomas looked between them, something shifting in his typically reserved expression. "I need to check the fabrication specifications with the model shop," he said suddenly. "These dimensions seem slightly off. I'll be back in twenty minutes."

Before either could respond, he had gathered several drawings and departed, the glass door closing behind him with deliberate finality. The abrupt exit created an unexpected moment of privacy neither had anticipated.

"He knows," Liz said quietly, once Thomas was out of earshot.

"He suspects," James corrected. "Thomas is perceptive, but he's also discreet."

The distinction provided little comfort. "If he's noticed something, others might too. Catherine already warned me about our 'obvious chemistry' weeks ago."

"We're being careful," James reminded her, maintaining professional distance across the table. "And we're adults making conscious choices, not teenagers sneaking around."

The simple reassurance created unexpected warmth. How different from Mark's approach to complications, avoidance, deflection, resentment. James faced challenges directly, acknowledged complexity without minimizing it.

"How was the lawyer appointment?" he asked, his voice softening.

The question touched the vulnerability she'd been suppressing all morning. "Surreal," Liz admitted. "Discussing the dismantling of fifteen years in procedural terms. Asset division. Timeline projections. As if a marriage can be reduced to spreadsheets and checklists."

James nodded, understanding in his eyes. "The practical aspects feel almost offensive in their banality. I remember reviewing property assessments and thinking, 'This can't possibly capture what's being lost.'"

"Exactly." The simple acknowledgment loosened something tight in her chest. "It's simultaneously devastating and... oddly liberating. Making it real. Irrevocable."

"The beginning of the rebuilding phase," James observed. "After necessary demolition."

The architectural metaphor created a small smile despite her emotional fatigue. "Always the architect."

"Occupational hazard," he admitted, returning her smile. "But the parallel holds. Divorce is controlled demolition, painful but necessary when the existing structure can't be salvaged."

Liz studied him across the table, this man who had reappeared in her life at precisely the moment when everything was changing. "How did you handle it? The practical dismantling while processing the emotional upheaval?"

"Not always gracefully," James admitted, his honesty refreshing. "I buried myself in work. Designed three award-winning buildings during my divorce, probably my most productive period professionally and my most destructive personally."

"Destructive how?"

"I stopped sleeping. Barely ate. Refused to process what was happening emotionally." He shook his head at the memory. "Classic avoidance disguised as productivity. It caught up with me eventually, panic attacks in client meetings, insomnia so severe I hallucinated during presentations."

The vulnerability of his admission created a tightness in Liz's throat. "What changed?"

"Thomas, actually." James glanced toward the door where his protégé had exited. "Found me one night, passed out at my desk after forty-eight hours without sleep. Practically dragged me to his therapist the next morning. Said he wouldn't continue working for someone determined to self-destruct."

"That doesn't sound like the reserved Thomas I know."

"He contains multitudes," James smiled briefly. "But he was right. I was using work to avoid feeling the failure of my marriage. As if perfect buildings could compensate for a collapsed relationship."

The insight resonated uncomfortably. Hadn't she done something similar throughout her marriage's slow deterioration? Channeling energy into marketing campaigns rather than addressing the emptiness at home?

"The point is," James continued, "divorce is both simpler and more complicated than we expect. Simpler in legal mechanics, more complicated in emotional impact. Be patient with yourself through the process."

The genuine care in his voice created that familiar warmth in her chest. How long had it been since anyone had offered support without agenda? Mark's version of comfort had always come with implicit expectations, that she'd quickly "get over" whatever was bothering her, that emotional processing shouldn't interfere with household routines.

"Thank you," Liz said simply. "For sharing that. For understanding."

James nodded, maintaining professional distance despite the personal conversation. "I've been where you are. It gets better, though rarely in the timeline we expect."

The glass door opened as Thomas returned, architectural models in hand. "The fabrication specs were indeed incorrect," he announced, setting the revised models on the table. "These reflect the actual dimensions for the limestone integration."

The professional buffer restored, they returned to technical discussion. For another hour, they refined the junction details, the conversation flowing between architectural specifications and narrative implications. Yet beneath the professional exchange ran a current of something deeper, mutual understanding that transcended their project collaboration.

As they concluded the meeting, Thomas gathered the revised models. "I'll update the engineering team on these modifications," he said, heading toward the door. Then, pausing with uncharacteristic hesitation, he added, "I just want to say... your collaborative approach has evolved significantly since those first contentious meetings. It's... impressive how you've transformed competition into synergy."

The observation hung in the air as he departed, leaving Liz and James momentarily speechless. Thomas had never commented on their dynamic before, his focus typically remaining on technical details rather than interpersonal observations.

"Definitely suspicious," Liz said once he was out of earshot.

"But not disapproving," James noted. "That's as close to a blessing as Thomas gets."

They shared a small smile, the moment of connection brief but significant. James moved to his office, Liz following to collect her bag from where she'd left it earlier.

"I have something for you," he said unexpectedly, retrieving a book from his desk drawer. "I remembered you mentioned reconnecting with abandoned interests."

He handed her a slim volume, a collection of architectural sketches by famous architects, annotated with their personal observations about design inspiration. The thoughtfulness of the gift created a lump in her throat.

"I noticed your sketching has improved," he explained, a hint of self-consciousness in his tone. "Thought this might provide some additional inspiration."

"You've seen my sketches?" Liz asked, surprised. She'd been practicing in her notebook but hadn't shared the results with anyone.

"At the engineering meeting last week. You were drawing the atrium junction while Chen was presenting the load calculations." A small smile touched his lips. "Your perspective rendering was actually more accurate than the computer model he was showing."

The observation, that he'd noticed her casual sketching, recognized its quality, and sought to encourage her interest, touched something deep and long-neglected. Mark had never shown interest in her creative pursuits, viewing them as useless hobbies to be tolerated rather than nurtured.

"Thank you," she said, running her fingers over the book's cover. "This is... thoughtful."

Their eyes met across the small space of his office, the professional distance they'd maintained throughout the meeting momentarily dissolving. For a heartbeat, Liz felt the same magnetic pull that had characterized their earlier encounters, the recognition that transcended physical attraction or intellectual compatibility, encompassing both while adding something deeper neither could fully name.

James broke the connection first, stepping back with deliberate restraint. "I should let you go. You've had a full day already."

"Yes," Liz agreed, grateful for his sensitivity to her emotional state after the lawyer appointment. "Thank you again. For the book. And the perspective on divorce recovery."

At the studio entrance, they exchanged professionally appropriate goodbyes, nothing in their interaction revealing the complex connection beneath. Yet as Liz walked to her car, she felt strangely strengthened despite the emotional weight of the morning's legal consultation.

The lawyer had outlined procedures for dismantling her marriage, the technical specifications of separation. But James had offered something equally valuable, understanding of the emotional architecture of divorce and recovery. Both perspectives were necessary for rebuilding, just as both marketing narrative and structural engineering were essential to their project's success.

In her car, Liz opened the book to find an inscription on the first page in James's precise architectural handwriting:

Elizabeth—

True design emerges from understanding materials not just for their appearance, but for their inherent strength. The most beautiful structures honor what materials can bear.

—James

The message carried layers of meaning beyond architectural principle, acknowledgment of her current challenges, recognition of her resilience, belief in her capacity to build something new from the necessary demolition of what had failed.

Unlike the lawyer's procedural approach or Mark's emotional avoidance, James offered something she'd rarely experienced: the perfect balance of practical support and emotional understanding. He saw both her current vulnerability and her fundamental strength, accepting both without judgment.

As she drove away from the studio, Liz felt the strange combination of grief and possibility that characterizes major life transitions. The divorce process would be painful, complicated, emotionally taxing. But for the first time, she truly believed what lay beyond might be worth the difficult passage, not despite the challenges but because of the strength they revealed in her.

Material strength, she reflected, wasn't about avoiding pressure but about withstanding it, transforming force into form, stress into structure. Perhaps people weren't so different from the materials James worked with, their true capacity revealed not when life was easy, but when tested by circumstances that demanded their full resilience.

CHAPTER THIRTY-FIVE

"Public Façade"

The Regency Grand Hotel's ballroom glittered with industry power brokers, champagne flutes, and carefully constructed professional personas. Crystal chandeliers cast flattering light over clusters of architects, developers, and corporate executives gathered for the annual Urban Development Association gala. Liz paused at the entrance, scanning the room with practiced nonchalance while her heart performed an uncomfortable staccato against her ribs.

Four weeks into her separation from Mark, she still felt strangely exposed in public settings, as if everyone could somehow see the upheaval in her personal life written across her face. Tonight carried additional complications, her first industry event requiring both her and James to attend while maintaining appropriate professional distance.

"Elizabeth Donovan?" A photographer approached with press badge displayed. "Could I get a shot of Meridian's marketing director for the industry journal?"

Liz smiled with practiced ease, turning slightly to her best angle. The camera flashed, capturing her emerald silk dress and professional composure without revealing the complicated emotions churning beneath.

"The Meridian headquarters is generating significant buzz," the photographer continued. "Any comment on the innovative design approach?"

"The building embodies Meridian's 'progressive tradition' philosophy," Liz replied, slipping effortlessly into marketing mode. "The material narrative creates a physical experience of our company's evolution from established foundation to innovative future."

As the photographer moved on, Liz spotted Howard Meridian holding court near the bar, surrounded by board members and industry executives. She made her way toward him, navigating the crowd with deliberate pacing, quick enough to appear purposeful, slow enough to acknowledge acquaintances with appropriate nods.

"Elizabeth!" Howard's face brightened as she approached. "Perfect timing. I was just telling the commissioner about our atrium concept."

Liz seamlessly joined the conversation, explaining the marketing integration while Howard beamed with proprietary pride. She felt... rather than saw James enter the ballroom, a prickling awareness that had nothing to do with visual confirmation. When she allowed herself a casual glance in that direction, he stood near the entrance in perfect black tie attire, the formal wear emphasizing his height and lean strength in ways his usual professional clothing didn't.

Their eyes met briefly across the room, a moment of electric connection before both deliberately looked away, maintaining the careful public façade they'd established since her separation. They'd been scrupulously professional at project meetings, communicating primarily through team members, seeing each other privately only when absolutely necessary for the project.

"James!" Howard called, waving him over with enthusiastic disregard for Liz's sudden tension. "Come tell the commissioner about the limestone integration."

James approached with confident strides, nodding professional greetings to those he passed. "Commissioner Davis, good to see you again." He extended his hand, then acknowledged Liz with appropriate colle-giality. "Elizabeth."

"James." She returned the greeting with perfect pro-fessional distance, ignoring the ridiculous acceleration of her pulse.

Howard launched into enthusiastic praise of their collaboration, completely unaware of the undercur-rents between them. "These two have transformed our headquarters from standard corporate architecture to a genuine landmark. The synergy between design and marketing narrative is extraordinary."

James outlined the technical innovations while Liz explained the experiential journey, their presentation flowing with the practiced ease of frequent collabo-rators. Anyone observing would see only two profes-sionals with obvious respect for each other's expertise, nothing to suggest the complex personal connection carefully concealed beneath.

"Quite the mutual admiration society," a new voice observed, the subtle edge beneath its pleasant tone im-mediately recognizable to James.

Liz turned to find a striking blonde woman in a per-fectly tailored red dress approaching their circle. Even without introduction, she would have known this was Vanessa Calloway, the confident posture, the calcu-lating assessment behind her smile, the way James's shoulders instantly tensed.

"Vanessa," James acknowledged, his voice carefully neutral. "I didn't realize you were attending tonight."

"The Peterson Group is a major sponsor," she replied with practiced warmth. "Martin insisted I come represent the firm." Her gaze shifted to Liz with undisguised curiosity. "You must be Elizabeth Donovan. I've heard so much about your... collaborative approach with my ex-husband."

The slight pause before "collaborative" carried unmistakable subtext. Liz maintained her professional smile while mentally recalibrating. "Vanessa Peterson, I presume? Your firm's Westridge Tower has received well-deserved recognition."

"Calloway, actually," Vanessa corrected. "I kept James's name professionally. Better brand recognition in the industry." She turned to Howard. "Mr. Meridian, the Meridian headquarters is generating quite the buzz. James always did have a flair for the dramatic in his designs."

"The drama serves function in this case," Howard replied, oblivious to the tension. "The narrative journey through the space is revolutionary. These two have created something truly special together."

Vanessa's perfectly sculpted eyebrow rose fractionally. "I'm sure they have."

The commissioner excused himself to greet another arrival, giving Howard the opportunity to spot a potential investor across the room. "If you'll excuse me," he said, already moving away. "Elizabeth, James, I'll catch up with you later for the industry panel discussion."

Their departure left Liz in the uncomfortable position of standing with James and his ex-wife, the triangular configuration feeling symbolically appropriate for the awkwardness of the moment.

"So," Vanessa said, taking a deliberate sip of champagne, "how did you two reconnect after all these years? James mentioned you were high school rivals."

"Professional selection process," Liz replied smoothly. "Calloway Design Group's proposal aligned perfectly with Meridian's vision."

"How fortunate," Vanessa's smile didn't reach her eyes. "James always did enjoy intellectual sparring. It's so rare for him to find someone who can keep up."

The comment carried both compliment and warning, acknowledgment and territorial marking. James cleared his throat, clearly uncomfortable with the direction of conversation.

"The Meridian project represents a significant evolution in sustainable design," he said, deliberately redirecting to professional territory. "Elizabeth's marketing insights have transformed how we approach the visitor experience."

"Elizabeth," Vanessa repeated, studying Liz with renewed interest. "James always uses full names for people he respects. Or people he's keeping at a distance." She turned to a passing waiter, exchanging her empty glass for a full one. "Tell me, does he still work until 3 AM when he's stuck on a design problem? That was always a challenge in our marriage."

Before Liz could formulate a response that wouldn't reveal too much, a silver-haired man approached their group.

"There you are, Vanessa," he said, placing a proprietary hand at her waist. "The commissioner was asking about our Denver project."

"Martin Peterson," Vanessa introduced him with obvious pride. "My partner in both business and life. Martin, this is James Calloway, my ex-husband, and Elizabeth Donovan from Meridian."

Martin's handshake was firm, his assessment swift and thorough. "Ah, the famous Meridian headquarters team. Your material transition concept is being discussed in every design circle." His gaze lingered on James. "Though I found the atrium solution unnecessarily complex. We would have approached it with more straightforward engineering."

"Straightforward isn't always better," James replied, the professional critique clearly touching a nerve. "The complexity serves both structural integrity and narrative purpose."

"At significantly higher cost," Martin countered with the confidence of someone accustomed to having the final word. "But then, you've always prioritized design theory over practical considerations."

Vanessa placed a restraining hand on Martin's arm. "Darling, let's not turn this into a design debate. I'm sure James and Elizabeth have plenty of admirers to convince tonight." She turned to Liz with a smile that didn't quite disguise her assessment. "Elizabeth, would you mind if I borrowed James for a moment? There's an old client asking after him."

The transparent attempt to separate them created an awkward moment. James glanced at Liz, silently checking if she was comfortable with the arrangement.

"Of course," Liz replied with professional grace. "I should find Catherine anyway. We're presenting together on the panel."

"Perfect," Vanessa took James's arm with familiar ease. "Martin, why don't you tell Elizabeth about your sustainable approach while I introduce James to the Harrington group?"

Before anyone could object, Vanessa had steered James toward the far side of the ballroom, leaving Liz with Martin Peterson and a growing sense of having been outmaneuvered.

"Your marketing background is impressive," Martin observed, his tone suggesting he considered marketing secondary to architecture. "Though I imagine the technical aspects of the Meridian project must be challenging for someone without design training."

Liz's professional smile remained fixed despite the condescension. "Actually, I've always had an interest in architectural narrative. The technical and experiential elements are inseparable in truly successful design."

Martin launched into a detailed explanation of his firm's approach, clearly assuming Liz needed education rather than conversation. She maintained polite attention while surreptitiously tracking James and Vanessa across the room. They stood with a group of developers, James's posture revealing tension despite his professional expression. Vanessa remained close to his side, occasionally touching his arm for emphasis as she spoke.

"Quite the power couple, aren't they?" Martin observed, following her gaze. "Or were, I should say. Their divorce surprised everyone in the industry."

"I wouldn't know," Liz replied carefully. "I only reconnected with James through the Meridian project."

"Vanessa says they were fundamentally incompatible," Martin continued, seemingly oblivious to Liz's discomfort. "James is brilliant but rigid in his design philosophy. Vanessa understands that client needs sometimes require compromise."

The assessment aligned with what James had told her about their marriage's dissolution, though Martin's framing clearly favored Vanessa's perspective. Before Liz could formulate a neutral response, Catherine appeared at her elbow.

"Elizabeth, there you are," she said with evident relief. "Howard wants us to coordinate on the panel presentation. If you'll excuse us, Mr. Peterson."

Catherine steered Liz away with practiced efficiency, waiting until they reached a quiet corner before speaking again. "You looked like you needed rescue," she said quietly. "Though I wasn't sure if it was from Peterson's monologue or watching James with his ex-wife."

The observation was too perceptive to dismiss. "Martin does enjoy the sound of his own voice," Liz deflected, unwilling to acknowledge the second part of Catherine's comment.

"Mmm." Catherine's expression remained skeptical. "The panel starts in twenty minutes. Howard wants us to emphasize the ROI on the sustainability features."

They discussed presentation strategy, the professional focus providing welcome distraction from the complicated dynamics across the room. When Liz finally allowed herself another glance in that direction, she found James alone, Vanessa having apparently moved to another conversation group.

As if sensing her attention, James looked up, their eyes meeting across the crowded ballroom. For a moment, the carefully maintained professional distance dissolved, revealing genuine connection beneath. Then a server passed between them, breaking the visual link and restoring appropriate boundaries.

"I need to freshen up before the panel," Liz told Catherine, needing a moment of privacy to recalibrate.

The ladies' room provided temporary sanctuary, its elegant anteroom empty except for a woman applying lipstick at the marble vanity. Liz entered a stall, taking deep breaths to steady herself. The evening was proving more challenging than anticipated—not just maintaining appropriate distance from James, but witnessing him with Vanessa, seeing the history between them, wondering about their private conversation.

When she emerged, Vanessa stood at the vanity, reapplying her already perfect lipstick. Their eyes met in the mirror, Vanessa's calculating assessment barely disguised behind her pleasant expression.

"Elizabeth," she said, turning to face her directly. "I was hoping we might have a moment alone."

Liz maintained professional composure despite internal alarm bells. "Of course."

"I'll be direct," Vanessa said, closing her lipstick with a decisive click. "James seems different since starting the Meridian project. More engaged. Almost... happy." She studied Liz's face carefully. "That's unusual for him, especially with clients."

"The project is creatively challenging," Liz replied, moving to wash her hands at the sink. "We've developed an effective collaborative approach."

"I'm sure you have." Vanessa's tone carried knowing amusement. "James responds to intellectual stimulation. Always has. It's what attracted him to me initially—my design perspective challenging his assumptions."

Liz dried her hands, unsure where this conversation was heading but certain it wasn't somewhere she wanted to go. "The panel will be starting soon—"

"He'll work himself to death for the right project," Vanessa continued as if Liz hadn't spoken. "Seventy, eighty hours a week. Sleeping at the studio. Forgetting meals, birthdays, anniversaries." Her perfectly manicured hand adjusted a strand of blonde hair. "Just something to consider if your... collaboration extends beyond the professional."

The implication hung in the air between them. Liz met Vanessa's gaze directly, refusing to be intimidated. "James's work habits are his business. My interest is in completing the Meridian headquarters successfully."

"Of course." Vanessa's smile held no warmth. "Just offering perspective from someone who's been there. James is brilliant, dedicated, and completely incapable of balancing work with personal life. It destroyed our marriage. I'd hate to see anyone else make the same discovery too late."

Before Liz could respond, the door opened as another woman entered. Vanessa nodded a polite goodbye and departed, leaving Liz with the uncomfortable sensation of having been both warned and assessed by someone who knew James in ways she didn't.

The panel discussion provided welcome structure after the unsettling encounter. Liz sat between Catherine and Howard at the presenters' table, James positioned at the far end beside the Urban Development Association president. They maintained perfect professionalism throughout, addressing each other by title and surname when necessary, focusing on their respective areas of expertise.

"The marketing integration with architectural elements creates a seamless narrative experience," Liz explained in response to a question about visitor flow. "Mr. Calloway's design philosophy aligns perfectly with Meridian's vision of progressive tradition."

"Ms. Donovan's insights transformed our approach to spatial storytelling," James added, the formal address masking the personal connection beneath. "The material transition concept evolved significantly through our collaborative process."

Howard beamed between them, clearly delighted with their presentation and oblivious to the careful distance they maintained. "What makes this project exceptional is how marketing and architecture have become inseparable," he told the audience. "The building literally tells Meridian's story through its physical form."

From her seat in the front row, Vanessa watched with undisguised interest, her expression revealing neither approval nor criticism, merely careful observation. Beside her, Martin Peterson took notes with the focused attention of someone studying competitors.

After the panel concluded, Liz found herself surrounded by marketing executives eager to discuss the narrative integration approach. She fielded questions with professional expertise, maintaining awareness of James's location without obviously tracking him. He stood across the room in similar conversation with architects and developers, his tall figure easy to distinguish despite the crowd.

"Quite impressive," Howard said, appearing at her elbow as the group dispersed. "The industry is taking notice of our approach. Three developers have already asked about applying similar concepts to their projects."

"That's gratifying," Liz replied, genuinely pleased despite her personal complications. "The material narrative deserves recognition."

"James deserves significant credit," Howard acknowledged. "His willingness to integrate marketing concepts into architectural design is unusual in the industry. Most architects resist what they consider 'non-architectural' influences."

"He understands that buildings are experienced, not just occupied," Liz said, the assessment professional despite the personal knowledge behind it. "The narrative enhances rather than compromises his vision."

Howard studied her with unexpected perceptiveness. "You two have developed quite the synergy. Catherine mentioned there was initial tension, but you've clearly moved past it."

"Professional respect developed through successful problem-solving," Liz replied, echoing the explanation she and James had crafted months earlier.

"Well, whatever you're doing, keep it up," Howard said, clapping her shoulder before moving toward a group of board members. "The results speak for themselves."

As the evening progressed, Liz maintained appropriate circulation among industry contacts, careful to avoid extended proximity to James while ensuring their occasional interactions appeared naturally collegial. The dance required constant awareness, not too distant to suggest discord, not too familiar to raise questions.

She was discussing sustainability metrics with a trade journal reporter when she felt James approach before seeing him. That peculiar awareness had only strengthened since their relationship had evolved, as if her body had developed specialized radar for his presence.

"Excuse me," he said to the reporter with professional courtesy. "I need to borrow Ms. Donovan for a moment. Howard has questions about the atrium presentation for next week's board meeting."

The reporter nodded understanding, moving toward another conversation group. James maintained appropriate distance as they walked toward a quieter corner of the ballroom.

"Howard's across the room with the commissioner," Liz observed once they were relatively private. "No questions about the atrium presentation?"

"A necessary fiction," James admitted, his voice low. "Vanessa was approaching with that look she gets when she's about to create a scene. I thought you might appreciate rescue."

"Thank you." Liz glanced toward where Vanessa stood with Martin, her attention now focused on a conversation with board members. "She cornered me in the ladies' room earlier. Quite the interesting perspective on your work habits."

James's expression tightened. "I can imagine. Vanessa has a revisionist view of our marriage that conveniently omits her numerous affairs with clients and colleagues alike."

"She suggested your workaholic tendencies destroyed your relationship," Liz said carefully. "Among other warnings about our... collaboration."

"Of course she did." James's sigh carried resigned frustration. "Vanessa prefers narratives where she's the reasonable party and I'm the difficult genius who couldn't compromise. It's more flattering than acknowledging she betrayed our partnership."

The simple honesty created unexpected warmth in Liz's chest. How different from Mark's defensive deflection whenever she'd attempted to discuss their marital problems. James faced uncomfortable truths directly, acknowledged complexity without minimizing it.

"She's watching us now," Liz murmured, noticing Vanessa's attention shift in their direction. "We should maintain some professional distance."

"Agreed." James stepped back slightly, creating appropriate space between them. "Though I find it increasingly difficult to remember why we're being so careful when you look like that."

The unexpected compliment brought heat to her cheeks. "Professional reputations. Project integrity. Complicated timing," she reminded him, though the list felt increasingly insufficient against the connection between them.

"All valid reasons," James acknowledged, his eyes conveying what his professional demeanor concealed. "Though standing across the room watching Martin Peterson monopolize your attention tested my commitment to appropriate boundaries."

"Jealousy, Mr. Calloway?" Liz raised an eyebrow, keeping her tone light despite the serious undercurrent. "That seems unlike your rational approach."

"Not jealousy," James corrected. "Protective instinct. Martin specializes in undermining confidence to establish dominance. I've seen him reduce junior architects to tears with his particular brand of condescension... And yes maybe a touch of jealousy as well."

"I handled much worse at Preston Academy," Liz reminded him with a small smile. "Usually from you."

The reference to their academic rivalry created a moment of shared amusement, easing the tension of the evening. James's expression softened into something dangerously close to affection before he carefully restored professional distance.

"Howard is indeed looking for us," he observed, nodding toward where their CEO was scanning the room. "We should probably address actual atrium questions before our excuse becomes obvious fiction."

They moved toward Howard, maintaining careful distance while navigating the crowded ballroom. As they passed near Vanessa's group, she broke away to intercept them, her timing too precise to be coincidental.

"James, the commissioner was just asking about the Thomas Building sustainability features," she said, touching his arm with familiar ease. "I assured him you'd be happy to explain the kinetic facade system."

"Elizabeth is actually more familiar with the energy metrics," James replied, smoothly including Liz in the conversation. "The Meridian headquarters incorporates similar technology with significant improvements."

Vanessa's smile tightened almost imperceptibly. "How fortunate to have such a knowledgeable marketing director. Most wouldn't understand the technical specifications."

"Most marketing directors haven't written a comparative analysis of sustainable architectural approaches that was published in the industry journal," James countered, his defense of Liz's expertise clear despite his professional tone.

Liz felt a surge of appreciation for his recognition. Mark had never acknowledged her intellectual capabilities, treating her academic and professional achievements as curious quirks rather than fundamental aspects of her identity.

"I didn't realize you were published in the architectural field," Vanessa said, reassessing Liz with new interest. "How unusual for a marketing professional."

"The article focused on experiential narrative in sustainable design," Liz explained modestly. "James's Thomas Building was actually one of my case studies."

"Before we'd reconnected," James added, anticipating Vanessa's next question. "Elizabeth's analysis was remarkably insightful, especially for someone outside the architectural field."

The exchange had shifted the dynamic, Vanessa's attempt to establish superiority neutralized by their united front. She glanced between them, her calculation almost visible behind her composed expression.

"How fascinating," she said finally. "You must have been following James's career for some time, Elizabeth. Even while you were married to... Mark, was it?"

The deliberate mention of Liz's marriage created a momentary tension. "Professional interest," Liz replied smoothly. "The Thomas Building generated significant attention in marketing circles for its brand integration."

Before Vanessa could continue this line of inquiry, Howard appeared at James's side. "There you are! The commissioner wants to discuss the limestone sourcing before he leaves."

The interruption provided perfect escape from the increasingly dangerous conversation. As they moved away with Howard, Liz felt Vanessa's gaze following them, her assessment now colored with confirmed suspicion rather than mere speculation.

The remainder of the evening proceeded with careful navigation, professional conversations, appropriate networking, occasional necessary interactions that revealed nothing of their personal connection. By the time the event began winding down, Liz felt emotionally exhausted from maintaining the public façade.

"Early site meeting tomorrow," she explained to Catherine when declining an invitation to post-event drinks. "I should head home and review the material specifications before then."

Catherine's knowing expression suggested she wasn't entirely convinced by the excuse, but she didn't press. "The panel presentation was excellent. Howard's practically floating with all the positive industry feedback."

"That's good to hear." Liz gathered her evening bag, genuinely pleased with the professional success despite personal complications. "The project deserves recognition."

As she moved toward the exit, Liz felt rather than saw James tracking her departure. They'd agreed to leave separately, maintaining appropriate professional distance even in their comings and goings. The caution felt simultaneously necessary and increasingly artificial—a public façade that protected their professional reputations while constraining the connection they'd discovered.

In the hotel corridor outside the ballroom, she heard footsteps behind her and knew without turning who had followed.

"Elevator's this way," James said, catching up but maintaining appropriate distance. "I'll walk you down."

They moved in professional silence until reaching an empty elevator. As the doors closed, creating momentary privacy, the careful distance between them remained intact—a physical manifestation of their public commitment to appropriate boundaries.

"Vanessa was watching us all evening," Liz observed, breaking the silence. "She definitely suspects something."

"Vanessa always suspects something," James replied with a hint of weariness. "Her own infidelity made her hyper aware of potential relationships. But you're right—we should be careful at industry events."

"The irony is that nothing inappropriate happened tonight," Liz noted. "We maintained perfect professional distance."

"Physical distance, yes." James's eyes held hers with uncomfortable perception. "But Vanessa recognized something beyond professional collaboration. She always had a talent for identifying emotional connections, even when carefully concealed."

The elevator reached the lobby, doors opening to reveal a group of late-arriving attendees. James and Liz stepped out, resuming appropriate professional spacing as they moved toward the hotel entrance.

"I meant what I said about your article," James said as they waited for the valet to bring their respective cars. "Your analysis of the Thomas Building was remarkably insightful. I was impressed when I read it, even before knowing who'd written it."

The genuine compliment created that familiar warmth in her chest. "I never mentioned I'd written about your work?"

"It never came up," James replied with a small smile. "Though I should have guessed. Few people understood what I was attempting with the kinetic facade system. Your article captured the experiential intention perfectly."

The valet appeared with James's car first, creating a natural end to their conversation. They exchanged

professional goodbyes, nothing in their interaction revealing the complex connection beneath. Yet as Liz
watched him drive away, she felt the growing strain of
maintaining their public façade, the careful distance
that protected their professional reputations while
denying the reality of what existed between them.

Like the buildings they designed together, their relationship had developed both public façade and structural reality, the external appearance carefully managed while the internal connections grew increasingly
complex and substantial. The question was whether
the façade would continue serving its protective purpose, or whether, like Vanessa, others would begin to
recognize the truth beneath the carefully constructed
exterior.

As her own car arrived, Liz considered Vanessa's
warning about James's work habits, his single-minded
focus, his inability to balance professional and personal
priorities. Was there truth in her assessment? Or merely
the bitter perspective of someone justifying her own
betrayal?

The question followed her home, adding another
layer to the already complex equation of their relationship. Yet beneath the complications and questions ran
a current of certainty, not about future outcomes, but
about the fundamental connection they'd discovered.
Whatever challenges lay ahead, professional bound-

aries, public perceptions, personal histories, the foundation they'd established felt increasingly solid, capable of supporting whatever structure they might eventually build.

CHAPTER THIRTY-SIX

"Temporary Structures"

The elevator ascended silently to the twelfth floor of James's building, a converted warehouse in the arts district that housed a carefully curated selection of luxury lofts. Liz studied her reflection in the polished doors, smoothing an imaginary wrinkle from her silk blouse. Despite the deliberate casualness of her outfit, dark jeans and an emerald top that brought out the green in her hazel eyes, she'd spent an embarrassing amount of time selecting it.

This visit to James's apartment carried weight beyond a simple dinner invitation. After months of professional collaboration punctuated by moments of intense personal connection, after her separation from Mark and their careful navigation of boundaries, this crossing of thresholds felt significant. His private space would reveal dimensions of him she hadn't yet seen.

The elevator doors opened to a minimalist hallway with exposed brick and industrial lighting. Only three doors occupied the entire floor. James waited at the middle one, leaning against the frame with casual grace that belied the slight tension in his posture.

"You found it," he said, a smile warming his features as she approached.

"Your directions were architect-precise," Liz replied, returning his smile.

He stepped aside to let her enter, his hand briefly touching the small of her back, a gesture both intimate and restrained. The contact sent awareness streaking across her skin despite its innocence.

The apartment opened before her, and Liz paused just inside, taking in the space with appreciation. Soaring ceilings with original beams. Floor-to-ceiling windows framing city views. Polished concrete floors softened by carefully placed rugs. The overall effect was minimalist but unexpectedly warm, industrial bones humanized by thoughtful details.

"This is beautiful," she said, moving toward the windows. "The light quality is extraordinary."

"That's what sold me on the place," James replied, following her gaze across the cityscape. "The western exposure creates this particular glow at sunset. I've redesigned everything else twice, but the windows remain the heart of the space."

Liz turned slowly, cataloging details that revealed the man beyond the professional façade. Bookshelves filled with architectural volumes but also poetry collections and literary classics. A baby grand piano in the corner that showed signs of regular use. Carefully selected art that favored abstract expression over architectural precision.

"Not what you expected?" James asked, watching her examination with amused perception.

"I'm not sure what I expected," Liz admitted. "Something more sterile, perhaps. More architect-perfect."

"Like a showroom rather than a home?" He moved to the open kitchen, pouring two glasses of wine from an already opened bottle. "I tried that after my divorce. Created a space that looked impressive but felt empty. This is the second iteration, designed for living rather than displaying."

He handed her a glass, their fingers brushing briefly. "Come, I'll give you the tour."

The apartment wasn't large by suburban standards, but the open layout and thoughtful design made it feel spacious. James showed her the main living area, the efficiently organized kitchen where he admitted to spending considerable time cooking, and a small home office with drafting table and computer station.

"I try to leave work at the studio," he explained, "but some ideas refuse to wait until morning."

The bedroom revealed the same careful balance between minimalism and comfort, platform bed with simple linens, nightstands holding books rather than electronics, a reading chair positioned to catch morning light.

"No TV?" Liz asked, noticing its absence throughout the apartment.

"In the media room," James replied, gesturing to a small space off the main living area she'd missed initially. "I prefer keeping it contained rather than making it the focal point of every room."

The observation carried no judgment but highlighted the contrast with her home with Mark, where televisions had occupied prominent positions in nearly every space. Another small difference that reflected larger philosophical divides.

They returned to the kitchen, where James began preparing dinner with practiced efficiency. Liz leaned against the counter, watching him chop vegetables with the same precision he brought to architectural drawings.

"You actually cook," she observed. "I thought that might have been theoretical when you mentioned it."

James smiled, not looking up from his careful knife work. "I find it meditative. Immediate results, unlike buildings that take years to complete." He added the vegetables to a sizzling pan. "And I discovered during my divorce that takeout becomes depressing after the third consecutive week. I found that I do love to cook. I will warn you though, I don't promise that I'm any good at it. I just feel...I don't know how to explain it, I feel when I cook for someone...I'm sharing myself? If that make any sense?"

Liz's heart pounded as his honesty, his vulnerability. "I think it makes perfect sense. How long did it take?" she asked, swirling wine in her glass. "To feel... normal again....after your divorce?"

James considered the question, his movements slowing. "You know, it's funny. When I first discovered her infidelity, I was devastated. I was so angry. I felt betrayed. I was lost." He glanced up, meeting her eyes. "We actually reconnected months later. She cheated on him, with me. It was my awakening. I finally realized this was about her insecurities...her issues...not mine. It was actually liberating. My anger was gone and it was replaced with, I dunno know, I think the best way to describe it is pity. My anger was gone and I was actually glad that we were no longer together. When I look back now, I am so happy I'm not with her. I don't mean to be cruel. I just can't imagine being with her now. It took me a couple of years to shed that identity of being her husband. You know she actually still had power over me for quite awhile. I remember one day she called and started ranting about something. My initial reaction was to try to soothe her, to fix the problem. She went on...blaming me for the problem. I suddenly had an epiphany, this wasn't my problem. I woke up. I said, you know what the best part of not being together anymore? This isn't my problem, and i hung up the phone. That was my liberation day. I finally realized we didn't work and we were better off apart."

The insight resonated deeply. "That's exactly it," Liz said quietly. "Staying with Mark would have been the real failure, continuing to pretend we hadn't grown into completely different people with different needs."

"How's the separation proceeding?" James transferred the vegetables to a serving dish, his attention seemingly on the task but his question carrying genuine concern.

"Surprisingly civil, now that the initial anger has passed," Liz replied. "The mediation session went better than expected. Mark's finally acknowledged that our problems existed long before..." She trailed off, uncertain how to reference their relationship.

"Before complications arose?" James suggested with a small smile, echoing her own careful phrasing from months earlier.

"Exactly." Liz smiled back, grateful for his understanding. "We're negotiating asset division now. The house will be sold, proceeds split evenly."

James nodded, plating the main course with artful precision. "And emotionally?"

"Better than I expected," Liz admitted. "There's grief, of course. Fifteen years isn't nothing. But also relief, like setting down a burden I've been carrying so long I'd forgotten how heavy it was."

They moved to the dining table positioned near the windows, the city lights now visible as darkness had fallen during their conversation. James served the meal, a perfectly prepared salmon with roasted vegetables and quinoa, that revealed another layer of his capabilities.

"This is delicious," Liz said after her first bite. "You've been hiding talents."

"I find cooking similar to architecture," James replied. "Understanding materials, balancing elements, creating something greater than the sum of its parts." He refilled their wine glasses. "Though buildings rarely get consumed quite so quickly."

Their conversation flowed easily through dinner, moving from divorce logistics to project updates to books they'd recently read. The intellectual connection that had drawn them together from the beginning deepened through shared references and complementary perspectives.

As they cleared dishes together afterward, Liz found herself studying James with new appreciation. In his home environment, some of his professional armor had fallen away, revealing a man more nuanced than the brilliant architect who had reappeared in her life months earlier.

"What?" he asked, catching her observation as he loaded the dishwasher.

"I'm just... seeing new dimensions," Liz admitted. "James Calloway, domesticated."

"Temporary structures," he replied, gesturing around the apartment. "We build our lives in impermanent spaces, despite architects' pretensions of creating eternity in stone."

The philosophical turn surprised her. "That's rather poetic for someone who designs buildings meant to last generations."

"Perhaps that's why I'm acutely aware of impermanence." James led her back to the living area, where they settled on the sofa with fresh glasses of wine. "I design assuming permanence while knowing most structures will be repurposed, renovated, or demolished long before their materials fail."

"Like marriages," Liz observed. "We build them assuming forever, despite knowing most won't survive in their original form."

"Exactly." James turned slightly to face her. "The foundation matters more than the façade. Get that wrong, and nothing built atop it will stand, no matter how beautiful the design."

The architectural metaphor created a natural bridge to more personal territory. Liz took a sip of wine, gathering courage for the question she'd been wanting to ask.

"What happened with your marriage? Really. Beyond the affair."

James was silent for a moment, his expression thoughtful rather than defensive. "The affair was symptom, not cause," he said finally. "Vanessa and I built on insufficient understanding of who we both were and who we would become. We looked perfect on paper—two ambitious architects with shared professional interests. But we wanted different things at a fundamental level."

"Like what?"

"I was building for legacy; she was building for recognition." His eyes held a distant pain. "I wanted to create structures that would outlast me, that would serve their occupants with integrity. Vanessa wanted to win awards, see her name in industry publications, be recognized at events."

"That's why she kept your name professionally," Liz observed, remembering their encounter at the industry gala.

"Exactly. The Calloway brand had value she wasn't willing to surrender, even after betraying everything it stood for." James shook his head slightly. "But I didn't see any of that until it was too late. I was so focused on our shared professional identity that I missed the fundamental misalignment in our values."

The candor of his admission created an opening for her own vulnerability. "I'm afraid of making similar mistakes," Liz confessed. "Of rebounding from one failed relationship into another without understanding what went wrong."

"What do you think went wrong with Mark?" James asked, his tone gentle but direct.

Liz considered the question carefully. "We built on attraction and youthful optimism without examining whether we truly shared values or vision for the future. I compromised pieces of myself so gradually I barely noticed until there was almost nothing left of the person I'd been."

"And now?"

"Now I'm rediscovering that person," Liz said, surprising herself with the conviction in her voice. "Reconnecting with interests I abandoned, expressing thoughts I suppressed, making choices based on what I actually want rather than what maintains peace."

James nodded, understanding in his eyes. "That's the hardest part of rebuilding after a relationship ends, distinguishing between who you truly are and who you became to accommodate someone else."

"Exactly." Liz felt a rush of gratitude for his perception. "Mark never really saw me, not the whole me, anyway. He saw the parts that fit his expectations and ignored the rest."

"I see you," James said quietly, the simple declaration creating a flutter beneath her ribs. "I always have, even when we were competing at Preston. Maybe especially then."

The reference to their academic rivalry shifted the conversation into territory they'd only partially explored. "You were my measuring stick for years," Liz admitted. "Every achievement compared against the standard you set."

"That's ironic," James replied with a small smile. "Because the Beckman victory felt hollow without your acknowledgment."

The admission caught her off guard. "What do you mean?"

"I wanted your recognition more than the scholarship itself," James explained, vulnerability evident in his expression. "When you disappeared after graduation, no alumni events, no academic conferences where we might have crossed paths, it felt like losing something significant. A worthy opponent. A... counterpart."

James set down his wine glass, his expression growing serious. "I need to be honest about something," he said, the sudden shift creating a flutter of anxiety in her chest. "I'm afraid of repeating the same patterns. Of mistaking intellectual chemistry for deeper compatibility. Of building something that looks perfect but lacks proper foundation."

The candor of his admission demanded equal vulnerability in return. "I have the same fear," Liz acknowledged. "That I'm seeking escape rather than authentic connection. That what's happening between us is circumstantial rather than substantial."

"And what do you think?" James asked, his eyes holding hers with that focused attention that always made her feel truly seen. "Is this circumstantial?"

Liz considered the question with the seriousness it deserved. "I think what exists between us began long before my marriage started failing," she said carefully. "The intellectual connection, the mutual challenge, the recognition, those have been constants since Preston Academy. The timing of our reconnection might be circumstantial, but the foundation isn't."

James nodded slowly, relief evident in his expression. "That's how I see it too," he said. "We've been building toward this for twenty years, though neither of us recognized the blueprint."

The architectural metaphor created a small smile despite the seriousness of their conversation. "Always the architect," Liz teased gently.

"Occupational hazard," James admitted, returning her smile. "But the parallel holds. What we're creating together, professionally and personally, has integrity because it's built on mutual recognition rather than convenience or escape."

The distance between them on the sofa suddenly felt unnecessary. Liz moved closer, her hand finding his with deliberate intent. "I'm not running away from my marriage," she said quietly. "I'm moving toward something authentic. Something I've been seeking without realizing it."

"I never imagined this," James said finally, his voice soft in the darkness. "When I walked into that Meridian presentation and saw you across the conference table, I never thought we'd end up here."

"No?" Liz smiled against his chest. "Not even a flicker of possibility?"

"Well, perhaps a flicker," he admitted. "But buried beneath layers of professional caution and personal history. You were Elizabeth Mitchell, my academic nemesis, suddenly transformed into Elizabeth Donovan, marketing director and potential client."

"And now?" she asked, raising her head to meet his gaze.

"Now you're simply Elizabeth," he replied, brushing hair from her face with tender precision. "The woman who challenges my thinking, improves my designs, and sees me more clearly than anyone ever has."

The simple assessment created a lump in her throat. How long had she yearned for that kind of recognition without even knowing what she was missing?

They talked for hours, bodies entwined as conversation moved from professional complications to personal histories to possible futures neither was entirely sure of. The intellectual connection that had drawn them together from the beginning deepened through honest exchange, creating intimacy beyond the physical.

"We should sleep," James said eventually, noticing her stifled yawn. "It's nearly three."

"Mmm," Liz agreed, though she made no move to disentangle herself. "Morning will arrive too soon."

"Stay," he said, the single word carrying a question. "Not just tonight. For breakfast. For conversation that doesn't have to end because of early meetings or professional boundaries."

"I'd like that," Liz replied, settling more comfortably against him. "Though I should warn you I'm useless before coffee."

"Noted," James smiled, pulling the duvet over them. "Fortunately, I make excellent coffee."

Sleep claimed them gradually, conversation giving way to comfortable silence and then the steady rhythm of shared breathing. For the first time in longer than she could remember, Liz didn't stare at ceiling cracks wondering how her life had become so empty. Instead, she drifted into dreams still feeling the warmth of genuine connection, intellectual, emotional, and physical alignment she'd forgotten was possible.

Morning arrived with gentle insistence, sunlight streaming through the uncurtained windows. Liz woke to the scent of coffee and the sound of quiet movement in the kitchen. She stretched luxuriously, taking a moment to absorb her surroundings in daylight. James's bedroom revealed additional details morning illuminated, sketches on the walls that appeared to be his own work, a small collection of architectural models on shelves, books stacked on both nightstands.

She borrowed his robe, the soft material carrying his scent as she padded barefoot toward the kitchen. James stood at the counter in pajama pants and t-shirt, hair adorably mussed, focusing on what appeared to be an elaborate coffee preparation.

"Good morning," she said, leaning against the doorframe.

He looked up, his expression warming at the sight of her. "Good morning. Coffee's almost ready. I remembered your preference, black, no sugar."

The fact that he'd noticed and remembered such a detail created that familiar warmth in her chest. "Thank you."

"I'm making breakfast," he added, gesturing toward ingredients arranged on the counter. "Nothing fancy, just eggs and toast. Unless you'd prefer something else?"

"That sounds perfect." Liz moved to his side, accepting the mug he offered. The coffee was indeed excellent, rich and complex without bitterness.

They prepared breakfast together with easy coordination, moving around each other in the kitchen as if they'd done this countless times. The domesticity of the scene struck Liz with unexpected force, how natural it felt to share this simple morning ritual with James, how different from the parallel routines she and Mark had developed over years.

"What?" James asked, catching her thoughtful expression as they settled at the table.

"Just... processing," Liz admitted. "How different this feels from what I'm used to."

"Different good or different concerning?"

"Different good," she clarified. "Being present rather than performing. Actually wanting to be here instead of mentally reviewing work projects to avoid conversation."

James nodded, understanding in his eyes. "I had a similar realization after my divorce. How much energy I'd been expending maintaining a relationship that didn't actually nourish either of us."

They ate in comfortable conversation, discussing the day ahead, the project timeline, books they'd been reading. The intellectual connection that had initially drawn them together flowed naturally into this domestic setting, creating a sense of rightness Liz hadn't experienced in years.

After breakfast, she helped clear dishes, then wandered into the living room while James showered. Her attention was drawn to a bookshelf she hadn't fully examined the night before. Among architectural volumes and literary classics, a familiar spine caught her eye, the industry journal where she'd published her analysis of sustainable design approaches.

She pulled it from the shelf, surprised to find it dog-eared and annotated in James's precise handwriting. Her article had been highlighted extensively, his notes filling the margins with thoughtful responses to her observations. The publication date revealed he'd acquired this copy years before their reconnection at Meridian, when she was still Elizabeth Donovan, marketing director and stranger, not potential collaborator.

Next to the journal stood a framed article about a marketing campaign she'd developed for Meridian three years earlier, a piece that had won industry recognition but hardly seemed relevant to architectural interests. The frame was elegant, the placement deliberate, suggesting it held significance beyond casual collection.

"I've followed your career," James said from behind her, his voice carrying a hint of self-consciousness. "Since Preston."

Liz turned, the journal still in her hands. "This is from before the Meridian project. Before we reconnected."

"Yes." He approached, covered now simply in a towel wrapped around his waist. "Your analysis of the Thomas Building was remarkably insightful—especially coming from someone outside architecture. I was impressed before I knew who'd written it."

"You didn't recognize my name?" Liz asked, surprised.

"You were published as Elizabeth Donovan," he explained. "I didn't make the connection to Elizabeth Mitchell until I happened across that marketing award article with your photo."

The revelation created a flutter in her chest, that he had noticed her work, appreciated her perspective, followed her career from a distance without any expectation of reconnection.

"And this?" She gestured to the framed marketing article. "Hardly architectural content."

A hint of color touched James's cheeks. "Professional curiosity," he said, the explanation not quite convincing. "Keeping tabs on industry developments."

"Through a retail marketing campaign?" Liz raised an eyebrow, unexpected joy bubbling through her. "James Calloway, did you have a crush on me from afar?"

His laugh was sudden and genuine, transforming his features. "Not a crush," he protested, though his expression suggested otherwise. "Intellectual admiration. Professional respect."

"Mmm-hmm." Liz set down the journal, stepping closer to him. "And the framing? The prominent shelf placement? Also professional respect?"

"Perhaps slightly more than that," he admitted, his arms slipping around her waist. "I may have maintained a certain... awareness of your career trajectory."

"Stalking is such an ugly word," Liz teased, her hands resting on his chest. "Let's call it 'long-term professional monitoring.'"

James laughed again, the sound warming her from within. "You're never going to let me live this down, are you?"

"Not a chance." She rose on tiptoes to kiss him briefly. "Though I should confess I've kept all our competing thesis papers from Preston. In a box I've moved to every apartment and house since college."

"Really?" Surprise and pleasure mingled in his expression. "Even after swearing you were done measuring yourself against me?"

"Especially then," Liz admitted. "They were tangible proof I'd once been your intellectual equal. That the person I became with Mark wasn't the only version of me that existed."

James's expression softened into something dangerously close to tenderness. "You were never just my equal, Elizabeth. In many ways, you were ahead of me. Your analysis had depth mine often lacked. Your arguments had nuance I couldn't match."

The simple acknowledgment of her intellectual capabilities created a lump in her throat. How long had she waited to hear such recognition? How many years had she spent suppressing her academic interests because Mark found them pretentious or boring?

"Where do we go from here?" she asked, the question encompassing far more than the immediate future.

"Forward," James replied, his eyes holding hers with unwavering certainty. "Building something with proper foundation this time. No shortcuts, no assumptions, no compromise on essential structural elements."

The architectural metaphor created a small smile despite the seriousness of the moment. "Always the architect," she said softly.

"Always," he agreed, brushing a strand of hair from her face. "But I'm designing for permanence now, not temporary occupation. Creating space that accommodates growth rather than constraining it."

The simple declaration contained everything she needed to hear, acknowledgment of their shared past, recognition of their present complexity, commitment to future possibilities. Not a perfect resolution, but perfect understanding of what they were building together.

As Liz leaned into his embrace, she felt the strange combination of excitement and peace that accompanies genuine connection. The foundation inspection was complete, the structural assessment positive. Now came the more important, more rewarding work of building something designed to last, something that

honored both their shared history and the future they
might create together.

CHAPTER THIRTY-SEVEN

"Conflicting Specifications"

The law office of Meredith Campbell looked even more austere on Liz's second visit. The neutral tones and tasteful artwork designed to project both success and discretion now seemed to mock the messy reality of dismantling a fifteen-year marriage. She sat across from Meredith, watching her scan the latest mediation documents with practiced efficiency.

"These terms are surprisingly reasonable," Meredith observed, setting down the papers. "Your husband's attorney has taken a more conciliatory approach than I anticipated."

"Mark wants this over with," Liz replied, smoothing an imaginary wrinkle from her skirt. "At least, that's what he says in his texts."

Meredith nodded, making a note in her leather-bound portfolio. "Well, that attitude will certainly expedite matters. The house sale proceeds will be split equally, retirement accounts divided proportionally based on contribution years..." She flipped through another page. "Everything appears straightforward except for this notation about personal property still at the residence."

"I've only taken what I absolutely needed," Liz explained. "Most of my things are still there. We haven't discussed how to divide the furniture or household items."

"That's often where emotions resurface," Meredith warned. "Items with sentimental rather than monetary value can become surprising flashpoints."

Liz doubted that would be an issue. She'd been mentally cataloging their possessions for weeks, surprised by how little she actually wanted from the carefully curated life they'd built. The dining room table where they'd eaten thousands of meals in growing silence. The living room furniture arranged around the television that had become Mark's primary companion. The bedroom set where they'd performed the mechanical motions of intimacy without true connection.

"I don't anticipate much conflict there," she said simply.

"Good." Meredith checked her watch. "The mediation session begins in twenty minutes. Are you prepared?"

The question carried layers beyond the practical. Was she prepared to sit across from Mark for hours, negotiating the dismantling of their shared life? Was she prepared for the accusations she'd glimpsed in his texts, the bitterness barely contained beneath civil words?

"As prepared as I can be," Liz replied.

"Remember what we discussed," Meredith said, gathering her materials. "Focus on equitable division, not emotional vindication. No matter what your husband might say, this isn't about assigning blame."

They walked together to the elevator, Meredith briefing her on procedural details while Liz nodded at appropriate intervals, her mind already in the mediation room, anticipating Mark's expression when he saw her. They hadn't been in the same space since she'd moved to Rebecca's loft weeks earlier, all communication conducted through carefully worded texts and emails.

The mediation center occupied the building's fourth floor, its reception area designed with the same soothing neutrality as Meredith's office. Mark was already there, standing by the window in a navy suit that hung slightly loose on his frame. He'd lost weight, Liz noticed with a pang of something between guilt and concern.

He turned as they entered, his expression hardening into careful blankness. The man who had once looked at her with adoration now regarded her as a stranger, worse, an adversary.

"Elizabeth," he said, the formal use of her name creating immediate distance.

"Mark." She nodded, maintaining composure despite the sudden tightness in her chest. "You look well."

The mediator, a gray-haired woman with kind eyes and no-nonsense posture, ushered them into a conference room where Mark's attorney already waited. Introductions were exchanged, procedural explanations delivered, and then they were seated across from each other, legal representation flanking them like seconds in a duel.

"We're here to facilitate an equitable division of assets and formalize the dissolution of your marriage," the mediator began. "Both parties have expressed interest in an amicable resolution. Is that still the case?"

"Absolutely," Liz said.

Mark's jaw tightened. "Sure. Amicable. Why not?"

The bitter edge in his voice created an immediate tension that the mediator acknowledged with a slight nod. "It's natural for emotions to surface during this process. My role is to keep us focused on practical matters while respecting the emotional context."

For the next hour, they moved methodically through financial assets, bank accounts, retirement funds, investments, with surprising efficiency. Mark agreed to most proposals without argument, his attention seemingly elsewhere. It wasn't until they reached the section on personal property that his detachment cracked.

"You can have whatever you want from the house," he said abruptly, interrupting Meredith's detailed proposal about cataloging items. "Furniture, dishes, artwork, take it all. I don't care."

"Mark," his attorney cautioned, "we should approach this systematically—"

"What's the point?" Mark's voice rose slightly. "She's already taken what she really wanted. A new life. Freedom from our marriage. A chance to be with—"

"Mark," the mediator interjected firmly. "Let's keep our discussion focused on the assets being divided."

He laughed, a hollow sound that carried no humor. "Assets. Right. Fifteen years reduced to a spreadsheet of possessions." His eyes fixed on Liz with sudden intensity. "Tell me something. How long?"

The question hung in the air, its meaning unmistakable despite its vagueness. Liz felt Meredith tense beside her, ready to intervene.

"This isn't relevant to our mediation," Meredith said smoothly.

"It's relevant to me," Mark insisted, leaning forward. "I want to know how long you were seeing him before you decided our marriage wasn't worth saving."

Liz met his gaze steadily. "Our marriage was failing long before any outside influences, Mark. We both know that. We were going through the motions for years."

"Convenient narrative," he replied, bitterness sharpening each syllable. "Rewrite history to justify leaving for your architect."

"I didn't leave for anyone," Liz countered, maintaining her calm despite the accusation. "I left because staying meant continuing to pretend we were happy when neither of us had been for a very long time."

"And the timing? Just coincidence that you found your 'authentic self' right when he reappeared in your life?" Mark's fingers made air quotes around the phrase she'd used in their final conversation.

The mediator intervened before Liz could respond. "This line of discussion isn't productive for our current purpose. Mr. Donovan, your feelings are valid, but they won't help us reach an equitable division of assets."

Mark sat back, a muscle working in his jaw. "Fine. Let's divide the assets. That's all that's left anyway."

The remainder of the session proceeded with tense efficiency. Mark agreed to all proposed divisions with minimal discussion, his earlier anger giving way to resigned detachment. By the time they signed the preliminary agreements, he seemed exhausted, the brief flare of emotion completely extinguished.

As they gathered their materials to leave, Mark paused beside Liz's chair. "For what it's worth," he said quietly, "I think part of me knew we were done years ago. I just didn't want to admit it."

The unexpected acknowledgment created a lump in her throat. "I know," she replied. "Neither did I."

"Doesn't make it hurt any less." He straightened, professional mask sliding back into place. "I'll have the rest of your clothes boxed up by next weekend if you want to come get them."

"Thank you. I'll text you about timing."

They parted in the reception area with awkward nods, fifteen years of shared history reduced to polite gestures between near-strangers. Liz watched him walk to the elevator, shoulders rigid with contained emotion, and felt the strange combination of grief and relief that had characterized every step of their separation.

"That went better than expected," Meredith observed as they waited for the next elevator. "Despite that momentary detour into personal territory."

"He's hurting," Liz said simply. "And he's not entirely wrong about the timing."

Meredith studied her with shrewd eyes. "The timing of your separation may have coincided with other developments, but that doesn't change the underlying issues in your marriage. Remember that."

The advice echoed Dr. Farmer's guidance about distinguishing between catalyst and cause, James had accelerated her recognition of problems with Mark, not created them. Yet the guilt lingered, complicated by the knowledge that her connection with James had indeed influenced her courage to finally end her marriage.

Outside the building, Liz checked her phone to find a text from Rebecca: *Mediation survival coffee at Lakeside Café? I'm nearby.*

The invitation was exactly what she needed, a buffer between the emotional intensity of the mediation and returning to normal life. She texted back her acceptance and headed toward the café three blocks away.

Rebecca was already there, occupying a corner table with two steaming mugs. Her auburn hair was pulled into a casual ponytail, her expression warming as Liz approached.

"That bad?" she asked, pushing a mug toward her sister.

"Actually, surprisingly civil," Liz replied, settling into the chair opposite. "Mark agreed to everything without much argument. Though he did ask how long I'd been seeing James before leaving."

Rebecca's eyebrows rose. "And what did you tell him?"

"That our marriage was failing long before James showed up." Liz wrapped her hands around the warm mug. "Which is true, even if not the complete picture."

"Mmm." Rebecca's noncommittal sound carried volumes of skepticism. "Speaking of the complete picture, when exactly did things with James move beyond professional collaboration? You've been remarkably vague about the timeline."

The direct question deserved honesty, especially after Rebecca had provided both emotional support and physical sanctuary during the separation. Liz took a fortifying sip of coffee before answering.

"It started during a business trip," she admitted. "About three weeks before I left Mark. We'd been keeping our distance despite a growing awareness, but..." She trailed off, unsure how to describe the seismic shift that had occurred in that hotel room.

"But proximity and alcohol broke those boundaries?" Rebecca suggested, her tone free of judgment.

"Something like that." Liz met her sister's gaze directly. "I'm not proud of that part. But our marriage was over long before anything happened with James. We were just living a lie at that point, both of us."

"I know, I could see it," Rebecca said, studying her sister's face. "But timing matters in these situations, Liz. Mark's not entirely wrong to question it."

"I know." Liz sighed, running a finger around the rim of her mug. "That's why I've been trying to proceed carefully with James, to make sure any decision comes from clarity, not reaction."

"And how's that going?" Rebecca's skepticism was evident. "The 'proceeding carefully' part?"

Heat rose to Liz's cheeks. "It's... complicated. We've been focusing on the project while exploring our connection more deliberately. Trying to understand what's happening between us beyond physical attraction or convenient timing."

"And what is happening between you?" Rebecca leaned forward, genuine curiosity replacing skepticism. "Beyond the obvious chemistry I've witnessed firsthand."

Liz considered the question seriously. How to explain the profound recognition she'd experienced with James? The intellectual challenge matched with emotional understanding? The sense of being truly seen for the first time in her adult life?

"It's like finding a missing piece I didn't know was absent," she said finally. "The connection isn't just physical or emotional, it's intellectual, creative, values-based. He challenges my thinking, values my perspective, sees me as an equal partner rather than some accessory."

Rebecca nodded slowly, her expression softening. "That's what I hoped for after my divorce, finding someone who saw me completely, not just the parts that fit their expectations." She studied Liz over the rim of her mug. "Just be careful about the narrative you're creating, sis. It's easy to idealize someone new when they're being compared to a failing relationship."

"I'm not idealizing James," Liz protested, though a small voice wondered if that was entirely true. "He has flaws, he's a workaholic, occasionally arrogant, sometimes too focused on design theory over practical concerns."

"Yet you're lighting up just talking about him," Rebecca observed with a knowing smile. "Even his flaws sound like compliments."

"That's not—" Liz began, then stopped herself. Was she creating an idealized version of James to justify her choices? Or was she simply experiencing the natural excitement of a relationship built on genuine compatibility rather than youthful attraction and shared logistics?

"I'm trying to be honest with myself," she said finally. "About what went wrong with Mark, about what I want moving forward, about whether James is part of that future or just a catalyst for necessary change."

"And what conclusions have you reached?" Rebecca asked.

"That my marriage would have ended regardless of James," Liz replied without hesitation. "That the connection we've found deserves exploration without rushed expectations. That I need to complete one chapter before fully beginning another."

Rebecca reached across the table, squeezing her hand briefly. "That sounds remarkably healthy, considering the circumstances. Just remember, whatever you decide about James should have nothing to do with your divorce. Build something new because it's right, not because it's an escape from what was wrong."

The advice resonated deeply, echoing Dr. Farmer's guidance about distinguishing between escape and growth. Was her relationship with James an escape route from her failed marriage? Or the natural evolution of a connection that had existed in some form since they were teenagers?

As they finished their coffee, conversation shifted to practical matters, the continued house sale preparations, Liz's search for her own apartment, Rebecca's latest dating disaster. The normalcy provided welcome respite from the emotional weight of the mediation and her own complicated reflections.

Back at Rebecca's loft that evening, Liz sat on the guest bed that had become her temporary home, phone in hand, James's contact information displayed on the screen. She'd promised to update him about the mediation, but hesitated over what to share and how much.

Their relationship had evolved into something both defined and undefined, more than colleagues, not quite partners, existing in the gray area between professional collaboration and personal commitment. They'd been careful to maintain appropriate boundaries at work while exploring their connection in private, neither rushing toward labels nor denying the significance of what was developing between them.

Finally, she pressed call rather than text, needing to hear his voice rather than interpret words on a screen.

"Elizabeth." He answered on the second ring, "How did it go?"

The simple question, asked with genuine concern rather than perfunctory politeness, loosened something tight within her. "Better than expected, actually. Mark agreed to all the proposed divisions without much argument."

"That's good," James said, relief evident in his tone. "Though I sense a 'but' coming."

"He asked how long we'd been involved before I left," Liz admitted, the honesty easier over the phone than it might have been face-to-face. "Implied that you were the reason our marriage ended."

James was silent for a moment. "How did you respond?"

"That our marriage was failing long ago." She sighed, leaning back against the headboard. "Which is true, but doesn't change the fact that my connection with you influenced my decision to finally end it."

"Are you having doubts?" The question carried no defensiveness, only genuine concern for her wellbeing.

"Not about ending my marriage," Liz clarified quickly. "That was the right decision regardless of us. But I do worry about the narrative Mark's created, that I left him for you rather than because our relationship had fundamentally failed."

"Does it matter what narrative he creates?" James asked gently. "You know the truth. I know the truth. The people who matter understand the complexities involved."

The simple perspective shifted something in her thinking. Did it matter what Mark believed about her reasons for leaving? His interpretation wouldn't change the reality of their failed marriage or the genuine connection she'd found with James.

"I suppose it doesn't," she acknowledged. "Though I hate being cast as the villain in his version of events."

"You can't control his interpretation," James said, his voice carrying the calm certainty that had always characterized his approach to challenges. "You can only be honest about your own experience and choices."

The wisdom of his response created a sudden lump in her throat. How different from Mark's defensive deflection whenever she'd attempted to discuss difficult topics. James faced emotional complexity directly, acknowledged uncertainty without minimizing it.

"Thank you," she said simply. "For listening. For understanding."

"Always." The single word carried more meaning than elaborate declarations might have. "How are you feeling otherwise? These processes can be emotionally draining even when they go smoothly."

"Strangely calm," Liz admitted. "Sad about what we couldn't salvage, but certain it was the right decision. There was a moment today when Mark acknowledged that part of him knew we were done years ago. That unexpected honesty was actually... healing, somehow."

"That makes sense," James replied. "Mutual recognition of reality, even painful reality, creates closure in a way that lingering denial never can."

They talked for nearly an hour, the conversation flowing naturally from divorce logistics to project updates to books they'd been reading. The intellectual connection that had drawn them together from the beginning deepened through honest exchange, creating intimacy that transcended any physical proximity.

"I should let you go," Liz said finally, noticing the time. "We both have early meetings tomorrow."

"The Westridge comparison analysis," James confirmed. "I've prepared the sustainability metrics you asked for."

"Always so efficient," she teased gently, warmth spreading through her chest at his consistent thoughtfulness.

"Occupational hazard," he replied, the smile evident in his voice. "Sleep well, Elizabeth. I'll see you tomorrow."

After they disconnected, Liz sat with the phone in her lap, reflecting on the conversation. The ease of their exchange, the natural flow between personal and professional topics, the way he listened without immediately offering solutions, all created a stark contrast with her interactions with Mark in recent years.

Where Mark had dismissed her concerns, James acknowledged them. Where Mark had changed the subject when conversations became emotionally complex, James leaned into the discomfort. Where Mark had seen only the place she filled in his existence, James saw her completely, brilliant mind, creative spirit, professional ambition, and personal vulnerabilities all recognized and valued.

Rebecca's warning about idealizing new relationships echoed in her mind. Was she creating a perfect version of James by comparing him to Mark at his worst? Or was she simply recognizing genuine compatibility after years of fundamental mismatch?

As she prepared for bed, Liz considered the conflicting specifications that had characterized her marriage, the irreconcilable differences in values, goals, and vision that no amount of compromise could resolve. Like an architectural project with contradictory requirements, the structure had been doomed from the foundation stage, no matter how carefully they'd tried to accommodate opposing needs.

With James, the specifications aligned more naturally. Not perfectly, no relationship could claim that, but with fundamental compatibility in core values and vision. The intellectual connection that had begun as competitive rivalry had evolved into collaborative strength, each enhancing rather than diminishing the other's capabilities.

The mediation had confirmed what she'd known for months: her marriage had reached its natural conclusion long before James Calloway reappeared in her life.

His presence had been catalyst rather than cause, accelerating her recognition of truths she'd been avoiding for years.

Now, as one chapter concluded with surprising civility, another began with cautious optimism. Not an escape from what had failed, but a deliberate movement toward what might succeed, a relationship built on mutual recognition rather than convenient timing or physical attraction.

The path ahead remained complex, fraught with potential complications and uncertain outcomes. But for the first time in years, Liz felt genuinely hopeful about the possibilities, not just professionally, but personally as well. Whatever happened with James, whether their connection developed into lasting partnership or remained a transformative chapter in both their lives, she was finally moving forward authentically, aligned with her true self rather than performing a role that no longer fit.

As sleep claimed her, Liz's final thought was of the building rising from Meridian's construction site, no longer just foundation and framework, but taking tangible form day by day. Like that structure, her new life was emerging gradually from careful planning and honest assessment, each element placed with deliberate intention rather than habitual compromise.

The conflicting specifications that had doomed her marriage were being replaced by aligned vision and compatible values, not perfect alignment, but complementary strengths creating something neither could build alone.

CHAPTER THIRTY-EIGHT

"Certificate of Occupancy"

T he morning sun cast long shadows through the nearly completed Meridian headquarters as Liz made her way across the gleaming marble lobby. After eighteen months of construction, design revisions, and countless hours of collaboration, the building had transformed from architectural renderings to physical reality. Each column, each material transition, each carefully considered space represented both professional triumph and personal evolution.

She paused at the center of the atrium, tilting her head back to take in the soaring ceiling where limestone elements met innovative glass in the articulated junction that had caused so much debate. The morning light filtered through precisely engineered panels, creating patterns across the floor that would shift throughout the day, a living calendar marking time through illumination.

"Quite different from those first sketches, isn't it?" James's voice came from behind her.

Liz turned to find him standing a few feet away, portfolio tucked under his arm, eyes taking in the space with the mixture of pride and critical assessment that characterized his relationship with all his creations.

"Better," she replied. "The reality exceeds the renderings."

He moved to stand beside her, both of them gazing upward at the architectural achievement they'd created together. "The material transition is more nuanced in actual light. The renderings couldn't capture how the limestone seems to dissolve into the glass elements."

"Progressive tradition made physical," Liz observed. "Howard couldn't have asked for a more perfect embodiment of the company philosophy."

Their shoulders nearly touched as they stood in comfortable silence, professional pride momentarily overshadowing the personal connection that had developed alongside the building. In the eighteen months since groundbreaking, their relationship had evolved through crisis and resolution, separation and reconnection, always grounded in the intellectual foundation that had drawn them together from the beginning.

The sound of voices broke their reverie as Howard led the project team through the main entrance. Board members, engineers, construction managers, and marketing staff filed into the atrium, their exclamations of approval echoing through the space.

"There they are!" Howard called, spotting Liz and James. "The visionaries who made this possible."

He approached with the confident stride of a man seeing his legacy take physical form, arms spread wide to encompass the soaring space around them. "What do you think? Does it meet your expectations?"

"It exceeds them," James replied, professional mask sliding into place despite the genuine satisfaction in his voice. "The quality of light is even better than our models predicted."

"The visitor experience flows exactly as we intended," Liz added. "The narrative journey from traditional to innovative elements creates precisely the progression we envisioned."

Howard beamed, clapping them both on the shoulders. "This building is everything I hoped for, and more. The board is ecstatic. The press coverage has been phenomenal. And all thanks to your collaborative vision."

The pre-opening walkthrough began with Howard leading the assembled team through each area, James explaining architectural elements while Liz highlighted the marketing and narrative integration. They moved from the public lobby through client meeting spaces to the central atrium, where Howard paused to address the group.

"Before we continue to the office levels, I want to take a moment to acknowledge what's been accomplished here," he said, his voice carrying through the acoustically engineered space. "Eighteen months ago, this was an empty lot with ambitious plans. Today, it's a landmark that will define Meridian for generations."

He gestured to the surrounding architecture. "This building isn't just a headquarters, it's a physical manifestation of our company's evolution and values. The journey from traditional materials to innovative technologies mirrors our own business philosophy. That narrative integration was the unique genius of this project."

Howard turned to James and Liz, standing side by side at the edge of the group. "What these two accomplished goes beyond architecture or marketing. They created a synthesis that transforms how people experience our company. Their collaboration, sometimes contentious, often brilliant, always productive, has resulted in something neither could have created alone."

Liz felt James's hand brush against hers, a momentary contact invisible to others but electric in its significance. They had maintained careful professional boundaries in public settings, their private relationship kept separate from their work collaboration. Yet in moments like this, the division between professional and personal seemed arbitrary, artificial, their connection flowing seamlessly between domains.

The tour continued through office levels and specialized workspaces, each area revealing thoughtful integration of function and narrative. Board members nodded approvingly at innovative sustainability features, while marketing staff excitedly discussed how client experiences would unfold within the carefully crafted spaces.

As the group moved toward the executive floor, Catherine fell into step beside Liz. "Quite an achievement," she observed, her shrewd eyes missing nothing. "The building and... everything else."

"The project exceeded our initial vision," Liz replied carefully.

"I wasn't referring to the project," Catherine said, her voice low enough that only Liz could hear. "Though I'm impressed you both managed to maintain professional focus despite some obvious... entanglements."

Before Liz could respond, Howard called for Catherine's input on the board presentation space, sparing her from navigating that particular conversational minefield. She caught James watching the exchange, his expression revealing he'd understood the general content if not the specific words.

The executive floor showcased the most sophisticated integration of traditional and innovative elements, the limestone and wood of Howard's office contrasting with glass-walled conference rooms and collaborative spaces. As the group dispersed to explore different areas, James approached Liz in the empty executive reception area.

"Howard wants us to check the east corner office," he said, professional tone belying the warmth in his eyes. "Something about the lighting specification."

The pretext was transparent but necessary. Liz nodded, maintaining appropriate distance as they walked down the corridor to the furthest office, a corner space with spectacular city views that had been designated for a future executive yet to be hired.

Inside, sunlight streamed through floor-to-ceiling windows, illuminating a space that existed in that perfect moment between completion and occupation, finished but untouched, full of possibility rather than history.

James closed the door behind them, the soft click creating sudden privacy amid the bustling pre-opening activities. "We did it," he said simply, professional mask falling away to reveal genuine wonder. "Sometimes I still can't believe we pulled this off."

"Which part?" Liz asked, moving to the windows. "The building or everything else?"

"Both." He joined her at the window, their reflection visible in the glass against the backdrop of the city beyond. "We built something that will last."

"In more ways than one," she replied, the double meaning intentional.

Their eyes met in the reflection, eighteen months of shared creation, professional and personal, flowing between them. From contentious rivals to reluctant collaborators to intellectual partners to something deeper neither had anticipated, their journey had paralleled the building's evolution from concept to reality.

"I keep thinking about that first presentation," James said, his voice softening with memory. "When you challenged my approach to the entrance sequence. I was so irritated by your questions, and secretly impressed by how quickly you'd identified the weak points in my design."

"I was trying to prove I could match you intellectually," Liz admitted. "After all those years measuring myself against your success, I needed to show I was still your equal."

"You were never just my equal, Elizabeth." His use of her full name still made her heart thump. "In many ways, you were ahead of me. Your understanding of how people experience space transformed my approach to design."

The simple acknowledgment of her professional contribution meant more than elaborate declarations might have. How different from Mark's dismissive characterization of her work, his inability to see beyond her function in his life to her intrinsic value.

"We should rejoin the group," Liz said reluctantly, aware of their extended absence. "Howard will be looking for us."

"In a moment." James took her hand, a gesture both tender and decisive. "I want to appreciate what we've created first. Not just the building, but this partnership. This connection that neither of us expected."

The professional achievement and personal evolution had become inseparable, each informing and strengthening the other. The building around them stood as physical testimony to what was possible when intellectual challenge transformed into collaborative creation, when competition gave way to recognition of complementary strengths.

James drew her closer, his free hand tracing the line of her jaw. "I never imagined this outcome when I walked into that first presentation at Meridian," he said quietly. "Finding you again. Building this together. Discovering that my academic rival would become my most essential partner."

"Partner," Liz repeated, the word encompassing both their professional collaboration and personal relationship. "I like that term."

"It's accurate," James replied. "In every sense that matters."

His kiss carried the certainty of deliberate choice, of connection built on genuine understanding rather than circumstantial attraction.

Liz responded with equal certainty, her arms sliding around his neck as the kiss deepened. The physical attraction that had complicated their professional relationship from the beginning had evolved into something more profound, desire grounded in intellectual respect and emotional recognition.

"We should stop," she murmured against his lips, though she made no move to create distance. "The team is waiting."

"They can wait another minute," James replied, his hands moving to her waist with possessive intent.

The sound of voices in the corridor broke the moment, professional awareness reasserting itself. They stepped apart with practiced efficiency, composure restored by the time Howard knocked briefly before opening the door.

"There you are," he said, oblivious to the charged atmosphere. "What do you think of the lighting specification? Does it need adjustment?"

"It's perfect," James replied, his professional mask firmly in place despite the slight roughness in his voice. "The eastern exposure creates exactly the quality we intended."

"The material integration is particularly effective in this space," Liz added, gesturing to where limestone elements met more innovative components. "The narrative transition is most visible here."

Howard nodded approvingly. "Excellent. We're heading to the rooftop garden next. Join us when you've finished your inspection."

After he departed, closing the door behind him, James and Liz exchanged glances that combined amusement and relief. The moment of privacy had passed, professional obligations reclaiming priority.

"Later," James said, the single word carrying promise rather than question.

"Later," Liz agreed, straightening her blouse with deliberate movements.

They rejoined the group, maintaining appropriate professional distance as the tour continued through the remaining areas. The rooftop garden provided spectacular views of the city, sustainable plantings creating an oasis above urban congestion. Howard delivered another speech about vision and execution, board members nodded appreciatively, and photographs were taken for the annual report.

Throughout the remainder of the walkthrough, Liz remained acutely aware of James's presence, his authoritative explanations of architectural elements, his gracious acknowledgment of team contributions, his occasional glance in her direction that carried private meaning beneath his public professionalism.

As the event concluded and team members dispersed to their respective tasks, Howard approached them one final time. "I'd like you both to check the fifth-floor storage area," he said. "There's some concern about the shelving installation. Nothing urgent, but it should be addressed before the official opening."

The transparent pretext would have been comical if not for the genuine appreciation in Howard's eyes. "And take your time," he added, his tone shifting to something more personal. "You've earned a moment to appreciate what you've created."

After he walked away, James raised an eyebrow at Liz. "Fifth-floor storage?"

"Apparently needs our immediate attention," she replied, matching his tone of mock seriousness.

They took the elevator to the fifth floor, the doors opening to reveal a corridor still in final stages of completion. Unlike the executive areas and public spaces, this utilitarian section remained partially unfinished, painters' tarps covering flooring, some light fixtures yet to be installed.

The storage area Howard had mentioned was a large room at the corridor's end, metal shelving units lining the walls and creating aisles through the center. The space was functional rather than aesthetic, designed for efficiency rather than impression.

"I'm not seeing any installation issues," James observed, closing the door behind them. "Though I suspect Howard wasn't actually concerned about shelving."

"His subtle way of giving us a moment alone," Liz agreed, moving further into the room. "He's more perceptive than he lets on."

"Catherine too," James added, following her between shelving units. "That conversation earlier wasn't about the board presentation space, was it?"

"No." Liz turned to face him, the utilitarian surroundings creating stark contrast to the emotional significance of the moment. "She was impressed we maintained professional focus despite 'obvious entanglements.'"

"Are we that transparent?" James asked, closing the distance between them.

"Apparently to those who know us well." Liz's hands found his chest, feeling his heartbeat accelerate beneath her touch. "Though we've been scrupulously professional in public."

"And now?" His voice dropped to that lower register that never failed to send awareness skittering across her skin.

"Now we're alone in a storage room that won't be used for weeks," Liz replied, fingers moving to the buttons of his shirt with deliberate intent. "In a building we created together. On what is essentially the culmination of eighteen months of collaboration."

"A moment worth marking," James agreed, his hands finding the zipper of her dress. "A milestone in our professional partnership."

The pretense of professional justification dissolved as quickly as their clothing, desire that had been contained during the public walkthrough now unleashed in private celebration. James lifted her against one of the metal shelving units, its industrial strength easily supporting their weight as his mouth found the sensitive spot below her ear that never failed to make her gasp.

Unlike their first encounter in the hotel room, fueled by argument and suppressed attraction, or even their later experiences as their relationship evolved, this connection carried the confidence of established partnership. No hesitation, no uncertainty, just the pure pleasure of bodies that knew each other intimately, minds that challenged each other intellectually, hearts that had found unexpected alignment.

"We built this," James murmured against her skin, the double meaning intentional as his hands mapped familiar territory with renewed appreciation. "Together."

"Equal partners," Liz agreed, her fingers threading through his hair as his mouth traced a path along her collarbone. "Though I believe I contributed that particular design element."

His laugh vibrated against her skin, the moment of playfulness deepening their connection beyond physical desire. This was what had been missing from her marriage to Mark, the integration of intellectual challenge and physical attraction, the ability to be completely herself rather than performing a role to maintain someone else's comfort.

When they finally came together, Liz felt the same synthesis that characterized their professional collaboration, complementary strengths creating something neither could achieve alone. James watched her with unwavering focus, his blue eyes reflecting the same wonder that had characterized his expression when viewing the completed building.

"Elizabeth," he whispered, her full name on his lips creating intimacy that transcended their physical connection.

The release when it came was mutual and profound, neither leading nor following but moving in perfect synchronization. Afterward, they remained entwined, breathing gradually slowing, neither willing to break the connection that felt simultaneously powerful and delicate.

"Technically," James said finally, his voice rough with lingering desire, "I believe we've now christened the building."

Liz laughed despite herself, the absurdity of their surroundings, metal shelving units and painters' tarps, contrasting with the significance of what had just transpired between them. "Howard did tell us to take our time appreciating what we created."

"I doubt this is what he had in mind," James replied, though his expression suggested he had no regrets. "Though it seems fitting somehow. This building represents both our professional collaboration and personal evolution."

As they helped each other dress, the gesture carried tenderness rather than embarrassment or regret. Their relationship had developed alongside the building's construction, foundation work giving way to structural elements, then interior spaces, finally the finished form that would stand for decades.

"Do you ever wonder what would have happened if you hadn't won that scholarship?" Liz asked as James buttoned his shirt. "If we'd both gone to Rice instead of taking such different paths?"

He considered the question thoughtfully. "I used to think we missed an opportunity, that those twenty years between Preston Academy and the Meridian project were wasted time." His hands stilled on the buttons. "But now I wonder if we needed those years to become who we are. If we'd connected at eighteen instead of thirty-eight, would we have recognized what we'd found?"

The insight resonated deeply. "Probably not," Liz acknowledged. "I was so focused on proving myself, on competing rather than collaborating. And you—"

"I was arrogant and single-minded," James finished with rueful self-awareness. "Too convinced of my own brilliance to recognize complementary strengths in others."

"So perhaps the timing wasn't wrong after all," Liz suggested, smoothing her dress into place. "Perhaps we needed those separate journeys to appreciate the intersection when it finally came."

They finished dressing in companionable silence, the room transformed from utilitarian storage to significant space by what had transpired within it. Before opening the door to return to public areas, James drew Liz into one final embrace.

"Certificate of occupancy," he murmured against her hair.

"What?"

"The final approval that declares a building safe for occupation," James explained. "The moment when potential becomes reality, when a structure is officially ready for its intended purpose."

Liz smiled against his chest, understanding the metaphor. "And have we received our certificate?"

"I believe we have," he replied, his arms tightening slightly around her. "And like buildings, relationships require continuous inspection and maintenance."

"Always the architect," Liz teased gently, looking up to meet his gaze.

"Always," he agreed, brushing a strand of hair from her face. "But I'm designing for permanence now, not temporary occupation. Creating space that accommodates growth rather than constraining it."

The simple declaration contained everything she needed to hear, acknowledgment of their shared past, recognition of present connection, commitment to future possibilities. Not a perfect resolution, but per-

fect understanding of what they were building together.

They returned to the main level, where team members were engaged in final preparations for the official opening. If anyone noticed their extended absence
or slightly disheveled appearance, no comments were
made. Howard merely nodded approvingly when they
reported the storage shelving was "structurally sound."

As evening approached and the building emptied
of all but security personnel, Liz and James found
themselves once more in the soaring atrium where their
journey had begun. The setting sun cast different patterns now, the material transitions highlighted in amber and gold rather than morning silver.

"Hard to believe we started with just sketches and
arguments," Liz observed, looking up at the space
they'd created together. "Remember that first meeting
in the temporary trailer?"

"When you criticized my entrance sequence concept and I questioned your understanding of spatial
dynamics?" James smiled at the memory. "I was so irritated by your precise identification of the design's
weaknesses."

"And I was determined to give you a run for your
money, intellectually," Liz admitted. "After all those
years measuring myself against your success."

They stood side by side, watching the changing light transform the space they'd designed together. The building around them represented both their professional achievement and personal evolution, the physical manifestation of a connection that had begun as competitive rivalry and transformed into something neither could have anticipated.

"Shall we?" James extended his hand, the gesture both question and invitation.

Liz placed her hand in his, fingers interlacing with familiar ease. "We shall."

Together they walked toward the entrance, their reflections visible in the glass doors that separated their creation from the world beyond. Behind them stood the building they'd designed together, its structure solid yet dynamic, traditional elements flowing into innovative forms. Before them lay whatever future they chose to build, not perfect, not without challenges, but grounded in the recognition that had transformed rivals into partners.

The certificate of occupancy had been granted. The building was ready for its purpose. And so, at last, were they.

CHAPTER THIRTY-NINE

"Final Inspection"

The courtroom's austere wood paneling and formal atmosphere seemed designed to drain emotion from even the most significant life events. Liz sat beside Meredith Campbell, hands folded in her lap to hide their slight trembling. Across the aisle, Mark occupied a similar position beside his attorney, his face a careful mask of indifference that didn't quite conceal the hurt beneath.

"Donovan dissolution of marriage," the clerk announced, voice echoing through the half-empty chamber.

The judge, a woman in her sixties with silver-streaked hair and reading glasses perched on her nose, reviewed the documents before her with practiced efficiency.

"I see all financial matters have been settled through mediation," she observed, glancing between the two attorneys. "Property division is complete, and there are no children requiring custody arrangements. Is there anything either party wishes to address before I finalize this dissolution?"

Meredith shook her head. "Nothing from the petitioner, Your Honor."

Mark's attorney began a similar response, but Mark leaned forward, whispering something that made his lawyer pause.

"Your Honor, my client would like to make a brief statement, if permitted."

The judge nodded. "Proceed, Mr. Donovan."

Mark stood, straightening his tie with nervous fingers. Liz braced herself for recrimination or bitterness, the emotions that had characterized their early separation conversations.

"I just wanted to say..." Mark began, his voice steadier than she expected. "I think we both made mistakes. Not just recently, but years ago when we started growing apart and neither of us was willing to admit it."

The simple acknowledgment caught Liz off guard. She looked up, meeting his gaze directly for the first time that morning.

"We held on too long to something that wasn't working," he continued. "And while I wish things had ended differently, I understand now that they needed to end."

The words carried no accusation, only a weary acceptance that mirrored her own feelings. In that moment, Liz saw beyond the hurt and anger to the young man she'd once loved, someone who had also been trapped in a relationship that no longer served either of them.

"Thank you, Mr. Donovan," the judge said, her expression softening slightly. "Ms. Donovan, would you like to respond?"

Liz hadn't planned to speak, but Mark's unexpected grace deserved acknowledgment. She stood, conscious of how final this moment truly was.

"I appreciate Mark's words," she said. "We built a life together for fifteen years, and there was love there, even if we eventually grew in different directions. I hope we can both find happiness moving forward."

The judge nodded, seemingly satisfied by this civil exchange. "Based on the agreement before me and the testimony provided, I hereby dissolve this marriage." The gavel struck with quiet finality. "You are both free to proceed with your separate lives."

Those words, "separate lives", hung in the air as Liz gathered her purse and documents. Freedom, she realized, felt both exhilarating and terrifying.

In the courthouse corridor, Mark approached as she was texting Rebecca.

"So that's it," he said, hands in his pockets. "Fifteen years undone in twenty minutes."

"Not undone," Liz corrected gently. "Just... concluded. We can't erase the past, Mark."

"No, I suppose not." He studied her face, something like resignation in his eyes. "You look good, Liz. Better than I've seen you look in years, actually."

The observation surprised her. "Thank you. I feel... more myself."

"That's it exactly," he nodded slowly. "You seem like yourself again. Not the version that was trying so hard to fit into our marriage."

The insight, that he had noticed her self-diminishment even if he hadn't understood it, created an unexpected lump in her throat.

"The house closing is next week," Mark continued, practical as always. "The realtor said everything's on track."

"Good. I'll sign whatever they need electronically."

An awkward silence fell between them, the kind that occurs when people who once shared everything now struggle to find common ground for conversation.

"Well," Mark said finally, "good luck with everything. The building looks amazing, by the way. I drove past it yesterday."

The mention of the Meridian headquarters, her professional triumph intertwined with her personal evolution, created a moment of tension. They both knew James existed, though Mark had stopped mentioning him directly after their mediation session.

"Thank you," Liz said simply. "Good luck to you too, Mark. I mean that."

They parted with an awkward half-hug that felt like the appropriate punctuation mark for their relationship, not the passionate embrace that had begun it nor the cold distance of recent months, but something in between. Acknowledgment of shared history without pretense of ongoing connection.

"To freedom!" Rebecca declared, raising her coffee mug in mock toast. They sat at their favorite corner table in Lakeside Café, autumn sunlight streaming through the windows.

Liz clinked her own mug against her sister's. "To closure," she countered. "And new beginnings."

"How does it feel?" Rebecca asked, studying her face. "Being officially divorced?"

Liz considered the question carefully. "Surreal. Sad. Relieving. All at once." She traced the rim of her mug with one finger. "Mark was surprisingly... decent. Said we'd been growing apart for years and just didn't want to admit it."

"Moments of self-awareness from Mark Donovan? Will wonders never cease." Rebecca's tone softened. "Though I'm glad he didn't make it harder than necessary. That speaks well of him."

"It does," Liz agreed. "I think he's finally accepted that this wasn't about James, that our problems existed long before."

Rebecca's eyebrow rose at the mention of James. "Speaking of the brilliant architect, how is he handling your newfound legal freedom?"

"Carefully," Liz replied, warmth spreading through her chest at the thought of him. "We've been... deliberate about our relationship. Taking time to understand what we're building rather than rushing into something new."

"Mmm-hmm," Rebecca's skepticism was evident. "And this careful approach includes him helping you move into your new apartment today?"

"It's practical," Liz protested weakly. "He has a truck."

"Of course. Very practical." Rebecca's knowing smile made further denial pointless. "So what's next for the two of you? Now that the divorce is final and you're officially a free woman?"

The question carried weight beyond casual curiosity. What was next? They'd maintained their connection through divorce proceedings and project completion, professional collaboration enhancing rather than compromising their personal bond. But they'd never explicitly discussed what would happen after these external structures no longer defined their relationship.

"I don't know exactly," Liz admitted. "We haven't really talked about... labels or definitions."

"But you're exclusive? Committed?"

"Yes," Liz said without hesitation. "There's no one else for either of us. We're just... taking our time figuring out what that looks like long-term."

Rebecca nodded, her expression softening. "That's actually healthy, considering everything you've both been through. No need to rush into defining something that's still evolving."

"Exactly." Liz felt a surge of gratitude for her sister's understanding. "And we still have the professional side to navigate. The Meridian project is complete, but there are already discussions about future collaborations."

"The personal and professional, forever intertwined," Rebecca observed. "Though I have to say, sis, I've never seen you this... alive. Even when you were first with Mark, there was always something held back. Some part of yourself you kept contained."

The observation struck with unexpected force. Had she always compartmentalized herself, even before her marriage began deteriorating? Had she ever been fully authentic with anyone before James?

"I think..." Liz began carefully, "I've spent most of my adult life trying to fit into spaces others created for me. Mark's expectations. Meridian's corporate culture. Even our parents' academic legacy. With James, I don't have to fit myself into anything. There's just... recognition. Of who I actually am."

"That's what we all want, ultimately," Rebecca said, reaching across the table to squeeze her hand. "To be seen completely and valued for what's seen. I'm happy you've found that, whether it came through complicated circumstances or not."

Their conversation shifted to practical matters—the apartment Liz had purchased in a converted warehouse building not unlike James's, the furniture she'd selected that reflected her aesthetic rather than compromise, the professional opportunities emerging from the Meridian project's success.

As they prepared to leave, Rebecca paused, her expression turning serious. "Just remember something, Liz. The house you shared with Mark wasn't just a building, it was a symbol of the life you constructed together. Selling it isn't just a financial transaction; it's letting go of that particular dream completely."

"I know," Liz nodded, understanding her sister's concern. "But I'm ready. The dream wasn't wrong, just incomplete. I've learned what I actually need in a home, and in a relationship."

"Which is?"

"Space to expand rather than contract," Liz said simply. "Room to become more myself, not less."

James's truck was already parked outside her new building when Liz arrived that afternoon. He stood beside it, sleeves rolled up, helping the movers unload boxes from the small moving van she'd hired.

"Perfect timing," he called as she approached. "We just finished bringing up the larger furniture. Your bed and dresser are assembled in the bedroom."

The casual domesticity of the scene, James directing movers, making decisions about furniture placement, already familiar with her new space, created a flutter in her chest. How different from Mark's reluctant participation in household matters, his view that such tasks were obligations rather than shared projects.

"Thank you," she said, accepting the brief kiss he offered. "You didn't have to oversee all this."

"I wanted to," James replied, his eyes warm with something that made her pulse quicken despite the mundane setting. "Besides, I couldn't risk them mishandling your book collection. I know how precisely you organize them."

The thoughtful observation, that he'd noticed and remembered such a detail, created that familiar warmth in her chest. Mark had never understood her meticulous book organization, viewing it as an unnecessary quirk rather than an expression of how her mind worked.

They spent the next hour directing the movers, unpacking essentials, and transforming the empty apartment into the beginning of a home. The space itself was perfect for Liz, high ceilings, exposed brick, windows that flooded the rooms with natural light. Unlike the suburban colonial she'd shared with Mark, this urban loft reflected her aesthetic sensibilities without compromise.

When the movers finally departed, Liz and James stood in the center of the main living area, surrounded by boxes and partially arranged furniture.

"What do you think?" she asked, gesturing to the space around them.

"It suits you," James replied, his gaze taking in the room before returning to her face. "Open, thoughtfully designed, with character beneath the surface details."

The description, of both apartment and occupant, created a small smile. "Always the architect, seeing beneath façades to structural elements."

"I keep telling you, it's an occupational hazard," he admitted, returning her smile. "Though in this case, the assessment is entirely positive."

They moved to the kitchen, where James produced a bottle of champagne he'd hidden in her refrigerator earlier. "I thought a celebration might be in order," he explained, locating glasses among the newly unpacked kitchenware. "Not just for the new apartment, but for the official fresh start."

The thoughtfulness of the gesture touched her deeply. He understood the significance of this day, not just a move, but a symbolic transition from one life chapter to another.

"To new beginnings," James said, handing her a filled glass. "And solid foundations."

"To recognition," Liz countered, clinking her glass against his. "And building something authentic."

They settled on the couch, one of the few pieces she'd purchased new rather than bringing from her previous life. James's arm draped comfortably around her shoulders, their bodies fitting together with the ease that still surprised her after months of connection.

"I spoke with Howard this morning," he said after a comfortable silence. "He's already talking about a satellite office project for Meridian's west coast expansion. Wants both of us involved if we're interested."

"Another collaboration?" Liz raised an eyebrow. "Are you sure that's wise, given our... complications?"

"I think we've proven we can maintain professional focus despite personal connection," James replied. "The Meridian headquarters exceeded expectations precisely because of our combined perspective."

"True," Liz acknowledged. "Though Catherine might have different opinions about our 'professional focus' if she knew about certain incidents in unfinished storage rooms."

James laughed, the sound warming her from within. "A minor deviation from professional protocol. The building was essentially complete."

"Is that what we're calling it? A 'minor deviation'?" Liz teased, setting down her champagne glass. "I seem to recall it being rather significant."

His expression shifted from amusement to something more intense. "Very significant," he agreed, his voice dropping to that lower register that never failed to send awareness skittering across her skin. "Though perhaps we should conduct further analysis to confirm that assessment."

The playful suggestion carried serious undertones, acknowledgment that their relationship had evolved beyond careful exploration to something more established, more certain. As his hand traced the line of her jaw, Liz felt the familiar magnetic pull that had characterized their connection from the beginning.

"James," she said, his name both question and answer. "Where do we go from here? Now that everything's official, now that the project's complete... what are we building?"

He studied her face with that focused attention that always made her feel truly seen. "Something designed for permanence rather than temporary occupation," he replied, echoing words he'd spoken months earlier. "A structure that accommodates growth rather than constraining it."

"But are we rushing?" Liz voiced the concern that had lingered despite their deepening connection. "Moving from one relationship directly into another? Is the timing still wrong?"

"I don't believe timing is ever perfect," James said thoughtfully. "There are always complications, always reasons to wait for some mythical 'right moment' that never seems to arrive." His hand found hers, fingers interlacing. "The question isn't whether the timing is perfect, but whether what we're building has integrity regardless of when construction began."

The architectural metaphor created a small smile despite the seriousness of their conversation. "And does it? Have integrity?"

"I believe so," James replied without hesitation. "We've established a foundation based on mutual recognition rather than convenience or escape. We've created supporting structures through honesty about our past patterns and present fears. We've designed space that accommodates both our individual needs and shared vision."

The simple assessment resonated deeply, articulating what made their connection different from her marriage to Mark or his to Vanessa. They had begun as intellectual rivals, evolved into reluctant collaborators, then partners in creation, both professional and personal. Each stage building upon the previous, creating something neither could have designed alone.

"I'm afraid of repeating patterns," James admitted, vulnerability evident in his expression. "Of mistaking initial compatibility for a lasting relationship. Of building something that looks perfect but lacks proper foundation."

"I have the same fear," Liz acknowledged. "That I've moved too quickly from one relationship to another without fully processing what went wrong."

"And what do you think now?" James asked, his eyes holding hers with unwavering focus. "Having completed that processing?"

Liz considered the question with the seriousness it deserved. "I think what failed in my marriage wasn't timing or circumstances, but fundamental incompatibility. Mark and I wanted different things, valued different qualities, moved in different directions. No amount of effort or therapy could have bridged that growing divide."

"And us?" James's question carried weight beyond the simple words.

"We challenge each other intellectually, support each other emotionally, see each other completely," Liz replied, the truth flowing easily. "The connection we've found isn't about escaping failed relationships or convenient timing. It's about recognition, finding someone who values all of me, not just the parts that fit their expectations."

Relief flickered across James's features. "That's exactly how I see it," he said. "What we're creating together, professionally and personally, has integrity because it's built on genuine understanding rather than projection or idealization."

As they continued unpacking boxes together, conversation flowing between practical matters and deeper reflections, Liz felt the strange combination of excitement and peace that accompanies genuine connection. They sorted kitchenware, arranged furniture, debated bookshelf organization, domestic tasks transformed by shared purpose and mutual respect.

"What's in this one?" James asked, opening a box labeled simply "Preston."

Liz glanced over, recognition dawning. "Oh, that's ... just old school papers. You can put it in the office."

But James had already removed the lid, revealing neatly preserved academic documents from their shared past. On top lay two bound thesis papers, his on architectural narrative in modernist literature, hers on spatial metaphors in contemporary fiction. The competing papers that had once defined their academic rivalry, preserved for nearly twenty years.

"That's right, you said you kept these?" he smiled, genuine wonder in his voice as he lifted the papers carefully.

"I did," Liz admitted, moving to his side. "They reminded me of who I was before... before I started making myself smaller to fit into Mark's world. Before I surrendered parts of myself for the sake of peace."

James opened her thesis, finding his own handwritten notes in the margins, critical but thoughtful commentary from their final class together. "I was unnecessarily harsh here," he observed, pointing to a particularly aggressive comment. "Your analysis was actually more nuanced than I acknowledged."

"And I was deliberately provocative here," Liz countered, indicating a passage in his thesis she'd heavily annotated. "Challenging your premise not because it was wrong, but because I knew it would spark your competitive response."

They sat on the floor surrounded by moving boxes, reading through their decades-old academic rivalry with new perspective. What had once been bitter competition now revealed itself as the first expression of intellectual connection, two minds recognizing worthy counterparts, challenging each other to greater depths of analysis and more precise articulation.

"We were defining ourselves in opposition to each other," James observed, turning a page filled with their competing marginalia. "Each trying to prove superiority rather than recognizing complementary strengths."

"And now?" Liz asked, the question encompassing far more than their academic past.

"Now we're defining ourselves through collaboration rather than competition," James replied, setting down the papers to meet her gaze. "Creating something neither could build alone."

The simple truth resonated deeply, articulating the evolution of their relationship from rivals to partners. Liz leaned forward, her hand finding his amid the scattered papers of their shared history.

"I think I've been keeping these all these years because they represented something I thought I'd lost," she said quietly. "The part of myself that was intellectually confident, academically ambitious, unwilling to diminish my light for someone else's comfort."

"You never lost that," James replied, his fingers tightening around hers. "It was always there, just waiting for the right conditions to reemerge."

"The right recognition," Liz corrected gently. "Someone who valued that light rather than being threatened by it."

As evening settled over the half-unpacked apartment, they continued sorting through boxes and arranging possessions, their conversation flowing between past insights and future possibilities. The competing thesis papers remained on the coffee table, tangible reminder of where they had begun and how far they had traveled.

Unlike her carefully coordinated house with Mark, this new space was emerging organically, James's suggestions enhancing rather than contradicting her vision, their different perspectives creating something more interesting than either would have designed alone.

"We should probably stop for tonight," James said eventually, noticing her stifled yawn. "The rest can wait until tomorrow."

"Stay," Liz said, the single word carrying a question beyond the immediate invitation. "Not just tonight. But... moving forward. Be part of this new chapter."

James studied her face, his expression softening into something dangerously close to tenderness. "Are you sure? We agreed to proceed carefully, to give you time after the divorce."

"The divorce was just legal confirmation of what ended years ago," Liz replied. "And we've been proceeding carefully for months. At some point, caution becomes avoidance of commitment rather than thoughtful consideration."

James's smile transformed his features, years of professional reserve giving way to genuine joy. "In that case, I accept your invitation. For tonight and... moving forward."

As they prepared for sleep in her new bedroom, James borrowing a toothbrush, Liz arranging pillows on a bed that was wholly hers rather than shared with Mark, Liz felt the strange combination of novelty and familiarity that characterized this transition. Everything was new, the apartment, her legal status, the open acknowledgment of their relationship, yet their connection felt established, grounded in months of careful exploration and genuine understanding.

"It feels strange," she admitted as they settled into bed together. "Starting over at thirty-eight. Building a new life from scratch."

"Not from scratch," James corrected, his arm drawing her closer. "From experience. From lessons learned and patterns recognized. From knowing what we need rather than just what we're expected to want."

The insight resonated deeply. This wasn't a reckless beginning but a deliberate continuation, the next logical phase in a relationship that had slowly evolved. Building blocks assembled, one by one.

As sleep approached, Liz found herself thinking of the competing thesis papers now resting on her coffee table. Those documents represented not just their academic past but the foundation of their current connection, the intellectual challenge and mutual respect that had eventually transformed into something deeper neither could have anticipated.

The architectural metaphors that had characterized their relationship from the beginning remained apt. They had begun with careful foundation inspection, proceeded through structural assessment and necessary demolition, and were now engaged in the more rewarding work of building something designed to last, something that honored both their shared history and the future they might create together.

Not a perfect resolution, but perfect understanding of what they were constructing, a relationship built on recognition rather than projection, collaboration rather than competition, authenticity rather than performance.

CHAPTER FORTY

"Beyond Blueprints"

The morning light transformed the Meridian headquarters into a gleaming testament to architectural vision. Sunlight danced across the limestone base before traveling upward through innovative materials, the building itself embodying the "progressive tradition" philosophy that had guided its creation. Liz stood on the temporary platform erected for the ribbon-cutting ceremony, surveying the crowd of executives, board members, and press representatives gathering before the main entrance.

"Quite a moment, isn't it?" Howard appeared beside her, pride evident in his voice. "Eighteen months from concept to reality. And more magnificent than I dared hope."

"It exceeded our expectations," Liz agreed, her eyes drawn to the material transition points where traditional elements flowed seamlessly into innovative ones. "The reality is even more powerful than the renderings."

Howard nodded, following her gaze. "That's what James said this morning during the final walkthrough. Something about light quality and material dialogue that went over my head. But I understand the result, it's extraordinary."

At the mention of James, Liz felt the familiar awareness prickle across her skin. She spotted him across the gathering crowd, deep in conversation with the city commissioner. Even from this distance, she could read the passion in his gestures as he explained some architectural detail, his tall frame commanding attention without effort.

As if sensing her gaze, James looked up, their eyes meeting briefly across the space. A small smile passed between them, professional acknowledgment with personal warmth carefully contained beneath. They had perfected this public performance over months of collaboration, maintaining appropriate boundaries while building something far more complex than a corporate headquarters.

The ceremony proceeded with practiced precision. Howard delivered an inspiring speech about vision and future legacy. The mayor praised the building's contribution to urban renewal. Board members nodded approvingly at mentions of sustainability features and innovative design. Finally, Howard invited both Liz and James to join him for the symbolic ribbon cutting.

"This building represents the perfect synthesis of marketing vision and architectural brilliance," Howard announced as they positioned themselves on either side of him. "Elizabeth Donovan and James Calloway have created something extraordinary together, a physical manifestation of Meridian's philosophy that will define our company for generations."

As Howard raised the ceremonial scissors, Liz found herself standing closer to James than professional protocol strictly required. The brief contact of their shoulders sent a current through her that had nothing to do with the cool autumn air.

"Ready?" Howard asked, beaming for the photographers.

The ribbon fell, applause erupted, and Meridian's future officially began.

"The limestone integration is remarkable," Catherine observed hours later, champagne flute in hand as they surveyed the soaring atrium during the evening reception. "Even I didn't fully appreciate the narrative impact until seeing it completed."

"The material transition creates a physical journey through Meridian's evolution," Liz explained, professional pride momentarily overshadowing her awareness of James across the room. "Visitors literally experience progressive tradition as they move through the space."

Catherine studied her with that penetrating gaze she was known for. Her ability to see through everything. "You've received three job offers based on this project, I hear."

"Word travels fast."

"In our circles, always." Catherine sipped her champagne. "I hope you're considering our counter-offer. Howard is prepared to be quite generous to keep you."

"I haven't made any decisions yet," Liz replied carefully.

"Mmm." Catherine's gaze drifted meaningfully toward James, who was explaining some architectural detail to board members. "I imagine there are... various factors to consider."

Before Liz could respond to the veiled reference, Howard appeared, champagne making him more effusive than usual.

"The press coverage is phenomenal!" he declared. "Architecture journals, business publications, sustainability magazines, everyone wants to feature our building. And they all mention the innovative marketing-architecture integration." He beamed at Liz. "Your concept is revolutionizing how companies approach headquarters design."

"James's architectural vision made it possible," Liz replied, the credit genuine despite Catherine's knowing glance. "The narrative only works because the physical space supports it so perfectly."

"Which is why you two need to present together at next month's Urban Development conference," Howard continued. "The board wants to leverage this success into speaking engagements, industry recognition, the full package."

"Of course," Liz agreed, professionalism masking the complicated emotions beneath. More collaboration with James, more careful boundaries to maintain, more pretending their connection was purely professional.

As the evening progressed, Liz circulated among guests with practiced ease, accepting congratulations and explaining marketing concepts with polished precision. She maintained awareness of James's location without obviously tracking him, their paths occasionally crossing for brief, appropriate interactions that revealed nothing of their private connection.

The reception was winding down when Derek appeared at her elbow, offering a fresh glass of champagne.

"Quite the triumph," he said, clinking his glass against hers. "Though I'm still not sure which is more impressive, the building or the fact that you two maintained professional focus despite... everything."

"I have no idea what you're talking about," Liz replied, though her tone belied the denial.

Derek's knowing smile made further pretense pointless. "Right. Purely professional collaboration. Nothing to see here." He glanced across the room to where James was speaking with Howard. "Though I will say, watching you two transform from academic rivals to whatever you are now has been the most entertaining subplot of this project."

"We're colleagues who've developed mutual respect," Liz insisted, the description technically accurate if woefully incomplete.

"Of course you are." Derek's expression softened. "And I've never seen you happier, by the way. Divorced life clearly agrees with you."

Before she could respond, Howard's voice rose above the ambient conversation. "Ladies and gentlemen, before we conclude this evening, I'd like to invite James Calloway to say a few words about the architectural vision that has transformed Meridian."

The crowd quieted as James took position near the central atrium, the material transition elements creating a perfect backdrop for his remarks. His presence commanded attention without apparent effort, confident but not arrogant, passionate without excess.

"Architecture at its best isn't just about creating spaces," he began, his deep voice carrying effortlessly through the acoustically engineered room. "It's about shaping experiences, embodying values, telling stories through physical form."

As he spoke about sustainable design and innovative materials, Liz found herself watching his hands, those architect's hands that sketched with such precision, that knew her body with equal thoroughness. The professional and personal had become so intertwined she could no longer separate her admiration for his work from her feelings for the man.

"But the true innovation in this building isn't structural or material," James continued, his gaze finding Liz in the crowd. "It's the seamless integration of a marketing narrative with architectural experience. For that, I must acknowledge Elizabeth Donovan, whose vision transformed this building from mere headquarters to physical embodiment of Meridian's identity."

The unexpected credit created warmth that spread through her chest. Such a marked difference from her previous life.

"Elizabeth challenged conventional thinking about how buildings communicate," James continued, his professional tone belying the personal knowledge behind his words. "Her insight that architecture could literally tell Meridian's story through material transition created a visitor experience that will define this company for generations."

As applause followed his remarks, their eyes met across the crowded atrium. For a moment, the carefully maintained professional distance dissolved, revealing the connection beneath. Then Howard stepped forward for closing comments, and the moment passed.

The reception concluded with final handshakes and congratulations. Board members departed in luxury cars, executives drifted toward waiting taxis, and staff began the subtle process of clearing champagne flutes and appetizer trays.

"Quite a day," Catherine observed, appearing beside Liz as she gathered her things. "You should be proud."

"I am," Liz replied, the simple truth encompassing both professional achievement and personal evolution. "It's been quite a journey."

"Indeed." Catherine's shrewd eyes missed nothing. "And speaking of journeys, I believe James mentioned something about showing you the rooftop lighting installation. Apparently there's some special effect only visible after dark."

The transparent pretext would have been comical if not for the genuine respect in Catherine's eyes. "And take your time," she added, her tone shifting to something more personal. "You've earned a moment to appreciate what you've created."

After Catherine departed, Liz found James waiting by the private elevator that accessed the rooftop garden.

"Shall we?" he asked, holding the door with a small smile.

The rooftop garden was transformed by night, subtle lighting highlighting sustainable plantings and creating intimate spaces amid the urban setting. The city spread below them like a constellation of lights, while above, stars punctuated the clear autumn sky.

"It's beautiful," Liz said, moving to the edge where a glass barrier provided safety without obstructing the view.

"The lighting designer integrated the same narrative progression we used throughout the building," James explained, standing beside her. "Notice how the traditional elements are illuminated with warmer tones, gradually transitioning to cooler, more contemporary lighting as you move through the space."

"Progressive tradition in illumination," Liz observed. "The attention to detail is remarkable."

"That was your influence," James said, his voice softening as he turned toward her. "You taught me to consider how every element contributes to the overall experience. My designs were technically proficient before, but you brought the human element, the narrative that makes spaces meaningful."

The simple acknowledgment of her professional contribution meant more than elaborate declarations might have. In the privacy of the rooftop garden, with the building they'd created together spread below them, the artificial distance they'd maintained all day finally dissolved.

"We did it," Liz said, wonder in her voice. "Sometimes I still can't believe we pulled this off."

"Which part?" James asked, moving closer. "The building or everything else?"

"Both." She turned to face him fully. "Eighteen months ago, I was trapped in a marriage that had become empty, working on projects that didn't challenge me, ignoring parts of myself I'd surrendered years before. Now..."

"Now?" James prompted when she trailed off.

"Now I'm standing on top of a building I helped create, beside the man who reminded me who I really am." Liz reached for his hand, fingers interlacing with familiar ease. "It's quite a transformation."

"From academic rivals to reluctant collaborators to ..." James left the final definition unspoken, a question in his eyes.

"Partners," Liz supplied. "In every sense that matters."

James's smile transformed his features, years of professional reserve giving way to genuine joy. "We wasted twenty years trying to beat each other," he said, drawing her closer.

"I still believe we needed those years to become who we are now," Liz countered. "I think... I think we appreciate it more now at thirty-eight then we ever could have at eighteen."

"Probably so," James acknowledged. "I was too arrogant, too convinced of my own brilliance. And you—"

"I was defining myself by academic achievement rather than authentic passion," Liz finished. "Too focused on winning to recognize a potential partner."

The insight resonated between them, creating a moment of perfect understanding. James's hand rose to her face, tracing her cheekbone.

"So what happens now?" he asked, the question encompassing their professional and personal future. "Howard mentioned the west coast expansion project. And you've had other offers."

"I'm considering all options," Liz replied. "But whatever I decide professionally, I'm certain about us.

This connection we've found, it's not something I'm willing to surrender."

"Even with the complications?" James's voice carried no doubt, only practical consideration. "Working together while maintaining a personal relationship has its challenges."

"We've managed so far," Liz smiled. "And I think we've proven our collaboration produces extraordinary results, professionally and personally."

"True," James acknowledged, his arms encircling her waist. "Though Catherine might have different opinions about our 'professional focus' if she knew about certain incidents in unfinished storage rooms."

Liz laughed, the sound carrying across the rooftop garden. "I suspect Catherine knows more than she lets on. That comment about the lighting installation was hardly subtle."

"Howard too," James added. "He suggested I show you the 'special view' from up here. As if we needed an excuse to find a moment alone."

The realization that their relationship was an open secret among those who mattered most created unexpected relief. The pretense of purely professional connection had grown increasingly difficult to maintain as their personal bond deepened.

"I love you Liz," James said suddenly, the declaration simple yet profound in its certainty. "Not just your brilliant mind or creative vision or the way you challenge my thinking. All of you. The complete Elizabeth Mitchell Donovan."

The words created a surge of emotion that momentarily robbed her of speech. He had never called her Liz. It was as if the transformation was complete. How long had she waited to be seen so completely? How many years had she spent diminishing herself to maintain someone else's comfort?

"I love you too," she replied when she found her voice. "The arrogant, brilliant, occasionally infuriating James Calloway who sees me more clearly than anyone ever has."

Their kiss was long and deep.

When they eventually pulled apart, James gestured toward the edge of the rooftop. "Shall we take one last look at our creation?"

They moved to the glass barrier, arms around each other's waists, gazing down at the illuminated building below. From this height, the Meridian headquarters revealed its complete form, traditional elements flowing into innovative design, limestone base supporting soaring glass, past and future integrated into harmonious whole.

"It's beautiful," Liz said, her head resting against James's shoulder.

"It will stand for generations," James replied, pride evident in his voice. "Long after we're gone, this building will remain as evidence of what we created together."

The simple truth resonated deeply. Like the building below them, their relationship had evolved from careful foundation work through structural development to finished form, each phase building upon the previous, creating something neither could have designed alone.

As they stood together under the autumn stars, Liz felt the strange combination of achievement and anticipation that accompanies completion of one significant project and the beginning of another. The building was finished, but their story was still unfolding, not perfect, not without challenges, but grounded in the recognition that had transformed rivals into partners.

The certificate of occupancy had been granted. The building was ready for its purpose. And so, at last, were they.

About Julie Freebush

Passionate and Dedicated

Ever wondered what it's like to live a life filled with passion, desire, and forbidden love?

Meet Julie Freebush, the author who knows no bounds when it comes to exploring the realms of ***eroticism***.

Julie has had an intense fascination with ***seduction*** and ***temptation*** since her childhood, when an innocent skinny dipping experience sparked something deep inside her.

Her stories are filled with *seduction*, *temptation*, and *illicit encounters* that will leave you *breathless*.

Julie spends her days *writing* and her nights "*Researching*".

As an author who knows no bounds.

Julie's experiences range from the *scandalous* to the downright *explicit*, and her writing is a testament to her *insatiable appetite for pleasure*.

Julie's works are filled with *secrets, lust, and explicit encounters* that will leave your heart racing. So, if you're ready to embark on a journey of *sensuality* and *illicit pleasure*, join *Julie Freebush* in her world of *Short & Steamy Tales of Erotica*.

For all the latest releases and current happenings with Julie, stop by her website. JulieFreebush.com